WITCH
WOOD

WITCH WOOD

BY
JOHN BUCHAN

"And Asa did that which was right in the eyes of the Lord . . . and removed all the idols that his fathers had made. . . . But the high places were not removed."

1 KINGS xv. 11–14.

THOMAS NELSON AND SONS, Ltd.
LONDON, EDINBURGH, NEW YORK
TORONTO, AND PARIS

First published in this edition September 1929.
Reprinted March 1930.

TO

WALTER BUCHAN

CONTENTS

WITCH WOOD

PROLOGUE

TIME, my grandfather used to say, stood still in
that glen of his. But the truth of the saying did
not survive his death, and the first daisies had scarcely
withered on his grave before a new world was knocking
at the gate. That was thirty years ago, and to-day
the revolution is complete. The parish name has been
changed; the white box of a kirk which served the
glen for more than two centuries has been rebuilt in red
suburban gothic; a main railway line now runs down
the Aller and the excellent summer service brings
holiday-makers from a hundred miles distant: houses
and shops have clustered under the Hill of Deer; there
may be found a well-reputed boarding school for youth,
two inns—both of them reformed—a garage, and a
bank agent. The centre of importance has moved from
the old village to the new town by the station, and
even the old village is no more a clachan of thatched
roofs straggling by a burnside. Some enemy of the
human race has taught the burn to run straight like a
sewer and has spanned it with a concrete bridge, while
the thatch of the houses has been replaced by slates of a
metallic green. Only the ruins of the old kirkton have
not been meddled with; these stand as I remember

them, knee-deep in docks and nettles, defended by a crumbling dry-stone dyke against inquisitive cattle from Crossbasket.

The old folk are gone, too, and their very names are passing from the countryside. Long before my day the Hawkshaws had disappeared from Calidon, but there was a respectable Edinburgh burgess family who had come there in the seventeenth century; now these have given place to a rawer burgess graft from the West. The farmers are mostly new men, and even the peasant, who should be the enduring stock, has shifted his slow bones. I learned from the postman that in Woodilee to-day there was no Monfries, no Sprot, but one Pennecuik, and only two bearers of the names of Ritchie and Shillinglaw, which had once been plentiful as ragwort. In such a renovated world it was idle to hope to find surviving the tales which had perplexed my childhood. No one could tell me when or why the kirk by the Crossbasket march became a ruin, and its gravestones lay buried in weeds. Most did not even know that it had been a kirk.

I was not greatly surprised by this, for the kirk of Woodilee had not been used for the better part of three centuries; and even as a child I could not find many to tell me of its last minister. The thing had sunk from a tale to an " overcome," a form of words which every one knew but which few could interpret. It was Jess Blane, the grieve's daughter, who first stirred my curiosity. In a whirl of wrath at some of my doings she prayed that the fate of the minister of Woodilee might be mine—a fate which she expounded as to be " claught by the Deil and awa' wi'." A little scared, I carried the affair to my nurse, who was gravely scandalized, and denounced Jess as a " shamefu' tawpie, fyling the wean's mind wi' her black lees." "Dinna you be feared, dearie," she reassured me. "It wasna the Deil that cam for the Minister o' Woodilee. I've aye heard tell that he was a guid man and a kind man. It was the Fairies, hinny. And he leev'd happy wi' them and dee'd happy and never drank out o' an empty cup." I took my information, I remember, to the clan of children who were my playmates, and they spread it among their households and came back with confirmation or contradiction. Some held for the Devil, some for the Fairies—a proof that tradition spoke with two voices. The Fairy school slightly outnumbered the others, and in a battle one April evening close to the ruined kirk we routed the diabolists and established our version as the canon. But save for that solitary fact —that the Minister of Woodilee had gone off with the Fairies—the canon remained bare.

Years later I got the tale out of many books and places ; a folio in the library of a Dutch college, the muniment-room of a Catholic family in Lancashire, notes in a copy of the second Latin edition of Wishart's *Montrose*, the diaries of a captain of Hebron's and of a London glove-maker, the exercise book of a seventeenth-century Welsh schoolgirl. I could piece the story together well enough, but at first I found it hard to fit it to the Woodilee that I knew—that decorous landscape, prim, determinate, without a hint of mystery ; the bare hilltops, bleak at seasons, but commonly of a friendly Pickwickian baldness, skirted with methodically-planned woods of selected conifers, and girdled with mathematical stone dykes ; the even, ruled fields of the valley bottom ; the studied moderation of the burns in a land meticulously drained ; the dapper glass and stone and metal of the village. Two miles off, it was true, ran the noble untamed streams of Aller; beyond them the hills rose in dark fields to mid-sky, with the glen of the Rood making a sword-cut into their heart. But Woodilee itself—whither had fled the savour? Once, I knew from the books, the great wood of Melanudrigill had descended from the heights and flowed in black waves to the village brink. But I could not re-create the picture out of glistening asphalted highway, singing telegraph wires, spruce dwellings, model pastures, and manicured woodlands.

Then one evening from the Hill of Deer I saw with other eyes. There was a curious leaden sky, with a blue break about sunset, so that the shadows lay oddly. My first thought, as I looked at the familiar scene, was that, had I been a general in a campaign, I should have taken special note of Woodilee, for it was a point of vantage. It lay right in the pass between the Scottish midlands and the south—the pass of road and water—yes, and—shall I say?—of spirit, for it was in the throat of the hills, on the march between the sown and the desert. I was looking east, and to my left and behind me the open downs, farmed to their last decimal of capacity, were the ancient land of Manann, the capital province of Pictdom. The colliery headgear on the horizon, the trivial moorish hilltops, the dambrod-pattern fields, could never tame wholly for me that land's romance, and on this evening I seemed to be gazing at a thing antique and wolfish, tricked out for the moment with a sheep's coat. . . . To my right rose the huddle of great hills which cradle all our rivers. To them time and weather bring little change, yet in that eerie light, which revealed in hard outline while it obscured in detail, they seemed too remote and awful to be the kindly giants with whose glens I daily conversed. . . . At my feet lay Woodilee, and a miracle had been wrought, for a gloom like the shadow of an eclipse seemed to have crept over the parish. I saw an illusion, which I knew to be such, but which my mind accepted, for it gave me the vision I had been seeking.

It was the Woodilee of three hundred years ago. And my mind, once given the cue, set out things not presented by the illuded eye. . . . There were no highways—only tracks, miry in the bogs and stony on the braes, which led to Edinburgh on one hand and to Carlisle on the other. I saw few houses, and these were brown as peat, but on the knowe of the old kirkton I saw the four grey walls of the kirk, and the manse beside it among elders and young ashes. Woodilee was not now a parish lying open to the eye of sun and wind. It was no more than a tiny jumble of crofts, bounded and pressed in upon by something vast and dark, which clothed the tops of all but the highest hills, muffled the ridges, choked the glens and overflowed almost to the edge of the waters—which lay on the landscape like a shaggy fur cast loosely down. My mouth shaped the word " Melanudrigill," and I knew that I saw Woodilee as no eye had seen it for three centuries, when, as its name tells, it still lay in the shadow of a remnant of the Wood of Caledon, that most ancient forest where once Merlin harped and Arthur mustered his men. . . .

An engine whistled in the valley, a signal-box sprang into light, and my vision passed. But as I picked my way down the hillside in the growing dusk I realized that all memory of the encircling forest had not gone from Woodilee in my childhood, though the name of Melanudrigill had been forgotten. I could hear old Jock Dodds, who had been keeper on Calidon for fifty years, telling tales for my delectation, as he sat and smoked on the big stone beside the smithy. He would speak of his father, and his father's father, and the latter had been a great hero with his flintlock gun. "He would lie in the moss or three on the winter mornin's, and him an auld man, and get the wild swans and the grey geese when they cam ower frae Clyde to Aller. Ay, and mony's the deer he would kill." And when I pointed out that there were no deer in the countryside, Jock shook his head and said that in his grandfather's day the Black Wood was not all destroyed. "There was a muckle lump on Windyways, and anither this side o' Reiverslaw." But if I asked for more about the wood, Jock was vague. Some said it had been first set by the Romans, others by Auld Michael Scott himself. . . . "A grand hidy-hole for beasts and an unco bit for warlocks." . . . Its downfall had begun long ago in the Dear Years, and the last of it had been burnt for firewood in his father's day, in the winter of the Sixteen Drifty Days. . . .

I remembered, too, that there had been places still sacrosanct and feared. To Mary Cross, a shapeless stone in a field of bracken, no one would go in the spring or summer gloaming, but the girls decked it with wild flowers at high noon of Midsummer Day. There was a stretch of Woodilee burn, between the village and the now-drained Fennan Moss, where trout, it was believed, were never found. Above all, right in the heart of Reiverslaw's best field of turnips was a spring, which we children knew as Katie Thirsty, but which the old folk called the Minister's Well, and mentioned always with a shake of the head or a sigh, for it was there, they said, that the Minister of Woodilee had left the earth for Fairyland.

CHAPTER I

THE COMING OF THE MINISTER

THE Reverend David Sempill began his ministry in Woodilee on the twenty-sixth day of August in the year of grace sixteen hundred and forty-four. He was no stranger to the glen, for as a boy he had spent his holidays with his grandfather, who was the miller of Roodfoot. In that year when the horn of the Kirk was exalted the voice of a patron mattered less; Mr. Sempill had been, as they said, "popularly called," and so entered upon his office with the eager interest of the parish which had chosen him. A year before he had been licensed by the presbytery of Edinburgh; he was ordained in Woodilee in the present year on the last Sabbath of June, and "preached in" on the third Sabbath of August by the weighty voice of Mungo Muirhead, the minister of Kirk Aller. His plenishing —chiefly books—had come from Edinburgh on eight pack-horses, and, having escaped the perils of Carnwath Moss, was now set out in an upper chamber of the little damp manse, which stood between the kirk and Woodilee burn. A decent widow woman, Isobel Veitch by name, had been found to keep his house, and David himself, now that all was ready, had ridden over on his grey cob from his cousin's at Newbiggin and taken seisin of his new home. He had sung as he came in sight of Woodilee; he had prayed with bowed head as he crossed the manse threshold; but as he sat in the closet which he named his "study," and saw his precious books on the shelf and the table before him on which great works would be written, and outside the half-glazed window the gooseberry bushes of the garden and the silver links of the burn, he had almost wept with pure gratitude and content.

His first hour he had spent exploring his property. The manse was little and squat and gave lodging in its heather-thatched roof to more than one colony of bees. The front abutted on the kirkton road, save for a narrow strip of green edged with smooth white stones from the burn. The back looked on a garden, where stood a score of apple trees, the small wild fruit of which was scarcely worth the gathering. There was also a square of green for bleaching clothes, a gean tree, a plot of gillyflowers and monkshood, and another of precious herbs like clary, penny-royal, and marjoram. At one end of the manse stood a brewhouse and a granary or girnel, for the storing of the minister's stipend meal; at the other a stable for two beasts, a byre with three stalls, a hen-house of mud, and, in the angle of the dykes of the kirk loan, a midden among nettles.

Indoors the place was not commodious, and even on that warm August day a chill struck upward from the earthen floors. The low-ceiled lobby had no light but the open door. To the right of it was the living-room with a boarded ceiling, a wooden floor, and roughly plastered walls, where the minister's eight-day clock (by John Atchison, Leith, 1601) had now acclimatized itself. To the left lay Isobel's kitchen, with a door leading to the brewhouse, and Isobel's press-bed at the back of it, and a small dog-hole of a cellar. The upper story was reached by a wooden staircase as steep as a ladder, which opened direct into the minister's bedroom—an apartment of luxury, for it had a fireplace. One door led from it to the solitary guest-chamber ; another to a tiny hearthless room, which was his study or closet, and which at the moment ranked in his mind as the most miraculous of his possessions.

David ranged around like a boy back from school, and indeed with his thick sandy hair and ruddy countenance and slim straight back he seemed scarcely to have outgrown the schoolboy. He spilt the browst in the brewhouse and made a spectacle of himself with pease-meal in the girnel. Isobel watched him anxiously out of doors, where he sampled the fruit of the apple trees, and with various rejected specimens took shots at a starling in the glebe. Then in response to his shouts she brought him a basin of water and he washed off the dust of his morning ride. The August sun fell warm on the little yard ; the sound of the burn in the glen, the clack of the kirkton smithy, the sheep far off on Windyways, the bees in the clove gillyflowers, all melted into the soothing hum of a moorland noontide. The minister smiled as he scrubbed his cheeks, and Isobel's little old puckered apple-hued face smiled back. " Ay, sir," she said, " our lines is fallen intil a goodly place and a pleasant habitation. The Lord be thankit." And as he cried a fervent amen and tossed the towel back to her, a stir at the front door betokened his first visitors.

These were no less than three in number, neighbouring ministers who had ridden over on their garrons to bid the young man welcome to Woodilee. Presently stable and byre were crowded with their beasts, and the three brethren had bestowed themselves on the rough bench which adjoined the bleaching-ground. They would have

their dinner at the village ordinary—let not Mr. Sempill
put himself about—they would never have come thus
unannounced if they had thought that they would be
pressed to a meal. But they allowed themselves to be
persuaded by the hospitable clamour of Isobel, who saw
in such a function on her first day at the manse a
social aggrandisement. "Mr. Sempill would think black
burnin' shame if the gentlemen didna break breid. . . .
There was walth o' provender in the house—this moment
she had put a hen in the pot—she had a brace of muir-
fowl ready for brandering that had been sent from
Chasehope that very morn. . . ." The three smiled
tolerantly and hopefully. "Ye've gotten a rare Abigail,
Mr. Sempill. A woman o' mense and sense—the manse
o' Woodilee will be well guidit."

The Reverend Mungo Muirhead had a vast shaven
face set atop of a thick neck and a cumbrous body.
He had a big thin-lipped mouth which shut tight like a
lawyer's, a fleshy nose, and large grey eyes which at
most times were ruminant as a cow's, but could on
occasion kindle to shrewdness. His complexion was
pale, and he was fast growing bald, so the impression at
first sight was of a perfect mountain of countenance, a
steep field of colourless skin. As minister of Kirk Aller
he was the metropolitan of the company, and as became
a townsman he wore decent black with bands, and
boasted a hat. The Reverend Ebenezer Proudfoot from
the moorland village of Bold was of a different cast.
He wore the coarse grey homespun of the farmer, his
head-covering was a blue bonnet, his shoes were thick
brogues with leather ties, and he had donned a pair of
ancient frieze leggings. A massive sinewy figure, there
was in his narrow face and small blue eyes an air of
rude power and fiery energy. The third, Mr. James

Fordyce from the neighbouring parish of Cauldshaw,
was slight and thin, and pale either from ill-health or
from much study. He was dressed in worn blue, and
even in the August sun kept his plaid round his shoulders. In his face a fine brow was marred by the
contraction of his lean jaws and a mouth puckered
constantly as if in doubt or pain, but redeemed by
brown eyes, as soft and wistful as a girl's.

At the hour of noon they sat down to meat. Mr.
Muirhead said a lengthy grace, which, since he sniffed
the savour from the kitchen, he began appropriately
with "Bountiful Jehovah." All the dishes were set
out at once on the bare deal table—a bowl of barley
kail, a boiled fowl, the two brandered grouse, and a
platter of oatcakes. The merchant in the Pleasance of
Edinburgh had given his son a better plenishing than
fell to the usual lot of ministers, for there were pewter
plates and a knife and a fork for each guest. The
three stared at the splendour, and Mr. Proudfoot, as if
to testify against luxury, preferred to pick the bones
with his hands. The home-brewed ale was good, and
all except Mr. Fordyce did full justice to it, so that the
single tankard, passed from hand to hand, was often
refilled by Isobel. "Man, Mr. David," cried Mr.
Muirhead in high good-humour, "this is a great differ
from the days of your predecessor. Worthy Mr. Macmichael had never muckle but bannocks to set before
his friends. But you've made us a feast of fat things."

David inquired about his predecessor, whom he
remembered dimly from his boyhood as a man even
then very old, who ambled about the parish on a white
shelty.

"He was a pious and diligent minister," said Mr.
Muirhead, "but since ever I kenned him he was sore

fallen in the vale of years. He would stick to the same 'ordinary' till he had thrashed it into stour. I've heard that he preached for a year and sax months on Exodus fifteen and twenty-seven, the twelve wells of water and three score and ten palm trees of Elim, a Sabbath to ilka well and ilka tree. I've a notion that he was never very strong in the intellectuals."

"He wrestled mightily in prayer," said Mr. Proudfoot, "and he was great at fencing the Tables. Ay, sirs, he was a trumpet for the pure Gospel blast."

"I doubt not he was a good man," said Mr. Fordyce, "and is now gone to his reward. But he was ower auld and feeble for a sinful countryside. I fear that the parish was but ill guided, and, as ye ken, there was whiles talk of a Presbytery visitation."

"I differ!" cried Mr. Muirhead. "I differ *in toto*. Woodilee has aye been famous for its godly elders. Has it not Ephraim Caird, who was a member of Assembly and had a hand in that precious work of grace done in the East Kirk of St. Giles's two years syne? Has it not Peter Pennecuik, who has a gift of supplication like Mr. Rutherford himself? Ay, and in the Bishops' War you'll mind how Amos Ritchie was staunch to uphold the Covenant with the auld matchlock that had been his gudesire's. There's no lack of true religion in Woodilee."

"There's no lack of carnal pride, Mr. Mungo. The folk of Woodilee are ready enough for any stramash in Kirk or State. But what of their perishing souls, I ask? Are they striving to get a grip of Christ, as a bird scrapes with its claws at a stone wall? And do they bring forth works meet for repentance?"

"There was no clash of cauld morality in worthy Mr. Macmichael," said Mr. Proudfoot sourly.

" Is there the spirit of God in the people ? That's what I want to ken. There's ill stories in the country-side anent Woodilee. The Black Wood could tell some tales if the trees could talk."

Mr. Muirhead, having finished his meal and said a second grace, was picking his teeth in great good-humour.

" Hoots toots, Mr. James, you'll give our young brother a scunner of the place, to which it has pleased the Almighty to call him, before he has had a look at it himself. I'm not denying that the Wood is ower near Woodilee. It's a wanchancy thing for any paro-chine to have a muckle black forest flung around it like a maud.* And no doubt the Devil walks about like a roaring lion in Woodilee as in other bits. But there's men of God here to resist him. I tell you, sirs, there have been more delations to the Presbytery for the sin of witchcraft in Woodilee than in any other parish on the water of Aller."

" And what does that prove, Mr. Mungo ? "

" That there's wealth of prayerful and eident † folk to confound the Adversary. This is no season to despair of Kirk and Covenant, when this day they hold the crown of the causeway. You'll no have heard of the astonishing mercy vouchsafed to us in England ? A post came to Kirk Aller yestreen, and it seems that three weeks syne there was a great battle beside the city of York, where our Scots wrought mightily, and our own Davie Leslie gave the King's horsemen their kail through the reek. What does that portend ? "

" It portends," said Mr. Proudfoot, whom food did not mellow, " that our pure and reformed Kirk of Scotland is linked more than ever with sectaries

---

* Plaid. † Careful.

and antinomians and those, like the bloody and
deceitful Cromwell, that would defile the milk of the
Word with the sour whey of their human inventions.
What avails a triumphant Kirk if its doctrine be
sullied ? ''

Mr. Muirhead laughed. " It portends nothing of
the kind. The good work goes cannily on, and the
noble task to which the Assembly of Divines at Westminster set itself is advanced by a long mile. Man,
Eben, you folk at Bold live ower far from the world.
It's the Kirk of Scotland that holds the balance to-day
and can enforce its will on both King and sectaries.
Two days back I had a letter from that gospel-loving
nobleman, the Earl of Loudoun . . .''

Mr. Muirhead was mounted on his high horse. He lit
his pipe and for the space of half an hour dealt compre-
hensively with politics, labouring to show the happy
posture of affairs for what he called the " good cause."
The Solemn League and Covenant bound all Scotland in
a pact with the Lord, and presently all England would
follow suit. There would be soon that comfortable sight
which had been foretold by their godly fathers, a uniform
Kirk and a pure Gospel established by law from London
to the Orkneys, and a covenanted Sion to which all the
peoples of the earth would go up. Mr. Muirhead was
eloquent, for he repeated a peroration which he had once
used in the General Assembly.

" I have heard," he concluded, " that in Woodilee
there was a signing of the Covenant by every soul that
could make a scart with a pen. That for your encouragement, Mr. David."

Mr. Fordyce shook his head. " How many appended
their names out of fear or from mere carnal policy ?
Mankind will run like jukes after a leader. . I much mis-

doubt if there is any spiritual health to be got from following a multitude under duress. I would have left the choice to every man's conscience."

"You're not sound," cried Mr. Muirhead. "You're shaky on the fundamentals, Mr. James. I will confound you out of the Word. When King Josiah made a solemn covenant, did he leave it to ilka man's fancy to sign or no? Nay, he caused all—all, I say—in Jerusalem and Benjamin to stand to it. See Second Chronicles thirty-four and thirty-two."

There was a touch of asperity in the one disputant and of recalcitrance in the other, so David for good-fellowship's sake suggested that he might show them the manse in its new guise. But at that moment Isobel appeared with word that Chasehope was at the door seeking speech with the minister of Kirk Aller. At her back appeared the fiery head of the visitor, who was that Ephraim Caird whom Mr. Muirhead had already praised as a pillar of the Covenant and who farmed the largest tack in the parish. He was a big fellow, red as a fox, with a white freckled face, no eyebrows and greenish blue eyes, a man of over forty, whose muscular frame was now somewhat overlaid by flesh. His mouth was small and generally puckered together, a habit which gave him an air of thought and gravity. He had been an opponent of David Sempill before the call, but had acquiesced in the majority vote and had welcomed the new minister at the "preaching in" with a great show of goodwill. To-day he was apologetic and affable. He asked pardon for his intrusion—he would take neither bite nor sup—he had heard that the ministers were at the manse and he begged a word with Mr. Muirhead on Presbytery matters which would save him a journey to Kirk Aller, when he was busy with the bog hay. So

David took the other two to his closet and left Chasehope and Mr. Muirhead to their colloquy.

Mr. Proudfoot eyed with disapproval the books in the little dark chamber. He was content, he said, with the Bible and the Institutes of John Calvin and old Robert Rollock's commentary on the Prophet Daniel. He read the lettering on one volume, *Sancti Clementi Opera*, and on another, a work by a Dutch theologian, *De Sancti Pauli Epistolis*. The word " Saint " roused his ire. " Rags of Popery," he muttered, as he banged the books back on their shelves. " What for ' Saint ' Paul and not ' Saint ' Moses or ' Saint ' Isaiah ? It's a queer thing that Antichrist should set himself to miscall the godly Apostles of the New Testament and let the auld prophets alone. You're a young man, Mr. Sempill, and, as is natural in youth, with but a small experience of religion. Take the advice of an older man, and no clog yourself on the road to Heaven with ower much printit lear, when you can put the whole Word of God in your pouch."

But Mr. Fordyce looked at the shelves with greedy eyes. The moor-fowl at dinner had loosened a tooth, and now it came out in his hand and was wrapped carefully in his kerchief. " I have kept ilka tooth I have ever cast," he told the others, " and they will go into my coffin with me that my bodily parts may be together at the Resurrection." " Would you shorten the arm of the Lord ? " Mr. Proudfoot had asked testily. " Can He no gather your remnants from the uttermost parts of the earth ? " " True, true," the other had answered gently, " but it's just my fancy to keep all my dust in the one place." This ceremony over, he flung himself on the books like a hungry man on food. He opened them lovingly, read their titles, fingered them as if he could scarcely bear to part with them. "You're no half my age," he told the owner, "but you've twice as many books as there are in the Cauldshaw manse. You start well provided, Mr. David."

The theology he knew already and approved, but there were other works over which he shook a moralizing head. "You've a hantle of Pagan writers, Mr. David. I would counsel a young minister to apply himself rather to the Hebrew than to the Greek, for though the Greek was the tongue of the New Testament, it was also the tongue of lascivious poets and mocking philosophers, whereas the Hebrew was consecrate wholly to God. . . . But you have the Hebrew too, I see. Losh, here's the lexicon of Bamburgius, of which I have read but have never seen. We must consult, Mr. David. I've a new theory of the Hebrew accents on which I would like your judgment."

As he ran over the list he suddenly cried aloud with pleasure, and then checked himself almost shamefacedly. "Preserve us, but here's Hieronymus Cardanus, and other astrologic works. Man, I've diverted myself whiles with the science of the stars, and can make a shape at calculating a nativity. I cannot see why the thing should not be turned to holy uses, as when the star guided the Wise Men of the East to Bethlehem. You and me must have long cracks some day. These books will be like the Pole Star to draw me to Woodilee, and I'm looking to see you soon at Cauldshaw. It's but a poor desert bit, but there have been precious occasions there and many an outpouring of grace. I'm sore troubled with the gravel, Mr. David, and the goodwife has had a flux in the legs this twelvemonth back, but the Lord has showed me singular favour and my damps are lightened since a leech in Edinburgh prescribed a hyperion of bourtree and rue. . . . We're a childless household, for we had but the one bairn and sax year syne the Lord gathered her to Himself."

Downstairs Mr. Muirhead had finished his talk and the three ministers took their leave—they of Bold and Cauldshaw to jog the moorland miles to their homes, he of Kirk Aller to take his " four-hours " with Chasehope at Lucky Weir's in the clachan. Each of the three kissed David on the cheek and blessed him after his fashion. " May you live to be a pillar of the Kirk," said Mr. Muirhead. " Keep a Gospel walk," said Mr. Proudfoot, " on the narrow rigging of the truth." But Mr. Fordyce took the young man's hand, after saluting him, and held it with a kind of wistful affection. " I pray," he said, " that your windows may be ever open towards Jerusalem."

When his guests had gone David Sempill explored once more his little domain, like a child who counts his treasures. Then, as the afternoon mellowed into evening, the slopes of the Hill of Deer, red with flowering heather, drew him for a walk. He wanted a wide prospect, to see his parish in its setting of hill and glen, and recall the landmarks now blurred in his childhood's memory. His black coat and breeches were of Edinburgh make and too fine for moorland work, but he had stout country shoes and hose of ram's wool, the gift of his cousin's wife at Newbiggin, and he moved over the bent with the long stride of a shepherd. He crossed the burn of Mire, and saw below him the farm-town of Mirehope, with barley and nettles at strife in the infield, and the run-rigs of the outfield feathered with very green oats. Presently he was on the Hill of Deer, where the long stacks of peats were drying so well that every breath of air sent up from them a fine flurry of dust. The Mirehope cattle, wretched little black beasts, were grazing under the charge of a herd-boy, and the Mirehope sheep, their coats matted with tar till they looked like monstrous slugs, were picking up an uneasy livelihood among the heather bushes, leaving tufts of smelly wool behind them on the scraggy twigs which were still charred from the March moorburn. He reached the low summit, and flung himself down on a patch of thymy turf between the whinstone screes, with his face to the valley.

His holiday mood still held. The visit of his ministerial brethren had not dashed him, for he saw their prosiness through a golden haze. Mr. Muirhead was a stout warder on the walls of Sion, Mr. Proudfoot a guardian of the purity of the Temple, and Mr. Fordyce beyond question a saint, with his haggard face and his wistful eyes. It was Mr. Fordyce who stuck in his memory: a lovable saint, with his cast teeth saved up to make easy the business of a bodily resurrection, his love of the stars, his pathetic bookishness. David was full of the zest of his calling, but for himself he was ready to circumscribe its duties. Not for him to uphold the Kirk against its ill-wishers in the State ; in that cause he would do battle when the need arose, but not till then. He left to others the task of keeping the canon of truth pure from alloy : he accepted the Kirk's doctrine loyally, but let others do the dogmatizing. The work for which he longed was to save and comfort human souls.

Seen on that hilltop the minister of Woodilee was a different figure from that beheld by his colleagues in the dim light of the manse. His active form, his colour, his tumbled hair, spoke of the boy, but his face was not boyish. In its young contours there were already thought and resolution and spiritual fineness, and there was a steady ardour in the eyes. If his chin was the fighter's, his mouth was the comforter's. Five years before he had been set on a scholar's life. At the college he had been a noted Grecian, and in Robert Bryson's bookshop at the Sign of the Prophet Jonah in the West Bow his verses, Latin and English, had been praised by the learned. When religion called him it was as a challenge not to renounce but to perfect his past. A happy preoccupation with his dream made him blind to the harshness and jealousies which beset the Kirk, and he saw only its shining mission. The beauty which was to be found in letters seemed in very truth a part of that profounder beauty which embraced all earth and Heaven in the revelation of God. He had not ceased to be the humanist in becoming the evangelist. Some had looked askance at him as too full of carnal learning for the sacred office, some as too cheerful for a shepherd of souls in a perishing world. But his critics as yet were few, for David carried with him a light and warmth which it was hard for the sourest to resist. " He is a gracious youth," an old minister had said at his ordination. " May the Lord deal tenderly with him ! "

David's eyes from his perch on the hilltop rested first on the kirkton of Woodilee. He saw the manse among its trees, and the church with its thatched roof—the roof had been lead till Morton the Regent stripped it and melted it down for bullets. He saw the little beehive cottages in the clachan with the taller gable-end of Lucky Weir's ale-house. He saw the adjoining farm-towns—the Mains, Chasehope, Nether Windyways, Crossbasket, the two Fennans, each with its patches of crops lifted well above the bogs of the glen. He saw the mill of Woodilee at present idle by the burn, and hay being cut on the side of Windyways hill, and what looked like the clipping of the miller's sheep. In the bright evening the scene was all of peace and pastoral and David's heart kindled. There dwelled his people, the little flock whom God had appointed him to feed. His heart yearned over them, and in a sudden glow of tenderness he felt that this sunset prospect of his parish was a new and more solemn ordination.

It was long before he lifted his eyes beyond the glen to the great encircling amphitheatre of the hills. At first he gazed at them in an abstraction, till childish memories came back to him and he began to name the summits to himself one by one. There was the bald top of the Lammerlaw, and the peak of the Green Dod, and far beyond the long line of the great Herstane Craig, which in that childhood had been the synonym for untravelled mystery. He saw the green cleft in the hills where the Aller came down from its distant wells, and the darker glen of the Rood where bent was exchanged for rock and heather. He saw the very patches of meadow by Roodside which he had made his boyish playground. Such a hilltop prospect he had never before known, for a child lives in a magnified world, and finds immensity in short vistas. One thing struck hard on his mind. Never before had he realized the extent of the forest ground. He remembered travelling to Roodfoot through trees, and all up the water of Rood there had been a drift of scrub. But it was the meadows and the open spaces that had been his kingdom, and his recollection was of a bare sunny land where whaup and peewit cried and the burns fell headlong from windy moors. But now, as he gazed, he realized that the countryside was mainly forest.

Everywhere, muffling the lower glen of the Woodilee burn and the immediate vale of the Aller, and climbing far up the hillside, was the gloom of trees. In the Rood glen there was darkness only at the foot, for higher up the woods thinned into scrub of oak and hazel, with the knees of the uplands showing through it. The sight powerfully impressed his fancy. Woodilee was a mere clearing in a forest. This was the *Silva Caledonis* of which old writers spoke, the wood which once covered all the land and in whose glades King Arthur had dwelt. He remembered doggerel Latin of Merlin the Bard and strange sayings of True Thomas—old wives' tales which concerned this sanctuary. He had grown up beside it and had not known of it, and now he had come back to a revelation. *Silva Caledonis !* Up the Rood water lay the house of Calidon. Were the names perhaps the same ?

The young man's fancy was quick to kindle, and he looked with new eyes at the great cup of green, broken only at one spot by Aller side with the flash of water. At first in the soft evening light it had worn a gracious and homely air, even the darkness of the pines seemed luminous, and the feathery top of a patch of birches was like the smoke of household fires. . . . But as the sun sank behind the Rood hills a change seemed to come over the scene. The shade became gloom, a hostile impenetrable darkness. The birches were still like smoke, but a turbid smoke from some unhallowed altar. The distant shallows of Aller caught a ray of the dying sun and turned to blood. . . . The minister shivered, and then laughed at himself for his folly.

The evening deepened in the hollows, though the hilltops were still faintly bright. The great wood seemed now to be a moving thing, a flood which lapped

and surged and might at any moment overflow the sand-
spit which was Woodilee. Again the minister laughed
at himself, but without conviction. It must be an eerie
life under the shadow of that ancient formless thing.
Woodilee could not be quite as other parishes, or its folk
like other folk. The Wood, this hoary Wood of Caledon,
must dominate their thoughts and form their charac-
ters. . . . Had not some one called it the Black Wood?
—Yes, they had spoken of it that afternoon. Mr. Muirhead had admitted that it must be queer to live so near
it, and Mr. Fordyce had shaken his head solemnly and
hinted at tales that would be told if the trees could
speak. . . . Did the Devil use the place as a stronghold
and seduce the foolish into its shadows? Could it be
said of a lost soul, *Itur in antiquam silvam*?

David was less superstitious than most men, but he
had too ready a fancy and a mind too well stored with
learning to be easy at the thought. Already he felt that
he had found an antagonist. Was Woodilee to prove
a frontier-post for God's servant against the horrid
mysteries of heathendom? . . . He gave a sudden start,
for a voice had sounded behind him.

The voice was singing—a charm against bogles which
he remembered himself using as a child :

> " Wearie, Ovie, gang awa',
>   Haste ye furth o' house an' ha',
>   Ower the muir and doun the burn,
>   Wearie, Ovie, ne'er return."

A grotesque figure emerged from the dusk. It was
a tall fellow, who seemed to have been broken in the
middle, for he walked almost doubled up. His face,
seen in the half-light, was that of a man of thirty or
so, with a full black beard and red protuberant lips.

His clothes were ruinous—an old leather jerkin which gaped at every seam, ragged small-clothes of frieze, and for hosen a wrapping of dirty clouts. There were no shoes on his feet, and his unwashed face was dark as a berry. In his hand he had a long ash pole, and on his head a blue cowl so tight that it was almost a skull-cap.

David recognized the figure for Daft Gibbie, the village natural, who had greeted him with mewing and shouting at his ordination. In the clachan street he had seemed an ordinary deformed idiot—what was known locally as an " object "—but up on this twilight hilltop he was like an uncouth *revenant* from an older world. The minister instinctively gripped his staff tighter, but Gibbie's intention was of the friendliest.

" A braw guid e'en to ye, Mr. Sempill, sir. I saw ye tak' the hill and I bode to follow, for I was wantin' to bid ye welcome to Woodilee. Man, ye gang up the brae-face like a maukin.* Ower fast, I says to mysel', ower fast for a man o' God, for what saith the Word, ' He that believeth shall not make haste ! ' "

The creature spoke in a voice of great beauty and softness—the voice rather of a woman than of a man. And as he spoke he bowed, and patted the minister's arm, and peered into his face with bright wild eyes. Then he clutched David and forced him round till again he was looking over the Wood.

" The Hill o' Deer's a grand bit for a prospect, sir, for is it no like the Hill o' Pisgah from which ye can spy the Promised Land ? Ye can lift up your eyes to the hills, and ye can feast them on the bonny haughs o' the Aller, or on the douce wee clachan o' Woodilee, wi' the cots sittin' as canty round the kirk as kittlins round an auld cat."

---

* A hare.

" I was looking at the Wood," said David.

The man laughed shrilly. " And a braw sicht it is in the gloamin' frae the Hill o' Deer. For ye can see the size o' the muckle spider's wab, but doun in the glen ye're that clamjamphried wi' michty trees that your heid spins like a peery and your e'en are dozened. It's a unco thing the Wud, Mr. Sempill, sir ? "

" Do you know your ways in it, Gibbie ? "

" Me ! I daurna enter it. I keep the road, for I'm feared o' yon dark howes." Then he laughed again, and put his mouth close to the minister's ear. " Not but what I'll tak' the Wud at the proper season. Tak' the Wud, Mr. Sempill, like other folk in Woodilee."

He peered in the minister's face to see if he were understood. Satisfied that he was not, he laughed again.

" Tak' Gibbie's advice, sir, and no gang near the Wud. It's nae place for men o' God, like yoursel', sir, and puir Gibbie."

" Do they call it the Black Wood ? "

Gibbie spat. " Incomin' bodies, nae doot," he said in contempt. " But it's just the Wud wi' nae ' black ' aboot it. But ken ye the name that auld folk gie'd it ? " He became confidential again. " They ca'd it Melanudrigill," he whispered.

David repeated the word. His mind had been running on heathen learning and he wondered if the name were Greek.

" That might mean the ' place of dark waters,' " he said.

" Na, na. Ye're wrong there, Mr. Sempill. There's nae dark waters in Melanudrigill. There's the seven burns that rin south, but they're a' as clear as Aller. But dinna speak that name to ither folk, Mr. Sempill, and

3

dinna let on that Gibbie telled ye. It's a wanchancy
name. Ye can cry it in a safe bit like the Hill o' Deer,
but if ye was to breathe it in the Wud unco things
micht happen. I daurna speak my ain name among
the trees."

" Your name is Gibbie. Gibbie what ? "

The man's face seemed to narrow in fear and then to
expand in confidence. " I can tell it to a minister o'
the Word. It's Gilbert Niven. Ken ye where I got
that name ? In the Wud, sir. Ken ye wha gie'd it
me ? The Guid Folk. Ye'll no let on that I telled ye."

The night was now fallen, and David turned for home,
after one last look at the pit of blackness beneath him.
The idiot hobbled beside him, covering the ground at a
pace which tried even his young legs, and as he went he
babbled.

" Tak' Gibbie's advice and keep far frae the Wud,
Mr. Sempill, and if ye're for Roodfoot or Calidon haud
by the guid road. I've heard tell that in the auld days,
when there was monks at the kirkton, they bode to
gang out every year wi' bells and candles and bless the
road to keep it free o' bogles. But they never ventured
into the Wud, honest men. I'll no say but what a
minister is mair powerfu' than a monk, but an eident
body will run nae risks. Keep to fine caller bits like
this Hill o' Deer, and if ye want to traivel gang west by
Chasehope or east by Kirk Aller. There's nocht for a
man o' God in the Wud."

" Are there none of my folk there ? "

For a second Gibbie stopped as if thunderstruck.
" Your folk ! " he cried. " In the Wud ! " Then he
perceived David's meaning. " Na, na. There's nae
dwallin' there. Nether Fennan is no far off and Reiverslaw is a bowshot from the trees, but to bide in the

Wud !—Na, na, a man would be sair left to himsel'
ere he ventured that ! There's nae hoose biggit * by
human hand that wadna be clawed doun by bogles
afore the wa' rase a span frae the grund."

At the outfield of Mirehope Gibbie fled abruptly,
chanting like a night bird.

---

* Built.

CHAPTER II

THE ROAD TO CALIDON

THE minister sat at his supper of porridge and butter-milk when Isobel broke in on him, her apple-hued face solemn and tearful.

"There's ill news frae up the water, Mr. Sempill. It's Marion Simpson, her that's wife to Richie Smail, the herd o' the Greenshiel. Marion, puir body, has been ill wi' a wastin' the past twalmonth, and now it seems she's near her release. Johnnie Dow, the pack-man, is ben the house, and he has brocht word that Richie is fair dementit, and that the wife is no like to last the nicht, and would the minister come up to the Greenshiel. They've nae bairns, the Lord be thankit; but Richie and Marion have aye been fell fond o' ither, and Richie's an auld exercised Christian and has been many times spoken o' for the eldership. I doot ye'll hae to tak' the road, sir."

It was his first call to pastoral duty, and, though he had hoped to be at his books by candlelight, David responded gladly. He put his legs into boots, saddled his grey cob, flung his plaid round his shoulders, and in ten minutes was ready to start. Isobel watched him like a mother.

"I'll hae a cup o' burned yill * waitin' for ye to fend off the cauld—no but what it's a fine lown † nicht. Ye

* Ale. † Mild.

ken the road, sir ? Up by Mirehope and round by the Back o' the Hill."

" There's a quicker way by Roodfoot, and on this errand there's no time to lose."

" But that's through the Wud," Isobel gasped. " It's no me that would go through the Wud in the dark, nor naebody in Woodilee. But a minister is different, nae doot."

" The road is plain ? " he asked.

" Aye, it's plain eneuch. There's naething wrong wi' the road. But it's an eerie bit when the sun's no shinin'. But gang your ways, sir, for a man o' God is no like common folk. Ye'll get a mune to licht ye back."

David rode out of the kirkton, and past the saughs and elders which marked the farm of Crossbasket, till the path dipped into the glen of the Woodilee burn and the trees began. Before he knew he was among them, old gnarled firs standing sparsely among bracken. They were thin along the roadside, but on the hill to his right and down in the burn's hollow they made a cloud of darkness. The August night still had a faint reflected light, and the track, much ribbed by tree roots, showed white before him. The burn, small with the summer drought, made a far-away tinkling, the sweet scents of pine and fern were about him, the dense boskage where it met the sky had in the dark a sharp marmoreal outline. The world was fragrant and quiet ; if this be the Black Wood, thought David, I have been in less happy places.

But suddenly at a turn of the hill the trees closed in. It was almost as if he had stripped and dived into a stagnant pool. The road now seemed to have no purpose of its own, but ran on sufferance, slinking furtively haunts, tearful with excited joy. The Wood was on him again, but a different wood, his own wood. The hazels snuggled close to the roadside, and the feathery birches and rowans made a canopy, not a shadow. The oaks were ancient friends, the alders old playmates. His horse had recovered its sanity, and David rode through the dew-drenched night in a happy rapture of remembrance.

He was riding up Rood—that had always been the thing he had hoped to do. He had never been even so far as Calidon before, for a boy's day's march is short. But he had promised himself that some day when he was a man he would have a horse and ride to the utmost springs—to Roodhopefoot, to the crinkle in Moss Fell where Rood was born. . . . "Up the water" had always been like a spell in his ear. He remembered lying in bed at night and hearing a clamour at the mill door : it was men from up the water, drovers from Moffat, herds from the back of beyond, once a party of soldiers from the south. And up the water lay Calidon, that ancient castle. The Hawkshaws were a name in a dozen ballads, and the tales of them in every old wife's mouth. Once they had captained all the glens of Rood and Aller in raids to the Border, and when Musgrave and Salkeld had led a return foray it was the Hawkshaws that smote them mightily in the passes. He had never seen one of the race ; the men were always at the wars or at the King's court ; but they had filled his dreams. One fancy especially was of a little girl— a figure with gold hair like King Malcolm's daughter in the "Red Etin of Ireland" tale—whom he rescued from some dire peril, winning the thanks of her tall mail-clad kin. In that dream he too had been mail-clad, and he laughed at the remembrance.

It was a far cry from that to the sedate minister of Woodilee.

As he turned up the road to the Greenshiel he remembered with compunction his errand. He had been amusing himself with vain memories when he was on the way to comfort a bed of death. Both horse and rider were in a sober mood when they reached the sheiling, the horse from much stumbling in peat-bogs, and the man from reflections on his unworthiness.

Rushlights burned in the single room, and the door and the one window stood open. It was a miserable hut of unmortared stones from the hill, the gaps stuffed with earth and turf, and the roof of heather thatch. One glance showed him that he was too late. A man sat on a stool by the dead peat-fire with his head in his hands. A woman was moving beside the box bed and unfolding a piece of coarse linen. The shepherd of the Greenshiel might be an old exercised Christian, but there were things in that place which had no warrant from the Bible. A platter full of coarse salt lay at the foot of the bed, and at the top crossed twigs of ash.

The woman—she was a neighbouring shepherd's wife —stilled her keening at the sound of David's feet.

"It's himsel'," she cried. "Richie, it's the minister. Wae's me, sir, but ye're ower late to speed puir Mirren. An hour syne she gaed to her reward—just slipped awa' in a fit o' hoastin'.* I've strauchten'd the corp and am gettin' the deid claes ready—Mirren was aye prood o' hers and keepit them fine and caller wi' gall and rosmry. Come forrit, sir, and tak' a look on her that's gane. There was nae deid-thraws wi' Mirren, and she's lyin' as peacefu' as a bairn. Her face is sair faun in,

* Coughing.

but I mind when it was the bonniest face in a' Rood-water.''

The dead woman lay with cheeks like wax, a coin on each eye so that for the moment her face had the look of a skull. Disease had sculptured it to an extreme fineness, and the nose, the jaw, and the lines of the forehead seemed chiselled out of ivory. David had rarely looked on death, and the sight gave him a sense first of repulsion and then of an intolerable pathos. He scarcely heard the clatter of the shepherd's wife.

'' She's been deein' this mony a day and now she's gane joyfully to meet her Lord. Eh, but she was blithe to gang in the hinner end. There was a time when she was sweir to leave Richie. ' Elspet,' she says to me, ' what will that puir man o' mine dae his lee lane ? ' and I aye says to her, ' Mirren, my wumman, the Lord's a grand provider, and Richie will haud fast by Him. Are not twa sparrows,' I says——''

David went over to the husband on the creepie by the fireside, and laid his hand on his shoulder. The man sat hunched in a stupor of misery.

'' Richie,'' he said, '' if I'm too late to pray with Marion, I can pray with you.''

He prayed, as he always prayed, not in a mosaic of Scripture texts, but in simple words ; and as he spoke he felt the man's shoulder under his hand shake as with a sob. He prayed with a sincere emotion, for he had been riding through a living coloured world and now felt like an icy blast the chill and pallor of death. Also he felt the pity of this lifelong companionship broken, and the old man left solitary. When he had finished, Richie lifted his face from his hands, and into his eyes which had been blank as a wall came the wholesome dimness of tears.

" I'm no repinin'," he said. " The Lord gave and
the Lord has taken away, and I bless His name. What
saith the Apostle—Mirren has gane to be with Christ,
whilk is far better. There was mony a time when the
meal-ark was toom,* and the wind and weet cam' in
through the baulks, and the peats wadna kindle, and
we were baith hungry and cauld. But Mirren's bye wi'
a' that, for she's bielded in the everlasting arms and
she's suppin' rich at the Lord's ain table. But eh, sir,
I could wish it had been His will to hae ta'en me wi' her.
I'm an auld man, and there's nae weans,† and for the
rest o' my days I'll be like a beast in an unco loan.‡
God send they binna mony."

" The purposes of the Lord are true and altogether
righteous. If He spares you, Richie, it's because He
has still work for you to do on this earth."

" I kenna what it can be. My fit's beginnin' to lag
on the hill, and ony way I'm guid for nocht but sheep.
Lambin's and clippin's and spainin's § is ower puir a
wark for the Lord to fash wi'."

" Whatever you put your hand to is the work of the
Lord, if you keep His fear before you."

" Maybe, sir." The man rose from his stool and
revealed a huge gaunt frame, much bowed at the shoulders. He peered in the rushlight at the minister's face.

" Ye're a young callant to be a minister. I was
strong on your side, sir, when ye got the call, for your
preachin' was like a rushin' michty wind. I mind I
repeated the heids o' your sermon to Mirren. . . .
Ye've done me guid, sir—I think it's maybe the young
voice o' ye. Ye wad get the word from Johnnie Dow.
Man, it was kind to mak' siccan haste. I wish—I wish

* Empty.   † Children.   ‡ Strange lane.
§ Weanings.

ye had seen Mirren in life. . . . Pit up anither petition afore ye gang—for a blessin' on this stricken house and on an auld man who has his title sure in Christ but has an unco rebellious heart."

It seemed to David as he turned from the door, where the shepherd stood with uplifted arm, that a benediction had been given, but not by him.

The moon had risen and the glen lay in a yellow light, with the high hills between Rood and Aller shrunk to mild ridges. The stream caught the glow and its shallows were like silver chased in amber. The young man's heart was full with the scene which he had left. Death was very near to men, jostling them at every corner, whispering in their ear at kirk and market, creeping between them and their firesides. Soon the shepherd of the Greenshiel would lie beside his wife ; in a little, too, his own stout limbs would be a heap of dust. How small and frail seemed the life in that cottage, as contrasted with the rich pulsing world of the woods and hills and their serene continuance. But it was they that were the shadows in God's sight. The immortal thing was the broken human heart that could say in its frailty that its Redeemer liveth. " Thou, Lord," he repeated to himself, " in the beginning hast laid the foundations of the earth, and the heavens are the work of Thy hands. They shall perish, but Thou shalt endure ; they all shall wax old as doth a garment, and as a vesture shalt Thou change them, and they shall be changed : but Thou art the same, and Thy years shall not fail."

But as the road twined among the birches David's mood became insensibly more pagan. He could not resist the joy of the young life that ran in his members, and which seemed to be quickened by the glen of his childhood. Death was the portion of all, but youth was still far from death. . . . The dimness and delicacy of the landscape, the lines of hill melting into a haze under the moon, went to his head like wine. It was a world transfigured and spell-laden. On his left the dark blotch which was Melanudrigill lay like a spider over the hillsides and the mouths of the glens, but all in front and to his right was kindly and golden. He had come back to his own country and it held out its arms to him. " Salve, O venusta Sirmio," he cried, and an owl answered.

The glen road was reached, but he did not turn towards Roodfoot. He had now no dread of the wood of Melanudrigill, but he had a notion to stand beside Rood water, where it flowed in a ferny meadow which had been his favourite fishing-ground. So he pushed beyond the path into a maze of bracken and presently was at the stream's edge.

And then, as he guided his horse past a thicket of alders, he came full upon a little party of riders who had halted there.

There were three of them—troopers, they seemed, with buff caps and doublets and heavy cavalry swords, and besides their own scraggy horses there was a led beast. The three men were consulting when David stumbled on them, and at the sight of him they had sprung apart and laid hands on their swords. But a second glance had reassured them.

" Good e'en to you, friend," said he who appeared to be the leader. " You travel late."

It was not an encounter which David would have sought, for wandering soldiery had a bad name in the land. Something of this may have been in the other's mind, for his next words were an explanation.

" You see three old soldiers of Leven's," he said, " on the way north after the late crowning mercy vouchsafed to us against the malignants. We be Angus men and have the general's leave to visit our homes. If you belong hereaways you can maybe help us with the road. Ken you a place of the name of Calidon ? "

To their eyes David must have seemed a young farmer or a bonnet-laird late on the road from some errand of roystering or sweethearting.

" I lived here as a boy," he said, " and I'm but now returned. Yet I think I could put you on your way to Calidon. The moon's high."

" It's a braw moon," said the second trooper, " and it lighted us fine down Aller, but the brawest moon will not discover you a dwelling in a muckle wood, if you kenna the road to it."

The three had moved out from the shade of the alders and were now clear under the sky. Troopers, common troopers and shabby at that, riding weary ill-conditioned beasts. The nag which the third led was a mere rickle of bones. And yet to David's eye there was that about them which belied their apparent rank. They had spoken in the country way, but their tones were not those of countrymen. They had not the air of a gaunt Jock or a round-faced Tam from the plough-tail. All three were slim and the hands which grasped the bridles were notably fine. They held themselves straight like courtiers, and in their voices lurked a note as of men accustomed to command. The leader was a dark man with a weary thin face and great circles round his eyes ; the second a tall fellow, with a tanned skin, a cast in his left eye and a restless dare-devil look ; the third, who seemed to be their groom, had so far not spoken and had stood at the back with the led horse, but David had a glimpse above his ragged doublet of a neat small moustache and a delicate chin. "Leven has good blood in his ranks," he thought, "for these three never came out of a but-and-ben." Moreover, the ordinary trooper on his way home would not make Calidon a house of call.

He led them up to the glen road, intending to give them directions about their way, but there he found that his memory had betrayed him. He knew exactly in which nook of hill lay Calidon, but for the life of him he could not remember how the track ran to it.

"I'll have to be your guide, sirs," he told them. "I can take you to Calidon, but I cannot tell you how to get there."

"We're beholden to you, sir, but it's a sore burden on your good-nature. Does your own road lie in that airt?"

The young man laughed. "The night is fine and I'm in no haste to be in bed. I'll have you at Calidon door in half an hour."

Presently he led them off the road across a patch of heather, forded Rood at a shallow, and entered a wood of birches. The going was bad and the groom with the led horse had the worst of it. The troopers were humane men, for they seemed to have a curious care of their servant. It was "Canny now, James—there's bog on the left," or "Take tent of that howe"; and once or twice, when there was a difficult passage, one or the other would seize the bridle of the led horse till the groom had passed. David saw from the man's face that he was grey with fatigue.

"Get you on my beast," he said, "and I'll hold the bridle. I can find my way better on foot. And do you others each take a led horse. The road we're travelling

is none so wide, and we'll make better speed that
way."

The troopers docilely did as they were bidden, and
the weary groom was hoisted on David's grey gelding.
The change seemed to ease him and he lost his air of
heavy preoccupation and let his eyes wander. The
birch wood gave place to a bare hillside, where even
the grey slipped among the screes and the four horses
behind sprawled and slithered. They crossed a burn,
surmounted another ridge, and entered a thick wood of
oak which David knew cloaked the environs of Calidon
and which made dark travelling even in the strong
moonlight. Great boulders were hidden in the moss,
withered boughs hung low over the path, and now and
then would come a patch of scrub so dense that it had
to be laboriously circumvented. The groom on the
grey was murmuring to himself, and to David's amazement it was Latin. " Ibant obscuri sola sub nocte per
umbram," were the words he spoke.

David capped them.

> " Perque domos Ditis vacuas et inania regna,
>   Quale per incertam lunam . . ."

The man on the horse laughed, and David, looking
up, had his first proper sight of his face. It was a long
face, very pale, unshaven and dirty, but it was no face
of a groom. The thin aquiline nose, the broad finely
arched brow, were in themselves impressive, but the
dominant feature was the eyes. They seemed to be
grey—ardent, commanding, and yet brooding. David
was so absorbed by this sudden vision that he tripped
over a stone and almost pulled the horse down.

" I did not look," said the rider, in a voice low-pitched and musical, " I did not look to find a scholar in these hills."

" Nor did I know," said David, " that Virgil was the common reading of Leven's men."

They had reached a field of wild pasture studded with little thorns, in the middle of which stood a great stone dovecot. A burn falling in a deep ravine made a moat on one side of the tower of Calidon, which now rose white like marble in the moon. They crossed the ravine not without trouble, and joined the main road from the glen, which ended in a high-arched gate round which clustered half a dozen huts.

At the sound of their arrival men ran out of the huts and one seized the bridle of the leader. David and the groom had now fallen back, and it was the dark man who did the talking. These were strange troopers, for they sat their horses like princes, so that the hand laid on the bridle was promptly dropped.

" We would speak with the laird of Calidon," the dark man said. " Stay, carry this ring to him. He will know what it means." It seemed curious to David that the signet given to the man was furnished by the groom.

In five minutes the servant returned. " The laird waits on ye, sirs. I'll tak' the beasts, and your mails, if ye've ony. Through the muckle yett an it please ye."

David turned to go. " I've brought you to Calidon," he said, " and now I'll take my leave."

" No, no," cried the dark man. " You'll come in and drink a cup after the noble convoy you've given us. Nicholas Hawkshaw will be blithe to welcome you."

David would have refused, for the hour was already

4

late and he was many miles from Woodilee, had not the groom laid his hand on his arm. " Come," he said. " I would see my friend, the student of Virgil, in another light than the moon," and to his amazement the young man found that it was a request which he could not deny. There was a compelling power in that quiet face, and he was strangely loth to part from it.

The four dismounted, the three troopers staggering with stiff bones. The dark man's limp did not change after the first steps, and David saw that he was crippled in the left leg. They passed through the gate into a courtyard, beyond which rose the square *massif* of the tower. In the low doorway a candle wavered, under a stone which bore the hawk in lure which was the badge of the house.

The three men bowed low to the candle, and David saw that it was held by a young girl.

CHAPTER III

GUESTS IN CALIDON TOWER

"WILL you enter, sirs?" said the girl. She was clad in some dark homespun stuff with a bright-coloured screen thrown over her head and shoulders. She held the light well in front of her, so that David could not see her face. He would fain have taken his leave, for it seemed strange to be entering Calidon thus late at e'en in the company of strangers, but the hand of the groom on his arm restrained him. "You will drink a stirrup-cup, friend. The night is yet young and the moon is high."

A steep stairway ran upward a yard or two from the doorway. Calidon was still a Border keep, where the ground-floor had once been used for byres and stables, and the inhabitants had dwelt in the upper stories. The girl moved ahead of them. "Will you be pleased to follow me, sirs? My uncle awaits you above."

They found themselves in a huge chamber which filled the width of the tower, and, but for a passage and a further staircase, its length. A dozen candles, which seemed to have been lit in haste, showed that it was raftered with dark oak beams, and that the walls were naked stone where they were not covered with a coarse arras. The floor, of a great age, was bare wood black-ened with time and use, and covered with a motley of

51

sheepskins and deerskins. Two long oak tables and a
great oak bench made the chief furniture, but there
were a multitude of stools of the same heavy ancient
make, and by a big open fireplace two ancient chairs of
stamped Spanish leather. A handful of peats smouldered on the hearth, and the thin blue smoke curled
upward to add grime to an immense coat of arms carved
in stone and surmounted by a forest of deer horns and
a trophy of targes and spears.

David, accustomed only to the low-ceiled rooms of
the Edinburgh closes, stared in amazement at the size
of the place and felt abashed. The Hawkshaws had
made too great a sound in his boyhood's world for
him to enter their dwelling without a certain tremor
of the blood. So absorbed was he in his surroundings
that it was with a start that he saw the master of the
house.

A man limped forward, gathered the leader of the
party in his arms and kissed him on both cheeks.

"Will," he said, "Will, my old comrade! It's a
kind wind that has blown you to Calidon this night.
I havena clapped eyes on you these six year."

The host was a man about middle life, with the
shoulders of a bull and a massive shaggy head now in
considerable disorder from the fact that a nightcap had
just been removed from it. His clothes were of a
comfortable undress, for the tags of his doublet and the
points of his breeches were undone, and over all he
wore an old plaid dressing-gown. He had been reading,
for a pipe of tobacco marked his place in a folio, and
David noted that it was Philemon Holland's version of
the *Cyropædia*. His eyes were blue and frosty, his
cheeks ruddy, his beard an iron grey, and his voice as
gusty as a hill wind. He limped heavily as he moved.

"Man, Will," he cried, "it's a whipping up of cripples when you and me forgather. The Germany wars have made lameters of the both of us. And who are the lads you've brought with you?"

"Just like myself, Nick, poor soldiers of Leven's, on our way home to Angus."

"Angus is it this time?" The host winked and then laughed boisterously.

"Angus it is, but their names and designations can wait till we have broken our fast. 'Faith, we've as wolfish a hunger as ever you and me tholed in Thuringia. And I've brought in an honest man that guided us through your bogs and well deserves bite and sup."

Nicholas Hawkshaw peered for a moment at David. "I cannot say I'm acquaint with the gentleman, but I've been that long away I've grown out of knowledge of my own countryside. But ye shallna lack for meat and drink, for when I got your token I bade Edom stir himself and make ready. There's a good browst of yill, and plenty of French cordial and my father's Canary sack. And there's a mutton ham, and the best part of a pie—I wouldna say just what's intil the pie, but at any rate there's blackcocks and snipes and leverets, for I had the shooting of them. Oh, and there's whatever more Edom can find in the house of Calidon. Here's back your ring, Will. When I read the cognizance I had a notion that I was about to entertain greater folk——"

"Than your auld friend Will Rollo and two poor troopers of Leven's. And yet we're maybe angels unawares." He took the ring and handed it to the groom, who with David stood a little back from the others, while Nicholas Hawkshaw's eyes widened in a momentary surprise.

An ancient serving-man and a barefoot maid brought in the materials for supper, and the two troopers fell on the viands like famished crows. The groom ate little and drank less ; though he was the slightest in build of the three travellers he seemed the most hardened to the business. The lame man, who was called Will Rollo, was presently satisfied, and deep in reminiscences with his host, but the other required greater sustenance for his long wiry body, and soon reduced the pie to a fragment. He pressed morsels upon the groom—a wing of grouse, a giblet of hare—but the latter smiled and waved the food away. A friendly service, Leven's, David thought, where a servant was thus tenderly considered.

" Yon were the brave days, when you and me served as ensigns of Meldrum's in the Corpus Evangelicorum. And yon was the lad to follow, for there never was the marrow of the great Gustavus for putting smeddum into troops that had as many tongues and creeds as the Tower of Babel. But you and me were ower late on the scene. We never saw Breitenfeld—just the calamitous day of Lutzen, and the blacker day of Nordlingen where Bernhard led us like sheep to the slaughter. That was the end of campaigning for you, Will. I mind leaving you on the ground for dead and kissing your cheek, the while I was near my own end with a musketoon ball in my ribs. Then I heard you were still in life and back in Scotland, but I was off with auld Wrangel to Pomerania and had to keep my mind on my own affairs."

So the talk went on, memories of leaguers and forced marches and pitched battles, punctuated with the names of Leslies and Hamiltons and Kerrs and Lumsdens and a hundred Scots mercenaries.—" I got my quietus a

year syne serving with Torstensson and his Swedes—a
pitiable small affair in Saxonia, where I had the misfortune to meet a round shot on the ricochet which
cracked my shin-bone and has set me hirpling for the
rest of my days. My Colonel was Sandy Leslie, a
brother of Leslie of Balquhain, him that stuck Wallenstein at Eger, but a man of honester disposition and a
good Protestant. He bade me go home, for I would
never again be worth a soldier's hire, and faith ! when
the chirurgeon had finished with my leg I was of the
same opinion.—So home you find me, Will, roosting in
the cauld rickle of stones that was my forbears', while
rumours of war blow like an east wind up the glens.
I'm waiting for your news. I hear word that Davie
Leslie . . ."

"Our news can wait, Nick. We've a gentleman here
to whose ears this babble of war must sound out-
landish." It seemed to David that some secret intelligence passed between the two and that a foot of
one was pressed heavily on the other's toes.

"I am a man of peace," David said, for the talk had
stirred his fancy, "but I too have word of a glorious
victory in England won by the Covenant armies. If
you have come straight from the south you can maybe
tell me more."

"There was a victory beyond doubt," said the tall
man with the squint, "and that is why we of Leven's
are permitted to go home. We have gotten our pay,
whilk is an uncommon happening for the poor soldier
in this land."

"I have heard," said David, "that the ranks of the
Army of the Covenant fought for higher matters than
filthy lucre."

"For what, belike ? "

" For the purity of their faith and the Crown honours of Christ."

The other whistled gently through his teeth.

" No doubt. No doubt. There's a braw sough of the Gospel in Leven's ranks. But we must consider the loaves and fishes, good sir, as well as the preaching of the Word. Man canna live by bread alone, but he assuredly canna live without it, and to fill his belly he wants more than preaching. Lucre's none so filthy if it be honestly earned, and goes to keep a roof over the wife and bairns. I have served in many lands with a kennin' o' queer folk and, believe me, sir, the first thing a soldier thinks of is just his pay."

" But he cannot fight unless he has a cause to fight for."

" He'll make a very good shape at it if he has been learned his business by a heavy-handed sergeant. I have seen the riddlings of Europe stick fast as rocks before Wallenstein's horse, because they had been taught their trade and feared death less than their Colonel's tongue. And I have seen the flower of gentrice, proud as Lucifer and gallant as lions, and every one with a noble word on his lips, break like rotten twigs at the first musket volley. It's discipline that's the last word in war."

" But if the discipline be there, will not a conviction of the right of his cause make a better soldier ? "

" You have spoken a true word, and there's a man in England this day that knows it. That is what Cromwell has done. He has built up a body of horse that stand like an iron wall and move like a river in spate. They have the discipline of Gustavus's Swedes, and the fires of Hell in their hearts. I tell you, there is nothing in this land that can stand against them."

" I have no love for sectaries," said David. " But cannot our Scots do likewise, with the Covenant to nerve them ? "

The other shrugged his shoulders.

" The Covenant's but sour kail to the soldier. Davie Leslie has hammered his men into a wise-like army, because he learned his trade from Gustavus. But think you our bannock-fed foot-sentinels care a doit for the black gowns at Westminster ? A man will fight for his King and for his country and for liberty to worship God in his own way. But, unless he has a crack in his head, he will not fight for a fine point of Church government."

David was becoming ill at ease. He felt that it was his duty to testify, or otherwise he would be guilty of the sin of Meroz, the sin of apathy when his faith was challenged. But he was far from clear as to the exact nature of his faith. There was no blasphemy in questioning whether the Covenant were truly in the hearts of the people. Had not the minister of Cauldshaw that very afternoon expressed the same doubt ?

Nicholas Hawkshaw was peering at him intently.

" I should ken you, friend, for they tell me you belong to this countryside. And your face sticks in my memory, but I canna put a name to it."

" They call me David Sempill. I am the new-ordained minister of Woodilee."

Nicholas cried out. " Auld Wat o' the Roodfoot's grandson. I heard of your coming, sir, and indeed I'm your chief heritor. I'll have your hand on that. Man, I kenned your gudesire well, and many a pouchful of groats I had from him when I was a laddie. You're back among kenned folk, Mr. Sempill, and I wish you a long life in Woodilee."

The troopers did not seem to share their host's geniality. Quick glances passed between them, and the tall man shifted his seat so that he came between David and the groom. This latter had taken no part in the conversation, indeed he had not spoken a word, but after his meal was finished had sat with his head on his breast as if sunk in meditation. Now he raised his eyes to David, and it was he who spoke.

"I am not less loyal to the Kirk of Scotland than you, Mr. Sempill. You are a placed minister, and I am a humble elder of that kirk."

"In what parish?" David asked eagerly.

"In my native parish benorth of Forth."

The man's dress and station were forgotten by David when he looked at his face. Now that he saw clearly in the candlelight it was not the face of a common groom. Every feature spoke of race, the firm mouth of command, the brooding grey eyes of thought. The voice was sweet and musical, and the man's whole air had a gentle but imperious courtesy.

The movement of the tall trooper, while it had separated David from the groom, had brought the latter full into the view of Nicholas Hawkshaw. Then a strange thing happened. The host, after a long stare, during which amazement and recognition woke in his eyes, half rose from his seat and seemed on the verge of speaking. His gaze was fixed on the groom, and David read in it something at once deferential and exulting. Then the toe of the lame man's boot came down on his shin, and the lame man's hand was laid on his arm. The lame man too said something in a tongue which David could not understand. Nicholas subsided in his chair, but his face remained both puzzled and excited.

The groom spoke again.

" You are a scholar, and you are young, and you are full of the ardour of your calling. This parish is fortunate in its minister, and I would that all Scotland were as happily served. What is it that you and I seek alike ? A pure doctrine, and a liberated Kirk ? Is there no more ? "

" I seek above all things to bring men and women to God's mercy-seat."

" And I say Amen. That is more than any disputation about the forms of Presbytery. But you seek also, or I am mightily mistook in you, the freedom and well-being of this land of ours—that our Israel may have peace and prosperity in her borders."

" If the first be won, all the rest will be added unto us."

" Doubtless. But only if the first be truly won—if the Kirk attend to the work of salvation and does not expend her toil in barren fields. Her sovereign must be King Jesus. Take heed that instead it be not King Covenant."

The words recalled to David Mr. Fordyce's doubts, which had been so scornfully repelled by the ministers of Kirk Aller and Bold.

" Does it lie in the mouth of a minister or an elder of the Kirk to cavil at the Kirk's doings ? " he asked, but without conviction in his tone.

The other smiled. " You give due loyalty, as the Scripture enjoins, to the King, Mr. Sempill ? "

" I am faithful to His Majesty so long as His Majesty is faithful to law and religion."

" Even so. It is my own creed. The King must respect the limits of his prerogative—it is the condition on which he rules in a free land. My loyalty to the

Kirk is in the same case. I am loyal when she fulfils those duties which God has laid upon her—that duty above all of bringing mortal men to God. If she forget those duties and meddle arrogantly with civil matters that do not concern her, then I take leave to oppose her, as in a like case I would oppose His Majesty. For by such perversities both King and Kirk become tyrants, and tyranny is not to be endured by men who are called into the liberty of Christ."

" Or by Scots," added the tall trooper.

" I have no clearness on the point," said David after a pause. " I have not thought deeply on these matters, for I am but new to the ministry and my youth was filled with profane study."

" Nevertheless, such study is a good foundation for a wise theology. I judge that you are a ripe Latinist— maybe also a Grecian. You have read your Aristotle ? You are familiar with the history of the ancient world, which illumines all later ages ? I would point my arguments from that armoury."

" I cannot grant that the doings of ancient heathen- dom give any rule for a Christian state."

" But, sir, the business of government is always the same. We have our Lord's warning that there are the things of Cæsar and the things of God. The Roman was the great master of the arts of government, and he did not seek throughout his empire to make a single religion. He was content to give it the peace of his law, and let each people go its own way in matters of worship. It was in that tolerant world which he created that our Christian faith found its opportunity."

" Doubtless God so moved the Roman mind for His own purpose. But I join issue on your application. The Church of Christ is now in being, and the faith of

Christ is the foundation of a Christian state. Civil law is an offence against God unless it be also Christian."

The young man smiled. "I do not deny it. This realm of ours is professedly a Christian realm—I would it were more truly so. But that does not exempt it from obedience to those laws of government without which no realm, Christian or pagan, may endure. If a man is so ill a smith that he cannot shoe my horse, I will be none the better served because he is a good Christian. If a land be ill governed, the disaster will be not the less great because the governors are men of God. If His Majesty—to take a pertinent example—override the law to the people's detriment, that tyranny will be not the less grievous because His Majesty believes in his heart that he is performing a duty towards the Almighty. Honest intention will not cure faulty practice, and the fool is the fool whether he be unbeliever or professor."

David shook his head. "Where does your argument tend? I fear to schism."

"Not so. I am an orthodox son of the Kirk, a loyal servant of His Majesty, and a passionate Scot. Here, my friend, is my simple confession. There is but one master in the land and its name is Law—which is in itself a creation of a free people under the inspiration of the Almighty. That law may be changed by the people's will, but till it be so changed it is to be revered and obeyed. It has ordained the King's prerogative, the rights of the subject, and the rights and duties of the Kirk. The state is like the body, whose health is only to be maintained by a just proportion among its members. If a man's belly be his god his limbs will suffer, if he use only his legs his arms will dwindle. If therefore the King should intrude upon the subject's rights, or the subject whittle at the King's prerogative, or the

Kirk set herself above the Crown, there will be a sick state and an ailing people."

Nicholas Hawkshaw had been listening intently with a puzzled air, his eyes fixed on the groom's face, but the two troopers seemed ill at ease.

"Man, James," said the tall man, "you've mistook your calling. You should have been a regent in the college of St. Andrews, and hammered sense into the thick heads of the bejaunts."

Rollo, the lame man, shifted his seat and seemed inclined to turn the conversation.

"Patience, Mark," said the groom. "It's not often a poor soldier of Leven's gets a chance of a crack with a like-minded friend. For I'm certain that Mr. Sempill is very near my way of thinking."

"I do not quarrel with your premises," said David, "but I'm not clear about the conclusion."

"It's writ large in this land to-day. There are those that would make the King a puppet and put all authority in parliaments, and there are those who would make the Kirk like Calvin's at Geneva, a ruler over both civil and religious matters. I say that both ways lie madness and grief. If you upset the just proportion of the law you will gain not liberty but confusion. You are a scholar, Mr. Sempill, and have read the histories of Thucydides? Let me counsel you to read them again and consider the moral."

"What side are you on?" David asked abruptly.

"I am on the side of the free people of Scotland. And you by your vows are on the same side, for your concern is to feed the flock of God which is among us. Think you, sir, if you depress the balance against the King, that thereby you will win more for the people? Nay, nay, what is lost to the prerogative will go, not to the

people, but to those who prey on them. You will have
that anarchy which gives his chance to the spoiler, and
out of anarchy will come some day a man of violence
who will tyrannically make order again. It is the way
of the world, my friend."

" Are you for the Covenant ? "

At the question the others started. " Enough of
politics," cried Rollo. " These are no matters to debate
among weary folk." But the groom raised his hand
and they were silent.

" I am for the Covenant. Six years back I drew
word for it, and I did not sheathe that sword till we
had established the liberties of this land. That was
indeed a Covenant of Grace."

" There is another and a later. What say you of
that ? "

" I say of that other that it is a Covenant of Works in
which I have no part, nor any true lover of the Kirk.
It is a stepping of the Kirk beyond the bounds prescribed
by the law of God and the law of man, and it will mean
a weakening of the Kirk in its proper duties. And that
I need not tell you, as a minister of Christ, will be the
starvation and oppression of Christ's simple folk. *Quic-
quid delirant reges, plectuntur Achivi*. Is it not more
pleasing to God that His ministers should comfort the
sick and the widow and the fatherless and guide souls
to Heaven than that they should scrabble for civil pre-
eminence ? "

Into David's mind came two visions—that of the
complacent ministers of Kirk Aller and Bold as they had
discoursed at meat, and that of the old herd at the
Greenshiel sitting by his dead wife. The pictures belonged to different worlds, and at the moment he felt
that these worlds were eternally apart. He had the

disquieting thought that the one had only the husks of
faith and the other the grain. Dimly he heard the voice
of the groom. " I will give you a text, Mr. Sempill.
' The vineyard of the Lord of hosts is the house of Israel,
and the men of Judah His pleasant plant ; and He looked
for judgment, but behold oppression ; for righteousness,
but behold a cry.' "

He scarcely realized that the others had sprung to their
feet, and it was only when Nicholas Hawkshaw exclaimed
that he turned his head.

A girl stood before them, the girl who had opened
the door, but whose face he had scarcely seen at the
time in the poor light.

" Katrine, my dear, you've been long of coming." It
was Nicholas who spoke. " I thought you had slipped
off to your bed. This is my sister's child, sirs, who keeps
me company in this auld barrack—Robert Yester's
daughter, him that fell with Monro in the year 'thirty-
four. You see three gentlemen-troopers of Leven's, my
dear, and Mr. Sempill, the new minister of Woodilee."

The girl was dressed in a gown of blue velvet, the
skirts of which were drawn back in front to show an
embroidered petticoat of stiff yellow satin. It was cut
low at the neck and shoulders, and round the top ran a
broad edging of fine lace. Her dark hair was caught up
in a knot behind, but allowed to fall in curls on each
side of her face. That face, to David's startled eyes, was
like none that he had ever seen before, certainly like none
of the Edinburgh burgher girls whom he had observed in
their finery on the Saturday causeway. It was small
and delicately featured, the cheeks flushed with youth
and health, the eyes dark, brilliant, and mirthful. At
another time he would have been shocked at her dress,

for the fashion of a low bodice had not spread much beyond the Court, but now he did not take note of what she wore. He was gazing moonstruck upon a revelation.

She smiled on him—she smiled on them all. She curtsied lightly to her uncle, to Rollo, and to the dark man. But she did not curtsy to the minister. For suddenly, as she looked at the groom, her composure deserted her. Her mouth moved as if she would have spoken, and then she checked herself, for David saw that the groom had put his finger to his lips. Instead she curtsied almost to the ground, a reverence far more deep than she had accorded to the others, and when he gave her his hand she bent her head as if her impulse was to kiss it.

All this David saw with a confused vision. He had scarcely spoken ten words in his life to a woman outside his own kin, and this bright apparition loosened his knees with nervousness. He stammered his farewells. He had already outstayed the bounds of decency, and he had a long ride home—he wished his friends a safe conclusion to their journey—in the course of his pastoral visitations he would have the chance of coming again to Calidon. " 'Deed, sir, and you'll make sure of that," said the hospitable Nicholas. " There's aye a bite and a sup at Calidon for the minister of Woodilee."

He bowed to the girl, and she looked at him for the first time, a quizzical appraising look, and gave him a fleeting smile. Five minutes later he was on his horse and fording Rood.

He took the long road by the back of the Hill of Deer, riding in bright moonshine up the benty slopes and past the hazel thickets. His mind was in a noble confusion, for on this, his first day in his parish, experiences had thronged on him too thick and fast. Out of the welter

5

two faces stood clear, the groom's and the girl's. . . .
He remembered the talk, and his conscience pricked him.
Had he been faithful to his vows ?   Had he been guilty
of the sin of Meroz ?   Had he listened to railing accusations and been silent ? . . . He did not know—in truth
he did not care—for the sum of his recollection was not
of an argument but of a person.   The face of the young
man had been more than his words, for it had been the
face of a comrade, and an intimate friendliness had
looked out of his eyes.   He longed to see him again, to
be with him, to follow him, to serve him—but he did not
know his name, and they would doubtless never meet
again.   David was very young, and could have wept at
the thought.

And the girl . . . ?   The sight of her had been the
coping-stone to a night of marvels.   She was not like
the groom—he had been glad to flee from her company,
for she had no part in his world.   But a marvel beyond
doubt !   The recollection of her made him a poet, and
as he picked his way over the hill he was quoting to
himself the lines in Homer where the old men of Troy
see Helen approaching and wonder at her beauty. . . .
οὐ νέμεσις Τρῶας—how did it go ?   " Small wonder that
the Trojans and the mailed Greeks should endure pain
through many years for such a woman.   In face she is
strangely like to some immortal."

And then he felt compunction, for he remembered the
worn face of the dead woman at the Greenshiel.

CHAPTER IV

THE FAITHFUL SERVANT

FOR two days the minister of Woodilee was a man unbalanced and distraught. He sat at his books without concentration, and he wandered on the hills without delight, while Isobel's face puckered in dismay as she removed his scarcely tasted meals. It was hot thundery weather, with storms that never broke in rain grumbling among the glens, and to this she set down his indisposition to eat. But David's trouble was not of the body. He had thought himself the mailed servant of God, single in purpose, armed securely against the world, and lo ! in a single night he had been the sport of profane fancies and had rejoiced in vanities.

The girl he scarcely thought of—she had scared rather than enthralled him. But the Wood of Melanudrigill lay heavy on his conscience. Where was his Christian fortitude if a black forest at night could set him shivering like a lost child ? David had all his life kept a tight hand on his courage ; if he dreaded a thing, that was good reason why he should go out of his road to face it. His instinct was to return alone to Melanudrigill in the dark, penetrate its deepest recesses, and give the lie to its enchantments. . . . But a notion which he could not combat restrained him. That was what the Wood wanted, to draw him back to it through curiosity or fear.

If he yielded to his impulse he would be acknowledging
its power.   It was the part of a minister of God to deny
at the outset that the place was more than a common
wilderness of rock and tree, to curb his fancies as things
too vain for a grown man's idlest thought.

On this point he fixed his resolution and found some
comfort.   But the memory of Calidon and the troopers
and the groom's words remained to trouble him.   Had
he not borne himself in their company as a Laodicean,
assenting when he should have testified ? . . . He went
over every detail of the talk, for it stuck firmly in his
mind.   They had decried the Solemn League and Covenant in the name of the Kirk, and he had not denounced
them. . . . And yet they had spoken as Christian men
and loyal sons of that Kirk. . . . What meant, too, the
groom's disquisition on law and government?   David
found the argument hard to gainsay—it presented a
doctrine of the state which commended itself to his
reason.   Yet it was in flat contradiction of the declared
view of that Kirk which he was sworn to serve, and what
then became of his ordination vows ? . . . But was it
contrary to the teaching of the Word and the spirit of
his faith ?   He searched his mind on this point and
found that he had no clearness.

His duty, it seemed, was to go to some father-in-God
like the minister of Kirk Aller, and lay his doubts before
him.   But he found that course impossible.   The pale
fleshy face of Mr. Muirhead rose before him, as light-
giving as a peat-stack ; he heard his complacent tones,
saw the bland conceit in his ruminant eyes.   Nor would
he fare better with the militancy of his brother of Bold,
who classed all mankind as Amalekites, save the chosen
few who wore his own phylacteries.   Mr. Fordyce might
give him comfort, and he was on the point many times

of saddling his horse and riding to the manse of Cauld-shaw. . . . But each time he found it impossible, and when he asked himself the cause he was amazed at the answer. Loyalty forbade him—loyalty to the young man, habited as a groom, who had spoken both as counsellor and comrade. That was the enduring spell of that strange night. David as a youth in Edinburgh had had few familiar friends, and none that could be called intimate. For the first time he had met one from whom had gone forth an influence that melted his heart. He recalled with a kind of aching affection the gentle, commanding courtesy, the winning smile, the masterful and yet wistful grey eyes. " I wonder," he thought, " if I was not meant to be a soldier. For I could follow yon man most joyfully to the cannon's mouth."

On the third day peace returned to him, when he buried Marion of the Greenshiel. The parish coffin was not used, as was the custom for poor folk, since the farmer of Reiverslaw, Richie's master, paid the cost of a private one, and himself attended the " chesting " the night before. On the day David walked the seven miles to the cottage, where Richie had set out a poor entertainment of ale and oatcakes for the mourners. It was not the fashion for the minister to pray at the house or at the grave, as savouring of Popish prayers for the dead, nor was it the custom for a widower to attend the funeral ; but David took his own way, and prayed with the husband, the wailing women, and the half-dozen shep-herds who had assembled for the last rites. The light coffin was carried by four young men, and David walked with them all the way to Woodilee. The farmer of Reiverslaw joined them at a turn of the road—his name was Andrew Shillinglaw, a morose dark man not over-

well spoken of in the parish—and he and the minister
finished the journey side by side. The bellman, Nehe-
miah Robb, who was also the gravedigger and the
beadle, met them at the entrance to the kirkton, and
with him a crowd of villagers. Preceded by the jángling
of Robb's bell, the procession reached the shallow grave,
the women remaining at the kirkyard gate. The coffin
was lowered, the earth shovelled down, and the thing
in five minutes was over. There was no " dredgy " *
at the poor house of the Greenshiel to draw the mourners
back upon the seven moorland miles. The men adjourned to Lucky Weir's, the kirk bell was restored to
its tree, a woman or two sobbed, and the last of Marion
Smail was a thin stream of figures vanishing in the haze
of evening, one repeating to the other in funereal voices
that "puir Mirren had got weel awa'."

Yet the occasion, austere and bare as poverty could
make it, woke in David a mood of tenderness and peace.
The lowering clouds had gone from the sky, all morning
it had rained, and the afternoon had had a soft autumn
freshness. He had prayed with Richie, but his prayers
had been also for himself, and as he walked behind the
coffin on the path by the back of the Hill of Deer his
petition seemed to have been answered. He had an
assurance of his vocation. The crowd at the kirkyard,
those toil-worn folk whose immortal souls had been
given into his charge, moved him to a strange exultation.
He saw his duty cleared from all doubts, and there must
have been that in his face which told of his thoughts,
for men greeted him and then passed on, as if unwilling
to break in on his preoccupation. Only Reiverslaw,
who was on his way to Lucky Weir's whence he would
depart drunk in the small hours, was obtuse in his per-

* Funeral feast.

ceptions. He took the minister's hand and shook it as he would a drover's at a fair, seemed anxious to speak, found no words, and left with a grunted farewell.

It was a fine, long-drawn-out back-end, the best that had been known for twenty years. All September the sun shone like June, and it was well into October before the morning frosts began, and the third week of November before the snow came. The little crops—chiefly grey oats and barley, with an occasional rig of peas and flax—were well ripened and quickly reaped. The nettie-wives were busy all day in the fields, and the barefoot children made the leading in of the harvest a holiday, with straw whistles in their mouths and fantastic straw badges on their clothing. Then came the threshing with jointed flails, and the winnowing on barn roofs when the first east winds blew. There were no gleaners in the empty stubbles, for it was held a pious duty to leave something behind for the fowls of the air. Presently the scanty fruits of the earth were under cover, the bog hay in dwarfish ricks, the unthreshed oats and bear in the barns, the grain in the girnels, and soon the wheel of the Woodilee mill was clacking merrily to grind the winter's meal. In that parish the burden of the laird lay light. Nicholas Hawkshaw asked no more than his modest rental in kind, and did not exact his due in labour, but for a week the road by the back of the Hill of Deer saw a procession of horses carrying the " kain " meal to the Calidon granary. As the minister watched the sight one day, Ephraim Caird, the Chasehope tenant, stood beside him, looking gloomily at his own beasts returning. " That's the way our puir crops are guided," he said. " As the auld folk used to say, ' Ane part to saw, ane part to gnaw, and ane to pay the

laird witha'.'" His eyes showed that he had no love
for Calidon.

Hallowmass that year was a cheerful season. The
elders shook their heads at the Hallowe'en junketings,
and the severe Chasehope was strong in his condemnation. But on the night of Hallowe'en, as David
walked in the bright moonlight and saw the lights in
the cottages and heard laughter and a jigging of fiddles,
he did not find it in his heart to condemn the ancient
fashions. Nor apparently did Chasehope himself, for
David was much mistaken if it was not Ephraim's great
shoulders and fiery head that he saw among the cabbage-
stalks in Nance Kello's garden. He had been to Hallow-
e'en frolics himself in past days when he stayed with his
cousin at Newbiggin, but it seemed to him that here in
Woodilee there was something oppressed and furtive
in the merriment. There was a secrecy about each lit
dwelling, and no sign of young lads and lasses laughing
on the roads. He noticed, too, that for the next few
days many of the people had a look of profound weariness—pale faces, tired eyes, stealthy glances—as if behind the apparent decorum there had been revels that
exhausted soul and body.

With the reaping of the harvest the ill-conditioned
cattle were brought from the hills to the stubbles, and
soon turned both outfield and infield into a miry wilderness. David, whose knowledge of farming was derived
chiefly from the *Georgics*, had yet an eye in his head and
a store of common sense, and he puzzled at the methods.
The land at its best was ill-drained, and the trampling
of beasts made a thousand hollows which would be
puddles at the first rains and would further sour the rank
soil. But when he spoke on the matter to the farmer
of Mirehope, he was answered scornfully that that had

been the " auld way of the land," and that those who were proud in their own conceit and had tried new-fangled methods—he had heard word of such in the West country—could not get two bolls from an acre where he had four. " And Mirehope's but wersh * land, sir, and not to be named wi' the Clyde howms."

When the November snows came all live stock was gathered into the farm-towns. The cattle were penned in yards with thatched shelters, and soon turned them into seas of mud. The milking cows were in the byre ; the sheep in paddocks near-by ; the draught-oxen and the horses in miserable stables of mud and heather. It was the beginning of the winter hibernation, and the chief work of the farms was the feeding of the stock on their scanty winter rations. The hay—coarse bog grasses with little nutriment in them—went mainly to the sheep ; horses and cattle had for fodder straw and messes of boiled chaff ; while Crummie in the byre was sometimes regaled with the débris of the kailyard and the oddments left from the family meals. Winter each year was both for beast and man a struggle with famine, and each was rationed like the people of a besieged city. But if food was scarce at the best, Woodilee did not want for fuel. It had been a good year for peats, for they had ripened well on the hills, and the open autumn had made them easy to carry. Each cottage had its ample peat-stack, and when harvest was over there had been also a great gathering of windfalls from the woods, so that by every door stood a pile of kindlings.

Melanudrigill in the bright October days had lost its menace for David. He had no occasion to visit it by night, but more than once he rode through it by day on his pastoral visitations to Fennan or the Rood valley,

* Sour.

and once in a flaming sunset he returned that way from Kirk Aller. The bracken was golden in decay, and the yellowing birches, the russet thorns, and the occasional scarlet of rowans made the sombre place almost cheerful. In his walks on the hill the great forest below him seemed to have grown thin and open, no longer a vast enveloping cloak, but a kindly covering for the ribs of earth. Some potency had gone from it with the summer, as if the tides of a fierce life had sunk back into the ground again. He had seen deer in the glades, and they looked innocent things. . . . But he noticed as curious that none of the villagers in their quest for wood penetrated far into it, and that on its fringes they only gathered the windfalls. Up at the back of the Hill of Deer and in the Rood glen men were busy all day cutting birch and hazel billets, but no axe was laid to any tree in the Black Wood.

A week before Yule came the great snow. It began with a thin cold fog which muffled every fold of the hills. "Rouk's * snaw's wraith," said the parish, and saw to its fuel-stacks and lóoked gloomily at its shivering beasts. The thick weather lasted for three days and three nights, weather so cold that it was pain to draw breath, and old folk at night in their box beds could not get warmth, and the Woodilee burn was frozen hard even in the linns. It was noted as a bad omen that deer from Melanudrigill were seen in the kirkton, and that at dawn when the Mirehope shepherd went out to his sheep he found half-frozen blue hares crouching among the flocks. On the fourth morning the snow began, and fell for three days in heavy flakes, so that it lay feet deep on the roads and fields. Then the wind rose and for six furious hours a blizzard raged, so that the day was like night, and few

* Fog.

dared stir from their doors. David, setting out to visit
Amos Ritchie's wife, who was sick of a congestion, took
two hours over a quarter of mile of road, wandering
through many kitchen middens, and had to postpone
his return till the wind abated in the evening, while
Isobel in the manse was demented with anxiety. The
consequence was that the snow was swept bare from the
knowes, but piled into twelve-foot drifts in the hollows.
It was an ill time for the sheep in the paddocks, which
were often one giant drift, where the presence of the
flock could only be detected by the yellowish steaming
snow. Chasehope lost a score of ewes, Mirehope half
as many, and Nether Fennan, where the drifts were deep,
the best part of his flock. To David it seemed that the
farmers' ways were a tempting of Providence. Had the
sheep been left on the hill they would have crowded in
the snow to the bare places ; here in the confined paddocks they were caught in a trap. Moreover, on the hill
in open winter weather there was a better living to be
picked up than that afforded by the narrow rations of
sour bog hay. But when he spoke thus his hearers
plainly thought him mad. Sheep would never face a
winter on the hills—besides, the present practice was
the " auld way."

The snow lay till the New Year was a week old, and
when the thaw came and the roads ran in icy streams,
David took to his bed for two days in utter exhaustion.
All through the storm he had been on his legs, for there
were sick folk and old folk in Woodilee who would perish
miserably if left alone. The farm-towns could look after
themselves, but in the scattered cottages of the kirkton
there was no one to take command, and neighbourliness
languished when each household was preoccupied with
its own cares. Peter Pennecuik, a ruling elder, whose

gift of prayer had been commended by Mr. Muirhead, had lost a tup and had his byre roof crushed in by the drift, so he became a fatalist, holding that the Lord had prepared a visitation which it would be impiety to resist, and sat lugubriously by his fireside. David's fingers itched for his ears. From Amos Ritchie the blacksmith he got better assistance. Amos was a shaggy black-bearded man of thirty-five, a great fiddler and a mighty putter of the stone, whose godliness might have been suspect but for his behaviour in the Bishops' War. His wife was at death's door all through the storm, but he nevertheless constituted himself the minister's first lieutenant and wrought valiantly in the work of relief. There were old women too chilled and frail to kindle their fires in the morning and melt snow for water; there were households so ill provided that they existed largely on borrowed food; there were cots where the weather had broken roof or wall. Isobel in the manse kitchen was a busy woman and her girdle was never off the fire. David had looked forward to the winter snows as a season of peace, when he could sit indoors with his books; instead he found himself on his feet for fourteen hours out of the twenty-four, his hands and face chapped like a ploughman's, and so weary at night that he fell off his chair with sleep while Isobel fetched his supper.

Yet it was the storm which was David's true ordina-tion to his duties, for it brought him close to his people, not in high sacramental things like death, but in their daily wrestling for life. He might visit their houses and catechize their families, but these were formal occasions, with all on their best behaviour, whereas in the intimate business of charity he saw them as they were.

The new minister was young and he was ardent, and his duties were still an adventure. His Sabbath sermons were diligently meditated. For his morning lecture he took the book of the prophet Amos, which, as the work of a herdsman, seemed fitting for a country parish. His two weekly discourses dealt laboriously with the fourfold state of man—his early state of innocence, his condition after the Fall, his state under grace, his condition in eternity. That winter David did not get beyond the state of innocence, and in discoursing on it he exhausted his ingenuity in piecing texts together from the Scriptures, and in such illustrations as he believed would awaken his hearers' minds. Profane learning openly used would have been resented, but he contrived to bring in much that did not belong to the divinity schools, and he escaped criticism, it may be, because his Kirk Session did not understand him. His elders were noted theologians, and what was strange to them, if it was weightily phrased, they took for theological profundity.

At ten o'clock each Sabbath morning Robb the beadle tinkled the first bell ; at the second the congregation moved into the kirk, and Peter Pennecuik, who acted as precentor, led the opening psalm, reading each line before it was sung. When Robb jerked the third bell, David entered the pulpit and began with prayer. At one o'clock the people dispersed, those who came from a distance to Lucky Weir's ale-house ; and at two fell the second service, which concluded at four with the coming of the dark. The kirk with its earthen floor was cold as a charnel-house, and the dimness of the light tried even David's young eyes. The people sat shivering on their little stools, each with the frozen decorum and strained attention which was their Sabbath ritual. To the minister it seemed often as if he were speaking to sheeted tombstones, he felt as if his hearers were at an infinite distance from him, and only on rare occasions,

when some shining text of Scripture moved his soul and
he spoke simply and with emotion, did he feel any contact with his flock.

But his sermons were approved. Peter Pennecuik
gave it as his verdict that he was a "deep" preacher
and sound in the fundamentals. Others, remembering
the thrill that sometimes came into his voice, called
him an "affectionate" preacher, and credited him
with "unction." But there were many that longed
for stronger fare, something more marrowy and awful,
pictures of the hell of torment which awaited those who
were not of the Elect. He had the "sough," no doubt,
but it was a gentle west wind, and not the stern Euroc-
lydon which should call sinners to repentance. Their
minister was a man of God, but he was young; years
might add weight to him and give him the thunders
of Sinai.

To David the Sabbath services were the least of his
duties. He had come to Woodilee with his heart full
of the mighty books which he would write in the solitude
of his upper chamber. The chief was that work on the
prophet Isaiah which should be for all time a repository
of sacred learning, so that Sempill on Isaiah would be
quoted reverently like Luther on the Galatians or Calvin
on the Romans. In the autumn evenings he had sketched
the lines of his masterpiece, and before the great snow
he had embarked on its prolegomena. But the storm
made a breach in his studies. He felt himself called to
more urgent duties, for he was a pastor of souls before
he was a scholar. His visitations and catechizings
among his flock were his chief care, and he began to win
a name for diligence. On nights when even a shepherd
would have kept the ingleside, David would arrive at
a moorland cottage, and many a time Isobel had to

welcome in the small hours a dripping or frozen master, thaw him by her kitchen fire, and feed him with hot ale and bannocks, while he recounted his adventures. He was strong and buoyant and he loved the life, which seemed to him to have the discipline of a soldier. His face high-coloured by weather, his cheerful eyes, and his boyish voice and laugh were soon popular in the length of the parish. " He is a couthy lad," said the old wives, "and for a man o' God he's terrible like a plain body."

Also he took charge of the children. In Woodilee there was no school or schoolmaster. There were three hundred communicants, but it was doubtful if more than a dozen could read a sentence or write their names. In the Kirk Session itself there were only three. So David started a school, which met thrice a week of a morning in the manse kitchen. He sent to Edinburgh for horn-books, and with them and his big Bible taught his class their rudiments. These were the pleasantest hours of the day for master and children, and weekly the gathering grew till there was not a child in the kirkton or in the farm-towns of Mirehope and Chasehope that would have missed them. When they arrived blue with cold and often breakfastless, Isobel would give each a bowl of broth, and while the lesson proceeded she would mend their ragged garments. Indeed more than one child emerged new clad, for the minister's second-best cloak and an old pair of breeches were cut up by Isobel— expostulating but not ill-pleased—for tattered little mortals.

David was more than a private almoner. He and his Session had the Poor Box to administer, the sole public means of relieving the parish's needs. Woodilee was better off than many places, in that it possessed

a mortification of a thousand pounds Scots, bequeathed
fifty years earlier by a certain Grizel Hawkshaw for the
comfort of the poor. Also there was the weekly collec-
tion at the kirk services, where placks and doits and
bodles and a variety of debased coins clinked in the
plate at the kirk door, and there were the fines levied
by the Session on evil-doers. In the winter the task
of almoner was easier, for there were few beggars on
the roads, and those that crossed the hills came as a
rule only to die, when the single expense was the use
of the parish coffin. Yet the administration of the
scanty funds was a difficult business, and it led to David's
first controversies with his Session. Each elder had his
own favourites among the poor, and Chasehope and
Mirehope and Nether Fennan wrangled over every grant.
The minister, still new to the place, for the most part
held his peace, but now and then, in cases which he knew
of, he asserted his authority. There was a woman
none too well reputed, who lived at Chasehope-foot, with
a buxom black-eyed daughter, and whose house, though
lamentably dirty and ill guided, seemed to lack nothing.
When he opposed Chasehope's demand that she should
receive a benefaction as a lone widow, he had a revelation of Chasehope's temper. The white face crimsoned,
and the greenish eyes looked for a moment as ugly as a
snarling dog's. " Worthy Mr. Macmichael . . ." he
began, but David cut him short. " These moneys are
for the relief of the helpless poor," he said, " and they
are scant enough at the best. I should think shame to
waste a bodle except on a pitiful necessity. To him or
her that hath shall not be given, while I am the minister
of this parish." Chasehope said nothing, and presently
he mastered his annoyance, but the farmer of Mirehope
—Alexander Sprot was his name—muttered something

in an undertone to his neighbour, and there was tension in the air till the laugh of the Woodilee miller broke it. This man, one Spotswood, reckoned the richest in the parish and the closest, had a jolly laugh which belied his reputation. "Mr. Sempill's in the right, Chasehope," he cried. "Jean o' the Chasehope-fit can manage fine wi' what her gudeman left her. We daurna be lovish wi' ither folks' siller." "I am overruled," said Chasehope, and spoke no more.

Little news came in those days to Woodilee. In the open weather before the storm the pack-horses of the carriers came as usual from Edinburgh, and the drovers on the road to England brought word of the doings in the capital. Johnnie Dow, the packman, went his rounds till the snow stopped him, but in January, when the weather cleared, he broke his leg in the Tarrit Moss and for six weeks disappeared from the sight of men. But Johnnie at his best brought only the clash of the farm-towns and the news of Kirk Aller, and in the dead of the winter there was no chance of a post, so that David was buried as deep as if he had been in an isle of the Hebrides. It was only at Presbytery meetings that he heard tidings of the outer world, and these, passed through the minds of his excited brethren, were all of monstrous portents.

The Presbytery meetings in Kirk Aller were at first to David a welcome break in his quiet life. The one in November lasted two days, and he, as the youngest member, opened the exercises and discoursed with acceptance on a Scripture passage. The business was dull, being for the most part remits from the kirk sessions of contumacious heritors and local scandals and repairs to churches. The sederunt over, the brethren

adjourned to the Cross Keys Inn and dined off better
fare than they were accustomed to in their manses.
It was then that Mr. Muirhead in awful whispers told
of news he had had by special post from Edinburgh.
Malignancy had raised its head again, this time in their
own covenanted land. Montrose, the recusant, had
made his way north when he was least expected, and
was now leading a host of wild Irish to the slaughter of
the godly. There had been battles fought, some said
near Perth, others as far off as Aberdeen, and the victory
had not been to the righteous. Hideous tales were told
of these Irish, led by a left-handed Macdonald—savage
as Amalekites, blind zealots of Rome, burning and
slaughtering and sparing neither sex nor age. The
trouble, no doubt, would be short-lived, for Leven's
men were marching from England, but it betokened
some backsliding in God's people. The Presbytery held
a special meeting for prayer, when in lengthy supplications the Almighty was besought to explain whether the
sin for which this disaster was the punishment lay with
Parliament or Assembly, army or people.

To David the tale was staggering. Montrose was to
him only a name, the name of a great noble who had at
first served the cause of Christ and then betrayed it.
This Judas had not yet gone to his account, was still permitted to trouble Israel, and now he had crowned his
misdeeds by leading savages against his own kindly
Scots. Like all his nation he had a horror of the Irish,
whose barbarity had become a legend, and of Rome,
whom he conceived as an unsleeping Anti-Christ, given
a lease of the world by God till the cup of her abomina-
tion was full. The news shook him out of his political
supineness, and for the moment made him as ardent
a Covenanter as Mr. Muirhead himself. Then came the

storm, when his head was filled with other concerns, and it was not till February that the Presbytery met again. This time the rumours were still darker. That very morning Mr. Muirhead had had a post which spoke of Montrose ravaging the lands of that light of the Gospel, Argyll—of his fleeing north and, at the moment when his doom seemed assured, turning on the shore of a Highland sea-loch and scattering the Covenant army. It was the hour of peril, and the nation must humble itself before the Lord. A national fast had been decreed by Parliament, and it was resolved to set apart a day in each parish when some stout defender of the faith should call the people to examination and repentance. Mr. Proudfoot of Bold was one of the chosen vessels, and it was agreed that he should take the sermon on the fast-day in Woodilee in the first week of March.

But David was now in a different mood from that of November. He repressed with horror an unregenerate admiration for this Montrose, who, it seemed, was still young, and with a handful of caterans had laid an iron hand on the north. He might be a fine soldier, but he was beyond doubt a son of Belial. The trouble with David was the state of his own parish, compared with which the sorrows of Argyll seemed dim and far-away.

January, after the snows melted, had been mild and open, with the burns running full and red, and the hills one vast plashing bog. With Candlemas came a black frost, which lasted the whole of February and the first half of March. The worst of the winter stringency was now approaching. The cattle in the yards and the sheep in the paddocks had become woefully lean, the meal in the girnels was running low, and everybody in the parish, except one or two of the farmers, had grown thin and pale-faced.   Sickness was rife, and in one week the kirk-yard saw six burials. . . . It was the season of births, too, as well as of deaths, and the howdie * was never off the road.

Strange stories came to his ears.   One-half of the births were out of lawful wedlock . . . and most of the children were still-born.   A young man is slow to awake to such a condition, and it was only the miserable business of the stool of repentance which opened his eyes.   Haggard girls occupied the stool and did penance for their sin, but in only one case did the male paramour appear. . . . He found his Session in a strange mood, for instead of being eager to enforce the law of the Kirk, they seemed to desire to hush up the scandals, as if the thing was an epidemic visitation which might spoil their own repute. He interrogated them and got dull replies ; he lost his temper and they were silent.   Where were the men who had betrayed these wretched girls ?   He repeated the question and found only sullen faces.   One Sabbath he abandoned his ordinary routine and preached on the abominations of the heathen with a passion new to his hearers.   His discourse was appreciated, and he was congratulated on it by Ephraim Caird ; but there was no result, no confession, such as he had hoped for, from stricken sinners, no cracking of the wall of blank obstinate silence. . . . The thing was never out of his mind by day or night.   What was betokened by so many infants born dead ?   He felt himself surrounded by a mystery of iniquity.

One night he spoke of it to Isobel, very shamefacedly, for it seemed an awful topic for a woman, however old. But Isobel was no more communicative than the rest. Even her honest eyes became shy and secretive.   " Dinna

* Midwife.

you fash yoursel', sir," she said. "The Deil's thrang in this parochine, and ye canna expect to get the upper hand o' him in sax months. But ye'll be even wi' him yet, Mr. Sempill, wi' your graund Gospel preachin'." And then she added that on which he pondered many times in the night watches. "There will aye be trouble at this time o' year so long as the folk tak' the Wud at Beltane."

The fast-day came and Mr. Proudfoot preached a marrowy sermon. His subject was the everlasting fires of Hell, which awaited those who set their hand against a covenanted Kirk, and he exhausted himself in a minute description of the misery of an eternity of torment. "They shall be crowded," he said, "like bricks in a fiery furnace. O what a bed is there! No feathers, but fire; no friends, but furies; no ease, but fetters; no daylight, but darkness; no clock to pass away the time, but endless eternity; fire eternal that ever burns and never dies." He excelled in his conclusion. "Oh, my friends," he cried, "I have given you but a short touch of the torments of Hell. Think of a barn or some other great place filled up top-full with grains of corn; and think of a bird coming every thousand years and fetching away one of those grains of corn. In time there might be an end of all and the barn might be emptied, but the torments of Hell have no end. Ten thousand times ten millions of years doth not at all shorten the miseries of the damned."

There was a hush like death in the crowded kirk. A woman screamed in hysterics and was carried out, and many sobbed. At the close the elders thronged around Mr. Proudfoot and thanked him for a discourse so seasonable and inspired. But David spoke no word, for his heart had sickened. What meant these thunders against public sin when those who rejoiced in them were ready to condone a flagrant private iniquity ? For a moment he felt that Montrose the apostate, doing evil with clean steel and shot, was less repugnant to God than his own Kirk Session.

The frost declined in mid-March, there was a fortnight of weeping thaw and a week of bitter east winds, and then in a single night came a south wind and Spring blew up the glens.

Isobel chased the minister from his books.

"Awa' to the hill like a man, and rax * your legs. Ye've had a sair winter and your face is like a dish-clout. Awa' and snowk up the caller air."

David went out to the moors, and on the summit of the Hill of Deer had a prospect of the countryside, the contours sharp in the clear April light, and colour stealing back after the grey of winter. The Wood of Melanudrigill seemed to have crowded together again, and to have regained its darkness, but there was as yet no mystery in its shadows. The hill itself was yellow like old velvet, but green was mantling beside the brimming streams. The birches were still only a pale vapour, but there were buds on the saughs and the hazels. Remnants of old drifts lay behind the dykes, and on the Lammer Law there was a great field of snow, but the breeze blew soft and the crying of curlews and plovers told of the spring. Up on Windy-ways and at the back of Reiverslaw the heather was burning, and spirals of blue smoke rose to the pale skies.

The sight was a revelation to a man to whom Spring had come hitherto in the narrow streets of Edinburgh.

* Stretch.

He had a fancy that life was beating furiously under the brown earth, and that he was in the presence of a miracle. His youth, long frosted by winter, seemed to return to him and his whole being to thaw. Almost shamefacedly he acknowledged an uplift of spirit. The smoke from the moorburn was like the smoke of sacrifice on ancient altars—innocent sacrifice from kindly altars.

That night in his study he found that he could not bring his mind to his commentary on the prophet Isaiah. His thoughts ranged on other things, and he would fain have opened his Virgil. But, since these evening hours were dedicate to theology, he compromised with Clement of Alexandria, and read again the passage where that father of the Church becomes a poet and strives to mingle the classic and the Christian.— "*This is the Mountain beloved of God, not a place of tragedies like Cithæron, but consecrate to the dramas of truth, a mount of temperance shaded with the groves of purity. And there revel on it not the Mænads, sisters of Semele the thunderstruck, initiate in the impure feast of flesh, but God's daughters, fair Lambs who celebrate the holy rites of the Word, chanting soberly in chorus.*"

In these days his sermons changed. He no longer hammered subtle chains of doctrine, but forsook his "ordinary," and preached to the hearts of the people. Woodilee was in turn mystified, impressed, and disquieted. One bright afternoon he discoursed on thankfulness and the praise due to God. "Praise Him," he cried, "if you have no more, for this good day and sunshine to the lambs."

"Heard ye ever the like?" said Mirehope at the kirk door. "What concern has Jehovah wi' our lambin'?"

"He's an affectionate preacher," said Chasehope, "but he's no Boanerges, like Proudfoot o' Bold."

The other agreed, and though the tone of the two men was regretful, their eyes were content, as if they had no wish for a Boanerges in Woodilee.

CHAPTER V

THE BLACK WOOD BY DAY

On the 22nd day of April the minister went for a walk on the Hill of Deer. He had heard news from Isobel which had awakened his numbed memory. All the long dark winter Woodilee had been severed from the world, and David had also lived in the cage and had had no thoughts beyond the parish. Calidon and its people were as little in his mind as if they had been on another planet. But as Spring loosened the bonds word of the neighbourhood's doings was coming in.

"Johnnie Dow's ben the house," Isobel had said as he sat at meat. "He's come down the water frae Calidon, and it seems there's unco changes there. The laird is awa' to the wars again. . . . Na, Johnnie didna ken what airt he had ridden. He gaed off ae mornin' wi' his man Tam Purves, baith o' them on muckle horses, and that's the last heard o' them. It seems that the laird's gude-sister, Mistress Saintserf frae Embro, cam' oot a fortnight syne to tak' chairge o' Calidon and the young lassie—there's a lassie bides there, ye maun ken, sir, though nane o' the Woodilee folk ever cast een on her—and the puir body was like to be smoored * in the Carnwath Moss. Johnnie says she's an auld wumman as straucht as a wand and wi'

* Smothered.

an unco ill tongue in her heid. She fleyed Johnnie
awa' frae the door when he was for daffin' wi' the
serving lasses.''

It was of Calidon that David thought as he took the
hill. Nicholas Hawkshaw, lame as he was, had gone
back to the wars. What wars? Remembering the
talk of that autumn night he feared that it could not
be a campaign of which a minister of the Kirk would
approve. Was it possible that he had gone to join
Montrose in his evil work? And the troopers and the
groom? Were they with Leven again under the Covenant's banner, or were they perilling their souls with
the malignants? The latter most likely, and to his
surprise he felt no desire to reprobate them. Spring
was loosening other bonds than those of winter.

It was a bright warm day, which might have been
borrowed from June, and the bursting leaves were
stirred by a wandering west wind. David sat for a
little on the crest of the hill, gazing at the high summits,
which, in the April light, were clear in every nook and
yet infinitely distant. The great Herstane Craig had
old snowdrifts still in its ravines, and he had the fancy
that it was really built of marble which shone in places
through the brown husk. The Green Dod did not now
belie its name; above the screes and heather of its
flanks rose a cone of dazzling greenness. The upper
Aller glen was filled with pure sunshine, the very quin-
tessence of light, and the sword-cut of the Rood was
for once free from gloom. There was no gold in the
landscape, for the shallows, even when they caught the
sun, were silver, the bent was flushing into the palest
green, the skies above were an infinity of colourless light.
And yet the riot of Spring was there. David felt it in
his bones and in his heart.

The herd of Reiverslaw was busy with his late lambs. The man, Prentice by name, was a sour fellow whom an accident in childhood had deprived of a leg. In spite of his misfortune he could move about on a single crutch at a good pace, and had a voice and a tongue which the parish feared. He was a noted professor, with an uncanny gift of prayer, and his by-names in Woodilee were " Hirplin' Rab " and the " One Leggit Prophet." But to-day even Prentice seemed mellowed by the Spring. He gave David a friendly good-day. " The voice o' the turtle is heard on the yirth," he announced, and as he hobbled over a patch of old moorburn, sending up clouds of grey dust, Prentice too became a figure of pastoral.

David had rarely felt a more benignant mood. The grimness of winter had gone clean out of his mind, and he had entered on a large and gracious world. He walked slowly like an epicure, drinking in the quintessential air of the hills, marking the strong blue swirl of the burns, the fresh green of the mosses, the buds on the hawthorns, the flash of the water-ouzels in the spray of the little falls. Curlews and peewits filled the moor with their crying, and as he began to descend into the Rood glen a lark—the first he had heard—rose to heaven with a flood of song.

His eyes had been so engaged with the foreground that he had not looked towards Melanudrigill. Now he saw it, dark and massy, the only opaque thing in a translucent world. But there was nothing oppressive in its shadows, for oppression could not exist in a scene so full of air and light and song. For a moment he had a mind to go boldly into its coverts by way of Reiverslaw and make for the lower course of the Woodilee burn. But the sight of the wild wood in the Rood glen detained him. It was a day not for the pines but for the hazels and birches, where in open glades a man would have always a view of the hills and the sky. So he slanted to his right through the open coppice, meaning to reach the valley floor near the foot of the path which led to the Greenshiel.

The coppice was thicker than he had imagined. This was no hillside scrub, but a forest, a greenwood, with its own glades and hollows, its own miniature glens and streams. He was in the midst of small birds who made a cheerful twittering from the greening boughs, cushats too were busy, and the thickets were full of friendly beasts. He saw the russet back of a deer as it broke cover, and the tawny streak of a hill-fox, and there was a perpetual scurrying of rabbits. Above all there was a glory of primroses. The pale blossoms starred the glades and the sides of the dells, clung to tree-roots, and climbed into crannies of the grey whinstone rock. So thick they were, that their paleness became golden, the first strong colour he had seen that day. David was young and his heart was light, so he gathered a great clump of blooms for his manse table, and set a bouquet in his coat and another in his bonnet. These latter would have to go before he reached the highway or the parish would think that its minister had gone daft. But here in the secret greenwood he could forget decorum and bedeck himself like a child.

Presently he had forgotten the route he had planned. He found himself in a shallow glade which ran to the left and away from the Greenshiel, and down which leaped a burn so entrancing in its madcap grace that he could not choose but follow it. Memory returned to him; this must be the burn which descended near the mill at Roodfoot; he knew well its lower course, for he had often guddled trout in its pools, but he had never explored its upper waters. Now he felt the excitement of a discoverer. . . . The ravine narrowed to a cleft where the stream fell in a white spout into a cauldron. David made the passage by slithering down the adjacent rocks and emerged wet to the knees. He was as amused as a boy playing truant from school, and when he found a water-ouzel's nest in the notch of a tree-root he felt that he had profit of his truancy. There came a more level stretch, which was a glory of primroses and wood-anemones, then another linn, and then a cup of turf rimmed with hazels, where the water twined in placid shallows. . . . He looked up and saw on the opposite bank a regiment of dark pines.

He had come to the edge of Melanudrigill. The trees rose like a cloud above him, and after the open coppice of birch and hazel he seemed to be looking into deep water where things were seen darkly as through a dull glass. There were glades which ran into shadows, and fantastic rocks, and mounds of dead bracken which looked like tombs. Yet the place fascinated him. It, too, was under the spell of Spring, and he wondered how Spring walked in its recesses. He leapt the stream and scrambled up the bank with an odd feeling of expectation. He was called to adventure on this day of days.

The place was not dark, but dim and very green. The ancient pines grew more sparsely than he had imagined, and beneath them were masses of sprouting ferns—primroses too, and violets which he had not found among the hazels. A scent of rooty dampness was about, of fresh-turned earth, and welling fountains. In every tree-root wood-sorrel clustered. But there were no small birds, only large things like cushats and hawks which made a movement in the high branches. A little farther and he was in a glade, far more of a glade than the clearings in the hazels, for it was sharply defined by the walls of shade.

He stood and gazed, struck silent by its beauty. Here in truth was a dancing-floor for wood nymphs, a playground for the Good Folk. It seemed strange that the place should be untenanted. . . . There was a rustling in the covert, and his heart beat. He was no longer the adventurous boy, but a young man with a fancy fed by knowledge. He felt that the glade was aware and not empty. Light feet had lately brushed its sward. . . . There was a rustling again, and a gleam of colour. He stood poised like a runner, his blood throbbing in a sudden rapture.

There was the gleam again and the rustle. He thought that at the far end of the glade behind the red bracken he saw a figure. In two steps he was certain. A green gown fluttered, and at his third step broke cover. He saw the form of a girl—nymph, fairy, or mortal, he knew not which. He was no more the minister of Woodilee, but eternal wandering youth, and he gave chase.

The green gown wavered for a moment between two gnarled pines and then was lost in the dead fern. He saw it again in the cleft of a tiny rivulet which came down from a pile of rocks, but he missed it as he scrambled up the steep. It seemed that the gown played tricks with him and led him on, for, as he checked at fault, he had a glimpse of it lower down where an aisle in the trees gave a view of the bald top of a mountain. David was young and active, but the gown was swifter than he, for as he went down the slope in great leaps it vanished into the dusk of the pines. He had it again, lost it, found it suddenly high above him —always a glimmer of green with but a hint of a girl's form behind it. . . . David became wary. Nymph or human, it should not beat him at this sport of hide-and-seek. There was a line of low cliffs above, up which it could not go unless it took wings. David kept the lower ground, determined that he would drive that which he followed towards the cliff line. He succeeded, for after twice trying to break away, the gown fluttered into a tiny ravine, with thick scrub on both sides and the rock wall at the top. As David panted upward he saw in a mossy place below the crags a breathless girl trying to master her tumbling tresses.

He stopped short in a deep embarrassment. He had been pursuing a fairy, and had found a mortal—a mortal who looked down on him with a flushed face and angry eyes. He was furiously hot, and the pace and his amazement bereft him of speech. It was she who spoke first.

" What does the minister of Woodilee in the Wood— and bedecked with primroses ? "

The voice was familiar, and as he brushed the sweat from his eyes the face too awoke recollection. She was far cooler than he, but her cheeks were flushed, and he had seen before those dark mirthful eyes. Mirthful they were, for her anger seemed to have gone, and she was looking down on him with a shy amusement. She had recognized him too, and had spoken his name. . . . He had it. It was the girl who had curtsied to Nicholas Hawkshaw's guests in the candlelight at Calidon. His abashment was increased.

" Madam," he stammered, " madam, I thought you were a fairy."

She laughed out loud with the abandonment of childhood. " A fairy ! And, pray, sir, is it part of the duties of a gospel minister to pursue fairies in the woods ? "

" I am shamed," he cried. " You do well to upbraid me. But on this spring day I had forgot my sacred calling and dreamed I was a boy once more."

" I do not upbraid you. Indeed I am glad that a minister can still be a boy. But folks do not come here, and I thought the wood my own, so when I saw you stumbling among the fern I had a notion to play a trick on you, and frighten you, as I have frightened intruders before. I thought you would run away. But you were too bold for me, and now you have discovered my secret. This wood is my playground where I can pick flowers and sing ballads and be happy with birds and beasts. . . . You were a man before you were a minister. What is your name ? "

" They call me David Sempill. I lived as a child at the Mill of the Roodfoot."

" Then you have seisin of this land. You too have played in the Wood ? "

" Nay, madam, the Wood is strange to me. I have but ridden through it, and till to-day I have had some dread of it. This Melanudrigill is ill reputed."

" Old wives' havers ! It is a blessed and innocent place. But I do not like that name—Melanudrigill. There is dark magic there. Call it the Wood, and you will love it as I do. . . . See, I am coming down. Make room, please, and then I will take you to Paradise. You do not know Paradise ? It is the shrine of this grove, and none but me can find the road."

This was not the stately lady in the gown of yellow

satin and blue velvet who had abashed him that night
in Calidon tower. It was a slim laughing girl in green
who presently stood beside him, her feet in stout
country shoes, her hair bound only by a silk fillet and
still unruly from the chase. He suddenly lost his
embarrassment. His reason told him that this was
Katrine Yester of Calidon, a daughter of a proud and
contumacious house that was looked askance at by the
godly, a woman, a beauty—commodities of which he
knew nothing. But his reason was blinded and he saw
only a girl on a spring holiday.

She led him down the hill, and as she went she
chattered gaily, like a solitary child who has found a
comrade.

" I saw you before you saw me, and I hoped you
would follow when I ran away. I liked you that night
at Calidon. They told me that ministers were all sour-
faced and old, but you looked kind. And you are
merry, too, I think—not sad, like most people in
Scotland."

" You have not been long in this land ? " he asked.

" Since June of last year. This is my first Scottish
spring, and it is different from France and England. In
those lands summer comes with a rush on winter's
heels, but here there is a long preparation, and flowers
steal very softly back to the world. I have lived
mostly in France since my father died."

" That is why your speech is so strange to my ears."

" And yours to mine," she retorted. " But Aunt
Grizel is teaching me to be a good Scotswoman. I am
made to spin till my arms are weary, and to make
horrid brews of herbs, and to cook your strange dishes.
'Kaatrine, ye daft quean, what for maun ye fill the
hoose wi' floorish and nesty green busses ? D'ye think

7

we're nowt and the auld tower o' Calidon a byre?
That is Aunt Grizel. But she is like a good dog and
barks but does not bite, though the serving-maids wail
in terror. I play with her at the cartes, and she tells
me tales, but not such good ones as Uncle Nick's.
Heigho! I wish the wars were over and he were home
again. . . . Now, sir, what do you think of this? It
is the gate of Paradise."

She had led him into a part of the wood where the
pines ceased and a green cleft was lined with bursting
hazels and rowans and the tassels of birch. The place
was rather hill than woodland, for the turf was as fine
as on a mountain-side, and in the centre a bubbling
spring sent out a rivulet, which twined among the
flowers till it dropped in a long cascade to a lower shelf.
Primroses, violets, and anemones made it as bright as a
garden.

"I call this Paradise," she said, "because it is hard
for mortals to find. You would not guess it was here
till you stumbled on it."

"It's away from the pines," he said.

She nodded her head. "I love the dark trees well
enough and on a day like this I am happy among them.
But they are moody things, and when there is no sun
and the wind blows they make me sad. Here I am gay
in any weather, for it is a kindly place. Confess, sir,
that I have chosen well."

"You have chosen well. It is what the poet wrote
of—*Deus hæc nobis otia fecit.*"

"La, la! That is Latin and I am not learned. But
I can quote my own poets." And in a voice like a
bird's she trilled a stanza of which David comprehended
no more than that it was a song of Spring and that it was
Flora the goddess herself who sang it.

" O fontaine Bellerie,
  Belle fontaine chérie
De nos Nymphes, quand ton eau
Les cache au creux de ta source,
Fuyantes le Satyreau
Qui les pourchasse à la course
Jusqu'au bord de ton ruisseau,
Tu es la Nymphe éternelle
De ma terre paternelle——"

Some strange and cataclysmic transformation was going on in David's mind. He realized that a film had cleared from his sight and that he was looking with new eyes. This dancing creature had unlocked a door for him—whether for good or ill, he knew not, and did not care. He wanted the world to stand still and the scene to remain fixed for ever—the Spring glade and the dark-haired girl singing among the primroses. He had the courage now to call her by her name.

" You have a voice like a linnet, Mistress Katrine. Can you sing none of our country songs ? "

" I am learning them from the serving-maids. I know ' The Ewebuchts ' and ' The Yellow-hair'd Laddie ' and—ah, this is the one for Paradise," and she sang :

" The King's young dochter was sitting in her window,
  Sewing at her silken seam ;
She lookt out o' a bow-window,
  And she saw the leaves growing green,
    My luve ;
  And she saw the leaves growing green."

" But Jean, the goose-girl who taught it me, remembered just the one verse. I wish I was a poet to make others."

Above the well was one of those circles of green mounds which country people call fairy-rings. The girl seated herself in the centre and began to make posies of

the flowers she had picked. David lay on the turf at
her feet, watching the quick movement of her hands, his
garlanded hat removed and the temperate sun warm-
ing his body. Never had he felt so bathed in happy
peace.

The pixie seated above him spared time from her
flowers to glance down at him, and found him regarding
her with abstracted eyes. For he was trying to fit this
bright creature into his scheme of things. Did the
world of the two of them touch nowhere save in this
woodland ?

" Your uncle is the chief heritor in Woodilee parish,"
he said, " but you do not come to the kirk."

" I was there no longer back than last Sunday——"
she said.

" Sabbath," he corrected.

" Sabbath, if you will have it so. Calidon is in Cauldshaw parish, and it was to Cauldshaw kirk we went.
Four weary miles of jogging on a plough-horse, I riding
pillion to Aunt Grizel. Before that the drifts were too
deep to take the road. . . . I have heard many a sermon
from Mr. Fordyce."

" He is a good man."

" He is a dull man. Such a preachment on dismal texts.
' Seventhly, my brethren, and in parenthesis——' " she
mimicked. " But he is beyond doubt good, and Aunt
Grizel says she has benefited from his words, and would
fain repay him by healing his disorders. He has many
bodily disorders, the poor man, and Aunt Grizel loves
sermons much but her simples more."

" You do not love sermons ? "

She made a mouth.

" I do not think I follow them. You are learned
theologians, you of Scotland, and I am still at the horn-

book. But some day I will come to hear you, for *your* sermons I think I might understand."

" I could not preach to you," he said.

" And wherefore, sir ? Are your discourses only for wrinkled carls and old rudas wives ? Is there no place in your kirk for a girl ? "

" You are not of our people. The seed can be sown only in a field prepared."

" But that is heresy. Are not all souls alike ? "

" True. But the voice of the preacher is heard only by open ears. I think you are too happy in your youth, mistress, for my solemnities."

" You do me injustice," she said, and her face was grave. " I am young, and I think I have a cheerful heart, for I can exult in a Spring morning and I cannot be very long sad. But I have had sorrows—a father slain in the wars, a mother dead of grieving, a bundling about among kinsfolk who were not all gracious. I have often had sore need of comfort, sir."

" You have found it—where ? "

" In the resolve never to be a faintheart. That is my creed, though I fail often in the practice."

To an ear accustomed to a formal piety the confession seemed almost a blasphemy. He shook a disapproving head.

" That is but a cold pagan philosophy," he said.

" Yet I learned it from a sermon, and that little more than a year back."

" Where was it preached ? "

" In England, and in no kirk, but at the King's Court."

" Was it by Mr. Henderson ? "

" It was by a Presbyterian—but he was no minister. Listen, and I will tell you the story. In March of last year I was taken to Oxford by my lady Grevel and was presented by her to the Queen, and her Majesty deigned to approve of me, so that I became a maid-of-honour and was lodged beside her in Merton College. There all day long was a coming and going of great men. There I saw "—she counted on her fingers—" his grace of Hamilton—him I did not like—and my lord of Nithsdale, and my lord of Aboyne, and my lord Ogilvy, and that very grave person Sir Edward Hyde, and my lord Digby, and the wise Mr. Endymion Porter. And all day long there were distracted counsels, and the King's servants plotting in side-chambers, and treason whispered, and nowhere a clear vision or a brave heart. Then there came among us a young man, who spoke simply. 'If the King's cause go down in England,' he said, 'it may be saved in Scotland.' When they asked him what he proposed, he said : 'To raise the North for his Majesty.' When they asked him by what means, he said : 'By my own resolution.' All doubted and many laughed, but that young man was not discouraged. 'The arm of the Lord is not shortened,' he said, 'and they who trust in Him will not be dismayed. . . .' That was the sermon he preached, and there was silence among the doubters. Then said Mr. Porter : 'There is a certain faith that moves mountains and a certain spirit which may win against all odds. My voice is for the venture !' . . . And then the Queen my mistress kissed the young man, and the King made him his lieutenant-general. . . . I watched him ride out of the city two days later, attended by but one servant, on his mission to conquer Scotland, and I flung him a nosegay of early primroses. He caught it and set it in his breast, and he waved his hand to me as he passed through the north gate."

"Who was this hero?" David asked eagerly, for the tale had fired him.

The girl's face was flushed and her eyes glistened.

"That was a year ago," she went on. "To-day he has done his purpose. He has won Scotland for the King."

David gasped.

"Montrose the malignant!" he cried.

"He is as good a Presbyterian as you, sir," she replied gently. "Do not call him malignant. He made his way north through his enemies as if God had sent His angel to guide him. And he is born to lead men to triumph. Did you not feel the compulsion of his greatness?"

"I?" David stammered.

"They told me that you had spoken with him and that he liked you well. Yon groom at Calidon was the Lord Marquis."

CHAPTER VI

THE BLACK WOOD BY NIGHT

WORD came of a great revival in the parish of Bold. Men called it a " work," and spoke of it in hushed voices, attributing it to the zeal and gifts of Mr. Ebenezer Proudfoot, the minister. For, after much preaching on fast-days in the shire, Mr. Ebenezer had fallen into a rapture and had seen visions and spoken with strange voices. The terror of the unknown fell upon his people, fasting and prayer became the chief business of the parish, and the most careless were transformed into penitents. For a season there were no shortcomings in Bold ; penny-bridals and fiddling and roystering at the change-houses were forgotten ; even swearing and tippling were forsworn ; the Sabbath was more strictly observed than by Israel in the Wilderness. To crown the Work a great field-preaching was ordained, when thousands assembled on Bold Moor and the sacrament was dispensed among scenes of wild emotion. In Bold there was a lonely field of thistles, known as Guidman's Croft, which had been held to be dedicate to the Evil One. The oxen of all the parish were yoked, and in an hour or two it was ploughed up and sown with bear for the use of the poor, as at once a thankoffering and a renunciation.

People in Woodilee talked much of the Work in Bold

and the Session sighed for a like experience. " Would but the wind blow frae that airt on our frostit lands ! " was the aspiration of Peter Pennecuik. But David had no ears for these things, for he was engrossed with the conflict in his own soul.

Ever since that afternoon in Paradise he had walked like a man half asleep, his eyes turning inward. His first exhilaration had been succeeded by a black darkness of doubt. He had adventured into the Wood and found magic there, and the spell was tugging at his heart-strings. . . . Was the thing of Heaven or of Hell ? . . . Sometimes, when he remembered the girl's innocence and ardour, he thought of her as an angel. Surely no sin could dwell in so bright a presence. . . . But he remembered, too, how lightly she had held the things of the Kirk, how indeed she was vowed to the world against which the Kirk made war. Was she not a daughter of Heth, a fair Moabitish woman, with no part in the commonwealth of Israel ? Her beauty was of the flesh, her graces were not those of the redeemed. And always came the conviction that nevertheless she had stolen his heart. " Will I too be unregenerate ? " he asked himself with terror.

The more he looked into his soul the more he was perplexed. He thought of the groom at Calidon, to whom had gone out from him a spark of such affection as no other had inspired. That face was little out of his memory, and he longed to look on it again as a lover longs for his mistress. . . . But the man was Montrose the recreant, who was even now troubling God's people, and who had been solemnly excommunicated by the very Kirk he was vowed to serve. . . . And yet, recreant or no, the man believed in God and had covenanted himself with the Almighty. . . . What were God's purposes, and

who were God's people ?   Where in all the round earth
should he find a solution of his doubts ?

The study, now warm in the pleasant Spring gloamings, saw no longer the preparation of the great work
on Isaiah. It had become a closet for prayer. David
cast his perplexities on the Lord and waited feverishly
for a sign. But no sign came. A horde of texts about
Canaanitish garments and idol worship crowded into
his mind, but he refused their application. A young
man's face, a girl's eyes and voice, made folly of
such easy formulas. . . . Yet there were moments
when in sheer torment of soul David was minded to
embrace them—to renounce what had charmed him
as the Devil's temptation, and steel his heart against
its glamour.

One day he rode over to Cauldshaw to see Mr. Fordyce. He was in the mood for confession, but he
found little encouragement. Mr. James was sick of
a spring fever, and though he was on his feet he had
been better in bed, for his teeth chattered and his hand
trembled.

They spoke of the household at Calidon. " Mistress
Saintserf has beyond doubt her interest in Christ," said
the minister of Cauldshaw. " When I have gone to
Calidon for the catechizing I have found her quick to
apprehend the doctrines of the faith, and her life is in
all respects an ensample, save that she is something of
a libertine with her tongue. But the lassie—she's but
a young thing, and has sojourned long in popish and
prelatical lands. Yet I detect glimmerings of grace,
Mr. David, and she has a heart that may well be attuned
to God's work. My wife pines for the sight of her
like a sick man for the morning. Maybe I fail in my
duty towards her, for she is lamentably ignorant, but

I cannot find it in me to be harsh to so gracious a bairn."

David returned with this purpose unfulfilled but a certain comfort in his soul. He would rather have Mr. Fordyce's judgment than that of the Boanerges of Bold or the sleek minister of Kirk Aller. His doubts were not resolved, but the very uncertainty gave him ease. He was not yet called to renunciation, and having reached this conclusion, he could let the memory of Paradise sweep back into his mind in a delightful flood.

Yet youth cannot be happy in indecision. David longed for some duty which would absorb the strong life that was in him. Why, oh why was he not a soldier ? He turned to his parish, and tried to engross himself in its cares. It may have been that his perception was sharpened by his own mental conflicts, but he seemed to detect a strangeness in Woodilee.

It had been a fine Spring, with a dry seed-bed, and the sowing of crops and the lambing had passed off well. The lean cattle had staggered out of byres and closes to the young grass and their ribs were now covered again. Up on the hills lambs no longer tottered on weak legs. There was more food in the place, for there had been feasts of braxy mutton, and the hens were laying again, and there was milk in the cogies. The faces of the people had lost their winter strain ; the girls had washed theirs, and fresh cheeks and bright eyes were to be seen on the roads. Woodilee had revived with the Spring, but David as he went among the folk saw more than an increase in bodily well-being. . . . There was a queer undercurrent of excitement—or was it expectation ?—and the thing was secret.

Every one did not share this. There seemed to be an inner circle in the parish which was linked together by some private bond. He began to guess at its membership by the eyes. Some looked him frankly in the face, and these were not always the best reputed. Amos Ritchie, the blacksmith, for instance—he was a profane swearer, and was sometimes overtaken in drink—and the farmer of Reiverslaw had, in addition to the latter failing, a violent temper, which made him feared and hated. Yet these two faced him like free men. But there were others, whose speech was often the most devout, who seemed to have shutters drawn over their eyes and to move stealthily on tiptoe.

Woodilee was amazingly well-conducted, and the Poor Box received the scantiest revenue in penalties. Apart from the lawless births in the winter, there were few apparent backslidings. David rarely met young lads and lasses at their hoydenish courtings in the gloamings. Oaths were never heard, and if there was drunkenness it was done in secret. Not often was a Sabbath-breaker before the Session, and there were no fines for slack attendance at the kirk. But as David watched the people thronging to service on the Sabbath, the girls in their clean linen, walking barefoot and only putting on shoes at the kirkyard gate, the men in decent homespun and broad bonnets, the old wives in their white mutches—as he looked down from the pulpit on the shoulders bent with toil, the heavy features hardened to a stiff decorum, the eyes fixed dully on his face—he had the sense that he was looking on masks. The real life of Woodilee was shut to him. " Ye are my people," he told himself bitterly, " and I know ye not."

This was not true of all. He knew the children, and

there were certain of the older men and women in the
parish who had given him their friendship. Peter
Pennecuik, his principal elder and session-clerk, he felt
that he knew to the bottom—what little there was to
know, for the man was a sanctimonious egotist. With
Amos Ritchie and Reiverslaw, too, he could stand as man
with man. . . . But with many of the others he fenced
as with aliens; the farmers, for example, Chasehope
and Mirehope, and Nether Fennan, and Spotswood the
miller, and various elderly herds and hinds, and the
wives of them. Above all he was no nearer the youth
of the parish than when first he came. The slouching
hobbledehoy lads, the girls, some comely and high-
coloured, some waxen white—they were civil and decent,
but impenetrable. There were moments when he
found himself looking of a Sabbath at his sober respectable folk as a hostile body, who watched him furtively
lest he should learn too much of them. . . . Woodilee
had an ill name in the shire, Mr. Fordyce had told
him the first day in the manse. For what? What
was the life from which he was so resolutely barred
—he, their minister, who should know every secret of
their souls? What was behind those shuttered eyes?
Was it fear? He thought that there might be fear in
it, but that more than fear it was a wild and sinister
expectation.

On the last day of April he noted that Isobel was ill at
ease. "Ye'll be for a daunder, sir," she said after the
midday meal. "See and be hame in gude time for
your supper—I've a rale guid yowe-milk kebbuck *
for ye and a new bakin' o' cakes—and I'll hae the
can'les lichtit in your chamber for you to get to your
books."

* Cheese.

He smiled at his housekeeper. " Why this carefulness ? " he said.

She laughed uneasily. " Naething by ordinar. But this is the day they ca' the Rood-Mass and the morn is the Beltane, and it behoves a' decent bodies to be indoors at the darkenin' on Beltane's Eve. My faither was a bauld man, but he wadna have stirred a fit over his ain doorstep on the night o' Rood-Mass for a king's ransom. There's anither Beltane on the aucht day of May, and till that's by we maun walk eidently."

" Old wives' tales," he said.

" But they're nane auld wives' tales. They're the tales o' wise men and bauld men."

" I thought of walking in the Wood."

" Mercy on us ! " she cried. " Ye'll no gang near the Wud. No on this day o' a' days. It's fou' o' bogles."

Her insistence vexed him and he spoke to her sharply. The heavy preoccupation of his mind had put him out of patience with folly. " Woman," he cried, " what concern has a servant of God with these heathen fables ? Think shame to repeat such folly."

But Isobel was not convinced. She retired in dudgeon to her kitchen, and watched his movements till he left the house as a mother watches a defiant child. " Ye'll be hame in guid time ? " she begged.

" I will be home when I choose," he said, and to show his independence he put some cheese and bannocks in his pockets.

The afternoon was warm and bright with a thin haze on the highest hills. Spring had now fairly come ; the yews in the kirkyard were russet with young shoots, the blossom was breaking on the hawthorn, and hazel and oak and ash were in leaf. His spirit was too laden to be sensible of the sweet influences of sky and moorland as on the walk which had first taken him to Paradise. But there was in him what had been lacking before—excitement, for he had tasted of magic and was in the constant expectation of finding it again. The land was not as it had once been, for it held somewhere enchantments—a girl's face and a girl's voice. From the summit of the Hill of Deer he looked towards Calidon hidden in the fold of the Rood hills. Was she there in the stone tower, or among the meadows whose green showed in the turn of the glen ? Or was she in her old playground of the Wood ?

He had resolved not to go near the place, so he set himself to walk in the opposite direction along the ridge of hill which made the northern wall of the Rood valley. As he strode over the short turf and scrambled through the patches of peat-bog his spirits rose. It was hard not to be light-hearted in that world of essential airs and fresh odours and nesting birds. Presently he was in view of Calidon tower, and then he was past it, and the Rood below him was creeping nearer to his level as its glen lifted towards its source. He strode along till he felt the sedentary humours leave his body and his limbs acquire the lightness which is the reward of the hill walker. He seemed, too, to gain a lightness of soul and a clearness of eye. In a world which God had made so fair and clean, there could be no sin in anything that was also fair and innocent.

The sun had set beyond Herstane Craig before he turned his steps. Now from the hilltops he had Melanudrigill before him, a distant shadow in the trough of the valley. Since that afternoon in Paradise awe of the Wood had left him. He had been among its pines and had found Katrine there. He watched the cloud of trees, growing nearer at each step, as earlier that day he had watched the environs of Calidon. It was her haunt ; haply she might now be there, singing in the scented twilight ?

When he stood above Reiverslaw the dusk was purple about him, and the moon, almost at her full, was climbing the sky. He longed to see how Paradise looked in this elfin light, for he had a premonition that the girl might have lingered there late and that he would meet her. There was no duty to take him home—nothing but Isobel's silly fables. But in deference to Isobel he took the omens. He sent his staff twirling into the air. If it fell with the crook towards him, he would go home. The thing lighted in a heather bush with the crook at the far end. So he plunged downhill among the hazels, making for the glade which slanted eastward towards the deserted mill.

He found it, and it was very dark in that narrow place. There was no light to see the flowers by, and there was no colour in it, only a dim purple gloom and the white of the falling stream, for the moon was still too low in the heavens to reach it.

In time he came to the high bank where the pines began. He was looking for Paradise, but he could not find it. It was not among the pines, he remembered, but among the oaks and hazels, but he had gone to it through the pines, led by a flitting girl. . . . He found the point where he had entered the darker Wood and resolved to try to retrace his former tracks.

The place was less murky than he had expected, for the moon was now well up the sky, so that every glade was a patch of white light. . . . This surely was the open space where he had first caught the glimmer of a green gown. . . . There were the rocks where she had stood at bay. . . . She had led him down the hill and then at a slant—but was it to right or left? Right, he thought, and plunged through a wilderness of fern. There had been briars, too, and this was surely the place where a vast uprooted trunk had forced them to make a détour.

Then he found a little stream which he fancied might be the outflow of the Paradise well. So he turned up-hill again, and came into a jungle of scrub and boulder. There was in most places a dim light to move by, but a dim light in a broken wood is apt to confuse the mind. David had soon lost all sense of direction, save that of the upward and downward slopes. He did not know east or west, and he did not stop to think, for he was beginning to be mesmerized by the hour and the scene. Dew was in the air and an overpowering sweetness of fern and pine and mosses, and through the aisles of the high trees came a shimmer of palest gold, and in the open spaces the moon rode in the dusky blue heavens—not the mild moon of April but a fiery conquering goddess, driving her chariot among trampled stars.

It was clear to him that he would not find Paradise except by happy chance, since he was utterly out of his bearings. But he was content to be lost, for the whole place was Paradise. Never before had he felt so strong a natural magic. This woodland, which he had once shunned, had become a holy place, lit with heavenly lights and hallowed by some primordial peace. He had forgotten about the girl, forgotten his scruples. In that hour he had acquired a mood at once serene and gay: he had the light-heartedness of a boy and the ease of a wise philosopher; his body seemed as light as air, and, though he had already walked some twenty miles, he felt as if he had just risen from his bed. But there was no

exuberance in him, and he had not the impulse to sing
which usually attended his seasons of high spirits. . . .
The silence struck upon him as something at once miraculous and just. There was not a sound in the Wood—
not the lightest whisper of wind, though there had been
a breeze on the hilltops at sundown—not the cry of a
single bird—not a rustle in the undergrowth. The place
was dumb—not dead, but sleeping.

Suddenly he came into a broad glade over which the
moonshine flowed like a tide. It was all of soft mossy
green, without pebble or bush to break its carpet, and in
the centre stood a thing like an altar.

At first he thought it was only a boulder dropped
from the hill. But as he neared it he saw that it was
human handiwork. Masons centuries ago had wrought
on it, for it was roughly squared, and firmly founded on
a pediment. Weather had battered it, and one corner
of the top had been broken by some old storm, but it
still stood foursquare to the seasons. One side was very
clear in the moon, and on it David thought he could
detect a half-obliterated legend. He knelt down, and
though the lower part was obscured beyond hope the
upper letters stood out plain. I. O. M.—he read : " Jovi
Optimo Maximo." This uncouth thing had once been
an altar.

He tiptoed away from it with a sudden sense of awe.
Others had known this wood—mailed Romans clanking
up the long roads from the south, white-robed priests
who had once sacrificed here to their dead gods. He was
scholar enough to feel the magic of this sudden window
opened into the past. But there was that in the discovery which disquieted as well as charmed him. The
mysteries of the heathen had been here, and he felt
the simplicity of the woodland violated and its peace

ravished. Once there had been wild tongues in the air, and he almost seemed to hear their echo.

He hurried off into the dark undergrowth. . . . But now his mood had changed. He felt fatigue, his eyes were drowsy, and he thought of the anxious Isobel sitting up for him. He realized that this was the night of Rood-Mass—pagan and papistical folly, but his reason could not altogether curb his fancy. The old folk said—folly, no doubt, but still—— He had an overpowering desire to be safe in his bed at the manse. He would retrace his steps and strike the road from Reiverslaw. That would mean going west, and after a moment's puzzling he started to run in what he thought the right direction.

The Wood, or his own mind, had changed. The moonlight was no longer gracious and kind, but like the dead-fires which the old folk said burned in the kirkyard. Confusion on the old folk, for their tales were making him a bairn again ! . . . But what now broke the stillness ? for it seemed as if there were veritably tongues in the air —not honest things like birds and winds, but tongues. The place was still silent so far as earthly sounds went— he realized that, when he stopped to listen—but never-theless he had an impression of movement everywhere, of rustling—yes, and of tongues.

Fortune was against him, for he reached a glade and saw that it was the one which he had left and which he thought he had avoided. . . . There was a change in it, for the altar in the centre was draped. At first he thought it only a freak of moonlight, till he forced himself to go nearer. Then he saw that it was a coarse white linen cloth, such as was used in the kirk at the seasons of sacrament.

The discovery affected him with a spasm of blind terror. All the tales of the Wood, all the shrinking he had once felt for it, rushed back on his mind. For the moment he was an infant again, lost and fluttering, assailed by the shapeless phantoms of the dark. He fled from the place as if from something accursed.

Uphill he ran, for he felt that safety was in the hills and that soon he might come to the clear spaces of the heather. But a wall of crag forced him back, and he ran as he thought westward towards the oaks and hazels, for there he deemed he would be free of the magic of the pines. He did not run wildly, but softly and furtively, keeping to the moss and the darker places, and avoiding any crackling of twigs, for he felt as if the Wood were full of watchers. At the back of his head was a stinging sense of shame—that he, a grown man and a minister of God, should be in such a pit of terror. But his instinct was stronger than his reason. He felt his heart crowding into his throat, and his legs so weak and uncontrollable that they seemed to be separate from his body. The boughs of the undergrowth whipped his face, and he knew that his cheeks were wet with blood, though he felt no pain.

The trees thinned and he saw light ahead—surely it was the glen which marked the division between pine and hazel. He quickened his speed and the curtain of his fear lifted ever so little. He heard sounds now— was it the wind which he had left on the hilltops ? There was a piping note in it, something high and clear and shrill—and yet the Wood had been so airless that his body was damp with sweat. Now he was very near air and sanctuary.

His heart seemed to stop, and his legs wavered so that he sunk on his knees. For he was looking again on the accursed glade.

It was no longer empty. The draped altar was hidden

by figures—human or infernal—moving round it in a slow dance. Beyond this circle sat another who played on some instrument. The moss stilled the noise of movement, and the only sound was the high mad piping.

A film cleared from his eyes, and something lost came back to him—manhood, conscience, courage. Awe still held him, but it was being overmastered by a human repulsion and anger. For as he watched the dance he saw that the figures were indeed human, men and women both—the women half-naked, but the men with strange headpieces like animals. What he had taken for demons from the Pit were masked mortals—one with the snout of a pig, one with a goat's horns, and the piper a gaping black hound. . . . As they passed, the altar was for a moment uncovered, and he saw that food and drink were set on it for some infernal sacrament.

The dance was slow and curiously arranged, for each woman was held close from behind by her partner. And they danced widdershins, against the sun. To one accustomed to the open movement of country jigs and reels the thing seemed the uttermost evil—the grinning masks, the white tranced female faces, the obscene postures, above all that witch-music as horrid as a moan of terror.

David, a great anger gathering in his heart, was on his feet now, and as he rose the piping changed. Its slow measure became a crazy lilt, quick and furious. The piper was capering; the dancers, still going widdershins, swung round and leaped forward, flinging their limbs as in some demented reel. . . . There were old women there, for he saw grey hair flying. And now came human cries to add to the din of the pipe—a crying and a sighing wrung out of maddened bodies.

To David it seemed a vision of the lost in Hell. The fury of an Israelitish prophet came upon him. He strode into the glade. Devils or no, he would put an end to this convention of the damned.

"In the name of God," he cried, "I forbid you. If you are mortal, I summon you to repent—if you are demons, I command you to return to him that sent you."

He had a great voice, but in that company there were no ears to hear. The pipe screeched and the dance went on.

Then the minister of Woodilee also went mad. A passion such as he had never known stiffened every nerve and sinew. He flung himself into the throng, into that reek of unclean bestial pelts and sweating bodies. He reached the altar, seized the cloth on it, and swept it and its contents to the ground. Then he broke out of the circle and made for the capering piper, who seemed to him the chief of the orgiasts.

In his flight through the wood David had lost his staff, and had as weapon but his two hands. "Aroynt you, Sathanas," he cried, snatched the pipe from the dog-faced figure, and shivered it on his masked head.

With the pause in the music the dance stopped suddenly, and in an instant the whole flock were on him like a weasel pack. He saw long-nailed claws stretched towards his face, he saw blank eyes suddenly fire into a lust of hate. But he had a second's start of them, and that second he gave to the piper. The man—for the thing was clearly human—had dealt a mighty buffet at his assailant's face, which missed it, and struck the point of the shoulder. David was whirled round, but, being young and nimble, he slipped in under the other's guard, and had his hands on the hound-mask. The man was very powerful, but the minister's knee was in his groin, and he toppled over, while David tore the covering of wood and skin from his head. It crumpled under his violent clutch like a wasps' nest, and he had a glimpse of red hair and a mottled face.

A glimpse and no more. For by this time the press was on him and fingers were at his throat, choking out his senses.

CHAPTER VII

THE FIRST BLAST

LATE in the forenoon of the next day David awoke in his own bed in the manse of Woodilee. He awoke to a multitude of small aches and one great one, for his forehead was banded with pain. The room was as bright with sunshine as the little window would permit, but it seemed to him a dusk shot by curious colours, with Isobel's head bobbing in it like a fish. Presently the face became clear and he saw it very near to him—a scared white face with red-rimmed eyes. Her voice penetrated the confused noises in his ears.

" The Lord be thankit, sir, the Lord be praised, Mr. David, ye're comin' oot o' your dwam. Here's a fine het drink for ye. Get it doun like a man and syne ye'll maybe sleep. There's nae banes broke, and I've dressed your face wi' a sure salve. Dinna disturb the clouts, sir. Your skin's ower clean to beal,* and ye'll mend quick if ye let the clouts bide a wee."

Her arm raised his aching head, and he swallowed the gruel. It made him drowsy, and soon he was asleep again, a healthy natural sleep, so that when he awoke in the evening he was in comparative ease and his headache had gone. Gingerly he felt his body. There were bruises on his legs, and one huge one on his right thigh.

* Fester.

His cheeks under the bandages felt raw and scarred, and there was a tenderness about his throat and the muscles of his neck, as if angry hands had throttled him. But apart from his stiffness he seemed to have suffered no great bodily hurt, and the effects of the slight concussion had passed.

With this assurance his mind came out of its torpor and he found himself in a misery of disquiet. The events of the night before returned to him only too clearly. He remembered his exaltation in the Wood—the glade, the altar. He recalled with abasement his panic and his flight. The glade again, the piping, the obscene dance— and at that memory he had almost staggered from his bed. He felt again the blind horror and wrath which had hurled him into the infernal throng.

Isobel's anxious face appeared in the doorway.

" Ye've had a graund sleep, sir. And now ye'll be for a bite o' meat ? "

" I have slept and I am well enough in body. Sit you down, Isobel Veitch, for I have much to say to you. How came I home last night ? "

The woman sat down on the edge of a chair, and even in the twilight her nervousness was manifest.

" It wasna last nicht. It was aboot the hour o' three this mornin', and sic a nicht as I had waitin' on ye ! Oh, sir, what garred ye no hearken to me and gang to the Wud on Rood-Mass ? "

" How do you know I was in the Wood ? "

She did not answer.

" Tell me," he said, " how I came home."

" I was ryngin' the hoose like a lost yowe, but I didna daur gang outbye. At twal hours I took a look up the road and again when the knock was chappin' twa. Syne I dozed off in my chair, till the knock waukened me.

That was at three hours, and as I waukened I heard steps outbye. I keekit oot o' the windy, but there was naebody on the road, just the yellow mune. I prayed to the Lord to strengthen me, and by-and-by I ventured out, but I fand naething. Syne I took a thocht to try the back yaird, and my hert gied a stound, for there was yoursel', Mr. David, lyin' like a cauld corp aneath the aipple tree. Blithe I was to find the breath still in ye, but I had a sair job gettin' ye to your bed, sir, for ye're a weary wecht for an auld wumman. The sun was up or I got your wounds washed and salved, and syne I sat by the bed prayin' to the Lord that ye suld wauken in your richt mind, for I saw fine that the wounds o' your body would heal, but I feared that the wits micht have clean gane frae ye. And now I am abundantly answered, for ye're speakin' like yoursel', and your een's as I mind them, and the blood's back intil your cheeks. The Lord be thankit ! "

But there was no jubilation in Isobel's voice. Her fingers twined confusedly and her eyes wandered.

" Do you know what befell me ? " he asked.

" Eh, sir, how suld I ken ? "

" But what do you think ? You find me in the small hours lying senseless at your door, with my face scarred and my body bruised. What do you think I had suffered ? "

" I think ye were clawed by bogles, whilk a'body kens are gi'en a free dispensation on Rood-Mass E'en."

" Woman, what is this talk of bogles from lips that have confessed Christ ? I was assaulted by the Devil, but his emissaries were flesh and blood. I tell you it was women's nails that tore my face, and men's hands that clutched my throat. I walked in the Wood, for what has a minister of God to fear from trees and darkness? And as I walked I found in an open place a heathen altar and that altar was covered with a linen cloth, as if for a sacrament. I was afraid—I confess it with shame—but the Lord used my fear for His own purpose, and led me back in my flight to that very altar. And there I saw what may God in His mercy forbid that I should see again—a dance of devils to the Devil's piping. In my wrath I rushed among them, and tore the mask from the Devil's head, and then they overbore me and I lost my senses. When I wrestled with them I wrestled with flesh and blood—perishing men and women wrapt in a lust of evil."

He stopped, and Isobel's eyes did not meet his. "Keep us a'!" she moaned.

"These men and women were, I firmly believe, my own parishioners."

"It canna be," the old woman croaked. "Ye werena yoursel', Mr. David, sir. . . . Ye were clean fey wi' the blackness o' the Wud and the mune and the wanchancy hour. Ye saw ferlies,* but they werena flesh and bluid, sir. . . ."

"I saw the bodies of men and women in Woodilee who have sold their souls to damnation. Isobel Veitch, as your master and your minister, I charge you, as you will answer before the Judgment Seat, what know you of the accursed thing in this parish?"

"Me!" she cried. "Me! I ken nocht. Me and my man aye keepit clear o' the Wud."

"Which is to say that there were others in Woodilee who did not. Answer me, woman, as you hope for salvation. The sin of witchcraft is rampant here, and I will not rest till I have rooted it out. Who are those in Woodilee who keep tryst with the Devil?"

* Marvels.

" How suld I ken ? Oh, sir, I pray ye to speir nae mair questions. Woodilee has aye been kenned for a queer bit, lappit in the muckle Wud, but the guilty aye come by an ill end. There's been mair witches howkit out o' Woodilee and brunt than in ony ither parochine on the Water o' Aller. Trust to your graund Gospel preachin', Mr. David, to wyse folk a better gait, for if ye start speirin' about the Wud ye'll stir up a byke that will sting ye sair. As my faither used to say, him that spits against the wind spits in his ain face. Trust to conviction o' sin bringin' evildoers to repentance, as honest Mr. Macmichael did afore ye."

" Did Mr. Macmichael know of this wickedness ? "

" I canna tell. Nae doot he had a glimmerin'. But he was a quiet body wha keepit to the roads and his ain fireside, and wasna like yoursel', aye ryngin' the country like a moss-trooper. . . . Be content, sir, to let sleepin' tykes lie till ye can catch them rauvagin'. Ye've a congregation o' douce eident folk, and I'se warrant ye'll lead them intil the straucht and narrow way. Maybe the warst's no as ill as ye think. Maybe it's just a sma' backslidin' in them that's pilgrims to Sion. They're weel-kenned to be sound in doctrine, and there was mair signed the Covenant——"

" Peace," he cried. " This is rank blasphemy, and a horrid hypocrisy. What care I for lip service when there are professors who are living a lie ? Who is there I can trust ? The man who is loudest in his profession may be exulting in secret and dreadful evil. He whom I think a saint may be the chief of sinners. Are there no true servants of Christ in Woodilee ? "

" Plenty," said Isobel.

" But who are they ? I had thought Richie Smail at the Greenshiel a saint, but am I wrong ? "

" Na, na. Ye're safe wi' Richie.''

" And yourself, Isobel ? "

Colour came into her strained face. " I'm but a broken vessel, but neither my man nor me had ever trokin's wi' the Enemy.''

" But there are those to your knowledge who have ? I demand from you their names.''

She pursed her lips. " Oh, sir, I ken nocht. What suld a widow-woman, thrang a' the day in your service, ken o' the doings in Woodilee ? "

" Nevertheless you know something. You have heard rumours. Speak, I command you.''

Her face was drawn with fright, but her mouth was obstinate. " Wha am I to bring a railin' accusation against onybody, when I have nae certainty of knowledge ? "

" You are afraid. In God's name, what do you fear ? There is but the one fear, and that is the vengeance of the Almighty, and your silence puts you in jeopardy of His wrath.''

Nevertheless there was no change in the woman's face. David saw that her recalcitrance could not be broken.

" Then listen to me, Isobel Veitch. I have had my eyes opened and I will not rest till I have rooted this evil thing from Woodilee. I will search out and denounce every malefactor, though he were in my own Kirk Session. I will bring against them the terror of God and the arm of the human law. I will lay bare the evil mysteries of the Wood, though I have to hew down every tree with my own hand. In the strength of the Lord I will thresh this parish as corn is threshed, till I have separated the grain from the chaff and given the chaff to the burning. Make you your market for that, Isobel Veitch, and mind that he that is not for me is against me, and that in the day of God's wrath the slack hand and the silent tongue will not be forgiven."

The woman shivered and put a hand to her eyes.

" Will you hae your bite o' meat, sir ? " she quavered.

" I will not break bread till God has given me clearness," he said sternly ; and Isobel, who was in the habit of spinning out her talks with her master till she was driven out, slipped from the room like a discharged prisoner who fears that the Court may change its mind.

David rose next morning after a sleepless night, battered in body but with some peace of mind, and indeed a comfort which he scarcely dared to confess to himself. He had now a straight course before him. There was an evil thing in the place against which he had declared war, an omnipresent evil, for he did not know who were the guilty. The thing was like the Wood itself, an amorphous shadow clouding the daylight. Gone were the divided counsels, the scruples of conscience. What mattered his doubts about the policy of the Kirk at large when here before his eyes was a conflict of God and Belial ? . . . For the first time, too, he could let his mind dwell without scruples upon the girl in the greenwood. The little glen that separated the pines from the oaks and the hazels had become for him the frontier between darkness and light—on the one side the innocency of the world which God had made, on the other the unclean haunts of devilry. . . . And yet he had first met Katrine among the pines. To his horror of the works of darkness was added a bitter sense of sacrilege—that obscene revelry should tread the very turf that her feet had trod.

That afternoon he set out for Chasehope. The

matter should be without delay laid before his chief
elder, and the monstrous suspicion which lurked at the
back of his mind dispelled. He was aware that his face
was a spectacle, but it should not be hidden, for it was
a part of his testimony. But at Chasehope there was
no Ephraim Caird. The slatternly wife who met him,
old before her time, with a clan of ragged children at
her heels, was profuse in regrets. She dusted a settle
for him, and offered new milk and a taste of her cheese,
but all the time with an obvious discomfort. To think
that Ephraim should be away when the minister came
up the hill ! . . . He had had to ride off that morn to
Kirk Aller upon a matter of a bull that Johnnie David-
son had brought from Carlisle—an English bull to
improve the breed—and he would not be home till the
darkening. The woman was voluble and hearty, but it
seemed to David that she protested too much. . . .
Was her husband all the while between the blankets in
the press-bed ?

On his way back, at the turn of the road from the
kirkton, he encountered Daft Gibbie. The idiot had
throughout the winter been a satellite of the minister,
and had had many a meal in the manse kitchen. When
they met it was " Eh, my bonny Mr. Sempill," or " my
precious Mr. David," and then an outpouring of grotesque but complimentary texts. But now the first
news he had of Gibbie was a small stone that whizzed
past his ear, and when he turned he saw a threatening
figure with a face twisted into a demoniac hate. A
second stone followed, very wide of the mark, and when
David threatened pursuit, the idiot shuffled off, shouting filth over his shoulder. A woman came out of a
cottage, and said something to Gibbie which caused
him to hold his peace and disappear into a kailyard.

. . . But the woman did not look towards the minister, but hurried in again and closed the door. Was the whole parish, thought David, banded in a tacit conspiracy? Was this poor idiot one of the misbegotten things of the Wood?

The next Sabbath, which was the fifth of May, the kirk of Woodilee showed a full congregation. That day, save for infants in arms, there were few absentees. Never had the place been more hushed and expectant. David preached from the text, "Enter into the rock, and hide thee in the dust for fear of the Lord," and he delivered his soul with a freedom hitherto lacking in his carefully prepared discourses. Not the Boanerges of Bold could have outdone the fiery vigour with which he described how Israel went astray after forbidden gods and how the wrath of the Almighty smote her with death and exile. But when he came to the application, which should have been as a nail fastened in a sure place, he faltered. The faces below him, set, composed, awful in their decency, seemed like a stone wall against which he must beat with feeble hands.

"I have the sure knowledge," he said, "that there are altars set up to Baal in this very parish, and that this little Israel of ours has its own groves where it worships the gods of the heathen—ay, the very devils from the Pit. Be assured that I will riddle out this evil mystery and drag it into the light of day, and on the priests of Baal in Woodilee, be they libertines or professors, I will call down the terrors of the Most High. I summon now in this place all poor deluded sinners to confession and repentance, for in the strength of the Lord I will go forward, and woe be to those that harden their hearts."

But his words seemed to be driven back upon him by

the steely silence. He saw his elders—the heavy white
face of Chasehope, the long sanctimonious jowl of Peter
Pennecuik, the impish mouth of Spotswood the miller
now composed in an alien gravity, the dark sullenness
of Mirehope—they relished his vigour, but their eyes
were hard as stones. And the folk behind them, men
and women, old and young, were attentively apathetic.
There was none of the crying and weeping and the
spasms of conviction which had attended the fast-day
service of the minister of Bold. Were they a congregation of innocents to whom his summons had no application ? Or were they so thirled to their evil-doing that
his appeals were no more than an idle wind ?

His Session congratulated him on his discourse.

" Ye had a gale on your spirit this day, Mr. Sempill,"
said Chasehope. " Yon was a fine waft o' the Word ye
gie'd us, and it's to be hoped that it will be blessed to
many."

As David looked at the pale cheeks and the red hair
of the man he had a sudden assurance. It was a mild
day, but Ephraim Caird wore a strip of flannel as if he
were nursing a cold. And was there not a discoloration
of the skin around his fleshy jaw and a dark bruise
below his left ear ?

Next day David sought out Amos Ritchie, the smith.
He learned that the man was on a job at Nether Windyways, and he watched for him on the hill-road as he
returned in the evening. The big loose-limbed figure of
Amos, striding down the twilit slopes with his bag of
tools slung on his shoulder, was a pleasant sight to eyes
that hungered for a friend. For with the smith David
had advanced far in friendliness since their partnership
in the winter snowstorm. The man was of a high
spirit and a complete honesty, and his professions were

9

well behind his practice.   Rough of tongue and apt in
a quarrel, he had a warmth of heart that did not fail
even those he despised.   He was no purveyor of edifying
speech, but the milk of human kindness ran strong in
him.   It was a saying in the village that there was
" mair comfort in an aith from Amos than a prayer
from Peter Pennecuik."

But on this occasion the smith's straightforward
friendliness seemed to have deserted him.   When David
appeared before him he looked as if he would fain have
avoided the meeting.   His eyes were troubled, and he
increased the pace of his walk when the minister fell
into step beside him.

" How's the wife ? " David asked.

" Fine, sir.   Her kist's stronger, and I'm hopin' the
simmer will pit colour intil her cheek."   But as he
spoke his eyes were on a distant hill.

" I want a word with you, Amos.   You and I are, I
believe, true friends, and I can speak to you as to a
brother.   I have become aware of a horrid evil in this
parish.   There is that in the Wood which tempts men
and women to abominations.   With these eyes of mine
I saw it on Beltane's Eve."

There was no answer.

" You were in the kirk yesterday, Amos, and you
heard my sermon.   The decision is on Woodilee to
choose whom they will serve.   You are my friend, and,
apart from certain backslidings, a man of a Christian
walk and conversation.   I summon you to my aid, and
conjure you by Christ who died for you, to tell me
what you know of this great sin and who are the
sinners ? "

Amos came to a standstill.   He laid down his tools,
and looked the minister in the face.

" Let it alane, sir. I rede ye, let it alane."

" In the name of God, what folly is this ? " David cried. " Are you, too, my own familiar friend, entangled in this wickedness ? "

The man's face crimsoned.

" Deil a haet ! Na, na, I never could abide thae trokin's wi' the Wud. But oh, Mr. Sempill, ye're but a callant, and ye kenna the wecht o' the principalities and poo'ers that are against ye. Hae patience, sir, and gang cannily. Trust in the Word, whilk it is your duty to preach, to bring conviction o' sin in the Lord's ain gude time, for if ye're ettlin' * to use the arm o' flesh it will fail ye."

It was the counsel which Isobel had given, and David's heart sank. What was it in Woodilee which made honest men silent and craven in the face of proved iniquity ?

" Man, Amos," he cried, " I never thought to get a coward's counsel from you. Am I to reckon you among my enemies, and among God's enemies ? I tell you I see my duty as clear before me as the Hill of Deer. I must unveil this wickedness and blast its practisers into penitence or I fail in my first duty as the minister of this parish. And from you, my friend, I get only silence and contumacy, and what is worse, the advice of a Laodicean. Alas ! that you who have fought stoutly in your country's battles should be such a poor soldier in God's battles."

There was no answer. The two had resumed their walk, and the smith strode at a pace which was almost a run, his eyes steadily averted from his companion.

" This is my last word to you, Amos," said David, as they reached the turn where the loan ran to the manse.

* Intending.

" Wednesday—the day after the morn—is the second Beltane, and I fear that that night there will be further evil in the Wood. I will go there and outface the Devil, but the flesh is weak, and I am one against many, and I would fain have a friend. Will you not bear me company ? "

The smith stopped again. " Deil hae me if I gang near the Wud ! Na, na, I'll no pit my heid intil ony sic wull-cat's hole. And, Mr. Sempill, be you guidit by an aulder man and bide at hame."

" You are afraid ? "

" Ay. I'm feared—but mair for you than for mysel'."

" You're like the men of Israel that failed Gideon at the waterside," David cried angrily as he turned away.

The next two days were spent by the minister in a strange restlessness. He walked each afternoon some violent miles on the hilltops, but for the rest he stayed in the manse, principally in his study. Isobel believed him to be at prayer, and indeed he prayed long and fervently, but he was also busied about other things. Among his belongings was a small-sword, for he had won some skill of fence in Edinburgh, and this he had out and saw to its point and edge. Also he read much in books which were not divinity, for he felt himself a soldier, and would brace his spirit with martial tales. With Isobel he exchanged no word save commonplaces, and the old woman, who had the air of a scolded child, showed no desire to talk. His meals were set before him in silence, and silently the table was cleared. Amos Ritchie came to the manse on some small repairing job, and he too seemed to be anxious to get his work done and leave. David saw him arrive as he set out for a walk, and when he returned, the shoulders of the smith were disappearing past the stable end.

Wednesday evening came, an evening of mellow light and a quiet sunset, and after his early supper David retired to his study to prepare himself for his task. He had already written out an account of what he had seen in the Wood and of what he proposed to do, and this he signed and directed under cover to Mr. Fordyce at Cauldshaw. Whatever mischance befell him, he had left a record. He had also written a letter to his father, setting forth what, in the event of his death, was to be the destination of his worldly goods. Then on his knees he remained for a while in prayer.

The clock struck nine, and he arose to begin his journey, strapping the sword to his middle, and taking also a great stick which the shepherd of the Greenshiel had made for him. The moon would rise late and there was ample time.

But he found that the door of his study would not open. It had no lock, and had hung on a light hasp, but now it seemed to have bolts and bars. It was a massive thing of oak, and when he shook it it did not yield.

He shouted for Isobel, but there was no reply. Then he assaulted it furiously with knees and feet and shoulder, but it did not give. There was no hope from the window, which was a small square through which a child could not have crept.

Further attacks on the door followed, and futile shouting. By the time the late light had faded from the little window David had acknowledged the fact that he was imprisoned and his first fury had ebbed from sheer bodily fatigue. But the clock had struck one before he attempted to make a bed on the floor, with for pillow a bag of chaff which Isobel had placed there for a winter footstool, and the dawn was in the eastern sky before he slept.

He was awakened by Isobel in the doorway.

"Peety on us," she wailed, "that sic a thing suld hae come to this hoose! Hae ye spent the nicht in this cauld chamber and no in your bed? The wyte's * on me, for I got Amos Ritchie yestereen to put a bar on the door, for there's walth of guid books here and I wad like to steek the place when ye're awa' to the hills and me maybe in the kitchen. I maun hae steekit it to see if it wad wark, no kennin' ye were in inside. And syne I gaed doun to my gude-brither's to speir after his bairn, and I was late in getting back, and, thinks I, the minister will be in his bed and I'll awa' to mine. Puir man, ye'll be as stiff as a wand, and ye'll maybe hae got your death o' cauld. . . . See and I'll get ye a het drink, and your parritch's on the boil. . . . Wae's me that I didn' tak' a thocht . . ."

"Silence, woman, and do not cumber your soul with lies." David's white face as he strode from the room did more than his words to cut short Isobel's laments.

* Blame.

CHAPTER VIII

THE SECOND BLAST

On the following Sabbath the minister's text was, " When the light within you is darkness, how great is that darkness ! " This time there was no faltering in the application. The congregation, men and women, were arraigned at the bar as sinners by deed or by connivance, and he had an audience hushed not in the ordinary Sabbath decorum, but in a fearful apprehension. Every moment he seemed to be about to name the sinner, and if he did not single out persons he made it blindingly clear that it was not for lack of knowledge. Never had he preached with greater freedom, never had passion so trembled in each sentence. Words seemed to be given him, stinging, unforgettable words that must flay the souls of the guilty. " Blinded self-deceivers," he cried, " you think you can tamper with devilry and yet keep your interest in Christ You are set up with covenants, public and private, but I tell you that your covenant is with Death and Hell. The man who believes he is elected into salvation, and thinks that thereby he has liberty to transgress and that his transgressions will be forgiven him, has sinned against the Holy Ghost—that sin for which there is no forgiveness." He declared that till there was a general confession and repentance there would be no Communion

in the parish of Woodilee, for those who sat down at
the Lord's Table would be eating and drinking damnation to themselves. . . . But at the end he broke
down. With tears in his eyes and a sob in his voice
he besought a people whom he loved to abase themselves before the Mercy Seat. " You poor folk," he
cried, " with your little dark day of life, with your few
years of toil and cold and hunger before the grave,
what have you if you have not Christ ? " He was
moved with an ecstasy of pity, and told them, like the
Apostle, that if he could but save their souls, he was
willing that his own should be cast away.

Not the oldest remembered such a sermon in the kirk
of Woodilee, and the fame of it was soon to go abroad
in the countryside. The place emptied in a strange
silence, as if the congregation went on tiptoe, and men
and women did not look at each other till they were
outside the kirkyard gates. The elders did not await
the minister in the session-house, and as David walked
the hundred yards to the manse he saw what looked
like the back of Peter Pennecuik, crouching behind a
turf dyke to avoid a meeting.

These were days of loneliness and misery for the
minister of Woodilee. He saw himself solitary among
enemies, for even those whom he thought his friends had
failed him. It was clear that Amos Ritchie had con-
spired with Isobel to imprison him in his study on the
eve of the second Beltane, and though their motive was
doubtless affection it but emphasized the hopelessness of
his task. He had to bring conviction of sin into a parish
where even the innocent were ready to cumber his arm.
These honest creatures feared for him—what ? Anger
would choke him at the thought of such contempt for
his sacred mission, and then awe would take its place,

awe at the immensity of the evil with which he fought. "Principalities and powers," Amos had said—yes, the Powers of the Air and the Principalities of Darkness. He had no doubt that the Devil and his myrmidons were present in the Wood in bodily form, mingling with the worshippers, and that the tongues which he had heard were in very truth mutterings of the lost. There were times when ordinary human fear loosened his knees, and he longed to flee from the parish as from a place accursed. But his courage would return, and his faith, for he knew that the armies of Heaven were on his side, and wrath would cast out fear, wrath and horror at the seducers of his flock. Nevertheless in these days his nerves were frayed, he lay awake of nights listening anxiously for noises without, and he would awake suddenly in the sweat of a nameless terror.

But his chief burden was that he did not know how to shape his course. The pulpit rang with his denunciations, but there was no response ; no stricken Nicodemus came to him by night. On the roads and at the house-doors people avoided his eyes. There were no more stones from Daft Gibbie—indeed Gibbie had resumed his fawning friendliness—but none waited to speak a word with him. Isobel had recovered her cheerfulness, and sought to atone for past misconduct by an assiduous attention to his comforts, but Amos Ritchie shunned him. And the children, too, who had been his chief allies. Perhaps their parents had warned them, for a group would scatter when he came near, and once when, coming up behind him, he laid a kindly hand on a boy's head, the child burst into tears and fled. What was the *fama* of the minister which had been put about in Woodilee ?

The worst of it was that he could contrive no plan of

campaign. Evidence which was overwhelming to his own mind would not convince the Presbytery or the Sheriff. He could not bring a reasoned charge against any man or woman in the parish. As the days passed he began to sort out his flock in his mind as the guilty and the abettors. Some were innocent enough, save for the sin of apathy; but others he could believe to have shared in the midnight debauches—heavy-browed sensual youths, women with shifty eyes, girls high-coloured and over-blown, whose sidelong glances seemed to hint at secrets, old wives, too, whose wild laughter he heard at cottage doors. But of one, his first certainty was giving way to doubt. Ephraim Caird's white face had got a wholesome tan from the summer sun, and he alone in the parish seemed to seek out the minister. He gave him a cheerful greeting when they met, spoke wisely of parish matters, had a word of humble commendation for the Sabbath discourses. "It's gaun to be a braw year for the aits," he said, "gin the weather hauds, and the lambs are the best I've yet seen on Chasehope hill. Let us hope, sir, that the guid seed ye've sown will come to as bountiful a hairst." The words were so simply spoken that they seemed no hypocrisy.

A plan of campaign! On that David could get no clearness, and the anxiety was with him at bed and board. He shrank from confessing himself to his brother-ministers, for what could they do to help him? Kirk Aller would pooh-pooh the whole thing, since Woodilee had been so forward in signing the Covenant. Bold would no doubt believe, but his remedy would be only a stiffer draught of doctrine. Even Mr. Fordyce at Cauldshaw seemed a broken reed, for Mr. Fordyce was an ailing saint, and this task was for the church militant. No, he must fight his battles

alone, and trust to God to send him allies. He wanted
men of violence, who would fight not with words but
with deeds, Israelitish prophets who with their own
hands cut down groves and uprooted altars and hewed
Agag in pieces. And where would he find them in a
countryside where the good were timid as sheep and
their pastors like loud voices in a fog?

June was a month of hot suns and clear skies, when
the hills were bone-dry and the deepest flowe-moss could
be safely passed. It was weather for the high tops, and
one afternoon David, walking off his restlessness on the
Rood uplands, stumbled unexpectedly on a friend. For
at the head of the glen where the drove-road crosses from
Clyde to Aller, he fell in with the farmer of Reiverslaw
leading his horse up a steep patch of screes.

This man, Andrew Shillinglaw, was something of a
mystery both to parish and minister. He was a long
lean fellow of some forty years, black-haired, black-
bearded, whose sullen face was redeemed by a humorous
mouth, so that the impression was of a genial ferocity.
He was reputed the most skilful farmer in the place, and
some held him a rival in worldly wealth to the miller, but
beyond the fact that he had in Reiverslaw the best of
the hill farms, there was no clue to his prosperity. He
had the only good riding-horse in Woodilee and was a
notable figure on the roads, for he travelled the country
like a packman. For weeks on end he would be away
from home, and he was heard of in Galloway and the
west and as far south as the Border, so that speculation
about his doings became a favourite pastime among his
neighbours. He neither sold nor bought in the parish,
and he kept his own counsel, but his profession was clear
enough had there been eyes to see. For he was dealer
and middleman as well as farmer, and in a day when

stock and produce scarcely moved beyond parish
bounds, he sold and bought in outlying markets. In
a district of home-keepers he was the sole traveller.

Few liked him, for there was always an undertone of
satire in his speech. But all feared him, for his temper
was on a hair-trigger. Drink made him quarrelsome,
and the spence at Lucky Weir's had seen some ugly
business, since with him blow followed fast on word.
Three years before he had buried his wife, there were
no children, and he lived at Reiverslaw with an aged
cousin for housekeeper, who was half blind and wholly
deaf. His attendance at the kirk was far from exemp-
lary; in winter there were the drifts and the full bogs to
detain him and in summer he was as often as not on his
travels. The Session, who did not love him, had talked
of citing him to appear before them, but in the end they
seemed to shrink from belling so formidable a cat.

At the head of the little pass, which in that country is
called a "slack," he halted and let David approach him.

"A guid day to ye, sir," he cried. "We'll let Bess
get her wind, for it's a lang gait frae Crawfordjohn. I
rade ower yestereen to see the sma' Cumberland sheep
that the Lowther herds are trying on yon hills. I hae
nae great broo o' them. They'll maybe dae on yon
green braes where the bite is short, but they're nae use
for a heather country. . . . Sit ye doun, sir. What
brings ye sae far ower the tops? Ye werena ettlin' to
gie me a ca' in at Reiverslaw?"

David gladly stretched himself on the bent beside
him. The man seemed willing to talk, and of late he
had had little speech with his fellows.

"I came here for the caller air," he said, "and to
drive ill humours from body and mind. There are
whiles when I cannot draw breath in Woodilee."

"Ay," said the man. "Ay! Just so." He pursed his lips and looked at the minister under half-shut eyes.

"Were you born in this parish?" David asked.

"Na, na. Far frae that. I'm but an incomer, though I've had the tack o' Reiverslaw for a dizzen years. My father, honest man, was frae the Glenkens, and my mither cam' frae the Cairn side. I was born at a bit they ca' Dunscore, but I was a stirrin' lad in my young days and I've traivelled the feck o' the Lawlands, frae the Forth to the Solway. But now I've got my hinderlands doun in Woodilee, and it's like I'll lay my banes here."

The man spoke in a different voice from the people of the place, and to David he seemed as one detached from the countryside, sharing neither its interests nor affections. As he looked at him, sprawling in the heather bush with one foot on his horse's bridle, he had a sense of something assured and resolute and not unfriendly.

"Ye're an incomer like mysel', sir," Reiverslaw said after a pause. "What think ye o' Woodilee?"

"I think that the Devil has chosen this miserable parish for his own."

"Ay. . . . Well, I wadna say ye were wrang. I jaloused * frae your last discourse that ye were per-plexed wi' the Enemy. And they tell me that ye've stirred up an unco byke against ye."

"Are you one of them?" David asked.

"No me. If there's fechtin' to be done, I'm on your side. I aye likit a bauld man, and it's a question, sir, if ye ken yoursel' how bauld ye are when ye offer to drive the Deil frae Woodilee."

* Guessed.

David had got to his feet, for these were the first words of sympathy he had had.

"Andrew Shillinglaw, I command you to tell me if you have kept yourself clean from this mystery of evil which scourges the parish."

The man still sprawled on the ground, and the face he turned to the minister was twisted in a grim humour.

"Ay. I'll swear ony aith ye like. I'll no deny my backslidin's, and, as ye may ken, my walk and conversation's no to boast o'. But as sure as God made me, I wad burn off my richt hand in the fire afore I wad file mysel' wi' the Babylonish abominations o' the Wud. I whiles drink a stoup ower muckle, and I whiles gie a waur straik than I ettle when my bluid's het, but these are honest stumblin's whilk I hope the Lord will forgie. But for yon——" and he spat viciously.

"Then, if you are yourself clean from this evil, tell me what you know of it, and who are its chief professors ?"

"That's easy speirin',* but ill to answer. How suld I ken the covens that rampage in the Wud ? I bide cheek by jowl wi' the muckle black thing, and often I wish it was a field o' strae in a dry back-end so that I could set fire to it and see it burn frae Reiverslaw to Windyways and frae Woodilee to the Aller side. But I've never entered the place in mirk or licht, for my wark's wi' sheep and the honest beasts will no gang near it."

"But you must have heard . . ."

"I've heard nocht. I have maybe guessed, but it's no like I wad hear a cheep. I never gang near the clachan except to kirk or to Lucky Weir's, and the

* Asking.

Woodilee folk are pawky bodies even when they're fou, and ony way I'm nae clatter-vengeance to be clypin' wi' auld wives at the roadside. But I've my ain notion o' what's gaun on, and I can tell ye, sir, it's gaun on in mony anither godly parochine in this kingdom o' Scotland, and it's been gaun on for hundreds o' years, long afore John Knox dang doun the Pape. But it's gotten a braw new tack in these days o' reformed and covenantit kirks. What do your Presbytries and Assemblies or your godly ministers ken o' the things that are done in the mirk ? . . . What do they ken o' the corps in the kirkyairds buried o' their ain wull wi' their faces downwards ? . . . They set up what they ca' their discipline and they lowse the terrors o' Hell on sma' fauts like an aith, or profane talk on the Sabbath, or giein' the kirk the go-by, and they hale to the cutty-stool ilka lass that's ower kind to her joe. And what's the upshot ? They drive the folk to their auld ways and turn them intil hypocrites as weel as sinners."

" Hush, man ! " said the scandalized David. " That is impious talk."

" It's true a' the same, though it's maybe no for a minister's lugs. The Kirk is set against witchcraft and every wee while a daft auld wife is brunt. But, God help us, that's but the froth on the pat. Na, na, Mr. Sempill. If you're lookin' to get to grips wi' the Adversary, it's no the feckless camsteery lad ye maun seek that likes a randan, or the bit lassie that's ower fond to wait for the Kirk's blessin', or the grannie that swears she rade to France on a kail-runt. It's the dacent body that sits and granes aneath the pu'pit and the fosy professor that wags his pow and deplores the wickedness o' the land.—Yon's the true warlocks. There's saunts in Scotland, the Lord kens and I ken mysel', but there's some that hae the name o' saunts that wad make the Deil spew."

Reiverslaw had risen, and in his face was such a flame of fierce honesty that David's heart kindled. He had found an ally.

"Give me names," he cried. "I will denounce the sinner, though he were one of my own elders."

"I speak nae names. I have nae proof. But ye've seen yoursel'. They tell me ye broke in on the coven at their wark."

"I had but a glisk of them, before they beat the senses out of me. But I intend to go back to the Wood, and this time I shall not fail."

"Ay. Ye've a stout heart, Mr. Sempill."

"But I must have help. Out of the mouths of witnesses I must establish the truth, and the innocent in Woodilee are very fearful. I have nowhere to look but to you. Will you come with me when I return to the Wood?"

"I'll no say that, for there's maybe better ways o' guidin' it. But this I will say—I'll stand by ye; for may the Deil flee awa' wi' me or I see a guid man beat. There's my hand on't. . . . And now I maun be takin' the road again. Come na near the Reiverslaw, sir, for that would set the bodies talkin'. If ye want word wi' me, tell Richie Smail at the Greenshiel."

The knowledge that he had found a friend lightened David's heavy preoccupation of mind. Athanasius now was not alone against the world, and his path was not towards martyrdom but to victory. He walked with a more assured step and turned a bolder face to the furtive hostility of the parish. When he met Amos Ritchie he looked on him not in reproach but in defiance. **His**

sermons were now less appeals than challenges, as of
one whose course was proclaimed and whose loins were
girded.

To his consternation he found that he now sat very
loose in his devotion to the Kirk. The profession of
religion was not the same thing as godliness, and he
was coming to doubt whether the insistence upon
minute conformities of outward conduct and the hair-
splitting doctrines were not devices of Satan to entangle
souls. The phrases of piety, unctuously delivered, made
him shudder as at a blasphemy. The fact that his only
supporter was one looked askance at by strict professors confirmed his shrinking. Had not Christ set the
publican and the sinner above the Pharisee ?

One consequence of his new mood was that his
thoughts turned again to the girl in Paradise. In
his season of desolation he had not dared to think
of her ; she belonged to a world of light and had
no part in his perplexities. To let her image fill his
memory seemed sacrilege, when that memory held so
many foul shadows. But as the skies cleared for him
her figure appeared again in the sunlight and he did
not banish it, for it was she who was the extreme
opposite of the horror of the Wood—she and her bright
domain of oaks and hazels. He would go again to
Paradise for his soul's comfort.

He chose a day when he was certain she would be
there. There was a week of fiery weather—moist heat
and heavy skies and flying thunderstorms, and after
it came a spell of long bright days, when the sunshine
had a dry tonic in it and the afternoons were mellow and
golden. On one such afternoon he crossed the Hill of
Deer and entered the glen which divided the pines from
the hazels.

Midsummer had changed the place. The burnside turf was all thyme and eyebright and milkwort, with the stars of the grass of Parnassus in the wet places. The water was clear and small, and the cascades fell in a tinkling silver. He had no doubts as to his road now. Paradise was among the hazels, but one could find it only by descending the glen to where the pines of the Wood began and then turning to the right towards the Greenshiel.

Presently the pines in a sombre regiment rose on the steep to the left. He looked at the beginning of the Wood with an awe which had now no fear in it. The place was hateful, but it could not daunt him. It was the battleground to which he was called. . . . On the edge of the trees was a great mass of dark foxgloves, the colour of blood, and they seemed to make a blood-trail from the sunlight into the gloom.

He turned up the right bank, and through hazel copses and glades breast-high with bracken he made his way as if by instinct. He found the shallow cup lined with birches and the blossoming rowans, and as he brushed through the covert he saw the girl sitting on the greensward by the well.

Motionless he watched her for a little, while his heart played strange pranks. She had a basket beside her full of flowers, and she was reading in a book. . . . She laid down the book, and shook her curls and dabbled her fingers in the water. She sang as she dabbled, low and clear in snatches, a song which he was to remember to his dying day :

> " There's comfort for the comfortless,
>   And honey for the bee,
> And there's nane for me but you, my love,
>   And there's nane for you but me."

She crooned the verse twice, broke off to watch a ring-
ouzel, and then sang again :

> " It's love for love that I have got,
>   And love for love again,
> So turn your high horse heid about
> And we will ride for hame, my love,
>   And we will ride for hame."

He would fain have lingered and watched her, but
he felt like an eavesdropper on her privacy. So " Mistress Katrine," he cried softly, and " Mistress Katrine "
a second time.

She sprang to the alert like a bird. Her face, when
she saw him, showed no welcome.

" I give you good-day, sir," she said. " Have you
maybe lost your road ? "

" I am seeking Paradise," he replied.

" It is the quest of all mortals, they tell me. But
the ministers say it is not to be found on earth."

" I was seeking the earthly one to which you yourself first led me."

" You entered then by my invitation, but I do not
think I bade you come again."

" Then I beg for admission, mistress, for indeed I
have sore need of Paradise."

She looked at him curiously. " You look older—and
sadder. I have not been to your kirk, but they tell me
that you are scorching the souls of your folk with your
terrors."

" Would to God I could scorch them into salvation ! . . . I have been in dire straits, Mistress Katrine.
For I came again to find Paradise and I found it not,
but stumbled into Hell."

The girl looked at him with compassionate eyes.

"You may sit down in Paradise," she said. "I permit you. And I will give you some of my wild strawberries. Tell me what has troubled you?"

He told her of the doings of Beltane Eve, stumblingly, with many omissions. He told her of his strife with his parishioners, of his loneliness, of the mission to which he was vowed. "I am resolved," he said, "that though I go on alone I will not fail in courage. Your Montrose's comfort is mine—that the arm of the Lord is not shortened."

The girl brooded.

"Did you come here to find me?"

"I had a conviction that you would be in Paradise. This is no tale for a maid's ear, but I came here to warn you, Mistress. The long glen that runs down to the Rood Mill is a frontier-line, which if you pass you are in the land of darkness. I found you first among the pines, and I beseech you go not again among them, though it were at high noon, for yon Wood is accursed."

She nodded. "I felt it too. When Spring was passing I felt a gloom come over me as I walked there, and one day a terror seized me and I ran and ran till I was among the hazels. I cannot bear even to be in sight of the dark trees. You say that there is witchcraft there." She lowered her voice and her eyes were solemn. "What is this witchcraft?"

"I cannot tell, save that it is the nethermost works of darkness and that it has seduced the hearts of my unhappy people. . . . God help me, but I have seen with my eyes what I cannot forget. . . . There is no smooth ministry for me, for now I am a soldier of Christ and must be fighting till I have got the victory."

"And you are alone?"

"I have one who will stand by me." And he told her of Reiverslaw.

"Nay, you have another," she cried. "You have me for a friend, and you have this greenwood for a sanctuary. If I cannot fight by your side, you will know that I am here and that I am wishing you well. See, I make you free of Paradise. It is yours now, as well as mine." She held out her hand.

He took off his hat.

"You were singing," he said, "and your song was true, for here's ' comfort for the comfortless.' You have put steel into my bones, Mistress Katrine. If I can come here and speak with you at times, it will be like the water beside the gate of Bethlehem to King David. . . . I will know when you are here without your sending me word."

"Then there is witchcraft in the greenwood," she said, smiling gravely, "for I too knew that you were coming to-day before you came."

CHAPTER IX

BEFORE LAMMAS

ONE day in July David saddled his horse and rode to Kirk Aller for a Presbytery meeting. He found a bewildered brotherhood. The usual "exercises" were omitted, there was no prelection on a set doctrinal theme for the benefit of the younger ministers, the sittings in the kirk were occupied mainly with prayers for a humbled Sion and a distracted country, and the dinner thereafter in the Cross Keys was not notable for good-fellowship. But it was a crowded gathering, and among the lay members in the kirk was Ephraim Caird.

At the meal Mr. Mungo Muirhead, primed with letters from Edinburgh, gave ill news of the war in the North. Montrose the recusant continued to win battles and was even now marching southward with his savage Irishry to strike at the citadel. "What for does Davie Leslie no hasten," he cried, "and what profits it to have a covenanted State and a purified Kirk if a mailed Amalekite can hunt our sodgers from Dan to Beersheba? I tell you, sirs, this war which has hitherto been fought among Hieland glens will soon be at our ain doorcheeks, and our puir folk will be called to testify not with voice and word and the scart of a pen, but with sufferings and revilings and bloody murderings. Forth and Aller may yet run red, and the hand of death be on the Lowdon

fields. Are we prepared, I ask, and I ask it yet again ?
Whatna gifts will we bring to the altar in the coming
day of sacrifice ? "

His fears had given dignity to the minister of Kirk
Aller. The man was a fighter, for his mouth shut tight
and there was a spark of fire in his heavy eyes. Nor
was Mr. Proudfoot of Bold less ready for the fray.
He had got himself a pair of great boots, and looked a
very Ironside as he expanded his big chest and groaned
assent to his leader's warning.

" Let us see that there is no Canaanitish thing in
our midst," Mr. Proudfoot cried, " for the purge of the
Lord is nigh. And let Israel dwell in unity, for a house
divided shall not stand. These are the twin counsels for
this day of wrath, a pure cause and a brotherly people.
These, I say, are the dams with which to stem the tide
of the heathen's rage."

" And that's a word in season for you, Mr. Sempill,"
said Mr. Muirhead. " I hear ye've set the haill parish of
Woodilee by the lugs with wanton accusations. You'll
admit none to the Table, says you, till there is public
confession of some unkenned iniquity. I applaud zeal
in a young minister, but it seems you've fair got your
leg ower the trams, and the serious folk of Woodilee
are troubled to ken what ye mean. Have a care,
Mr. Sempill, lest this zeal of yours be but human
impatience. This is no time to sow confusion among
God's people."

The minister of Kirk Aller had lost his air of rough
good-humour. It was a hard face and an inquisitorial
eye that he bent on David.

" I take my stand on the first of Mr. Proudfoot's
counsels," said the latter. " If the day of tria. is coming,
our cause must be pure, and there must be no Canaanitish

thing in our midst. When I am clear about the sins of Woodilee, the Presbytery will have further news of me."

The young man's speech was too assured to please Mr. Muirhead. He drew down his eyebrows till they formed a straight line bisecting his huge expanse of face. "Have a care, have a care, I counsel you," he said crossly. "I can tell you that there's many an auld exercised professor in Woodilee that's sore concerned about your doings."

Mr. Proudfoot added his reproof. "When I mind on the precious work I witnessed in that very parish in the month of March, I will not believe that the Devil has got the master hand. Examine yourself, I rede you, Mr. Sempill, and see if the beam be not in your own eye."

David rode away from Kirk Aller in the company of Mr. Fordyce of Cauldshaw, but they had not ridden a mile before there was a clatter of hoofs behind them and the minister of Bold joined himself to their company. His beast was fractious, having had an unaccustomed feed of oats in the Cross Keys stable, and Mr. Proudfoot, since he was an awkward horseman, had to spend much of his energy in keeping it to the road. But what time he could spare from this task he devoted to catechizing David, and for the three miles during which their course lay together his tongue never stopped.

"There's an ill *fama* of you gone abroad, Mr. Sempill, and it is my duty as your elder in the Lord's service to satisfy myself thereanent. It is reported that you pervert the doctrine of election into grace, maintaining that this blessed estate may be forfeit by a failure in good works, as if the filthy rags of man's righteousness were mair than the bite of a flea in face of the eternal purposes of God."

"I say that a man who believes that his redemption

through Christ gives him a licence to sin is more doubly damned than if he had never had a glimpse of grace."

" But ye maun distinguish. The point is far finer than that, sir. I will construe your words, for there is an interpretation of them which is rank heresy."

The task of construing and distinguishing did not fare well, for every few minutes the teeth of Mr. Proudfoot were shaken in his head by his horse's vagaries. He had just reached a point of inordinate subtlety, when the track to Bold branched off, and his animal, recognizing at last the road home, darted down it at a rough gallop. The last seen of the minister of Bold was a massive figure swaying like a ship in a gale, and still, if one might trust the echoes the wind brought back, distinguishing and construing.

Even Mr. Fordyce's grave face smiled as he watched the fleeing Boanerges.

" He is a wilful man, and he has a wilful beast. But what is this rumour in the countryside, Mr. David ? I fear that you are finding Woodilee a dour rig to plough."

" What do they say in Cauldshaw ? "

" I have been little about of late, for these last weeks I've been sore troubled with my bowels. I'm like the Psalmist—the Lord trieth my reins in the night watches —and I've never made out my visit to you to have a read of Cardanus. But I cannot but hear orra bits of news from the next parish, and the speak in the countryside is that you have uncovered the nakedness of Woodilee and preach siccan sermons that the een of the folk turn inward in their heads. What's the truth of it, Mr. David ? My heart yearns over you as if you were my own mother's son."

" I have uncovered a great wickedness—but not yet all. I wait and watch, and when I have fuller know-

ledge I will know better how to act. You told me the
first day we met that Woodilee had an ill reputation, and,
sorrow on me! I have proved the justice of your words.
And I greatly fear that it is the loudest professors that
are deepest in the mire."

"Man, David, that is a grievous business. Is it the
Wood?"

"It is the Wood, and the blackest kind of witchcraft.
Some old devilry of the heathen has lingered in that
place, and the soul of my miserable parish is thirled to it.
You will not find in Scotland a doucer bit, for there are
no public sins and shortcomings. Man, there's times
when Woodilee seems as quiet and dead as a kirkyard.
But there's a mad life in its members, and at certain
seasons it finds vent. In the deeps of night and in the
heart of the Wood there are things done of which it is
shameful even to speak."

"What witness have you?"

"My own eyes. I stumbled upon one of their hellish
Sabbaths."

"God be kind to us! I have heard tell of siccan
things and I have read of them in old books, but I never
experienced them. I'm positive they're not in Cauldshaw, for the place is ower bare and bright and the wind
blows ower clean on our braes. There's no cover for the
abominations which must be done in darkness. But I
have aye had a scunner of yon Wood. . . . It's a queer
thing the heart of man, Mr. David, and there's that in
my own that whiles terrifies me. The work of redemption is done in an instant, but the job of regeneration is
a lifetime's; and the holiest saint on his death-bed is but
a bag of rottenness compared to the purity to which he
shall yet attain. And at times I'm tempted to think that
our way and the Kirk's way is not God's way, for we're

apt to treat the natural man as altogether corrupt, and put him under over-strict pains and penalties, whereas there's matter in him that might be shaped to the purposes of grace. If there's original sin, there's likewise original innocence. When I hear the lassie Katrine Yester singing about the door at Calidon, I have an assurance of God's goodness as sharp as I ever got in prayer. If you ban this innocent joy it will curdle and sour, and the end will be sin. If young life may not caper on a Spring morn to the glory of God, it will dance in the mirk wood to the Devil's piping."

Mr. Fordyce stopped short with a rueful face. "That's for your own ear, Mr. David. If the bruit of what I have said came to the manse of Bold, Mr. Ebenezer would be for delating me to the Presbytery. But if it's not orthodox it's good sense."

"I doubt orthodoxy is no salve against sin," said David. "The devils, it is written, believe and tremble, and it's my surmise that the leader of the witches' coven in Woodilee could stand his ground with Bold himself on matters of doctrine."

"You have formidable foes."

"I have a whole parish, for even those who are free of guilt are too timid to lift a hand. Likewise I have my Kirk Session."

Mr. Fordyce exclaimed.

"And it looks like I will have the Presbytery. I'm in ill odour with Mr. Muirhead for dividing Israel, and to Mr. Proudfoot I smack of heresy."

"You've aye gotten me on your side," said Mr. Fordyce. "No that I'm much of a fighter, for my bowels melt and my speech sticks in my throat and I sit like a dumb ox, and syne mourn on my bed in the night watches that I have been found wanting. But my

heart is with you, Mr. David, and what voice my infirmities permit me, and you'll be never out of my prayers.
. . . Come to Cauldshaw whenever ye long for speech
with a friend. I can aye give you sympathy if I canna
give you counsel."

But when David three days later turned his horse in
the direction of Cauldshaw, it was not to the manse he
went but to the tower of Calidon. For Katrine Yester
had become for him the only light on his path. She
personified the cause for which he fought, the fair world
that stood in contrast to the obscene shades, and since
their last meeting in Paradise she was no longer a flitting
wood-nymph, but a woman of flesh and blood and heart.
He longed to see her in the house where she dwelt and
among her own people.

But there was no Katrine in Calidon that afternoon,
for she had gone to the greenwood. It was a still day
of July in which no cloud tempered the heat of the sun,
but the great upper chamber in the tower was cool and
dusky. He asked for Mistress Saintserf and was received by that grim lady in state, for she kept him waiting
while she donned a new toy and kerchief for the occasion.
She spoke a Scots as broad as any shepherd's wife, but
the sharp vowels of Edinburgh took the place of the
softer Border tones. Large and gaunt and domineering,
her high-nosed face and prim mouth were mellowed by
an audacious humour. Katrine had clearly never spoken
of him (at which he was glad), but she knew him by
repute and by his connection with the miller of the Roodfoot. She entertained him with shortcake of her own
baking and elder wine of her own brewing, and her tone
mingled the deference of a good woman towards a
spiritual guide and the freedom of an old woman towards
a young man.

"That gilpie o' mine suld have been here, but she's awa' to the hill. As weel try to keep a young jeuk frae the water as Katrine frae stravaigin' the countryside. And her bred denty in France and England whaur there are nae hills! If she had a joe * I wad say nocht, but she has nae joe but the whaups."

He asked concerning Nicholas Hawkshaw.

"And that's speirin'!" she cried. "He's fechtin' and him a lameter, but whaur he's fechtin' and in what cause the Lord alone kens! Since he gaed off wi' Tam Purves three months syne sorrow a word has come frae him. He's maybe in England and maybe in France, and maybe ryngin' with Montrose, and I'll wager wherever he is, him and his swird and Tam and his firelock are in the het o't. Ye'll no fetter a Hawkshaw, and they can nae mair bide in the ae place than a puddock on a brae, as my puir sister that was married on him kenned ower weel. And the same bluid's in Katrine, wha suld hae been a laddie, and a tinkler laddie, for it's no her that will mind her seam or watch the pot when the sun's shinin'. She's a fine lassie for a' that, but by ordinar' forgetfu'. I wish I saw her wed."

Of Woodilee she had many questions to ask.

"It's a' Hawkshaw land, but I never likit the folk. There's a wheen fosy bodies yonder, wha pray mair with their tongues than their hearts, and they're as keen at a niffer † as a Musselburgh wabster—aye wi' the puir face and the greetin' word when it comes to payin' siller. Auld Dobbie in Murchison's Close—he's our doer,‡ ye maun ken, as his father was afore him—he has had mony a sair tuilzie for our bits o' rents. Now that Nicholas is at the wars it's my shouther that has to carry the

---

* Sweetheart.   † Bargain.

‡ Man of business.

burden, and there's never a post frae Embro but brings
me Dobbie's scribin'. Ye'll ken that the mailin' o'
Crossbasket is to let, and whaur am I to get a guid
tenant wi' the land in siccan a steer?"

David told her the news he had heard at Kirk Aller.

"Keep us a'!" she cried. "God send Nicholas binna
wi' Montrose or we'll hae him and Tam Purves here
rauvagin' his ain lands, and if Argyll gets the upper hand
they'll be glorifyin' God at the end o' a tow in the Grass-
market. Hech, sir, we're surely faun on the latter days
when, it is written, confusion will be on the people. I'm
for the Kirk, but they tell me Montrose is likewise for
the Kirk as he conceives it, and between her twa well-
wishers it's like our auld Sion will get uncoly mishandled.
But I hae nae broo o' poalitics. My poalitics is just an
auld wife's poalitics that wants to be left in peace by her
fireside. . . . But ye say Montrose is mairchin' south?
He'll be for England, and that means the road by Aller
Water. I'll hae to kilt my coats and pit the tower o'
Calidon in a state of defence against Nicholas or ony
ither, for if I let the laird intil his ain house we'll hae to
answer for't before the Privy Council."

It was plain that Mistress Saintserf was not ill-pleased
with David, for she talked freely and would hardly let
him go.

"Ye're ower young for the sacred callin'," she told him
when at last he took his leave. "And ye're ower wise-
like a man for a minister. Saunts suld hae weak
stomachs, like our ain Mr. Fordyce; it gars them sit
loose to earthly affections."

"I would put up with his affliction if I could get one-
half of his goodness," said David.

"'Deed that's weel spoken. I'm sure o' Heaven if I
can get haud o' the strings of Mr. James's cloak. Never

heed an auld wife's clavers. Come back and prie our grosarts when they're ripe, and if ye see that lass o' mine on the hill tell her I'm waitin' for her wi' a besom."

On his way home David had no sight of Katrine, but the next afternoon he met her in Paradise. She came to him smiling and friendly as a boy.

"You have been to Calidon and seen Aunt Grizel. I congratulate you on your conquest, sir, for my aunt is now your devout partisan and you have won another friend in this countryside. But what is this news of the Lord Marquis?"

They whiled away the summer afternoon with talk, rambling sometimes through the oak glades, but always returning to the nook by the spring, while David kept a jealous eye on the declining sun. The girl must be well on her way to Calidon before the first dusk began. When he came again they did not talk of his troubles, nor even of Montrose, but of little things, her childhood in France, her kin, the tales of the glen, his own youth at Edinburgh College. For she was not an ally so much as a refuge. When he was with her he was conscious that the world was still large and sunlit, the oppression lifted from his spirit, he saw himself not only victor in the quarrel but a messenger of God with a new gospel to perplexed mankind.

One evening, when he had seen the girl descend through the hazels to the Rood vale, and had turned back towards the shoulder of the Hill of Deer, he saw a man's figure slanting across the hill as if coming from Melanudrigill. It was Reiverslaw, but though their paths all but intersected the farmer did not stop to talk. He waved a hand in greeting. "Ye suld gie a look in at the Greenshiel," he shouted. "They tell me Richie Smail is in need of consolation."

David took the hint, passed word to Richie, and the next evening met Reiverslaw in the herd's cottage. "Tak' a look round the faulds, Richie," said the master. "Me and the minister has something to say to ither," and the two were left alone in the dim sheiling.

"I've been spyin' oot the land," said Reiverslaw, "like the lads that Joshua sent afore him into Canaan. I canna say I likit the job, but I've been through the Wud east and west and I've found the bit whaur the coven meets aside the auld altar. I think I could find the road till't on the blackest nicht. And I've been speirin' judeeciously in Woodilee."

"But surely they did not answer?"

The dark face of the farmer had a crooked grin.

"Trust me, I was discreet. But I've a name for takin' a stoup ower muckle, and when the folk thocht I was fou, my lugs were as gleg as a maukin's. They're preparin' for another Sabbath, and it fa's on the Lammas Eve. On that nicht you and me maun tak' the Wud."

David shivered, and the man saw it.

"The flesh is weak," he said, "and I'm feelin' like that mysel'. But you an' me are no the anes to pit our hand to the plew-stilts and turn back. Mr. Sempill, are ye young enough to speel a tree?"

"I was a great climber as a laddie."

"Weel, ye'll hae to be a laddie aince again. And I'll tell ye mair. Ye'll hae to leave this place afore the Lammas-tide. Is there ony bit ye can bide at, not abune twenty miles frae Woodilee?"

"There is my cousin at Newbiggin."

"Weel, to Newbiggin ye gang, and your departure maun be public. Crack about it for days afore. Tell the auld wife at the manse and deave her wi' your preparations. For if you're no oot o' the parish in guid time ye'll be lockit in your chamber, as ye were on the second Beltane. And ye maun be in the Wud that nicht as a witness, for there's just us twasome, you and me, and we maun be witnesses that the Presbytery and the Sheriff and the Lords in Embro cannot deny."

"I see that. But have you found out nothing more in Woodilee?"

"I've gotten a hantle o' suspeecions. Man, ye'd wonder to see how chief me and Chasehope are these days. I've been ower to see his English bull, and I've ta'en his advice about sheep, and I've sell't him a score o' gimmers at a price that made me voamit. He thinks I'm a dacent, saft, through-ither body, wi' his wits sair fuddled by strong drink, and has nae back-thochts o' ane that's just clay in his hands. . . . Ay, and I've been payin' muckle attention to his hen-house. His wife, ye maun ken, is a notable hen-wife, and she has a red cock that there's no the like o' in the countryside. I took Rab Prentice up wi' me to Chasehope toun, and I bade Rab tak' special note o' the red cock."

"But I do not see the purpose . . ."

"Ye needna—yet. Ye'll be tell't in guid time. I'm thinkin' o' the process afore the Presbytery, and it's witnesses I'm seekin'. I hae twa honest men, my herds Richie Smail and Rab Prentice, but Richie's ower auld to tak' the Wud and Hirplin' Rab wad dee afore he would pit his neb inside it. So there's just you and me for the chief job, though the ither twa will hae their uses."

The imminence of the trial made David's heart sick, for he had now brooded for three months on the mysteries of the Wood, whereas at Beltane he had stumbled upon them in hot blood unwittingly. He was confident in his cause, but he believed most firmly that the Devil

11

in person would be his antagonist, and the cool tones of Reiverslaw struck him with admiration and awe.

" Man, you speak as calm as if you were making ready for a clipping. Is it that you do not believe in the power of Satan ? "

" I believe in God," said the man, " and I've seen ower muckle o' the world no to believe in the Deil. But I'll no be feared o' a Deil that misguides auld wives and tak's up wi' rotten peats like Chasehope, and though he comes in a brimstane lowe I'll hae a nick at him."

Then began for David a time of doubt and heart-searching. He could not share the robust confidence of Reiverslaw, for his memory of Beltane was too clear and he had lived too long under its shadows. His imagination, always quick and easily kindled, ran riot, and he saw the Wood as an abode of horrid mysteries, which spread into subtle ramifications of evil the more he pondered them. His secular learning was so much fuel to this fire. Courage did not fail him, but brightness died out of his world, and he knew himself condemned to tread a dark winepress alone.

It was the thought of Katrine that most disquieted him. The Wood, the whole parish, the very mission on which he was engaged, seemed to him one vast pollution, to be kept hidden for ever from youth and innocence. The girl must not be allowed to come within sight of the skirts of it. There could be no friendship between them, and it was his first duty to warn her.

So when they met in Paradise it was a shamefaced young man that stood before her, a young man with a white face who kept his eyes on the ground and spoke terrible things. Words came unreadily, but his broken speech was more moving than eloquence. He bade her keep to the clean precincts of Calidon and come not even near the greenwood. God's curse was on the parish, and in the judgment preparing innocent might share with guilty. As for himself, he was no friend for such as she.

" I am too heavily burdened," he stammered. " I must touch pitch and my hands will be defiled. I will blight your youth with my dark duties. . . . I will never come again to this place, and I plead with you to come no more, for it is too near the Enemy's country. . . . Go now, I beg of you, and forget that you have ever seen me and called me friend. You will torture me if you bide. . . ."

There was more of the same sort, and then David stopped, confident that he had done his purpose, and that no proud girl would linger in the face of such a warning. He waited, very cold and lonely at heart, and he thought he heard her departing feet on the grass.

But when he raised his eyes, she had not moved, and her face was smiling.

CHAPTER X

WHAT THE MOON SAW

THERE was great heat at the end of July—sultry, thunderous weather when the hills drowsed under a haze and the sun's beams seemed to be the more torrid for the screen of vapour through which they fell. The heavens were banking up for the Lammas rains. But each evening the skies cleared, and the night was an amethyst dome sprinkled with stars.

David made a great to-do about his visit to Newbiggin. On the Monday morning he announced it to Isobel, and in an hour the word had gone through the village. His housekeeper seemed to receive the news with relief. "Blithe I am to hear it, sir. Folk suld whiles change their ground like bestial, and ye've been ower lang tethered to this parochine. Newbiggin will be a caller bit in this lown weather, and while ye're awa' I'll get your chamber cleaned and the stairs washed doun. Dinna haste to come back, for I'll no look for ye or Setterday."

He set off on the Tuesday after midday and there were many eyes in Woodilee to mark his going. That night he duly slept at Newbiggin, but the next day, which was Lammas Eve, he left his cousin's house and rode up Clyde water into the farthest moors. It was a wide circuit, which brought him in the afternoon to the uplands which separate Rood from Annan. All day he had been out of sight of human dwelling, and the first he saw was in the dusk when he descended upon the tower of Calidon by the glen of the Calidon burn. At Calidon he left his horse with the grieve, promising to return for it on the morrow, and with one look at the lit windows of the tower he set out on foot to ford the Rood. About nine o'clock in the mulberry gloaming he reached the cottage of the Greenshiel.

Three figures greeted him there. One was the herd of the outer hirsel, Richie Smail; another was Rab Prentice, the herd of the home hirsel, who sat on the turf deas at the cottage-end with his crutch beside him; the third was Reiverslaw himself, who was also seated, smoking a pipe of tobacco.

"Ye're in braw time, Mr. Sempill," said the last. "Did ye pass ony folk on the road?"

"I have seen no man since the morning, except the Calidon grieve half an hour syne."

"And that's just as weel. Richie, kindle the cruisie, for our job is better done indoors."

The feeble light in the hut revealed a curious assembly. The two shepherds had faces of portentous gravity, and their twitching mouths and restless eyes were proof of an extreme discomfort. Reiverslaw wore his usual frieze small-clothes and boot-hose, but he had no coat, though he had slung on his arm what might have been that garment. He flung this on the settle. "It's ower het to wear that muckle maud till the time comes. We maun get to business, Mr. Sempill, for you should be on the road afore the moon rises. We're here to get our plan strauchtit oot and there's jimp * time. Rab Prentice, ye've been twice wi' me to Chasehope in the

* Scarcely.

last se'en days. Ye mind the braw red cock the wife has gotten ? "

" Fine," said the shepherd.

" There's no sic another fowl in the countryside ? "

" That I'll engage."

" Therefore if I show ye the morn a pluckin' o' red feathers, ye'll jalouse it's the Chasehope cock ? "

" Ay. But I'm no gaun intil the Wud . . . not even in braid daylicht."

" If I bid ye, ye'll gang, Rab Prentice, though I suld carry ye mysel'. . . . Now, secondly, as the ministers say. Do ye see this bottle ? Smell it, a' three of ye. That's a smell ye never fand afore ? It's what they call oil of hennyseed, and I got it frae a horse-doctor at Carlisle. I'll wager there's no anither phial o' the same between here and Embro. It's a smell ye'll no sune forget. Pit a dab on yer sleeves to remind ye o't. If the three o' us gangs to Chase-hope the morn and finds Chasehope's breeks and Chasehope's sark stinkin' o' this oil, ye'll be able to swear to it, and to swear that I showed it you this verra nicht and that ye kenned the smell when ye fand it again."

The two men agreed, sniffing the drop on their sleeve.

" Thirdly," said Reiverslaw, " I'm gaun to turn mysel' intil a guisyard."

He picked up the thing he had been carrying and revealed it as a cloak of deerskins which fitted like a loose jerkin. Over his head he drew a cap of skin with slits for his eyes, a roughly shaped nozzle like a deer's, and on the top the horns of a goat.

" Save us a' ! " Richie cried, as he saw his master stand up, his lean, active body surmounted by a beast's head. " Save us a', ye're no gaun to tamper wi' the accursed thing?"

"That's what I ettle, but the intention is guid, and it's by our intentions we'll be judged, as Mr. Sempill will tell ye. Look at me, ye daft auld fules, for there's naething to be feared o'. I'm for the Wud the nicht, and it's my purpose to bide in cover till the folk are half dementit, and syne when their een are blind to join them. I've a notion that there will be some wark wi' the red cock, and I'd like a feather or twa as a keepsake. And I've a sort of notion that my auld friend Chasehope will be there; so as a token o' friend-ship I'll pit saut on his tail—whilk means that if I get the chance I'll anoint his dowp wi' the hennyseed. Now, you twa, take tent and listen to me. Ye will swear that I telled ye what I have telled ye, and that ye saw me at the Greenshiel dressed up like a merry-andrew. The horns suld hae been a stag's; but I was feared o' hankin' them in the busses, so the puir auld Reiverslaw billy-goat had to dee."

He was a crazy sight with the goat's head on him, and a formidable sight without it, for as he stood in that dusk beside two men bent with labour, the one maimed and the other past the allotted span of human years, David had an impression of something desperate and fearless and light-hearted. The shepherds were clearly torn between loyalty and terror, and he himself, while firm enough in his resolve, had to keep his thoughts battened down to prevent his knees knocking. But Reiverslaw seemed to have no fears. He had set about the thing as cannily as if it were selling sheep at Locker-bie fair, and now, with a venture before him which not two other men in Scotland would have contemplated, he was notably the least embarrassed of the party.

"I saw three pyets * flee intil the Wud this morning," said Prentice, "and but ane cam' back. That's an unco freit † for the beginnin' o't !"

"Haud your tongue, ye auld wife," said Reiverslaw. "Freits fa' to them that fear them, and I'm no gaun to fash my heid about twa jauds o' birds. . . ."

"I had a vision yestereen," Richie put it. "I saw the haill land o' Scotland like a field of aits, white until the harvest, the haill land frae John o' Groats to Galloway, a' but the parish o' Woodilee, whilk was unplewed and rough wi' briars and thrissles. An' says I to mysel', ' Whatever place is yon ? ' and says a voice to me, ' That's what we ca' the Deil's Baulk in the gospel field o' Scotland.' "

"And a very true observe, for Deil's Baulk is just what the Wud is, and it's for us to pit a plew intill't and mak' a fire o' the wastry. Set bite and sup afore the minister, Richie."

The shepherd produced some oatcakes, of which David ate only a mouthful, for though he had had no food since morning, his throat was dry and his tongue like a stick. He drank, however, a pint of buttermilk.

"Kirn-milk for you ? " the host asked of Reiverslaw. "I hae nae yill, but Rab has brocht a flask o' aquavitty ye gied him at the lambin'."

"I'll hae spring water. Nae strong drink for me, for this nicht I'm like Jonadab the son of Rechab. . . . Are ye ready, Mr. Sempill ? Ye maun start first, for ye've a tree to speel. There's nae hurry for me till the Deil begins his pipin'."

"You are either strong in the faith, or of a very stout heart," said David admiringly.

"No as strong as I might be," was the answer.

* Magpies.   † Omen.

" Afore we part, wad it no be weel for you to pit up a prayer ? "

The minister prayed—and it was as if he confessed alone to his God in his closet. He himself was strengthened by it, and the comfort of Richie and Rab was visibly enlarged. But Reiverslaw stood through the devotions in no very devout position, and from him came none of the responses which flowed from the others. Before the " Amen " he had his goat-cap on, and was peering at the rising moon. He made his staff sing as he whirled it.

David took his strange confederate's hand, and his own shook. Reiverslaw noted his trepidation.

" Fear nocht, sir. It'll gang ill wi' the wirriecow gin we meet him. But what brocht a man o' peace like you into this tuilzie ? "

" Jealousy for the honour of my God. And you ? For it is less your quarrel than mine."

The man grinned. " Write it down that Andra Shillinglaw couldna see an honest man beat, and that he didna like kail-worms."

David had many times gone over in his mind the route to the glade of the altar, and had compared notes with Reiverslaw that very night. The distance was less than three miles, and he had a couple of hours to reach the place and still be in position well before midnight. As on all the nights of the past week, the oppressive haze of the day had lifted, and the sky rose to an infinite height, thick studded with stars, for the moon was only new risen. David made his way to the dividing glen between the pines and the hazels in a miserable disquiet. He had lost the first fierce anger which had stiffened him for his frustrated expedition on the eve of the second Beltane, and his tacit ostracism all summer by the folk of Woodilee had engendered a profound self-distrust. Even the thought of Katrine Yester did not nerve him; she belonged to a world separated by impassable gulfs from that black necromancy which he warred against. Nor did the fact that he had an ally comfort him, for Reiverslaw, he greatly feared, fought in his own strength and not in that of the Lord, and in such a strife the arm of flesh could not avail them. As he stumbled through the dark undergrowth David's lips moved in anxious prayers.

He entered the pines, and, shaping his course by the low line of cliffs, came to the place where he had first met Katrine. Thus far he felt that he was not wholly outside the pale of kindly things. But after that he was in enemy country, and the moon was still too low to give him help. He wasted half an hour in the thickets, till by a strong effort of will he forced himself to take his bearings and remember Reiverslaw's instructions. He scrambled uphill again till he was in touch with the outcrop of rock, and then suddenly found himself looking down on the glade where stood the altar.

It was very dark, and the stone was only a ghostly blur. But the darkness was a blessing, for the place was not as he had seen it before, and the sight of it did not revive the terrors he had feared. It looked no more than a woodland glade, and the fact that a rabbit scurried from under his feet seemed a friendly omen. On the far side the trees grew thick, and he selected a gnarled Scots fir as his perch for the night. Its trunk, branchless for sixty feet, was too thick to climb, but he found a younger and slimmer tree, up which he could squirm and from its upper branches traverse to the other. He had not tried the game since he was a boy, and at first his legs and arms seemed too feeble ; but the exercise warmed him, and after twice sliding back to the ground, he at last reached the umbrella-like spread of the crest. To gain the other tree proved more difficult than he had thought, and he was compelled to let his body swing and make a long stretch with his right arm. But the task was accomplished in the end, and he found himself on a platform of crooked fir boughs, hidden from everything but the stars, and with a view through the gaps of the branches to the glade below him.

He had now a clear sight of the sky. The moon was three-quarters up, and the whole of Melanudrigill with its slopes and valleys was washed in silver. He was in it and yet above it and outside it, like a man on a hillside looking into a cleft. He made his body comfortable in a crutch of the tree, and looked down on the stage beneath him. It was now lighting up, and the altar was whitened by a stray moonbeam. For the first time that night he felt his spirits returning. The oppression of the Wood was not realized on this outer shell of it, for here only winged things dwelt, and the unclean things of the dark had no wings.

In this happier mood his eyes sought the whereabouts of Calidon. It was hidden by a ridge, the ridge to the west where lay Paradise. The thought gave him an unreasoning pleasure. He was not cut off from the world of light, for, whatever befell on the earth beneath him, he had but to lift up his eyes and they rested on a happier country.

As the moon rose, the multitudinous little noises of a wood at night were hushed. There was a sleepy muttering of cushats to the south of him, and then, with a clatter which made him jump, the birds rose in a flock and flew across the valley. After that there was no sound until the music began.

There was no fixed moment for its beginning, for it seemed to steal insensibly into the air. And it was scarcely music, but rather a delicate babble of tongues which made a crooning like the low notes of a pipe. The sound was all beneath him near the ground, and gathering from different quarters to one centre. Suddenly in the midst of it came a sharp liquid note, several times repeated, a note with authority in it like a trumpet, and yet ineffably faint and distant as if it were the echo of an echo. It did not flutter David's heart, for there was no threat in it, but it had a strange effect upon his mind. For it seemed familiar, and there was that in him which answered it. He felt a boy again, for in the call there was the happy riot and the far horizons of childhood, and the noise of hill winds and burns, and the scent of heather and thyme, and all the unforgotten things of memory.

The silver trumpet did not speak again, but the soft babble was creeping nearer, and suddenly just beneath him it broadened and deepened into the sound of pipes. He looked down and saw that the dance had begun. As before, the piper with his hound mask sat cross-legged beyond the altar, and the dancers revolved widdershins around him. . . .

To his amazement he found himself looking on not in terror, but in curiosity. It was a graver dance than that of Beltane, not the mad riot of the bursting life of Spring, but the more sober march of summer and the hot suns bringing on the harvest. . . . Seen from above, the figures were only puppets, moving at the bidding of a lilt that rose and fell like a lost wind. The passion of wrath with which he had watched the former Sabbath had utterly gone from him. He felt a curious pity and friendliness, for there was innocence here, misguided innocence.

"Will this be the way God looks down upon the follies of the world?" he asked himself. What was it that Reiverslaw had said?—If the Kirk confines human nature too strictly, it will break out in secret ways, for men and women are born into a terrestrial world, though they have hopes of Heaven. . . . That was blasphemy, and he knew it, but he did not shudder at it.

How long these gentle dances continued he did not know, for he was in a dream and under the spell of the piping. . . . Then suddenly there came a change. The dancing-floor became dark, and he saw that clouds were coming over the moon. A chill had crept into the air. Lights sprang up out of nowhere, and though the wind had begun to sigh through the trees, he noted that these lights did not flicker. . . . The music stopped, and the dancers crowded together around the altar.

The hound-faced leader stood above them with something in his hand. The mysterious light seemed to burn redly, and he saw that the thing was a bird—a cock which was as scarlet as blood. The altar top was bare, and something bright spurted into the hollow of the stone. From the watchers came a cry which chilled David's marrow, and he saw that they were on their knees.

The leader was speaking in a high shrill voice like a sleepwalker's, and David caught but the one word often repeated—Abiron. Every time it was uttered the man dabbled his finger in the blood on the altar and marked a forehead, and as each received the mark he or she fell prostrate on the ground. . . .

There was no innocence now in that spectacle of obscene abasement. Terror entered into David's soul, and his chief terror was that he had not been afraid before. He had come very near falling himself under the spell.

There followed what seemed to be a roll-call. The leader read names out of a book and the prostrate figures answered. The names seemed like an idiot's muttering, not good Scots words, but uncouth gutturals. And always like an undercurrent came the word Abiron.

Then with an unholy cry the whole coven was on its feet. The pipes began again, and music other than pipes, which seemed to soak out of the ground and the adjacent coverts. Gone was every trace of gentleness and innocency. It was witch-music made by the Devil himself on the red-hot chanter-reeds of Hell, and the assembly capered as if their feet were on the lake of burning marl. The Israelitish prophet in David awoke, and he saw it all with clear eyes and horror-stricken soul.

If the Beltane dance had been hideous, this was the very heart of bestial lust. Round and round it swept, a fury and yet an ordered fury, in which madness and obscenity were mingled. He recognized the faces of women, old and young, who sat devoutly beneath him in kirk of a Sabbath. The men were all masked, but he knew that if he could tear off the beast coverings he would see features which were normally composed into a pious decency. Figure would clasp figure and then fling apart, but in each circuit he noted that the dancers kissed some part of the leader's body, nozzling him like dogs on the roadside.

Up in his tree-top the minister had now an undivided mind. He had the names of several of the females of the coven firm in his memory, and for the men he must trust to Reiverslaw. There were some of the dancers with goat-horns, but as the rout swung round it seemed to him that a new goat-mask had appeared, a taller wilder figure, who was specially devout in his obeisance before Houndface. Was it Reiverslaw with his aniseed?

The night had become very dark and the only light in the glade came from the candles which burned in its hidden hollows. And then suddenly a colder wind blew, and like the burst of a dam came a deluge of rain. The Lammas floods had broken, stealing upon the world, as is their fashion, out of a fair sky.

It seemed to David—and he held it part of the infernal miracle—that the torrent did not quench the lights. In a trice he himself was soaked to the skin, but the candles still burned, though the rain beat on the floor of the glade with a sound like a whip-lash. . . . But it ended the dance. The silver pipe sounded again, and as the wind rose higher and the falling water slanted under it to search out even the bield of the trees, he saw figures moving hurriedly off. The next time he looked down through the spears of rain—for the hidden moon still made a dim brightness in the world—the glade was empty. Above the noise of the storm he thought he heard the strange babble of tongues, but now it was departing to the far corners of the Wood.

He waited for a little and then tried to descend. But he found it harder to get down than to get up, for he could not find the branch by which he had swung himself from the lesser tree, and in the end had to drop a good twenty feet into the bracken, whence he rolled into the

empty glade. . . . He scrambled to his feet and made
haste to get out of it, but not before he had sniffed the
odour of unclean pelts.—And yes—surely that was the
stink of Reiverslaw's aniseed.

He had no difficulty about his homeward course.
Most of the way he ran, but fear had completely left his
heart. The rain in his face seemed to cleanse and in-
vigorate him. He had looked upon great wickedness,
but he had looked down on it, like the Almighty, from
above, and it seemed a frail and pitiful thing—a canker
to be rooted out, but a thing with no terror for a servant
of God. The Devil was but a botcher after all. And
then he remembered how the first notes of the music
had melted him, and he felt humbled.

Reiverslaw had arrived at the Greenshiel before him.
The place was filled with the reek of burning hides, and
David saw that the goat-mask and cloak had been laid
on the peats. His ally, a weird dripping figure, sat on
a stool sipping the aqua vitæ which Rab Prentice had
brought with him. He, who had started the night's
venture with such notable sang-froid, was now in a sweat
of fright.

" Be thankit ye're safe," he stuttered, while the spirits
spilled over his beard. " I never thocht to see ye mair,
for I never thocht to win out o' yon awesome place. My
legs are a' gashed and scartit, for I cam' here through
stane and briar like a dementit staig.* Oh, sir, siccan
a sicht for mortal een ! "

" Saw ye the Foul Thief ? " asked the awed Prentice.

" I saw ane in his image, and I got a drap o' the red
cock's bluid, and I loupit like the lave, but it wasna wi'
their unholy glee. Sir, I was fair wud wi' terror—me
that am no gien to fear muckle—for I got a cauld grue

* Young horse.

in my banes and my een turned back in their sockets. I tell ye, I forgot the errand I had come on, I forgot my name and my honest upbringing, and I was like a wean forwandered among bogles. . . . I've burnt thae skins, and when I get hame I'll burn every stitch o' cleading, for the reek o' the Pit is on it."

" Did you recognize many ? " David asked.

" No me. I had nae een to see wi'. I spun round like a teetotum and I wadna say but I let out skellochs wi' the best—may God forgie me ! "

" But the oil—the aniseed ? "

Reiverslaw held up something which David saw was an empty bottle.

" I didna fail ye there. For the ae man I kenned in the coven was him that piped. When I cam' near him I felt a stound o' black hate, and there's but the ae man on God's earth that can gar me scunner like yon. So when it was my turn to bow down afore him, he gat mair frae me than a kiss. Unless he burns his breeks this very nicht there'll be a queer savour aboot the toun o' Chasehope the morn."

CHAPTER XI

THE MINISTER GIRDS UP HIS LOINS

NEXT day David returned to the manse in time for the
noontide meal. He was greeted by Isobel with a hospitable bustle, in which was apparent a certain relief. She
had known of the Lammas festival; she guessed, no
doubt, that David too was aware of it, and she evidently
took his visit to Newbiggin as a sign that he had at last
taken her prudent counsel. But from her master she
got no response. When questioned as to the welfare of
his kin at Newbiggin he answered in civil monosyllables,
ate his dinner in silence, and thereafter secluded himself
in his study.

That evening he walked to the Greenshiel, where
Reiverslaw and Prentice met him. The former was in
an excited state and had clearly been drinking—to the
scandal of the two shepherds, who wore portentous faces.
Richie Smail had the air of an honest man compelled to
walk in abhorred paths; he had been reading his Bible
before their arrival, and sat with a finger in the leaves,
saying nothing, but now and then lifting puzzled eyes
to his master. Prentice's hard jaw was set, and he
swung his crutch as if it had been a pikestaff.

"We were at Chasehope by eleven hours this mornin',"
Reiverslaw announced. "I took Richie and Rab, as
I forewarned Ephraim, to have a look at his new tups.

But I needna tell you there was nae word of Ephraim.
The wife said he was awa' to Kirk Aller, but she was like
a hen on a het girdle a' the time, and I think we wad hae
found him if we had ripit the press-beds. If he was
lurking there he maun hae gotten a sair fricht, for I spak'
that loud ye could hae heard me on the tap o' Chasehope
hill."

"Did you find what you sought?" David asked.

"I fand eneuch." He drew from a pocket a bunch
of feathers. "I got these last nicht in the Wud. Doubtless there'll be mair in the same place, if they havena
been soopit up. But there's nae red cock the day in
the toun o' Chasehope. I admired the wife's hens and
speired what had become o' the cock, and was telled that
it was deid—chokit last nicht on a grosart. I ken the
kind o' grosart that ended the puir beast."

"And the aniseed?"

Reiverslaw laughed tipsily.

"We were just in time, sir. The wife had a fire lowin'
in the yaird. 'What's burnin', mistress?' says I.
'Just some auld clouts,' says she. 'There was a gangrel
body sleepit ae nicht in the loft,' says she, 'and he left
some duds ahint him, as fu' o' fleas as a cadger's bonnet.
I'm haein' them brunt,' says she, 'for fear o' the weans.'
Weel, me and Richie and Rab stood aside the fire, and it
loupit as if an oil can had been skailed on it, and the reek
that rase frae it was just the reek o' my wee bottle.
Mair nor that, there was a queer smell ayont the hallin—
Richie and Rab fand it as weel as me. What name wad
ye gie it, Rab?"

"It was the stink o' the stuff ye showed us in this
house last nicht," said Prentice solemnly.

"Sae muckle for that," said Reiverslaw. "We've
proof that the lad in the dowg's cap was nae ither than

him we ken o'. Na, na, I never let on to the wife. I was jokesome and daffin' wi' her, and made a great crack o' the tups, and praised a' I saw about the toun, and Rab and Richie were as wise as judges. I had a dram inside me, and was just my canty ordinar'. But my een and my nostrils werena idle, and I saw what I've telled ye. . . . My heid was in sic a thraw last nicht that I canna sweir wi' ony certainty to ither faces, though I hae my suspeecions about the weemen. But you, sir, sittin' aloft on the tree-tap, ye maun hae had a graund view, for there was licht eneuch to read prent."

" I recognized certain women, to whom I can swear on my oath. About some I dare not be positive, but there were five of whom I have no doubt. There were Jean Morison and her daughter Jess."

"The folk o' the Chasehope-fit," Reiverslaw cried. " Ay, they wad be there. They've aye been ill-regarded."

" And old Alison Geddie in the kirkton."

" A daft auld wife, that skellochs like a sea-maw ! "

" And Eppie Lauder from Mirehope road-end."

Richie Smail groaned. " The widow of a tried Christian, Mr. Sempill. A dacenter body than Wattie Lauder never walked the roads. It's terrible to think o' the Deil's grip on the household o' faith."

" And Bessie Tod from the Mains."

" Peety on us, but I sat neist her at the March fast-day when Mr. Proudfoot preached, and she was granin' and greetin' like a bairn. Ye surely maun be in error, sir. Bessie was never verra strong in the heid, and she hasna the wits for the Deil's wark ! "

" Nevertheless she was there. I am as certain of it as that I was myself in the tree-top. Of others I have suspicions, but of these five I have certainty."

Reiverslaw rubbed his great hands. " Our business

gangs cannily forward.   We've gotten the names o' six
o' the coven and can guess at ithers.   Man, we'll hae
a riddlin' in Woodilee that will learn the folk no to be ill
bairns.   Ye'll be for namin' them frae the pu'pit, sir ? "

" I must first bring the matter before the Presbytery.
I will prepare my dittay, and bring it before Mr. Muirhead
of Kirk Aller as the Presbytery's moderator, and I must
be guided by him as to the next step.   It is a matter for
the courts of the Kirk and presently for the secular law."

Reiverslaw cried out.   " What for maun ye gang near
the Presbytery ?   If ye stir up yon byke ye'll hae com-
missioners of justiciary and prickers and the haill clam-
jamphrie, and in the lang end an auld kimmer or twa
will suffer, and the big malefactors will gang scot free.
Chasehope's ower near the lug o' the law to tak' ony
scaith, and yon's the kailworm I wad be at.   Be guidit
by me, Mr. Sempill, and keep the thing inside the pairish.
As the auld saying gangs, bleach your warst hanks in
your ain yaird, for I tell ye if the Kirk and the Law hae
the redding o't it's little justice will be done.   Name
and upbraid and denounce a' and sindry, but dinna
delate to the Presbytery.   A man may like the kirk
weel eneuch, and no be aye ridin' on the riggin' o't. . . .
I'll tell ye my way o't.   Now that we ken some o' the
coven, the four o' us can keep our een open, and watch
them as a dowg watches a ratton ; and at their next
Sabbath, as they ca' it, we'll be ready for them.   I can
get a wheen Moffat drovers that fear neither man nor
deil, and aiblins some o' Laird Hawkshaw's folk frae
Calidon, and we'll break in on their coven and tear the
masks frae the men, and rub their nebs in their ain mire,
and dook the lot in the Water o' Aller.   I'll wager that's
the way to get rid o' witchcraft frae the parochine, for
we'll mak' it an unco painfu' business to tak' the Wud.

A witch or a warlock is a fearsome thing to the mind
o' man, but they're bye wi't gin we mak' them gowks
and laughing-stocks."

The two shepherds stared at the speaker with up-
braiding eyes, and David's face looked as if a blasphemy
had been spoken.

"You would fight the Devil in your own carnal
strength," he said sadly. "It's little you would make
of it. You talk as if this wickedness of the Wood were
but a natural human prank, when it is black sin that
can only be combated by the spirit of God and such
weapons as God has expressly ordained. Man, man,
Reiverslaw, you've but a poor notion of the power of the
Adversary. I tell you last night I was trembling like
a weaned child before yon blast that blew out of Hell,
and you yourself were no better when I found you here.
I durstna have entered the Wood except as a soldier
of the Lord."

Reiverslaw laughed.

"I was sair fleyed,* I'll no deny, but I got a juster
view o' things wi' the daylicht."

"It would appear that you got courage also from
Lucky Weir."

"True. I had my mornin' and my meridian and an
orra stoup or twa sinsyne. I'm a man that's aye been
used wi' a guid allowance o' liquor. But the drink, if so
be ye're no fou, whiles gi'es ye a great clearness, and I
counsel ye, sir, to keep wide o' the law, whether it be of
the Kirk or the State. It's a kittle thing, and him that
invokes it is like to get the redder's straik.† It's like a
horse that flings its heels when ye mount and dings out
the rider's teeth. . . . But hae your ain way o't, and
dinna blame me if it's a fashious way. There's me and

* Frightened.   † The peacemaker's blow.

Rab Prentice and Richie Smail waitin' to sweir to what's in our knowledge, and if there's mair speirin' to be done in the Wud, I'll no fail ye. But keep in mind, Mr. Sempill, that I'm a thrang body, and maun be drawin' my crocks and sellin' my hog-lambs afore the back-end, and it's like I'll hae to traivel to Dumfries, and maybe to Carlisle. Richie will aye hae word o' my doings, and if ye want me it wad be wise to tell Richie a week afore."

That night on his return David summoned Isobel to his presence. The housekeeper appeared with a more cheerful countenance than she had worn for weeks, but the minister's first words solemnized her.

" Isobel Veitch, I asked you a question after Beltane and you refused me an answer. I, your minister, besought your aid as a confessing Christian, and you denied it me. I told you that I would not rest until I had rooted the idolatry of the Wood from this parish. Since then I have not been idle, and I have found men who did not fail me. Three days back I rode to Newbiggin, as I told you, but I returned on Lammas Eve, and on Lammas Eve I was a witness a second time to the abominations of the heathen. Not only myself, but another with me, so that the thing is established out of the mouths of two witnesses, while Robert Prentice and Richard Smail can speak in part to confirm me. Now I have got my tale complete, and it is to the Presbytery that I shall tell it. Will you implement it with such knowledge as you possess, or do you continue stiff in your recusancy ? "

The old woman's eyes opened like an owl's.

" Wha went with you—wha was sae left to himsel' ? " she gasped.

" Andrew Shillinglaw in Reiverslaw. . . . One man

and five women stand arraigned on our witness. I will
speak their names, and I care not if you put it through
the parish, for soon the names will be thundered from the
pulpit. The man was Ephraim Caird."

"I'll no believe it," she cried. "Chasehope's aye
been a polished shaft in Christ's kirk. . . . He's o' your
ain Session. . . . He cam' here, ye mind, when ye first
broke bread in this house. Ay, and he was here when
ye were awa' at Newbiggin. I was seilin' the milk when
I heard his voice at the door—cam' here wi' ane o' his
wife's skim-milk kebbucks that she kens weel how to
mak', for she's frae the Wastlands—spoke sae kind and
neeborlike, and was speirin' after the health o' the gude
man my maister. . . . Tak' it back, sir, for ye maun be
mistook. Ephraim's weel kenned for a fair Nathaniel."

There was no doubt about her honesty, for the mention
of Chasehope had staggered her.

"Nevertheless he is a whited sepulchre, painted without but inside full of bones and rottenness."

"Oh, sir, bethink ye afore ye mak' this fearsome
accusation. Your een may have played ye fause. And
wha in their senses wad lippen to Reiverslaw? A
muckle, black-avised, grippy incomer that nae man kens
the get o' . . . sweirs like a dragoon when the maut's
abune the meat. Ye'll never gang to the Presbytery
in siccan company wi' siccan a tale! And Hirplin' Rab
is a thrawn deevil, though I'll no deny he hae a gift o'
prayer—and Richie Smail is sair failed in body and mind
since last back-end when Mirren dee'd."

"There are also five women," David went on. "There
are Jean and Jess Morison from Chasehope-foot."

"Sae that's where ye get your ill-will at Chasehope—
because he's ower kind to turn twa randies intil the road!
I hae nothing to say for the Morisons. They come oot o'

a dirty nest, and they may ride on a saugh ilka nicht to Norroway for a' I ken."

" There is Eppie Lauder at Mirehope."

" Tut, man, as dacent a body as ever boiled sowens. And her man, Wattie, that dee'd in Aprile o' the year thretty-nine, was weel thocht o' by a'body. Ye've come till a frem'd toun wi' Eppie."

" And Alison Geddie."

" A tongue like a bell-clapper, but ettles nae hairm."

" Likewise Bessie Tod of the Mains."

" She's weak in her mind, sir. Lang syne she had a bairn to a sodger and it dee'd, and she never got ower it. Ye'll no convince me that there's ony ill in Bessie forbye the want o' sense."

" I have evidence of ill. I accuse, I do not condemn. It is for others to do the judging."

Isobel's timidity, which had been notable during the Beltane interview, seemed now to have left her. There was a sincere emotion in her voice.

" I plead wi' ye, sir, to halt while yet there's time, and if needs be content yoursel' wi' private examination. It's verra weel for Andrew Shillinglaw, that's but an incomer, and rakes the country gettin' as he gangs like a cadger's powny. But you're the minister o' Woodilee, and the fair fame o' the parochine suld be as dear to you as your ain. If ye tak' the gait ye speak o', ye'll mak' it a hissing and a reproach in a' the water of Aller. It's a quiet bien bit, wi' douce folk weel agreed, and ye wad mak' it a desolation, and a' because some daft lads and a wheen hellicat lassies dance their twasomes in the Wud. It's no as if they did ill things like garrin' the kye rin dry and the weans dwine."

" Then you admit knowledge of the sin ? "

" I admit nocht, for I ken nocht. Young folk will

be young folk, peety though it be. . . . But for Chasehope and my auld gossip, Eppie Lauder, the man's gyte
that wad chairge them wi' idolatry—and you can tell
that to your drucken Reiverslaw."

For the first time since he had known her Isobel flung
out of the room in a temper.

Next day he sought out Chasehope, and found him
alone on the hill. The man greeted him with effusion.

"The Lammas rains is weel-timed this year, Mr.
Sempill, nae ragin' flood but just eneuch to slocken the
ground. I start cuttin' the bog hay the morn. I heard
ye were at Newbiggin, sir, and I trust ye found your
friends in guid health. A blaw on the hills yonder is
fine for a body after the lown air o' Woodilee."

"I returned home on the Lammas Eve. I ask you,
Ephraim Caird, as you will answer to your God, where
were you in the mirk of that night?"

The heavy face, now brick-red with summer suns, did
not change.

"Where suld I be but in my bed? I gaed till't early,
for I had a long day wi' the hog-lambs."

"You know that that is a lie. You were in the Wood,
as you were in the Wood at Beltane, dancing away your
miserable soul to the Devil's piping. With my own eyes
I saw you."

The astonishment of Chasehope was admirably simu-
lated.

"Are ye daft, sir? Are ye gane clean gyte? Ye're
no weel, Mr. Sempill. Sit ye doun, and I'll fetch you
some water in my bonnet. Ye've got a blaff o' the
sun."

"I am not mad nor am I sick. I have preached
throughout the summer at the sin, and the time has now
come to get to grips with the sinner. This is your last

chance, Ephraim Caird. Will you confess to me, who
have been set in spiritual authority over you, or must
confession be wrung from you by other means?"

It was a warning which David felt bound to give, but
he was silent as to the rest of his purpose, for he had
decided that the time had not yet come to show his
hand. He looked sternly at Chasehope, and under his
gaze the man's face seemed to whiten, and his odd
greenish eyes to waver. But it might be in innocent
amazement.

"I kenna what ye speak o'," he stammered. "What
concern have I wi' the Wud? Ask the wife and she'll
tell you that I sleepit the Lammas nicht in my bed.
But oh—the thing fair coups the crans! . . . and me an
elder thae ten year! Ye're no weel or ye're dementit to
speak sic words to a man like me. Awa' hame, sir, and
humble yoursel' on your knees and pray that ye may
be forgiven. . . . I may cry out in the words of the
Psalmist, 'They opened their mouth wide against me,
and said Aha, our eye hath seen it.'"

David's hand clenched on his staff. "Before God,"
he cried, "I will strike you down if you utter another
blasphemous word. You neglect my warning? Then
your punishment be on your own guilty head."

He turned and strode away. Once he looked back
and saw Chasehope still staring, the very image of
virtuous dismay.

There was no sermon in the kirk the next two Sabbaths. Robb the bellman had orders not to ring the
bell, but few came to the kirkyard gate, for the rumour
had spread that the minister would conduct no ordinances until he had taken counsel with the Presbytery.
David waited, hoping for he knew not what—some
thaw to melt this icy impenitence. At last on the

sixteenth day of August he rode to Kirk Aller to visit Mr. Muirhead.

He found the Moderator in his parlour in the little stone manse, which stood below the kirk on the knowe at the west gate above the brig of Aller. The room had few books, but a mass of papers, for Mr. Muirhead was an active ecclesiastic and noted for his conduct of church business. Also, as if to meet the disturbed times in which he lived, a pair of spurred boots, still with the mud on them, stood beside the table, on it lay a brace of ancient pistols, and from the peg of the door hung a great horseman's cloak.

Mr. Muirhead bent a preoccupied brow on David as he entered, but his face was well content. There were open letters before him, and it seemed that he had just been the recipient of welcome news.

"Come awa' in, Mr. David," he cried. He saw his visitor's eye stray to the pistols. "Ay, I've got me to the auld weapons. I had them with me at the memorable assembly in Glasgow in '38 when we dang down the Bishops. . . . I have a crow to pyke with you, but first I have some braw tidings for your ear. At the last Presbytery we met under the shadow of calamity, but the Lord has mercifully turned again the captivity of Sion. Yon devil's spawn, Montrose—alas that he should take his name from a burgh of which worthy Mr. Saunders Linklater was so long the faithful minister ! —yon Montrose, I say, approaches the end of his tether. It has been a long tether, and he has ravened like a hungry hound, but he will soon be back on his haunches with the rope tightening at his thrapple. The Almighty has wysed him with a sure hand intil the snare that was prepared for him."

"Has he been defeated ? " David asked.

" By this time there is good hope that he has been scattered to the four airts of Heaven. After his savageries in the north he marches south to rend the fair fields of Stirling and the Lennox, and summon the towns of Glasgow and Embro, whilk are the citadels of our faith. Like Jeshurun he has waxed fat and kicked, but his pride will have a fearful fall ; for long ere he wins to Clyde the trap will be sprung. He is bye Perth and at this moment, I trow, at the skirts of the Ochils. Before him lie Argyll and Baillie with horse and foot, which are to his heathen hirelings as four men to one. The faithful folk of Fife are marching cannily against his left flank, and mustering from the Glasgow airt against his right are the braw lads of the West, led by those well-disposed noblemen, the Earl of Eglinton, the Earl of Cassilis, and the Earl of Glencairn. More—all the gentry of Clydesdale are on the road, commanded by the Earl of Lanark, and him and his Hamiltons are waiting to soop up the remnants of that which Argyll will shatter. Isna that a bonny tale, Mr. Sempill ? Isna that a joyful recalling of our bondage, even as streams of water in the south ? "

David assented, but to his surprise his interest was faint. He had more pressing problems than the public captivity of Israel.

" And now for other matters," said Mr. Muirhead, setting his mouth again in severe lines. " I have word of grave mishandling at Woodilee. You have created a stramash in the doucest and most God-regarding parish in the presbytery of Aller. You are sinning away your mercies, sir."

" It is of that I came to speak," said David. " I have to submit to you, and through you to the Presbytery, proofs of a dreadful wickedness among professing

Christians in that unhappy place. Will you be pleased to run your eye over these papers? You will see certain names subscribed as witnesses."

Mr. Muirhead began to read the depositions carelessly, as if he knew what to expect from them. Then his attention deepened and he wrinkled his forehead.

"Hoots! What's this?" he cried. "Ye were in the Wood? Ye saw this and that? Mr. Sempill, ye're not exempt from the charge of tampering with unlawful things."

"I went there as God's servant."

"Nevertheless——" He read on, and his brows darkened. He finished, flung the bundle on the table, and looked at David with a troubled and uncertain eye.

"Here's a bonny browst o' yill! You charge your chief elder with the sin of witchcraft—a man of noted godliness, as I myself can testify—and you conjoin in the libel five women who are unknown to me. What is your evidence, I ask? Your ain een, at a time when you were in no condition to see clear, and forbye you were on the top of a tree, and it was in the mid of the night. You have no corroboration. But I pretermit the women and come to Chasehope. You have cherished a suspicion of him since Beltane, says you, when you were present in the Wood. And what, I ask, did you there at that season, Mr. Sempill? I opine that your ain conduct wants some explanation."

"That I can give," said David.

"You have further the evidence of the man Andrew Shillinglaw, and the plot you prepared against Chasehope. Man, I see nothing in your red cock's feathers or your hennyseed, as you call it. The well is tainted, so how can you look for pure water? Your Reiverslaw is

notoriously a winebibber and a ruffler and a despiser of
ordinances. What hinders that he should be also a
lear ? The cock's feathers may all the time have been
in his pouch, and he may have played some prank at
Chasehope with the stinkin' oil. You have the witness
of the herds, says you, but it's easy enough to begowk
two landward simpletons. Your case will not hold
water, sir, before any competent court, and Reiverslaw,
your principal abettor, stands suspect. As the old
overcome has it, he suld bide still that has riven
breeks."

Mr. Muirhead spoke with a weighty assurance, and
as David looked at his shrewd coarse face he felt a
sudden helplessness. It would be hard to convince a
tribunal so prejudiced—in whose ears, perhaps, Chasehope had already spoken.

" My advice to you," the voice went on, " is to get
you home and let the steer settle. There's nothing in
these papers that calls for action by the Presbytery—
just hearsay and idle *fama*, the visions of an excited
young man and the lees of a drucken reprobate. No
doubt you mean well, but I will homologate no course
which fastens evil on a man whose righteousness has
been abundantly proven. Have mind of the virtue of
charity, sir, which thinketh no evil. I opine that you're
ower ready to think evil. Bring before me wise-like
evidence and I will be prompt to act, but not these
havers."

So far he had spoken with a kind of rough good-
humour, but now his voice became harsh.

" They tell me you have conducted no public worship these last two Sabbaths," he said fiercely.

" I will not lead my folk into deeper hypocrisy," said
David. " I will not preach or pray in the kirk till I

also denounce the sinners, and that I purpose to do on the next Lord's day."

"You will do no such thing!" said Mr. Muirhead sternly. "I, your elder, and father in God, forbid you."

"I must follow my own conscience," said David. "I am as convinced of the abominations of the Wood and of the persons that partake in them as that I am sitting with you here in Kirk Aller this August morning."

"You would add contumacy to your folly!" the other roared. "You would sow dissension in the Kirk when it is necessary to set a stout front against the Kirk's oppressors!"

"That," said David firmly, "is mere carnal policy. In the name of God, whose purity is a flame of fire, would you let gross wickedness go unchecked because it may knock a splinter off the Kirk? I tell you it were better that the Kirk should be broken to dust and trampled underfoot than that it should be made a cloak for sin. I refuse to obey you, Mr. Muirhead. Next Sabbath I will make every wall in Woodilee dirl under my accusation."

The two men were on their feet, David white with wrath, and the face of the other mottled with a like passion. "You rebellious schismatic!" the minister of Kirk Aller cried, when a knock at the door called both to a sense of the proprieties.

It was the minister's man, who entered with a letter held reverently with the tips of his fingers.

"A dispatch, sir, from Embro. Brocht this moment by a mounted messenger, wha wouldna stay for meat, but maun post off doun the water."

When the man retired Mr. Muirhead, still standing and puffing heavily, broke the seal. He seemed to have trouble with the contents, for he moved his spectacles, took them off and rubbed them, and then re-read the missive. His eyes stared, his face paled, and then at the last perusal reddened again. He turned to David in a flame of temper.

"The Kirk must suffer for you and your like!" he cried. "The Lord had prepared an abundant mercy whilk has been denied us because of the hardness of our hearts. Wae's me, wae's me for the puir sheep that have sic faithless shepherds! The auld and the bauld and the leal-hearted must go down because of conceited halflings like you that are Achans in the camp."

"You speak in riddles, sir," said David, whose sudden anger had gone at the spectacle of this strange transformation.

"It's a riddle you'll read or you're a month older in letters of blood and fire. . . . Riddle, says you? The riddle is why the Almighty should give our covenanted Kirk sic a back-cast of His hand, and to that you maybe ken the answer. Our deliverance has most lamentably miscarried, and our bondage is waxed more grievous. Get out of my sight, for I must be about the Lord's business, and there will be no rest for Mungo Muirhead this many a day. You have defied me, but wait on and see if you can defy your Creator."

"You have had bad tidings?"

"Bad, says you? Ay, bad for God's people and God's Kirk, but they're maybe blithe tidings for a schismatic like yourself. You'll maybe get Left-handed Coll and his Irishry to purge your parish and burn the honest folk with whilk you are unworthily blessed. Awa' to Montrose, man, for yon's the lad for you!"

"Montrose!"

"Ay, Montrose. Know that yesterday at Kilsyth

yon whelp of Satan was permitted to lay low the Covenant's banner, and rout the godly. This word I have
gotten is a scribe from Argyll on his road to Berwick,
written from a boat at the Queen's Ferry. This very
day it's like that Antichrist will be hammering on the
gates of Glasgow."

CHAPTER XII

THE MAN WITH THE SQUINT

THE sermon which was to indict by name the sinners was not preached in the kirk of Woodilee the next Sabbath.

For the day after his return from Kirk Aller a post reached the manse from the Pleasance of Edinburgh which in an hour set David on his horse riding hard for the capital. There was plague in the city and his father was sick of it. It was the plague in a new form, for death did not come quickly; the patient lay for days in a high fever, afflicted with violent headaches and shiverings and a contraction of muscles and nerves, and then, in nine cases out of ten, passed into a rigor which meant death. There was no eruption on the bodies, and the physicians were at a loss in the matter of treatment. But it was scarcely less deadly than the older visitations, and the dead-bell rang hourly and the dead-cart rumbled day and night on the cobbles.

David found the old man conscious, but very clear that he was near his end. The family doctor had bled him copiously, applied leeches to his head, and brought a horrid regiment of drugs and vomitories. The son pled with his father to receive them patiently. " God works by means," he told him, " as Christ cured the blind man with clay and spittle, and what remedy could be more rude than these ? ''

" Aye, but it was the Lord that laid them on, Davie," said the patient, " and no an auld wife like McGlashan." So he sent the physician packing, and engaged a new one, a certain young Crosbie from the Monk's Vennel, who had studied in France and had at least the merit of letting a sick man die in peace. Instead of smothering the patient under bedclothes, he kept him lightly covered, ordered the window to be open day and night, and let him drench his system with small ale. It is likely that under any treatment the old man would have died, for he was in his seventy-fourth year and had long been ailing, and the plague only speeded the decay of age. But under the new regimen his last days were less of a martyrdom. His head remained clear and he could speak with his son—chiefly of his mother and his childhood.

David lodged not in the city, but in the village of Liberton, and walked in daily to his father's bedside. He read the Scriptures to him and prayed with him, as his duty demanded, but he felt a certain shyness at inquiring into his father's state towards God. Nor was the old man communicative. " I've made my peace lang syne," he said, " and I read my title clear, so there's no need of death-bed wark for me." But he was full of anxiety for his son. " You've chosen a holy calling, Davie lad, and I'm blithe to think you've got a downsetting in our calf-country. Man, there were Sempills in the mill o' the Roodfoot since the says of Robert Bruce. But the ministry in these days is a kittle job, for the preachers are ower crouse, and the Kirk has got its heid ower high. . . . What's come o' this Montrose they crack about ? . . . Keep you humble before the Lord, my son, for Heaven's yett is a laigh yett."

He died peacefully on the third day of September, and David had a busy week settling his affairs—the sale of the business and the household effects and the payment of bequests to servants and distant kin. Hour after hour he sat with the lawyers, for there was a considerable estate, and to his surprise he found himself with worldly endowments such as few ministers of the Kirk possessed. There was money at the goldsmith's, and in his lawyer's boxes deeds and sasines and bonds on heritable property, and there would be more to come. His doer, a little old snuffy attorney of the name of Macphail, grew sententious as the business drew to its close. "You've both the treasure on earth, Mr. David, and the treasure in Heaven, and it's a pleasing thought that they're alike well-guided. Anent the latter, moth cannot corrupt, saith the Word, nor thieves break through and steal, and anent the former a moth will no do muckle ill to a wheen teugh sheepskins, and it would be a clever thief that got inside Georgie Gight's strong-room in the Canongate where your bonds are deposited. So you can keep an easy mind, Mr. David, while you wrastle for souls in Woodilee."

Those were strange days both for death in a bed and for conducting business, for the stricken city was the prey of wild fears. Scarcely a traveller entered her infected precincts, but rumour was as busy as the east wind in May. The battle of Kilsyth had worked a revolution in Scotland. Glasgow had surrendered and welcomed the conqueror, with enthusiasm for his person and largesse for his soldiers. The shires and the burghs were falling over each other in their haste to make submission. Edinburgh had been summoned, and a

delegation of the town council had gone out beyond
Corstorphine to capitulate to the young Master of
Napier. The imprisoned Lords went free from the
Tolbooth ; David saw the sight—pallid men shivering
with prison ague ; only the Castle still held for the
Covenant. Word came that the King had made Montrose Captain-general of all Scotland, and that soon the
victorious army would move towards the Border ;
already, on the haugh of Bothwell by Clyde side, Sir
Archibald Primrose had read the royal commission to
the troops. A summons had gone out for a Parliament
to be held presently in Glasgow—" for settling religion
and peace," said the proclamation, " and freeing the
oppressed subjects of those insufferable burdens they
have groaned under this time bygone."

The ministers who walked the Edinburgh causeway
wore gloomy faces. David had a sight of Mr. Muirhead,
who sternly inquired of him what he did in the city.
" I have come to bury my father," he replied. " If he
died in the hope and the promise," was the answer, " he
has gotten a happy deliverance, for the vials of wrath
are opened against this miserable land." It was a
phrase repeated like a password by others of his ministerial brethren, and he replied with a becoming gravity,
but he could not in his heart feel any great sorrow. For
he remembered the face of the groom at Calidon, and he
wondered how that face looked as a conqueror. Pride,
he was assured, would not be in it. . . . News came that
Montrose was at Cranstoun and moving by Gala Water
to the Border. For a moment David had a crazy desire
to follow him, to be in his presence, for he had a notion
that if he could but have speech again with that young
man the shadows and perplexities might lighten from
his mind.

At last he set off homeward, and under the rowans at Carlops brig he read a printed paper which had been circulated in the Edinburgh streets—torn across and cast away by many, but by others cherished and pondered. It was a manifesto of Montrose from the camp at Bothwell, and it set out his purpose. In it were the very words used by the groom that night at Calidon. The nobles had destroyed " lawful authority and the liberty of the subject," the Kirk had coerced men into a blind obedience worse than Popery. He took up arms, he said, for pure religion, "the restoration of that which our first reformers had "; for the King, and the establishment of a central authority: for the plain people and the " vindication of our nation from the base servitude of subjects." He confuted the timorous souls " who can commit nothing to God." He repudiated the charge of blood-guiltiness, for he had never " shed the blood of any but of such as were sent forth to shed our blood and to take our lives." And he concluded by pointing to the miracles that faith had wrought : " What is done in the land, it may sensibly seem to be the Lord's doing, in making a handful to overthrow multitudes." The words came to David with a remembered sound, like the echo of a speaking voice. Could this man be the bloody Amalekite of the Kirk's denouncing ? On which side, he asked his perplexed soul, did the God of Israel fight, for this man's faith was not less confident than that of the minister of Kirk Aller ?

Isobel received him with the reverential gloom which the Scots peasantry wear on an occasion of death.

" So it's a' bye, sir. We got the word from the Embro carrier, but I wasna looking for ye yet awhile, for we heard ye were like to be thrang wi' the lawyer bodies. . . . He just slippit awa', for how could an auld man stand out against yon wanchancy pestilence? It's a gait we maun a' gang, and he would be weel prepared Godward, and at ease in his mind about warldly things, for they tell me he was brawly set up wi' gear. And there's just yoursel' to heir it, Mr. David? . . . But shame fa' me to speak o' gear in this sorrowful dispensation, for a faither is a faither though he live ayont the threescore and ten years whilk is our allotted span."

"He died as he lived, Isobel, a humble but confident Christian. I think he was pleased to know that I was settled in his forebears' countryside."

"He wad be that, honest man. Fine I mind o' your gudesire, and mony a nievefu' o' meal I gat from him when I was a bairn. But I'm concerned for yoursel', Mr. David, and fearfu' lest ye have got a smittal o' the pestilence. Ye're fine and ruddy, but there's maybe fever in your veins. Drink off this wersh brew, sir—it was my mither's way to caller the blood—just kirnmilk boiled wi' soorocks."

David asked concerning the parish.

"Woodilee!" Isobel cried. "If Embro's a stricken bit, it's nae waur than this parochine. For the last se'en days it's been naething but wars and rumours o' war. Ye'll hae heard o' how Montrose has guidit our auld Sion, and now we've Antichrist himsel' on our waterside. Ay, he's no twenty miles across the hills, campin' with his Edomites somewhere on Yarrow, as welcome as snaw in hairst. The lads and lassies are a' fleyed out o' the sheilin's, for the Yerl o' Douglas—weary fa' him!—and his proud horsemen are drovin' ower frae Clyde like craws in the back-end. We canna move man nor bestial, and folk winna ride the roads except in a pack, and they tell me that Amos Ritchie wi' his auld firelock was sent for to convoy the minister o' Bold to Kirk Aller. The weans daurna keek past the doorstane, and Johnnie Dow winna gang his rounds, and he's been lyin' fou at Lucky Weir's thae three days. There's nae wark done in a' Woodilee, nor like to be done—it's a dowg's life we've gotten, muckle ease and muckle hunger."

" But the place has suffered no harm ? "

" No yet, forbye a wedder o' Richie Smail's that Douglas's dragoons brandered and ate yestreen at the Red Swire. But ony moment a vial may be opened.— What hinders Montrose to come rauvagin' this airt ? for if it's meat and drink he's seeking for his sodgers, Woodilee is a bien bit aside yon bare Yarrow hills. Forbye Calidon's no that far, and they tell me that our auld hirplin' laird, wha suld rather be thinkin' o' his latter end, is high in the command o' the ungodly, and him and yon sweirin' Tam Purves will be rampin' like lions in their pride. Hech, sir, our kindly folk are in the het o' the furnace, in whilk they will either be brunt to an ass, or come out purified as fine gowd. . . . But what am I claverin' here for, when ye're wantin' your denner ? It's little I hae for ye, for our meal ark is nigh toom, and there's no a kain hen left on the baulks."

That night David sat long in his study. It was now the sixteenth day of September, and the sultry weather, which had fostered the plague, was sharpening towards autumn. He had returned from his father's death-bed in something of the mood in which he had first entered the manse. The confusion in the State was to him only a far-off rumour ; he was not greatly concerned whether Covenant or King was a-top, for he had no assurance as to which had the right on its side. But

he longed for peace, that he might be about his proper
business, for the charge of Woodilee lay heavy on his
soul.   The wickedness against which he had raged
seemed now to him as pitiful as it was terrible, a cruel
seduction of Satan's against which he must contend,
not without pity for the seduced.   Charity filled him,
and with his new tenderness came hope.   He could not
fail in the struggle before him—God would not permit
his little ones to be destroyed.

He had not forgotten the minister in the crusader ?
His books caught his eye—he had touched them little
during the summer.   What had become of that great
work, Sempill on Isaiah ?   He pulled out his manuscript notes and for a little was happy in their contem-
plation. . . . The day's ride had been long and the sun
had been hot.   His head nodded, then dropped on his
arm, and he fell asleep.

He awoke to a sound below the window.   The manse
stood at the extreme southern end of the kirkton,
beyond the kirk, a long bowshot from the nearest
dwelling, which was Robb the bellman's.   To the west
of it lay the broomy slopes of the Hill of Deer, to the
east the glen of the burn and Windyways hill, and to
the south the rough meadows through which the road
dipped to the Wood.   It was a lonely spot, as Isobel
often testified, and after nightfall no soul came near it ;
even a traveller on the highway did not pass within
half a mile.

His study window opened on the garden, and the
sound seemed to come from some one knocking gently
on the back door.   David, still confused with sleep,
took his candle and descended the stairs.   Isobel had
heard nothing—for the muffled sound of her snores
came from the press-bed behind the kitchen. . . . Again

the soft knocking came, this time with a more insistent sound. In some trepidation David unbolted the door, telling himself that it might be a summons to attend a dying parishioner.

There was little moon and a thick autumn haze covered the ground. Rising out of it, like ships out of the water, were huge figures, and he saw that they were mounted men. One of them sat his horse, and held the other beasts; one was on his feet and supported a third who seemed very weary.

David raised his candle, and saw the figure of the standing man. The face was dark with sun, but darker under the eyes with fatigue; the dress, once rich and splendid, was both mired and torn; and one hand was wrapped in a blood-stained kerchief.

"Do I speak with the minister of Woodilee?" the man asked, and at the first word David knew him. That voice had been echoing all the year in his chamber of memory.

"I am the minister," was his reply. "In what can I serve my Lord Marquis?"

The face relaxed into a smile, which made it for the moment gay in spite of the heavy eyes.

"You have not forgotten me? Nor have I forgotten you, and therefore I come to you in sore need to beg a charity. I do not doubt but you are of the opposite faction, but I know also that you are a faithful minister of Christ, whose custom was to do good to His enemies. Will you give shelter to this wounded comrade of mine, and thereby save the life of one whom you consorted with a year back in Calidon?"

"But this is but a poor manse, my lord. Why do you come here when Calidon is so nigh?"

"Alas! Calidon is no port for me or mine in this

storm. Know, sir, that this day my army has been beaten on the Yarrow haughs and utterly scattered. Before morning Leslie's troopers will be knocking at Calidon door. I myself am a fugitive, and there is no safety till I cross the Highland line. But this comrade of mine has a broken leg, besides other hurts, and it is impossible that he should ride further. If he does, he will impede us and we shall be taken. But where can I leave him? for I am in an unfriendly country, and if he is captured it will be the gallows for an honest fellow. I bethought me that you were minister of this parish, and that your heart was not likely to be steeled to common humanity, and a manse is the one place that the pursuit will miss. Will you take him and let him lie hid till the hunt passes? After that he will fend for himself, for he is an old soldier of the German wars."

" He has done no evil . . . ? "

" None save what I have done myself. He has drawn the sword in a brave cause which this day has sorely miscarried. But, sir, it is not of politics I speak, but of charity. For the sake of Christ's mercy, I beseech you not to refuse."

" It is a heavy charge, my lord, but I cannot say you nay."

Montrose shifted the burden of the wounded man to David's arm. " Farewell, Mark," he whispered. " The good cause is down but not dead, old friend. You know where to get news of me." Then he kissed his cheek and gave his hand to David.

" May God bless and reward you, sir. I dare not linger. We will take the third horse with us, for it would be too kenspeckle in your stable. Think kindly of me, whatever my fate, as I think tenderly of you, and pray for a lonely man whose feet are set on a long road."

The next moment the riders had disappeared in the fog. David stood in a dream, for he would have given worlds to recall the speaker. His voice, the sight of his face, had brought back tenfold the longing to be with him which had haunted him after the Calidon meeting. The man had been a conqueror and was now a fugitive, but earthly fortunes had no meaning for such an one. Those calm eyes would look on triumph and disaster alike unperturbed.

He was roused by the wounded man going limp in his arms, and he saw that he had fainted. He carried him up the steep stairs—Isobel's snoring still making a chorus in the background—and laid him on the bedstead in the guest-room. The bed was not made up, and it was clear that he must wake Isobel. As the man's head drooped on the bolster David turned his candle on it. The face was grimed and blood-stained, but there was no mistaking the features: it was the tall trooper with the squint whom he had once guided to Calidon.

David sought the kitchen and hammered at the door of the press-bed. The snoring ceased and presently a scared and muffled voice demanded what was the trouble.

" Get up, woman," David ordered. " There's a sick man here that has need of you."

Three minutes later Isobel appeared, shawled and nightcapped. " Keep us, Mr. David, is't yoursel' that's seeck ? " she wailed. " I didna like the look o' ye the day and——"

He cut her short.

" A friend of mine has had a mischance. His leg is

broken and I think there is other trouble. Listen, Isobel. . . . The man is one of Montrose's soldiers and Montrose's army has suffered defeat. If he is found here by the pursuing troops he will die. He is my friend, and I would save him. You and I must nurse him between us, and no word of his presence here must pass these doors."

" Mercy on us ! A malignant ! " the old woman exclaimed.

" And my friend," said David curtly. " If I think it consistent with Christian duty to save his life, so well may you. You and I have no quarrel with stricken men. I appeal to the kind heart that is in you and your regard for me, and I do not think I will appeal in vain."

" Your wull be done," said Isobel. " Whaur is the body ? See and I'll get blankets and pillows, for the bed hasna been made up this sax months."

The sight of the figure on the bedstead, his quilted and brocaded coat, his light cuirass, his long untanned boots much scratched and frayed, his feathered hat beside him on the floor, caused Isobel to shrink.

" A rampin' Edomite," she said. " Look at the long hair and the murderin' sword, stained nae doot with the bluid of the saints. Your friend, says you, sir ? Weel, he's been walkin' ither than Gospel roads, I can see brawly, and gin he hadna been amang the craws he wadna hae been shot. . . . But the puir chield's in a dwam ! Haste ye, sir, and help me off wi' thae Babylonish garments, and that weskit o' airn— what for suld folk gang to the smith for cleading and no to a wabster ? And stap his swird aneath the bed, for I'm feared to look on't."

The man half recovered consciousness as they stripped

off his coat and cuirass, and when it came to the breeches he groaned aloud. So they left them on him and slit the boot on the broken leg. It was a clean break of the shin, and Isobel, who showed some skill in the business, set the leg, and bound it in firm splints made of the staves of an old cask. Then they searched for further damage and found that he was suffering from little except an extreme fatigue. There was a pike wound in his shoulder, which Isobel bathed and bandaged, and a pistol-ball had been turned by the mail he wore and had left a bruised rib. By the time the grime and blood were washed from his face he had got his senses sufficiently back to find his voice.

"You are the minister?" he asked. "I am crippled, as you see, sir—an accursed fail-dyke on Minchmoor did it—and you'll not be wanting this kind of merchandise long on your hands. A drink and six hours' sleep will set me up, and I'll make shift to take the road. Let me bide here till the morn's night and you'll be rid of me."

"You'll not be fit to move for a week. You can sleep here securely. You're in a friend's charge."

The sick man was an old soldier who took life as it came. After he had drunk a bowl of gruel laced with usquebagh he turned on his side and fell asleep. David and Isobel went down to the kitchen and with the candle between them looked at each other with something like consternation.

"We must burn those clothes," said David.

"Na, na. I'll make a bundle o' them and hide them in the cupples. It's braw raiment, gin it were cleaned. But oh, sir, this is a bonny kettle of fish! Who wad hae thocht to see such wark in the manse of Woodilee?"

" It is a work of mercy."

" There's some wad call it by anither name. There's some wad say it was a turnin' back from the gude fight and a faintin' and a backslidin' on the road. I'd be feared to think what yon thrawn minister o' Bold wad call it, but it wadna be mercy. He'd be for savin' the puir lad as Jael the wife of Heber the Kenite saved Sisera."

" I will be party to no such wickedness, which would be an offence against human charity as well as against the law of Christ."

" Ay, charity. I'm blithe to hear ye speak the word, sir." Isobel's eyes had an inclination to twinkle.

" I must follow the guiding of my own conscience. But I would not constrain you. If the thing offends you, I will even now, before it is light, carry the man to the Greenshiel . . ."

" A bonny gait that wad be. The avenger of blood will be chappin' ony hour at Richie's door and there's nae space at the Greenshiel to hide a mouse. Na, na, I'm no denyin' your duty, Mr. David. There never was woman yet, young or auld, that was ill-set to a sodger, forbye yon randy Jael, wha maun hae been an unco trial to her man. And the lad upbye seems a decent body, though he skellies * sair wi' his left ee. I'se do your bidding, sir, and I hope it winna be accounted to me for sin."

" Can we keep him here without any one knowing of it ? "

" Brawly. The folk o' Woodilee are sweir to come near the manse thae days. They're feared o' the glower they micht get from you."

" But if Leslie's troopers arrive and offer to search——"

* Squints.

"I'll search them! I'se warrant I'd be doun on them with my ten fingers like a gled on poutry. Isobel Veitch will learn the godless loons to mak' free with the house o' a man o' God. And mind, sir, if onybody speirs, ye maun brazen like a packman. Bleeze awa' about the needcessity o' speed in the guid cause and send them on their ways to Clyde, and maybe ye'll be spared the sin o' actual leein'."

"If need be I will not shrink from the false word, which will be forgiven in the cause of mercy."

"Fine, sir." Isobel grinned appreciatively on him; for this confederacy seemed to have ended the estrangement between servant and master. "There's a man ahint the minister in you, whilk is mair than ye can say for the feck o' the Presbytery."

"And, meantime, I must be up and doing."

"Ye'll awa' to your bed and sleep out your sleep. What's the need o' hurry when the body's leg is still to set. As my auld mither used to say, naething suld be done in haste but grippin' a flea. . . . But I'll look out some o' your auld garments, for our friend will hae to cast his braw coat and put on homespun or he wins forth o' Woodilee."

CHAPTER XIII

WHITE MAGIC

THE man upstairs slept for a round of the clock and then awoke and clamoured for food. Isobel reported that he was cured of his weakness and that the pike wound in his shoulder was no more than a scratch. "Forbye his leg, he's as weel as you or me, and he has the hunger o' a cadger's powny. It was an awesome sicht to see him rivin' my bannocks. He's speirin' to see ye, for nae doubt he has muckle on his mind." The old woman was in the best of tempers, and her wizened face was puckered in a secret smile, for she and her master were now restored to friendship as partners in conspiracy.

David found his guest clad in one of his own bed-gowns, the hue of health once more on his unshaven cheeks. His first request was for a razor and for shears, and when Isobel had shorn his hair and he had got rid of a three-days' beard, it was a head of a notable power and dignity that rested on the pillow. The high-boned weather-beaten face, the aquiline nose, the long pointed chin were no common trooper's, and the lines about mouth and eyes were like the pages of a book wherein the most casual could read of ripe experience. The brown eyes were dancing and mirthful, and the cast in the left one did not so much mar the expression as make it fantastically bold and daring. Here was one who had lived in strange places and was not used to fear.

"It's a sore burden I've brought on you, Mr. Sempill," he cried, "and it's you that's the good Samaritan. It was my lord's notion that I should throw myself on your compassion, for it's a queer thing, I own, for a cavalier to be seeking a hiding-place in a manse, though Mark Kerr has had some unco ports in his day. I mind in Silesia—— But there's no time for soldiers' tales. You'll be wanting me out of this as soon as I can put foot to ground, and it's blithe I'll be to humour you. My leg is setting brawly, says that auld wife who is my chirurgeon, and in less than a week I'll be fit to go hirpling on my road."

"That will be to walk into the fire," said David. "If Montrose's army is scattered throughout the hills, there will be such a hunt cried as will leave no sheiling unsearched."

"Just so. I'll not deny that this countryside is unhealthy for folk like me. You'll be well advised to bury or burn the clothes I had on last night, and if you can lend me a pair of grey breeks and an auld coat, I'll depart with a lighter mind."

"You'll be for the sea and the abroad?"

"No me. It's at the coast that they'll be seeking me, and a wise man that's in trouble will go where he's no expected. I think I'll just bide hereaways. Put me in a frieze jacket and I'll defy Davie Leslie himself to see Mark Kerr, the gentleman-cavalier of Mackay's, in the douce landward body that cracks of sheep and black nowt. You'll maybe have me in your congregation, Mr. Sempill. I'm thinking of taking a tack of Crossbasket."

David stared. "Are you mad?" he asked.

"Not so—only politic, as is the way of us soldiers of the Low Germany. One of my profession must think well into the future if he's to keep his craig unraxed. I've had some such escapado in mind ever since I travelled north a year syne, and I've had a word on the matter with Nicholas Hawkshaw, so when the glee'd * auld farmer body from Teviotside seeks the tack of Crossbasket the lawyer folk in Edinburgh will be prepared for him. Nicholas was like me—he kenned fine that our triumph in the North was fairy gold that is braw dollars one day and the next a nieve-full of bracken."

"Where is the laird of Calidon?"

"By a merciful dispensation we left him sick at Linlithgow, and Nicholas, being an eident soul, had a boat trysted at the Borrowstounness and by this time doubtless will be beating down the Forth on his way to a kinder country. He'll be put to the horn, like many another honest gentleman, and his braw estates may be roupit. Thank the Lord, I have nothing to lose, for I'm a younger son that heired little but a sword."

"A month ago," said David, "Montrose was lord of all Scotland. You tell me that everything has been lost in one battle, and that you and others were confident of its loss. Man, how did he succeed with such a rabble of the half-hearted behind him?"

"I wouldna just call it half-hearted. We won because James Graham is the greatest captain since Gustavus went to God at Lutzen, and because he has a spirit that burns like a pure flame. But he did not ken this land of Scotland as me and Nicholas kenned it. He had a year of miracles, for that happened which was clean beyond all sense and prevision, but miracles have

* Squinting.

an ugly trick of stopping just when they are sorest needed. . . . A year syne there were three men on Tayside, Montrose and Inchbrakie and me, and that was the King's army. By the mercy of Providence we fell in with Alasdair Macdonald on the Atholl braes, and got a kind of muster at our back. . . . There's no Hieland blood in you, Mr. Sempill ? No ? Well, it's a very good kind of blood in its way, but it's like the Hieland burns, either dry as the causeway or a roaring spate. It's grand in a battle, but mortal uncertain in a campaign, if you follow me—and that James should have held it in leash till he had routed Argyll and Baillie and Hurry and brought the Kirk and Estates to their knees is a proof of a genius for war that Gustavus never bettered. But for conquering Scotland and keeping the conquest fixed—na, na ! Hielands will never hold down Lowlands for long, and that Lowland support we reckoned on was but a rotten willow wand. My lord deceived himself, and it was not for me to enlighten him, me that had witnessed so many portents. So we kept our own thoughts—Nicholas and me—and indeed we had half a hope that a faith which had already set the hills louping might perchance remove the muckle mountains. But I tell you, sir, when we marched for the Borders I had a presage of calamity on me as black as a thundercloud."

" But you had the army that won Kilsyth ? "

" Not a third of it. Yonder on Bothwell haughs it melted away like a snow-wreath. Macdonald—he is Sir Alasdair now and a Captain-general, and proud of it as an auld gander—must march off with the feck of his Irishry to Argyll to settle some private scores with Clan Diarmaid. The Gordons took the dorts *—a plague on

* Sulks.

their thrawn heids—and Aboyne and his horse went off in a tirrivee. James looked for a Lowland rising, for, says he, the poor folk for whom I fight are weary of the tyranny of greedy lairds and presumptuous ministers. If so, they are ower weary to show it. What can be done with lads that grovel before a Kirk that claims the keys of Heaven and Hell ? . . . If that sounds blasphemy, sir, you'll forgive a broken man that is unlocking his heart and cannot wale * his words. . . . Forbye, the Irish were like a millstone round our necks, for what profit was it to plead that Munro used them in Ireland for an honest cause ? To the Lowland herds and cotters they were murdering savages, and the man that had them on his side was condemned from the beginning. The sons of Zeruiah were too strong for us."

"Is it true that they fight barbarously ? " David asked.

"So, so. I'll not deny that they're wild folk, but they havena your Kirk's taste for murder in cold blood. There were waur things done in Methven Wood than were done at Aberdeen, and it's like that Davie Leslie is now giving shorter shrift to the poor creatures than ever they gave to the Campbells in Lorne and Lochaber. . . . We'll let that be, for there was never an army that did not accuse its enemies of barbarity, and the mere bruit of it on our side was enough to keep the Lowlands behind steekit doors. There were some of the nobles that we counted on—my Lord Home, and my cousin Roxburghe, and the sly tod Traquair. James was in good heart at their promises, but I mistrusted the gentry, and I was most lamentably justified, for when we were on Teviotside, where were my lords but

* Pick.

in Leslie's camp?—prisoners, they said—but willing refugees, as I kenned braw and well."

"And the battle?"

A spasm of pain passed over the other's face.

"It was not, properly speaking, a battle, but more in the nature of a surprise and a rout. We were encamped on Yarrow at the gate of the hills, for the coming of Davie Leslie had altered our plans and we were about to march westward to the Douglas lands. We were deceived by false intelligence—it was Traquair's doing, for which some day he will get my steel in his wame—but I bitterly blame myself that an old soldier of the German wars was so readily outwitted and so remiss in the matter of outposts. . . . In the fog of the morning Davie was on us, and Douglas's plough-lads scattered like peesweeps. There were five hundred of O'Keen's Irish, and five score of Ogilvy's horse, and for three hours we held Davie's six thousand. These are odds that are just a wee bit beyond my liking, forbye that we had no meat in our bellies. Brawly they fought, the poor lads, fought as I never saw men fight in the big wars—but what would you have? . . . It's no tale for me to tell, though it will be in my mind till my last breath."

He sighed, and for a moment his face was worn and old.

"Well and on, sir," he continued. "The upshot is that the bravest of Scottish hearts is now, by God's grace, somewhere on the road to the Hielands, and the great venture is bye and done with, and here am I, a lameter, seeking sanctuary of a merciful opponent. If to shelter me does violence to your conscience, sir, say the word and I'll hirple off as soon as the night falls. You've **given me bite and sup, like a good Christian, and suffered** me to get my sleep, and you've no call to do more for a broken malignant."

"My conscience is at ease anent succouring the wounded and saving a man's life. And I have no clearness about this quarrel of Montrose and the Kirk, and would therefore give it the go-by. But I will exact the promise that, if you come off safe, you will fight no more in Scotland. In that much I am bound to serve my calling."

"You shall have the promise. Mark Kerr is for beating his sword into a ploughshare. What says the Word ? ' His speech shall be of cattle '—though now I come to think of it, that's from what you gentry call the Apocryphal books and think little of. . . . I'm one that has no great love for idleness on the broad of his back. Have you no a book to while away the hours ? Anything but divinity—I've lost conceit of divinity these last months when I've been doing battle with the divines."

David furnished his guest with reading which was approved, and then went forth into Woodilee. The village made holiday, and every wife was at her doorstep. A batch of troopers were drinking a tankard at Lucky Weir's, and saluted him as he passed. The people he met had an air of relief and good temper, and looked with a friendly eye on the minister, forgetting apparently the Lammas controversies and the shut kirk, for he was a representative of the winning cause.

Peter Pennecuik, sitting on a big stone outside the smithy, was the chief dispenser of tidings. His cheeks were swollen and his voice faltered with pride.

"What for do ye bide in your tent, Mr. Sempill, in this hour of our deliverance ? They tell me that Mr. Ebenezer of Bold has mounted his beast and ridden wi' the horsemen to harry the ungodly's retreat. Ay, and

baith Chasehope and Mirehope have ta'en the road, for
the haill land is fou o' the wreckage of the wicked, as the
sands o' the Red Sea were strewed wi' the chariots o'
Pharaoh. Our General Leslie is no ane to weaken in the
guid cause, for there's word that his musketeers hae shot
the Irish in rows on the Yarrow haughs, ilk ane aside
his howkit grave, and there's orders that their women
and bairns, whilk are now fleein' to the hills, are to be
seized by such as meet wi' them, as daughters of Heth
and spawn of Babylon, and be delivered up to instant
judgment. Eh, sir, but the Lord has been exceeding
gracious us-ward, and our griefs are maist marvellously
avenged. . . . Nae doot ye'll be proclaimin' a solemn
fast for praise and prayer."

David ate his dinner with a perturbed mind, for if
the countryside was being scoured for fugitives on this
scale, it was unlikely that the manse would remain long
inviolate. But Isobel reassured him. " They wad never
daur ripe the house, and for the lave I can speak them
fair in the gate." In the afternoon he set out to walk
to the Greenshiel, since the road would give him a far-
away glimpse of Calidon. Autumn was already chilling
the air, and the horizon was a smoky purple, the heather
was faded, the bracken yellowing, the rowan trees
plumed with scarlet, the corn in the valley already more
gold than green. To David, in whose ear was still the
gloating voice of Peter Pennecuik, the place seemed to
smell of death.

At the Greenshiel he found death in bodily form. On
the plot of turf outside the cottage half a dozen troopers
stared from their saddles at something that lay on the
ground. The men were mostly a little drunk, and had
the air of a pack of terriers who have chased a cat and
found it at bay—an air that was puzzled, angry, and

irresolute. David strode towards them, and they gave place to him, somewhat shamefacedly. On the turf lay a wretched draggle-tailed woman, her clothes almost torn off her back, her hair in elf-locks, her bare feet raw and bloody. Her face was emaciated and of an extreme pallor, her shrunken breast heaved convulsively, and there was blood on her neck. Richie Smail was on his knees attempting to force some milk between her teeth. But her lips shut and unshut with her panting and the milk was spilled. Then her mouth closed in that rigor from which there is no unloosing.

Richie lifted his head and saw the minister.

"She's bye wi't," he said. " Puir thing, puir thing! She ran in here like a hunted maukin." Then to the soldiers : " Ye had surely little to dae, lads, to mishandle a starvin' lassie."

There was no sign of compunction on the coarse faces of the troopers.

"An Irish b-bitch," one hiccoughed. " What's the steer for a bawbee joe ? "

" Tam Porteous kittled her wi' his sword point," said another. " Just in the way o' daffin, ye ken. She let out a skelloch and ran like the wund." The man put his hands to his sides and guffawed at the memory of it.

He did not laugh long, for David was on him like a tempest. The fuddled troopers heard a denunciation which did something to sober them by chilling their marrow. As men, as soldiers, as Christians, he left them no rag to cover them. " You that fight in God's cause," he cried, " and are worse than brute beasts ! Get back to your styes, you swine, and know that for every misdeed the Lord will exact punishment a thousandfold." He was carried out of himself in his wrath. " I see each one of you writhing on a coming field of battle, waiting to change the torments of the flesh for the eternal agonies of Hell. You are the brave ones—your big odds gave you a chance victory over one that for a year hunted you and your like round the compass—and you purge your manhood by murdering frail women."

It was not a discreet speech, and a sentence or two of it pierced through their befuddlement, but it sent them packing. They were too conscious of the power of a black gown in Leslie's army to dare to outface a minister. David marched homeward with his heart in a storm, to find an anxious Isobel.

"These are dreidfu' days," she moaned. "We were told that Montrose's sodgers were sons of Belial, but if they were waur than yon Leslie's they maun be the black Deil himsel'. Wae's me, bluid is rinnin' like water on Aller side. There's awfu' tales comin' doun from the muirs o' wild riders and deid lasses—ay, and deid bairns—a' the puir clamjamphry that followed the Irish. It canna be richt, sir, to meet ae bloodguiltiness wi' anither and a waur. And yon thrawn ettercap frae Bold ridin' wi' the sodgers and praisin' the Lord when anither waefu' creature perishes! And Chasehope, they tell me—black be his fa'—guidin' the sodgers to the landward buts-and-bens like a dowg after rattons! Catch yon lad frontin' an armed man, but he's like Jehu the son of Nimshi afore defenceless women."

David asked if any one had been near the manse.

"That's what fickles * me. There's been naebody at the door, but there's been plenty snowkin' round. There's a gey guid watch keepit. And waur than that, there's sodgers in the clachan—ten men and ane they ca' a sairgent at Lucky Weir's. I heard routin' as I gaed by the kirkton, and, judging by the aiths, there's sma'

* Puzzles.

differ between them that fechts for Montrose and them that uphauds the Covenant."

Next day the uneasiness of both increased. The place was thronged with troopers, among them the men whom David had denounced at the Greenshiel. It is probable that his hasty words had been reported, for dark looks followed him as he passed the ale-house. Moreover, Isobel had news in the village that Leslie's main forces were even now moving towards Woodilee, and that the triumphant general himself would lodge in the village. Where would such lodging be found except in the manse? At any moment the guest-room and its contents might lie bare to hostile eyes.

By the afternoon David had come to a decision. The wounded man must at all costs be moved. But where? Calidon would be as public as the street, and besides he had heard that a picket had been stationed there in case its laird came looking for shelter. . . . The hills were too open and bare. Reiverslaw would be suspect—in any case its tenant babbled in his cups. . . . Then he had an inspiration. Why not Melanudrigill, for its repute would at ordinary times make it the perfect sanctuary? He would be a bold man, it was true, who sought a lair in its haunted recesses, but this Mark Kerr did not lack for stoutness of heart. He found him yawning and extracting indifferent entertainment from a folio of Thuanus.

Kerr only grinned when he heard of the danger.

" I might have guessed that the place would soon be hotching with Davie's troops. And maybe I'm to have. Davie in bed aside me? Faith, I fear we wouldna agree, though I'll no deny that the man has a very respectable gift in war. . . . I must shift, you say, and indeed that is the truth of it, but hostelries are no that plenty in this

countryside for one like me that's so highly thought
of by his unfriends."

Melanudrigill was set before him, and he approved.

"The big wood. Tales of it have come down the
water, but I've never paid much attention to clavering
auld wives. . . . There's black witchcraft, you say—
you've seen it yourself? I care not a doit. There's
just the one kind of warlock that frichts me, and that's
a file of Davie Leslie's men. Find me a bed in a hidy-
hole and some means of getting bite and sup till I can
fend for myself, and I'll sit snug in Melanudrigill, though
every witch coven in Scotland sat girning round me
with the Deil playing the bagpipes."

David was clear that he must be moved that night,
but he was far from clear as to how it was to be done.
He did not dare to take any other into the secret, not
even Reiverslaw or Amos Ritchie, for hatred of Montrose
was universal among the Lowland country folk. He and
Isobel might make shift to get him to the Wood, for
Isobel was a muscular old woman, but there was much
to do besides that—a bed to be found, food transported,
some plan made for a daily visit. There was no help to
be found in Woodilee.

And then he remembered Katrine Yester.

For a long time he would not admit the thought.
He would not have the girl enter a place of such defile-
ments. The notion sickened him and he put it angrily
from him. . . . But he found that a new idea was growing in his mind. The Wood had been a nursery of evil,
but might it not be purified and its sorceries annulled
if it were used for an honest purpose? The thought of
Mark Kerr, with his hard wholesome face and his mirthful eye, eating and sleeping in what had been consecrated
to midnight infamies, seemed to strip from the place

its malign *aura*. . . . To his surprise, when he thought
of Mark in the wood, he found that he could think of
Katrine there also, without a consciousness of sacrilege.
The man was her uncle's comrade-in-arms—he was of
the cause to which she herself was vowed—she was a
woman and merciful—she was his only refuge. . . .
Before the dusk fell he was on the road to Calidon.

He had expected to find a house garrisoned and
dragooned, and had invented an errand of ministerial
duty to explain his presence.   He found instead a normal
Calidon—the evening bustle about the gates, an open
door, and Katrine herself taking the air in the pleasance
beside the dovecot.   She came towards him with bright
inquiring eyes.

" You have soldiers here ? " he asked breathlessly.

She nodded to a corner of the house, which had been
the shell of the old peel tower.

" They are there—three of them—since last night.
They arrived drunk—with two wretched women tied to
their stirrups. . . . We were most courteous to them,
and they were not courteous to us.   So Jock Dodds wiled
them into the place we call the Howlet's Nest and gave
them usquebagh and strong ale till they dropped on the
floor.   They are prisoners and woke up an hour ago, but
they may roar long and loud before a cheep is heard
outside the Howlet's Nest, and the door is stout enough
to defy an army."

" But Leslie himself will be here.   Other soldiers will
come, and how will you explain your prisoners ? "

The girl laughed merrily.   " Trust Aunt Grizel.   Two
lone women—violent and drunken banditti—locking
them up the only way—and then a spate of texts and a
fine passage about soldiers of the good cause setting an
ensample.   I will wager my best hawk that Aunt Grizel

will talk down General Leslie and every minister in
his train. . . . The women are safe in the garret, less
hurt than frightened. The poor things talk only the
Erse, and there's none about the town to crack with
them."

He told her of the midnight visit to the manse and
the lame man left on his hands.

"You saw him?" she whispered. "You saw the
Lord Marquis? How did he look? Was he very
weary and sorrowful?"

"He was weary enough, but yon face does not show
sorrow. There's an ardour in it that burns up all weakness. He would continue to hope manfully though his
neck were on the block."

"Indeed that is true, and that is why I will not despair. When I heard the news of disaster I did not
shed a single tear. . . . Whom did he leave behind?"

"The tall man—Mark Kerr is his name—who was in
this house of yours a year back. Him that has a cast
in his eye."

"But that is the Lord Marquis's most familiar friend,"
she cried. "The occasion must be desperate which
parts them."

"The occasion grows more desperate," he said, and
told her of the need for instant removal. When he spoke
of the Wood she showed no surprise.

"Where else so secret?" she said.

"Dare you go into it?" he asked. "For unless I
have your help the business is like to prove too hard for
me. I will confess that it sticks in my throat to stir one
step myself into the gloom of the pines, when I ken what
has been transacted there, and it sticks sorer to have you
in that unholy place. But if this Kerr is to be saved,
there's need of us both. The man will have to be fed,

and that would be done more easily from Calidon than from the manse."

"Why, so it must be. I have been pining for some stirring task, and here it is to my hand. I will be your fellow-labourer, Mr. David, and we begin this very night. For a mercy there is a small moon. . . . No, Aunt Grizel shall not hear of it. I have the keys and can leave and enter the house as I choose. When the dusk comes and our guests in the Howlet's Nest are quiet from hoarseness, I will bid Jock Dodds carry certain plenishing to Paradise."

A little before midnight, when even the clamour of Lucky Weir's was still, three figures stole from the manse, after David by many reconnaissances had assured himself that the coast was clear. Montrose's erstwhile captain was dressed like a small farmer, in David's breeches and a coat that had once belonged to Isobel's goodman. He had a rude crutch with which he managed to keep up a good pace, having learnt the art, he said, during an escape from a patrol of Wallenstein's, which for greater security had manacled the prisoners in pairs leg to leg. Isobel prospected the road before him like a faithful dog, while David steadied him with his arm. In such fashion they crossed the Hill of Deer, and in a darkness lit only by the stars came to the glade called Paradise. There they found awaiting them a glimmering girl, at the sight of whom Isobel's fears broke loose, for she prayed in words not sanctioned by any kirk, and her prayer was for mercy from the Good Folk.

Kerr made an attempt at a bow. "Mistress Yester, it is not the first time I have come for succour to women of your house. They say I must take to the shaws like Robin Hood, but the wildwood will be a palace if you are among its visitors."

"Yester," Isobel muttered to herself. "The young leddy o' Calidon! Wha wad have thocht that the minister was acquaint there? Certes, she's the bonny ane," and she bobbed curtsies.

Katrine was the general. "These bundles are bedding and food. Up with them, sir, and I will guide Captain Kerr. I have also brought a covered lantern, which will light us through the pines better than your candle, Mr. David. La, this is a merry venture."

The sense of company, the presence of Katrine and the soldier, the nature of the errand, above all the preposterous figure of Isobel, whose terrors of the Wood were scarcely outweighed by her loyalty to her master and her curiosity about the girl, took from the occasion for David all sense of awe, and even endowed it with a spice of fun and holiday. The mood lasted till they had crossed the boundary glen and entered the pines; it endured even when, feeling their way along the foot of the low cliffs, they looked downward and saw by the lantern light an eerie white stone in a dim glade. The girl guided them to a dry hollow where an arch of rock made a kind of roof, and where a yard off a spring bubbled among the stones. It was she and not Isobel who made a couch of branches and fir boughs on which she laid the deerskins and plaids she had brought. It was she and not David who gathered dry sticks against the morning fire and saw that Kerr had flint and steel and tinder. It was she, too, who made a larder of a shelf in the rock, where she stored the food, and fixed certain hours of the day for further provisioning, and enjoined a variation of routes to prevent suspicion. It was she finally who presented Kerr with a pistol, shot, and powder—belonging, it is to be feared, to one of the imprisoned troopers—and who saw him to bed like a nurse with a child.

"I'm as snug here as a winter badger," said Kerr contentedly. "I lack nought but a pipe of tobacco, and that I must whistle for, seeing that I left my spleuchan at Philiphaugh. . . . Mistress, you've the knack of an old campaigner. You might have been at the wars."

"The men of my race have always been at the wars and the women have always dreamed of them," she said, and on his forehead she kissed him good-night.

David Leslie came to Woodilee in the morning, but did not halt, pushing on to Lanark in the afternoon. His army was in less of a hurry, and three troop-captains made their beds in the manse, while the minister slept on his study floor. They were civil enough, cadets of small houses in Fife, who had had their training in arms abroad, and cared as little for the cause they fought for as any mercenary of Tilly's. Within two days the neighbourhood was clear of soldiery, save for the garrisons left as earth-stoppers at houses like Calidon, which might be the refuge of malignants.

For a week Mark Kerr lay in the recesses of Melanudrigill, and for David the days passed like a seraphic vision. Every night after the darkening he met Katrine in Paradise and the two carried to the refugee his daily provender —eggs and milk, ale from the Calidon buttery, cakes which were Mistress Grizel's, cheese which was Isobel's. For David the spell of the Wood had gone. He looked on it now as a man does at his familiar bedroom when he wakes from a nightmare, unable to reconstruct the scene of his terrors. His crusading fury, too, had sensibly abated, for part of his wrath against witchcraft had been due to his own awe of the Wood and his disgust at such awe. Now the place was a shelter for a friend, and a

meeting-ground with one he loved, and the cloud which
had weighed on him since he first saw it from the Hill
of Deer gave place to clear sky. Men might frequent
Melanudrigill for hideous purposes, but the place itself
was innocent, and he wondered with shame how he came
ever to think that honest wood and water and stone could
have intrinsic evil.

Nightly, in the light mists of the late September, when
pine trees stood up out of vapour like mountains, and
the smell of woodland ripeness was not yet tinged with
decay, David and Katrine threaded the aisles and clam-
bered among the long bracken, till a pin-point of light
showed from beside a rock and was presently revealed
as Kerr's bivouac. They would sit late with him,
listening to his tales and giving him the news of the
glens, while owls hooted in the boughs, and from the
higher levels came the faint crying of curlews. There
was much business to be done between Mark and Calidon
—business of Nicholas Hawkshaw's, who had been duly
put to the horn, and over whose goods, by the intrigues
of Mistress Grizel, a friendly curator had been appointed,
and business of his own anent the tack of Crossbasket
—and Katrine carried daily messages by letter and by
word of mouth. When his leg was healed there was a
certain polish to be given to his appearance, and the
ladies of Calidon were busy with their needles. When
he left his lair at last it was just before dawn—on foot,
with a blue coat instead of the hodden grey of Isobel's
goodman, and four miles on the Edinburgh road Jock
Dodds from Calidon waited with a horse for him.

David would fain have had the leg prove trouble-
some that the time of hiding in the Wood might be
prolonged, for that season passed for him with the
speed of a too happy dream. To be with Katrine was

at all times bliss, but to be her partner on these dark journeys and in these midnight conclaves was a rapture of happiness. If he had lost his awe of the Wood, he had lost also the sense that in letting his heart dwell on the girl he was falling away from duty. The standards of the Kirk meant the less to him since he was in declared controversy with its representatives, and a succourer by stealth of its enemies. His canons of conduct were dissolving, and in their confusion he was willing to surrender himself to more ancient instincts. The minister was being forgotten in the man and the lover.

The lover—though no word of love was spoken between the two. They were comrades only, truant children, boy and girl on a Saturday holiday. It was a close companionship, yet as unembarrassed as that of sister and brother. In her presence David caught her mood, and laughed with it, but when absent from her he was in a passion of worship. The slim green-gowned figure danced through his waking hours and haunted his dreams. He made no plans, forecast no future ; he was in that happy first stage of love which is content to live with a horizon bounded by the next meeting.

In such a frame of mind he may have grown careless, for he did not see what Isobel saw. His housekeeper, brisk with the consciousness of a partnership with her master in things unlawful and perilous, and under the glamour of Katrine's gentrice and beauty, was as unquiet as a hen with a brood of young ducks on the pond's edge. She clucked and fussed, and waited for David's return in an anxious tempest. " There's queer on-gaein's in this bit," she told him. " When I hearken in the sma' hours I hear feet trailin' as saft as a tod's,*

* Fox.

and whiles a hoast * or a gant † which never cam' frae a tod's mouth. And yestreen when ye set out, sir, there was something slipped atween the birks and the wa' and followed. I wish it mayna be your deid wraith." He pooh-poohed her fears, but on the last night, when he parted from Katrine in Paradise, and according to his custom watched her figure as, faint in the moonlight, it crossed a field of bracken above Rood, he saw something move parallel to her in the fern. On his way home, too, as he passed the kirkton road in the first light, there was a rustling among the elders and a divot fell mysteriously from the turf dyke.

* Cough.   † Yawn.

CHAPTER XIV

THE COUNTERBLAST

HE dreamed that night that he was being spied upon,
and next day—with no more meetings with Katrine
before him to fire his fancy—his cold reason justified
the fear. The conviction was presently confirmed by
a discovery of Isobel's. Mark Kerr's cast clothes had
been hidden at first in the gloom of the rafters in David's
camceiled bedroom, but the coming of Leslie's troops
compelled her to change this place of disposal to the
stable, where in the space between the wall and the
thatch she bestowed them, wrapped stoutly in sacking.
She kept an eye on the bundle, and one morning it had
disappeared. More, it had clearly been stolen and
hurriedly opened, for the sacking and a tarry rope which
bound it were found among the nettles beyond the
kirkyard wall. Compromising goods indeed to come
forth of a minister's house !

That same day Isobel returned from a visit to her
cousin with a queer tale.

"Something's gotten out, sir. The wives in the
kirkton are clatterin' like daws. 'What's this they
tell me, gossip,' says one, 'about Babylonish garments
found in the manse ?' 'Faith, I kenna,' says I.
'They're nane o' my findin', but wi' roarin' sodgers
quartered in ilka chamber ye'll no surprise me if some

unco gear were left behind.' 'But it's nae honest gear
o' Davie Leslie's lads,' she says, ' but the laced coats
and plumit hats o' the malignants. And there's a report
that ithers hae sleepit in the manse this past se'nnight
than our ain Covenant sodgers.' 'Wha tell't ye that,
my wumman,' I says, 'was a black leear, and a thief
forbye. I'd like brawly to ken wha has been snowkin'
round our doors and carryin' awa' leein' tales and maybe
some o' our plenishin'. Tell me the names, and man
or wumman I'll hae my fingers at their lugs.' It was
Jean of the Chasehope-fit that spoke to me and she
got mair frae me than she expeckit. There wasna ane
o' her auld misdaein's I didna fling in her teeth."

The name of the woman disquieted David and he
asked what she had answered.

"Her! She took my flytin' wi' downcast een, and
that angered me sae that I had muckle ado to keep my
hands frae her face. Syne she says, quietlike, 'Ye
needna get in a steer, Isobel Veitch. If Mr. Sempill's an
honest man, he'll get his chance to redd up the *fama*.'
Fama, says she, whatever yon may mean—there's a reek
o' Chasehope about the word. And she went on wi'
her saft een and her mim mou'.—' There's waur nor that,
Isobel wumman,' she says. 'Our minister, that's sae
fierce against warlocks, has been walkin' a queer gait.
There's them that hae seen him in the Wud, and wha
do you think he met wi' there? It's no a name that I
daur speak, but folk hae brunt for less than sic a ran-
dyvoo.' Ye may fancy, sir, what a stound I got, but
I just spoke the kimmer civil and speired for mair. She
wasna laith to tell. 'There's them,' says she, 'that
saw the green gown o' the Queen of Elfhame, and the
mune shinin' through her hair, and saw her gie a kiss
to the minister.' Ye never kissed the leddy, sir?"

" God forbid," cried David, startled as if at an impiety.

" I thocht ye werena just as far forrit as that. . . . Weel, that's the tale they've gotten, and may it stick in their thrapples ! I'm no feared for their blethers about fairies, but we'll need some stench lees to get the sodger's claes blawn over. I wish I kenned wha was the thief. I'll threip that they were left by Leslie's folk and that ye kenned nocht about them."

" For me," said David, " I shall tell the plain truth, save in the mentioning of names. I command you, Isobel, to do likewise. The man is by now out of danger, and a falsehood, which may be pardoned if it is to save another, is black sin if used by a coward to save himself."

Isobel looked at him uneasily. " There will be an awfu' speak in the parish, sir. Bethink ye, is it wise to gie sic a handle to them that wad bring ye doun ? . . . But I see your mind is made up and nae words o' mine will turn ye. We maun hope that the question will never be speired, and I daur ony man or wumman in the place to get sae far wi' *me* as the speirin'.''

During David's absence in Edinburgh Mr. Fordyce, by the command of the Presbytery, had preached in the afternoon in the Woodilee kirk—to but scanty audiences, for the news of Montrose's advance had inclined the people to keep inside their doors. On the first Sabbath after his return, when there were still troops in the place, the pulpit had been occupied by one of Leslie's chaplains, a stalwart member of the Church militant, who hailed from the Mearns and whose speech was consequently understood with difficulty in the Border parish. But on the next, when Mark Kerr had gone from his refuge in the Wood, David changed his mind, and himself filled the pulpit. At the news a great congregation assembled, for in that joyous day of delivery it was believed that the sins of the parish would be left on one side, and that the service, as in the other kirks in the land, would be one of thanksgiving and exultation. To the surprise of most of his hearers—and to the satisfaction of the suspicious—there was no word of the recent crowning mercies, save a perfunctory mention in the opening prayer.

David, as befitted one who had just buried his father, discoursed on death. He was in a mood which puzzled himself, for gentleness seemed to have come upon him and driven out his jealous wrath. He had seen the righteous die, the man who had begot him, the last near kin he possessed, and memories of childhood and something of the wistfulness of the child had flooded in on his soul. He had seen, too, the downfall of human pride, the descent of greatness to dust, and yet in that dust a more compelling greatness. Above all, his love for Katrine had mellowed and lit the world for him ; it had revealed depths of joy and beauty which he had never known, but the beauty and joy were solemn things, and of a terrible fragility. He felt anew the dependence of all things upon God and the need of walking humbly in His sight. So he preached not like an Old Testament prophet confident in his cause and eager to gather the spoil, but as one who saw from a high mountain the littleness of life against the vast background of eternity. He spoke of the futility of mortal hopes, the fallibility of man, the certainty of death. In a passion of tenderness he pled for charity and holiness as the only candles to light the short dark day of life—candles which, lit by a heavenly hand, would some day wax into the bright everlasting day of the New Jerusalem.

There were those among his hearers who were moved by his words, but to most they were meaningless, and to many they were an offence.   Peter Pennecuik was darkly critical.   " The man is unsound as a peat," he declared. " Whaur's the iron o' doctrine and the fire o' judgment in sic a bairnly screed ?   There's an ill sough there, sirs —he's ower fond o' warks and the rags o' our ain right-eousness.   Worthy Mr. Proudfoot will be garrin' the stour fly the day denouncin' the Laodiceans that wad be lukewarm in cuttin' off the horns o' the wicked.   Is there ony such godly zeal in our man ?   Whaur's the denunciation o' the sins o' Montrose and his covenant-breakers ?   It seems that he's mair convinced o' his ain sins."

" He has maybe cause," Chasehope observed drily.

It had been David's intention to visit the manse of Kirk Aller and obtain the answer of the Presbytery's moderator to the charges he had formulated.   This was a duty which could not be shirked, since he had put his hand to it, but at the moment the fire of battle had died in him and he had no zest in the task.   He found himself longing to take Isobel's view and believe that his senses had played him false, that the events of the Beltane and Lammas nights were no more than illusions.   So he had delayed journeying to Kirk Aller, hoping that his mood would change and that that which was now a cold duty would revive as a burning mission. . . . Suddenly a post brought him a summons from Mr. Muirhead to wait upon him without delay.

He rode down the riverside in a day of October glooms and shadows.   Sometimes a wall of haze would drop from the hills so that the water ran wan as in the ballads, and the withering fern and blanching heath had the tints of December.   Then a light wind would furl the shrouded sky into fantastic towers and battlements, through long corridors of which the blue heavens would shine like April at an infinite distance, and the bald mountain-tops, lit by sun gleams, would be revealed. When he rode over the crook-backed bridge of Aller past the burgh gallows he saw that the doomster had been busy at his work. Three ragged scarecrows hung in chains, the flesh already gone from their limbs, and a covey of obscene birds rose at his approach. Stragglers of Montrose, he guessed, and he wondered how many gallows-hills in Scotland showed the same grim harvest. The thought, and the fantastic October weather, deepened the gloom which all morning had been growing on him.

He found a new man in the minister's chair. The victory of his cause seemed to have expanded Mr. Muirhead's person, so that he loomed across the oaken table like a judge in his robes. Pride pursed his lips and authority sat on his forehead. Gone were the airs of tolerant good-humour, the assumption of meekness, the homeliness which had a greeting and a joke for all. This man sat in the seats of the mighty and shared in the burden of government, and his brow was heavy with the weight of it. He met David with a cold inquisitorial eye, and greeted him with a formal civility.

"I sent for you, Mr. Sempill," he said, "anent the charge which you have set out in these papers and on which you have already conferred with me. There has been no meeting of Presbytery, owing to the disturbances in public affairs, but I have shown the papers to certain of my brethren and obtained their mind on them. I have likewise had the privilege of the counsel of the godly laird of Wariston, who, as you no doubt ken, is learned alike in the law of God and the law of

man. I have therefore taken it upon myself to convey
to you our decision, whilk you may take to be the
decision of the courts of the Kirk, and that decision is
that there is no substance in your case. You are upset
on the relevancy, sir. There is nothing here "—and he
tapped the papers—" which would warrant me in occupying the time of folk who have many greater matters
in hand."

"I did not ask for a judgment, but for an inquiry,
and that I must continue to demand."

"Ay, but you must first show a *prima facie* case, and
that you have failed to do. You have brought grievous
charges against one noted servant of God, and sundry
women, of whom it can at least be said that they bear
a good repute. Your evidence—well, what is your
evidence ? You say that you yourself have seen this
and heard that, but you are a tainted witness—a matter
to which I shall presently revert. . . . You have the
man Andrew Shillinglaw in Reiverslaw, who, in the bit
of precognition with which you have furnished me, tells
a daft tale of dressing himself up like a mountebank,
visiting the wood of Melanudrigill, and sharing in certain
unlawful doings. I ask you, sir, what credence can be
given to such evidence ? *Imprimis*, he was himself engaged in wrongdoing, and so is justly suspect. *Item*,
he is a notorious wine-bibber, and when the maut is
in, the wits are out. Whatna condition was he in to
observe justly in the mirk of the night in the Black
Wood, where by his own account he was capering like
a puddock and was all the time in a grue of terror ?
He claims on that occasion to have laid a trap for the
accused and to have informed two men of undoubted
Christian conversation of his purpose, and he claims that
on the next day the same witnesses at the toun of Chase-

hope were cognizant of the success of his trap. As I live by bread and by the hope of salvation, this is the daftest tale that ever came to my ears. A smell of burning duds, and a missing hen! The veriest cateran that ever reived in the Hielands would be assoilzied on such a plea. There is not evidence here to hang a messan dog. Away with you, man, and let's hear no more of what I can only judge to have been a drunken cantrip."

"I demand that Ephraim Caird be interrogated by the Presbytery and confronted with me and my witnesses."

"You must first prove a *prima facie* case, as I say, for otherwise honest men might lose time and siller in being set to answer malicious libels. That is the law of Scotland, sir, and it is the law of every Christian land, and you have lamentably failed in that prior duty."

"There is my own evidence—the evidence of an eyewitness. You may account for Reiverslaw, but you have still to account for me."

"Just so." A grim humour seemed to lurk at the corner of Mr. Muirhead's mouth. "We have to account for you, Mr. Sempill, and it seems that it will be a sore business. For I have here"—he tapped a paper—"another dittay in which you yourself are named. It is painful for me even to give ear to accusations against a brother on whose head my own hands have been laid in holy ordination. But I have my solemn duty to perform and must consider the complaints of a kirk session against a minister as carefully and prayerfully as those of a minister against a kirk session."

The effect on David was of a sudden clearing of the air and a bracing of nerve. This was, then, to be no one-sided war, for his enemies had declared themselves, and met attack by counter-attack. He smiled at the portentous solemnity of Mr. Muirhead's face.

"I can guess one of the names appended to the charge," he said. "It is that of Chasehope."

Mr. Muirhead turned over the paper. "Ephraim Caird is there, and others no less weighty. There is Peter Pennecuik . . . and Alexander Sprot in Mirehope . . . and Thomas Spotswood in the mill of Woodilee. If godly elders are constrained to delate him who has been set over them in spiritual affairs, it's scarcely a thing to be met with a smirk and a grin."

"I am waiting to hear the charge."

"It is twofold. The complainants allege that you have had trokings with the Wood and the evil of the Wood—and indeed on your own confession we know that you have frequented it when decent folk were in their beds. There are witnesses to depone to following you to the edge of the thing, as you made your way stealthily at dead of night. On what errand, Mr. Sempill? And in what company?"

"That is what I would like fine to know," said David.

"You were seen to meet a woman. They were simple folk who saw you and not free from superstition, so they jumped to the conclusion that the woman was no mortal but the Queen of the Fairies. That's as it may be. You and me are not bairns to believe in fays and bogles. But the fact that emerges is that you were in the Wood at night, not once but many times, and that you were seen in a woman's company. That is a fine report on a minister of God, and it will want some redding up, Mr. Sempill."

"My movements were wholly innocent, and can be simply explained," said David. But the charge maddened him, he blushed deep, and he had much ado to keep his tongue from stammering. He wrestled with a pagan desire to buffet Mr. Muirhead violently on his large authoritative face.

" But can you explain *this* ? " the latter cried, for he was not unconscious of David's confusion. " There is a second charge, and its gravamen is the heavier, seeing that it alleges an offence both against the will of God and the governance of this land. On the 26th day of the month of September in this year of grace there was found in the appurtenances of the manse of Woodilee— to wit in the baulks of the stable atween the thatch and the wall—a bundle of garments, including a laced coat such as is worn by malignants, and sundry other habiliments strange to the countryside but well kenned in the array of caterans whereof Montrose was the late leader. It is argued therefore that shelter was given in the manse to a fugitive, and that a minister of the Kirk connived at the escape from justice of one of the Kirk's oppressors. What say you to that, sir ? "

" I say that it is true."

David was not prepared for the consternation in the other's face. Mr. Muirhead sat erect in his chair, his head was poked forward from between his shoulders like that of a tortoise from its shell, colour surged over cheeks and forehead and his bald crown, and his voice, when he found utterance, was of an unnatural smallness. His careful speech broke down into country dialect.

" Ye admit it ! God peety you, ye do not blench to admit this awful sin ! Have ye no shame, man, that ye sit there snug and canty and confess to a treason against Christ and His Kirk."

There was more in the man's face than anger and incredulous horror ; there was pity, regret, a sense of an unspeakable sacrilege done to all that he held most

dear. David saw that the minister of Kirk Aller,
though he might have little love for himself, would
have given much had this confession been unsaid—
that he felt that shame had been cast upon his calling
and even upon his own self-respect. So he answered
gently :

"A wounded man came to my door. I fed him and
nursed him, and he is now, I trust, in health and safety.
I would do the same thing again for any distressed
mortal."

Mr. Muirhead's eyes goggled.

"Have you no notion—have you no glimmering of
what you have done ? I speak patiently, for I'm driven
to think you're not right in the mind. You have loosed
on the world a malefactor, a slayer and despoiler of
God's people."

"I have his word that he will not again take up arms
in Scotland. He was a soldier of the great Gustavus."

"What's the word of a malignant to lippen to ? Man,
you're easy begowked. When the Lord's command
anent our enemy is Smite and spare not, you, an ordained minister, connive at his escape. . . . Ay, and
there's more to it. I have news that you molested
Leslie's troops in their pursuit of a light woman that
followed Montrose's camp, and that you took the name
of the Lord in vain in interdicting them from their
manifest duty. Have you not heard that at the brig
of Linlithgow the wantons were drowned in scores by
the command of the worthy General, whilk was a
notable warning to sinners and an encouragement to
God's people ? Are there not Commissions of the
Estates and of the Kirk appointed to judge the captured
malefactors in Edinburgh and St. Andrews, and gallows
set on every burgh knowe besouth of Forth ? And you

dare help to cheat the wuddy of one who was no doubt the blackest of them? There's no a presbytery in the land but has sent in a memorial to encourage those in authority in their righteous work. For shame, man! Even in your own parish you have Chasehope lending a hand and riding the hills like a moss-trooper—the very man you would delate for sin."

"I obey God's word and my own conscience. I can imagine no blacker sin than cruelty to the defenceless."

"God's word!" cried Mr. Muirhead. "You've been lamentably ill-instructed. What did Joshua to the people of Jericho, but utterly destroy them, both man and woman, young and old? What did Gideon to the kings Zeba and Zalmunna? What was the command of the Lord to Saul when he went out against Agag king of the Amalekites but to slay both man and woman, infant and suckling, and when Saul would have saved Agag, what said Samuel to him?—'Rebellion is as the sin of witchcraft and stubbornness is as iniquity and idolatry.' Your eyes are full of fatness if you canna see the Lord's will. And your conscience! You would set up your own fallible judgment against God's plain command and the resolved opinion of the haill Kirk."

"I am a minister of Christ first and of the Kirk second. If the Kirk forgets its Master's teaching, we part company."

"And what's that teaching, prithee?"

"To have mercy and not sacrifice."

The minister of Kirk Aller closed his eyes as if in pain.

"You're deep deep in the mire of your carnal conceits," he said. "I thought you were only wayward and mistaken, but I see you're firm on the rock of your impenitence. Troth, Mr. Ebenezer of Bold was in the

right—you've heresy in you as well as recalcitrance.
This is Presbytery business, sir—ay, and maybe matter
for the General Assembly. I would be a faithless
guardian of the sheepfold if I didna probe it to its
bottom. This complaint must go forward.—Meantime,
till the Presbytery has adjudged it, I forbid you to
conduct the ordinances in the kirk of Woodilee. I will
appoint some worthier person, lest the pure gospel milk
on your lips be turned to poison."

"I refuse to obey you," said David, "for you have
no power to command. I stand on my rights to continue my ministrations till such time as the lawful
authority sets me aside. Meantime I require that my
charge against Chasehope go to the Presbytery equally
with his charge against me."

Mr. Muirhead was on his feet, with the famous glower
on his face which had aforetime awed timid brethren.
It did not awe David, who gave him back stare for stare
with a resolution to which he was little accustomed.
Indeed the vigorous youth of his antagonist and something in the set jaw made the elder man pause. He
shuffled off as if to end the interview, and David strode
from the house with unseeing eyes and a burning heart.

All the way home his head was filled with a confusion of angry thoughts. He saw himself caught in
toils at once absurd and perilous. He could imagine
the prejudice which his sheltering of the fugitive would
raise against him ; he saw his indictment of Chasehope
nullified by this legend of his own visits to the Wood ;
above all the bringing in of Katrine made him clench
his hands with a sense of furious sacrilege. In that
moment he seemed to himself like a child without
friends battering at a wall as broad as the earth and as
high as the heavens. . . . But the consequent feeling

was not of hopelessness but of a tight-lipped rage. He longed to be in a world where blows could be struck swift and clean, and where hazards were tangible things like steel and powder. Not for the first time in his life he wished that he had been a soldier. He was striving against folly and ignorance, blind prejudice, false conventions, narrow covenants. How much better to be fighting with armed men ?

Isobel met him at the manse door with a portentous face.

"There's a new man come to Crossbasket," she announced. "His plenishin' cam' up the water this mornin'—four horse-loads—and the drovers are bringin' his sheep and kye. I saw the body himsel' in the kirkton an hour syne. He's the rale down-the-water fairmer breed, verra weel set up and no that auld, and he wears a maud like a herd. But, Mr. David, sir "— she lowered her voice—" guess ye wha he is ? I couldna be mistook, and when he cried me guid day I saw brawly that he kenned me and kenned that I kenned him. He ca's himsel' Mark Riddel, but it's the glee'd sodger man that lay in our best bed."

CHAPTER XV

HALLOWMASS

ILL news travels fast, and by noon next day word of the complaint against their minister, of Mr. Muirhead's suspension of him from the pulpit, and of David's defiance was in the mouth of every parishioner in Woodilee. David was aware of curious eyes following him as he went about the place, and of a new constraint on the part of most of his Kirk Session. Peter Pennecuik fled his approach and could be seen hobbling into the nearest kailyard, while Mirehope, when he met him, gave him greeting with averted face. But he noted, too, a certain sympathy in others. Women, who had formerly avoided him, had now a friendly word, especially the young ones, and Alison Geddie—whose name had appeared in his charge—was overheard, as he passed, to comment in her pea-hen voice to her gossip : " Peety for sae wise-like a lad, and him aye with the kind word and the open hand to puir folk."

Isobel, whose face was now always heavy with unspoken news, he kept at a distance, for in these days he was trying to make peace with his soul. By day and by night, on the hills and in his closet, he examined himself to find in his conscience cause of offence. He went over every step in his past course and could discover no other way than that he had followed. He

could not see matter for blame in an act of common
charity, though Old Testament precedents might be
quoted against it ; nor could he blame himself for his
war against the things of the Wood. If he read his
duty more by the dispensation of Christ than of Moses,
it was Christ whom he had been ordained to preach. . . .
Of Katrine he scarcely suffered himself to think. She
was a thing too fine and gracious to be touched with
such doleful cares. Yet it was the thought of her
which kept youth alive in him, and in his dreariest
moments gave him a lift of the heart. When he looked
down from the Hill of Deer on the dark shroud of
Melanudrigill and beside it the shaws of birch and
hazel which stretched towards Calidon, he saw his strife
as a thing natural and predestined, and he himself as
only a puppet in the grip of primordial powers. The
thought gave him the confidence which springs from
humility.

On the Sabbath he preached from a text in Ecclesi-
astes : " So I returned, and considered all the oppres-
sions that are done under the sun : and behold the
tears of such as were oppressed, and they had no
comforter ; and on the side of their oppressors there
was power ; but they had no comforter." His hearers
looked no doubt for some topical word, but they did
not find it ; few realized the meaning of a discourse
which David preached rather to himself than to others.
It was a confession of faith, a plea for personal religion,
and an anathema against shibboleths and formulas
which did not dwell in the heart. So long as religion
is a pawn in a game of politics—the argument ran—so
long will there be oppressors and oppressed, with truth
the perquisite of neither side, and therefore comfort to
none. . . . The congregation was notably reduced, for

the five elders and their families were absent. But there was one new figure who sat modestly in the back parts of the kirk. It was that of a man of middle age, dressed like the other farmers in homespun, but holding himself with a spruceness rare in a place where men and women were soon bowed in the shoulders by unremitting toil. His cheeks were shaven, so that he stood out from the others, since, besides the minister, only Chasehope was unbearded. His skin was as brown as a hazel-nut, and though the face was composed to a decent gravity, there was a vigour in the lines of it which spoke of a life not always grave. The man had a blue bonnet of a pattern common nearer the Border—smaller than the ordinary type which came from the Westlands—and after the fashion of Cheviot and Liddesdale he had a checked plaid of the kind called shepherds' tartan. But in the cast in the left eye, shown by a sudden lifting of the face, he revealed his identity.

The stranger did not wait to speak to the minister, but David found Amos Ritchie at the kirkyard gate, and asked concerning him. "It's the new man that has ta'en the tack o' Crossbasket," was the answer. "He's frae the far Borders—Jeddart way, they tell me —and it's no easy to understand the wild hill tongue o' him. But he's a decent, weel-spoken body, and it seems he's a skilly fairmer and a graund judge o' sheep. He has stockit his mailin' weel, and has a full hirsel on Windyways. . . . Na, he's a single man and hauds to himsel', though he has a name for a guid neebor."

Amos accompanied the minister to the manse, and there was a shy friendliness in his air, as if he regretted the estrangement of the summer. He spoke only of weather and crops, but his manner suggested a desire to say something by way of encouragement. Only at the manse gate, however, did he find utterance. "If there's deep waters to be crossed, sir, I'll ride the ford wi' ye," he muttered as he turned away.

Presently it was apparent that a change had come over the parish. David's doings in the summer had puzzled and alarmed it ; even those with a clear conscience had thought of him as a danger to their peace and good repute. But now that he was himself in dire trouble and indicted before the Presbytery, there was a revulsion in his favour ; his friendliness was remembered, his kindness in the winter storms, his good looks and his youth. He had his own party in the place, a party composed of strange elements. There were in it noted professors like Richie Smail and Rab Prentice ; Isobel and her kin were hot on his side ; Reiverslaw, of course, many of the frequenters of Lucky Weir's alehouse, and all who from poverty or misdeeds were a little blown upon. If the Pharisees and Scribes were against him, he had the publicans and sinners. Also he had the children. By some secret channel the word had gone round in the circles of childhood that their friend was in trouble, and in queer ways they showed their affection. The girls would bring him posies ; bowls of wild rasps and blaeberries would be left at the manse ; and often on the doorstep Isobel found an offering of guddled trout neatly strung on rushes. Daft Gibbie, too, had become a partisan. He would dog David's footsteps, and when spoken to would only reply with friendly pawings and incoherent gabble. He would swing his stick as if it were a flail. "Sned them, sir," he would cry, "sned them like thristles."

But the comfort of the atmosphere in which he now moved was marred for David by the conduct of Reiverslaw. That worthy had been absent in Nithsdale when

Philiphaugh was fought and did not return till the week after the battle. It would seem that the general loss of stock due to the disturbances had benefited his pocket ; he had sold his hog-lambs to advantage and had had a prosperous deal in black cattle with Leslie's quartermaster. By the middle of October the work on the hill farms was all but over for the year, and Reiverslaw was a leisured man. Whether the cause was the new access of wealth or the excitement of Lammas, he fell into evil courses. There was word of brawls in ale-houses as far apart as Lanark and Kirk Aller, and he would lie for days in Lucky Weir's, sleeping off potations, only to renew them in the morning. His language coarsened, his tongue grew more unbridled, his aptitude for quarrels increased till he became a nuisance in the village and a public scandal. " A bonny friend ye've gotten in Andra Shillinglaw," Isobel said bitterly. " For three days he has been as fou as the Baltic and cursin' like a cornet o' horse." David made several attempts to reason with him, penetrating to the back parts of the ale-house, but got no reply but tipsy laughter and owlish admonitions. It looked ill for the credit of his principal witness.

The call of Calidon was always in his ears, but he did not yield to it. October brought a fortnight of drenching rains, and Katrine came no more to Paradise. He could not bring himself to seek her in her home, for he dared not compromise her. Already a nameless woman appeared in the tales against him, and he would have died sooner than let the woman's identity be revealed. From her he had had kindness and comradeship, but these things were not love, and how could he ask for love when every man's hand was against him and he could offer nothing but companionship in disrepute ? . . . But loneliness weighed on him, and he longed to talk with two especially—the minister of Cauldshaw and the new tenant of Crossbasket. But when he rode one afternoon to Cauldshaw, it was not only the minister's self that drew him there, but the remembrance that the Calidon household were among his parishioners.

Mr. Fordyce was scarcely recovered of an autumn ague, and his little book-room was as bleak and damp as a grave. He sat in a wooden armchair propped up with pillows, nightcap on head, a coarse drugget dressing-gown round his shoulders, and two pairs of stockings on his thin shanks. His wife was sick a-bed, outside the rain dripped steadily, there was no fireplace in the chamber, and gloom muffled it like a shroud. Yet Mr. James was casting a horoscope, and mild and patient as ever.

"Tell me the whole story, Mr. David, for I've heard naught but rumour. They say you've fallen out sorely with Mr. Mungo at Kirk Aller."

David recounted the events of the past months, beginning with Lammastide in the Wood and ending with his last visit to Mr. Muirhead. The other heard him out with many sighs and exclamations, and mused for a little when he had finished.

"You havena been over-gentle with the Moderator," he said. "Far be it from me, that am so imperfect, to impute error to a brother, but you canna deny that you took a high line with Mr. Mungo."

"I was within my rights in refusing to obey his suspension. He had no resolution of the Presbytery behind him."

"Maybe no. But was there no excess of vehemence, Mr. David, in defying one who is your elder ? Would not the soft word have availed better ? You seem to have spoken to him like a dominie to a school bairn."

"Oh, I do not deny that I was in a temper, but if I was angry it was surely with a righteous anger. Would you have me let that black business of the Wood be smothered just because Chasehope with his sleek face and his cunning tongue has imposed on the Presbytery ? And for the charge against myself, would you, I ask you, have refused succour to any poor soul that came seeking it, though his sins were scarlet on him ? "

"I'll not say. I'm a timid man by nature, and I'm so deeply concerned with my own state towards God that I'm apt to give other duties the go-by—the more shame to me ! In the matter of the Wood I think you have done honestly and bravely, and I doubt I wouldna have had the courage to do likewise myself. The Lord be thankit that such a perplexity never came my way ! . . . As for Montrose's man, what am I to say ? Mr. Mungo will quote Scripture against you, and it's not for me to deny the plenary inspiration of the whole Word, though I whiles think the Kirk in Scotland founds a wee thing over much on the Old Testament and forgets the New. But I can see great trouble for you there, Mr. David, for the view of Kirk Aller will be the view of the Presbytery—and the view of the General Assembly, if the thing ever wins that far."

"But what would you yourself have done in like case ? Would you have turned the suppliant from your doors ? "

"I do not know. To be honest with you, I do not know. I am a weak vessel and very fearful. But in such a case I should pray—ay, I should pray to be given strength—to do as you did, Mr. David."

The young man smiled. "I've got the comfort I

wanted. I'm content to be judged by you, for you are nearer the Throne than the whole Presbytery of Aller and the Merse."

" No, no. Dinna say that. I'm the feeblest and poorest of God's servants, and at the moment I'm weakening on what I said and doubting whether a man should not bow to lawful authority and cultivate a humble spirit as the first of the Christian graces. What for did our Lord found the Kirk if it wasna to be obeyed ? "

" Bide where you were, Mr. James. What kind of a Presbyterian would you make yourself out ? By your way we should be still under the bondage of Rome, because Rome was once the lawful authority. A bonny Covenanter, you ! If the Kirk constrains conscience unduly and makes a tyranny out of Christian freedom, then the Kirk is no more to be respected than the mass the old priests mumbled in Woodilee."

Mr. Fordyce smiled wanly. " I daresay you're in the right. But what a tangle for an honest man ! You've taken the high road, Mr. David, and I must keep jogging along the low road, for there's but the two of them. A man must either jouk and let the jaw go bye, as the overcome says, or he must ride the whirlwind. I have been given the lown downsetting, where I can nourish my own soul and preach Christ to the best of my power, and let the great matters of Kirk and State pass me, as a man hears the blast when he sits by his fireside. It is for stronger spirits like you to set your face to the storm. Alack and alas, I'm no fierce Elijah to break down the temples of Baal, and I'm no John Knox to purge the commonwealth of Israel. If you go forward in God's name, my dear young man, you'll have a hard road to travel, but you'll have the everlasting arms to support you. . . . But oh, sir, see that you fight in the Lord's strength, and not in your own. Cultivate a meek and contrite spirit, for I suspect that there is a good leaven of the old Adam in your heart."

"That's a true word. There's an unregenerate heat of temper in me at which I often tremble."

"And you must keep your walk and conversation most pure and circumspect. Let there be no cause of reproach against you save what comes from following your duty." Mr. Fordyce hesitated a little. "There was word of another count in Mr. Mungo's complaint anent you. . . . Wasna there some tale of a woman?"

David laughed.

"The Queen of the Fairies, Mr. Muirhead says, though he does not believe in her. . . . I have a confession to make to you, Mr. James, which I would make to no other ear. I have met with a lady in the Wood, for indeed she was engaged with me in the same errand of mercy. I had met with her before that, and I count the days till I may meet with her again. It is one whom you know—Katrine Yester."

"Mistress Katrine!" Mr. Fordyce cried out. "The young lassie from Calidon! Mr. David, Mr. David, is this not a queer business for a minister of the Kirk? Forbye that she is of a house that is none too friendly to our calling—though far be it for me to deny her Christian graces—forbye that, I say, she is of the high gentrice. What kind of wife would she be for a poor Gospel preacher?"

"Oh, man, there's no question of wife. You make me blush to hear you. The lady would never think of me any more than an eagle would mate with a throstle. But a minister is a man like the lave,* and this one is

* Rest.

most deeply in love, though he has not the thousandth part of a hope. There's no shame in an honest love, which was a blessing given to man by God's own self in Eden."

"It's a matter I ken little of," said Mr. Fordyce shyly. "Me and Annie have been that long wedded that we've forgot what our wooing was like. She wasna by-ordinar in looks, I mind, but she had a bonny voice, and she had mense and sense and a fine hand for making apple jeely. . . . Mistress Katrine! You fly high, David, but I wouldna say—I wouldna say . . . Anyway you've a well-wisher in me. . . . But Katrine Yester!"

David left the minister of Cauldshaw ingeminating that name, and in a blink of fine weather set out on his way home. He was on foot and beyond Reiverslaw, where the road first runs out of the birks to the Hill of Deer, when he was overtaken by a horseman. The mount was no farmer's shelty or minister's garron, but a mettled chestnut mare, with marks of breeding in head and paces, and he who rode her was the new tacksman of Crossbasket.

In that open bright place there could be no eavesdropper. The rider dismounted and flung his arms round the minister.

"I pay my debt," he cried, "by becoming your dutiful parishioner, your next-door neighbour, and your faithful hearer ilka Sabbath. . . . Danger, you say. Man, the darkest hidy-hole is just under the light, and the best sanctuary for a hunted man is where he is not expected. They're riping the ports for Mark Kerr, once captain of Mackay's and till late a brigadier under the King's Captain-general, but they'll no trouble about honest Mark Riddel, a plain farmer-body from Teviotside, that comes up Aller seeking a better tack and has

mair knowledge of sheep than any herd on the hills.
And Mark will pay his way with good white siller, and
will be a kind neighbour at kirk and market. My
Roxburghe kin are buried deep, but there's folk in
Woodilee already that mind of my great-aunt that was
married into Annandale, and my cousin once removed
that was a herd in Megget. Trust an old soldier for
making a fine palisado around him of credible lees. I
run no risk save the new ones that I make for myself,
and I'm in no mind for that, for a peaceful year or two
will be good for my soul, till I see whatna way the
cat jumps. Montrose must get him abroad, and if I'm
to bide quiet let it be in my own countryside and not
in a stinking foreign city. . . . But for yourself, Mr.
David ? From all I hear you've been making an ill
bed to lie on."

They sat down in the roadside heather, and David
brought up to date the tale which he had first told him
in the deeps of the Wood. To unburden himself to this
man was a greater comfort than his talk at Cauldshaw,
for this was one accustomed to desperate straits and
chances and of a spirit more akin to his own. The
soldier whistled and looked grave.

"Faith, you've stirred up the hornets, and it's not
easy to see where you will get the sulphur to smoor
them. There's much in common between you and my
Lord Marquis. You see the ills of the land and make
haste to redd them, but you have no great notion of
what is possible."

"You would not have had me do otherwise ? "

"No, no. I like your spirit fine, and beyond doubt
you've taken the honest road. But we live in a pitiful
world, where honesty is an ill-requited trade ; and you've
let yourself be forced into defence, whilk is an unpleasant

position for a campaigner. . . . Count me on your side, but let me take my own gait. It winna do for you and me to appear to be chief * in public. I'll make haste to conciliate the mammon of uprighteousness—whilk I take to be Chasehope—so dinna wonder if you hear that the two of us are like brothers. But it's the Kirk I fear, your own sacred calling, Mr. David. One shilpit body in bands and a Geneva gown, the way things are guided now, is more powerful than a troop of horse and less easy to get upsides with. . . . Still and on, I'm at hand across the glebe, and we'll no be beat for lack of good contriving. The night's the time, when we can step across and collogue at our ease."

To have the soldier at Crossbasket gave a lift to David's spirit. But at first he saw him rarely, for it was wise to let the man settle down in the place before appearing in his company, lest people should suspect a previous friendship. Mark Riddel appeared to be for ever on the move, and the minister met him oftenest on the Rood road—generally in the early darkness. It pleased him to think that his neighbour was visiting Calidon, for it seemed to bring Katrine nearer. But he made no effort to see the girl himself. With the fall of the leaf the season for Paradise had gone, and he could not seek her at home till he had unravelled the tangle of his own perplexities.

The chief of them was the approach of Hallowmass. He was determined not for one moment to forgo his charge against Chasehope and his coven, whatever the counter-charge against himself might be, and if necessary to go in person again to the Wood. But his chief ally Reiverslaw spent his days drinking soddenly in the clachan, and when he sought him out at the ale-house he got nothing but fuddled laughter. Then one morning

* Friendly.

he found him on the hill, and apparently in a better mind.

"My ran-dan is bye," said Reiverslaw sullenly. "Ye've cause to upbraid me, sir, and no words o' yours can be waur than what I gie mysel'. It's apt to take me that way at this time o' year, and I think black burnin' shame that I should be sae thirled to the fauts o' the flesh—drinking like a swine in a stye among folk that, when sober, I wadna touch wi' a graip's end. I'm no better than the beasts that perish. But I've fand out ae thing in these humblin' days. There'll be nae Wud at Hallowmass. The folk we ken o' dinna fancy the Wud aince the Lammas is bye, and it's the clachan itsel' that will see their next cantrips."

"But there is no place that could contain them——" David began.

"I ken, but they maybe follow some ither gait. I'll be in the kirkton that nicht—na, na, ye needna fear for me, I'll no gang near the hostler-wife—the verra thocht o' yill and usquebagh staws * me. But I'll be there, and you maun be in the manse, and we'll guide our gait according to what the nicht brings forth. I'll wager Chasehope will no be long out o' my sicht, and if he meddles wi' me he'll find me waur than the Deil's oxter. . . . Keep a watch on yoursel' that day, sir, for there's mony will wish ye out o' the clachan."

The last day of October came and David rose to find that the rain had gone, and that over the drenched hills had dawned a morning as bright as April. He spent the forenoon in distracted study, striving to keep his mind on printed pages, but his restlessness was such that after dinner it sent him to the moors. He took his old road for the Rood tops, and by three o'clock

* Sickens.

had reached the pass from Clyde, where in July he had had his talk with Reiverslaw.

The earth was soaked with the October rains, and as the sun's power declined in the afternoon a mist began to creep out of the glens. Insensibly the horizon shortened, the bold summit of Herstane Craig became a blur and then was hidden in clouds, the light wind of the morning died away, and over the land crept a blind eerie stillness. David turned for home, and long before he had reached the crest above Reiverslaw the fog was down on him. It was still a gossamer covering through which it was possible to see a hundred yards ahead, but objects stood up in it in unfamiliar outlines —a sheepfold like a city wall, a scrag of rowan like a forest tree.

A monstrous figure appeared in the dimness which presently revealed itself as a man on horseback. David saw that it was Mark on his chestnut.

"Well met," the man cried. "I'm pushing for home, for I'm getting the yowes to the infield, but I saw you before the mist dropped and I guessed I would find you here. There's a friend of yours up bye that would be blithe to see you—up the rig from the auld aik on the road to the Greenshiel." With no further word Mark touched his mare and went off at a canter.

The friend, thought David, would be Richie Smail, who might have some message to him from Reiverslaw. So he turned as directed past the root of oak towards the ridge of the hill. In twenty yards a figure loomed before him, a figure on a horse. He fancied it was Mark returning, till as he drew nearer he saw that it was no man that sat the black gelding and peered into the thick weather.

It flashed through his mind that Mark had sent him

here on purpose. And then something came into his
soul which he had never known before, a reckless boldness, a wild joy which caught at his heart. The girl
was looking away from him and did not turn her head
till he was close on her and had spoken.

"Mistress Katrine," he cried breathlessly.

She looked down on him, her face rosy, her hair be-
dabbled with the mist jewels. She did not start at his
approach. Was it possible that she was expecting him?

"What does the minister on the hill?" she asked.

"What does Mistress Katrine? It will be a thick
night and you are still far from Calidon."

She was dressed all in green, with a kirtle which
scarcely reached her ankles and left her foot in the
stirrup clear. The feather from her green hat hung
low over her curls. David had never seen a woman
gloved and booted for the hunt, and in that hour and
in that wild place the apparition was as strange and
as beautiful as a dream.

"I took out the hawks this morning with Edie the
falconer, for the mallards were flighting over from Clyde.
Edie went back an hour ago with the birds, and I lingered
to watch the mist creep up. Maybe I have lingered too
long."

"That was good fortune for me," he said. "I have
not dared to come seeking you, but now that we are met
I will convoy you to Calidon. Presently the world will
be like the inside of a feather bed."

She made no protest when he laid his hand on her
bridle to turn her horse, and as he stole a look at her he
saw that she was smiling. That smile sent a tremor
through him so that he forgot every care and duty.
He and she were enclosed in a magical world—together
and alone as they had never been before. . . . He felt

that he could bring her safely through raging rivers and across mountains of stone, that for her he could scale the air and plough the hills, that nothing was impossible which she commanded. They two could make of the world a song and a rapture. So deep was his transport that he scarcely heard her voice when she spoke.

"I have been hearing of your troubles, Mr. David. He whom we must call Mark Riddel has told me."

"I have no troubles," he cried. "Now that I see you the world is altogether good."

"Will you tell that to the Presbytery?" she asked, laughing.

"I will tell it to the broad earth—if you give me leave."

A momentary confusion came over her. She slightly checked her horse, and as the ground shelved the beast stumbled. The slip brought her in contact with David's shoulder, and before she knew his hand was laid on hers.

"Oh, my dear, my dear," he cried. "Katrine, I must say it . . . I am daft for love of you. . . . Since I first saw you down in the greenwood your two eyes have been sun and moon to me. Your face—God forgive me—comes between me and the Word. There are times when I cannot pray for thinking of you. . . . It's nothing I ask of you, Katrine, but just leave to tell you. What was it your song said?—'There's nane for me but you, my love'—and oh! it's the gospel truth."

She did not reply, but her hand did not move under his. They were descending the hill towards Rood, and the fog had grown so thick that each to the other was only a shadow. Before it had enclosed them in a visible encirclement; now it seemed to have crept so near that it dislimned the outlines of horse and rider. He held her by touch and by sight, and this disembodiment seemed to give him courage.

"I seek nothing," he said, "but that you should know my love. I am perplexed with coming battles, but so long as you're in life there's nothing can daunt me. I would not have you smirched with the stour of them, but if you'll let me think of you and mind of you and whiles see you I'll be as strong as Samson. The papist cries on his saints, and you are the saint whose name is written on my heart."

Still she did not speak, and he cried out in alarm.

"Have I angered you? Forgive me—forgive me —but I had to speak. Not one other word more will I say till we are at Calidon door."

Her answer, when it came, was strange, for it was a song crooned very softly:

> "It's love for love that I have got,
> And love for love again."

A great awe came over David and checked his breath —the awe of one who sees and yet does not believe, the answer to a hopeless prayer. His hand tightened on hers, but she slipped it away. "So turn," she sang:

> "So turn your high horse heid about
> And we will ride for hame, my love,
> And we will ride for hame."

The hand which had moved from under his was laid on his head. Suddenly a face bent down towards him and a kiss as light as a bird's wing brushed his forehead. He caught her to him from the saddle.

CHAPTER XVI

THE WITCH HUNT

DAVID awoke next morning to a world which had been suddenly re-created. That Katrine should return his love upheaved for him the foundations of the globe. Nothing could be the same again, in face of this tremendous fact ; his troubles lifted like mist in the sun, for what ill could befall one whom Katrine loved ? Even the incubus of sin in Woodilee seemed to lighten, for evil could not prevail with such a lady walking the earth. He felt that he had come anew into the land of the living, and every fibre of him sang praises.

His new fortitude was proof against even the news which Reiverslaw brought. That worthy arrived at the manse with a long face. The coven in Woodilee had held their Hallowmass rites and to the best of his belief they had held them in the kirk. . . . He had lost sight of Chasehope early in the evening, and had gone to Mirehope on a false scent. . . . They had been watching the manse and knew that the minister was from home. . . . He had hastened up the road seeking David and had been overtaken by the fog, and when he got back to Woodilee the place had been under a blanket. Doubtless the Devil was protecting his own. . . . There had been no cruisies lit in the cottages, even of those who were known to be of the coven. But, as luck would have it, he had entered the kirkyard and had seen a speck of light in the kirk. The door was locked, but he was clear that there were folk inside. . . . He had roused Robb to get the key, but no key was to be found. He had gone for Amos Ritchie to break open the door, and though Amos had refused to stir, he had borrowed a mell and a crowbar; but when he reached the kirk, the place was quiet and dark again, and the keys were lying on Robb's doorstep.

The man was really shocked, for this was a superfluity of naughtiness for which he had not been prepared. To David, with a memory of his Kirk Session, the sacrilege was less of a surprise; if men and women could defy their Maker by sitting at the communion table and by taking in vain the Gospel words, they would not shrink from polluting God's house. But it proved the boldness and security of the evildoers. It was Chasehope of whom he chiefly thought—Chasehope, that darling of the Presbytery, the ally of the Kirk in hunting down malignants, the one in all the parish who flaunted most his piety. The man grew in stature as he contemplated him. Here was no feeble sinner, but a very provost in the craft, who turned all the uses of religion to his foul purposes. And at the thought David, fired by his new happiness, almost rejoiced; he was fighting not with human frailty, but against a resolute will to damnation.

That day he received a summons to attend on the following Monday upon a special meeting of Presbytery at Kirk Aller for a preliminary examination. The thing seemed to him now to have lost all terrors. He had no anger against his accusers, for were they not dull old men who knew nothing of the ravishing world that had been opened to him? He would be very meek with them, for he pitied them; if they chose to censure and

degrade him he would bear it patiently. His extreme
happiness made him feel more than ever in the hands of
the Almighty and disposed to walk softly before Him.
He had given many hostages to fortune, but he had won
something which could never be taken away. Thankful
and humble he felt, in love with life and with all humanity,
and notably less bellicose. His path of duty was clear,
but he would not court antagonisms. He owed much to
the less fortunate, he who daily met Katrine in the greenwood or on the hill in the soft noons which make a false
summer at autumn's end.

So on the Sabbath he preached a sermon which was
long spoken of in Woodilee. He discoursed of charity—
a topic not popular in the Kirk, and commonly left to
such as Mr. Fordyce who were afflicted with ill-health.
For a young minister, his face ruddy with the hill winds
and his figure as well set up as a dragoon's, to expand on
such a matter seemed a mere waste of precious time, when
so many more marrowy subjects lay to his hand. Yet
there was that in David's earnestness which impressed
his audience almost as much as if his sermon had been
on death and judgment. He had a new hearer. A man
sat beneath the pulpit whose eyes never moved from the
minister's face—a mere lath of a man, thin to emaciation,
with a narrow head and a much-freckled face, a ragged
beard, and eyes with red lights in them like a ferret's.
David noticed that as the kirk emptied the others seemed
to shun the new-comer's proximity. As he moved to the
door, there was a drift away from him, like sheep from
a collie.

That night Isobel gave him news of the stranger.

"The pricker has come," she announced in a solemn
voice. "He arrived yestreen and is bidin' wi' Chasehope. Yon was him in the kirk the day, yon body wi'

the fernietickles * and the bleary een. They ca' him
Kincaid—John Kincaid, and he's frae Newbottle way
—anither than a guid ane, if a' tales be true. Eh, sir,
this is a shamefu' business, routin' out puir auld bodies
and garrin' them gie daft answers, and syne delatin'
them on what they ca' their confessions. There's naebody safe that hasna a power o' keepin' a calm sough and
giein' back word for word. I wadna be feared mysel' o'
ony Kincaid, but if you was to cross-speir me, Mr. David,
wi' your searchin' een, I daresay ye could get me to own
up to ony daftness ye liked to pit to me. I dinna haud
wi' this prickin' o' witches, and I can find nae warrant
for it in the Word. Belike it's some device that thae
weary Embro lawyers hae howkit out o' their rotten
herts."

As he rode to Kirk Aller next day David reflected
much on Isobel's tale. Who could have brought a
pricker to Woodilee—and lodged him with Chasehope ?
Was it the work of the Presbytery ? Was it a plan to
cover up the major sin by hunting out minor sinners ?
He knew of the pricker class as of the worst repute,
knaves and quacks who stirred up popular superstition and were responsible often for hideous brutalities.
Even the Law looked askance at them. He did not
like to be absent from his parish when such a creature
was let loose in it.

The examination of the Presbytery lasted for two days.
He had gone lightly to face it, but he found it a formidable affair. Business began with long prayers and
prelections delivered to his address. The Moderator constituted the court with the formality of a Lord of Session
and the solemnity of a minister fencing the tables at the
Communion season. He announced that the matter for

* Freckles.

examination would be limited to the charge of assisting the Kirk's enemies. The prior charge of witchcraft preferred by the minister of Woodilee against certain parishioners would be relegated to a later day, since the Privy Council on his motion had issued a commission to inquire into the machinations of the Devil in that parish, naming as its members himself, the minister of Bold, and the Laird of Killiequhair. This, thought David, explains the pricker. Mr. Muirhead added that he had moved in the matter at the request of a godly elder, known to all of them, Ephraim Caird in Chasehope.

The court was composed of the two score of ministers in the Presbytery, and only Mr. Fordyce was lacking, for he was once more stretched upon a bed of sickness. As it was only a preliminary examination there were no witnesses, since the object was to give the accused a chance of stating his case and so narrow the issue to be ultimately tried. The Moderator read aloud sworn statements, to which no names were appended, the names, as he explained, being reserved for the time when the complainants should appear in person. To David it was obvious that, though one of the statements was by a soldier of Leslie's, the others must come from members of his own flock. There was nothing new in the details —the finding of the cavalier's clothes in the manse out-house, the interference with the troopers at the Green-shiel, and certain words spoken on that occasion ; but what surprised him was the fact that the avowal which he had made to Mr. Muirhead was not set down. It was clear from the Moderator's manner that he proposed to forget that episode, and was willing that David should deny any and every charge in the libel. Indeed he seemed to encourage such a course. " The Court will be glad," he said, " if our young brother can blow away these most

momentous charges. Everybody kens that among wars
and rumours of war daft tales spring up, and that things
are done in the confusion without ill intent, whilk are not
defensible. It is the desire of all his brethren that Mr.
Sempill shall go forth assoilzied of these charges, which
are maybe to be explained by the carelessness of a
domestic and the thoughtless words of a young man
carried for a moment out of himself, and no doubt in-
correctly reported."

But David did not take the hint. He avowed frankly
that he had entertained a fugitive of Montrose at the
manse, and had assisted him to escape. Asked for the
name, he refused to give it. He also confessed that he
had endeavoured too late to protect an Irishwoman at
the Greenshiel and had spoken with candour his opinion
of her persecutors.

"It is alleged," said a heavy man, the minister of
Westerton, "that you promised these poor soldiers
eternal torments, and them but doing their Christian
duty, and that you mocked at them as inferior in valour
to the reprobate Montrose."

"No doubt a false report, Mr. Archibald," said the
Moderator. "It's like that the worthy sodgers had been
looking at the wine when it was red and werena that clear
in their understanding."

"I cannot charge my memory with what I said,"
David replied, "but it may well have been as set forth.
That, at any rate, was what I had it in my mind to say."

A sigh of reprobation rose from the Court, and the
Moderator shook his head. He honestly desired to give
David a way of escape, not from any love he bore him,
but for the credit of the Kirk. This, too, was the general
feeling. As David looked over the ranks of his judges
he saw stupidity, arrogance, confusion, writ on many

faces, but on none malevolence. This Court would deal
mildly with him, if he gave them the chance, for the sake
of the repute of their common calling.

He laboured to be meek, but no answers, however
soft, could disguise the fact that he and they looked upon
things from standpoints eternally conflicting. It was
suggested to him again and again that the stranger at
the manse had been entertained by his housekeeper, an
ignorant woman and therefore the less reprehensible, for
had she not rolled up the clothes and hidden them in the
byre, as the accused admitted? But David refused to
shelter behind any misapprehension. He had admitted
the man, what was done had been by his orders, and—
this in reply to a question by the minister of Bold—what
he had done he was prepared to do again. The close
of the first day's sederunt found the charges proven in
substance by the admission, indeed by the vehement
proclamation, of the accused.

For David there was no share in the clerical supper
at the Cross Keys. He lay at a smaller inn in the Northgate, a resort of drovers and packmen, and spent such
time as remained before bed in walking by Aller side,
under the little hill crowned with kirk and castle, watching the salmon leap as they passed the cauld. Next day,
the facts having been ascertained by admission, the
Presbytery debated on principles. David was summoned to justify his conduct, and—with a prayer that
he might be given humility—complied. With every
sentence he rode deeper into the disapprobation of his
hearers. He claimed that the cause of the helpless,
however guilty, was the cause of Christ. Should a
starving enemy be turned from the door, even though
it was an enemy of the Kirk's?

"Man, can ye no distinguish?" thundered the

minister of Bold. " Have you no logic in your head ? "
And he quoted a dozen savage Scriptural precedents
against him.

Was the Court, David asked, in a time of civil strife
and war between brothers, clear that the precedent of
Israel and the tribes of Canaan held ? The men they
fought against were professing Christians, indeed pro-
fessed Presbyterians. Granted that they were in error,
was it an error which could only be extirpated in blood ?

It was an unlucky plea, for it brought forth a frenzied
torrent of denials. The appeal of his opponents was not
only to Scripture, but to the decisions of the Kirk. Was
there not here, one cried, that rebellion which was as
the sin of witchcraft ? What became, cried another, of
the deference which a young man was bound to show
to the authority of his fathers in God ? " Are we to
be like Rehoboam, who hearkened to callow and inex-
perienced youth, and not to those elders who partook
of the wisdom of his father Solomon ? "

Presently David was silent. He remembered that
meekness became him, and he had a sharp sense of the
futility of argument. Respectfully he bowed his head
to the blast, while a dozen of his brethren delivered
extracts from their recent sermons. The Moderator
confirmed the sense of the Court.

" Our young brother is lamentably estranged from
Christ," he said in a voice which was charged with
regret as well as with indignation. " He is like the
Church of Laodicea of whom it was written ' Because
thou art lukewarm, and neither cold nor hot, I will spue
thee out of my mouth.' I tell you, sir, he that is not
with us is against us, and that in the day of the Lord's
judgments there can be no halting between two opinions.
It is the duty of the Kirk to follow His plain command-

ment and to rest not till the evil thing be utterly destroyed from our midst, even as Barak pursued after the chariots to Harosheth of the Gentiles, and all the host of Sisera fell upon the edge of the sword, and not a man was left. You are besotted in your error, and till you repent you have no part in the commonwealth of Israel, for you are like Lot and have taken up your dwelling in the Cities of the Plain and have pitched your tents towards Sodom, whereas the Kirk, like Abram, dwelleth in the plain of Mamre which is in Hebron, and hath built there an altar to the Lord."

The Presbytery refrained from any judgment on the case, that being deferred till a later meeting, when, if necessary, evidence could be called ; but in view of the fact that the minister of Woodilee had acknowledged his fault and exhibited contumacy thereanent, he was by a unanimous decision suspended from occupying the pulpit and dispensing the Sacrament in the parish, and from all other pastoral rights and duties. As the winter was close on hand, when evil roads lessened church attendance, it was agreed that spiritual needs would be met if Mr. Fordyce were enjoined to conduct public worship alternately in Woodilee and Cauldshaw.

David rode home in a frame of mind which was neither sad nor glad. He felt no shame at his suspension, but he recognized with a pang the breadth of the gulf which separated him from his brethren and the ruin of those high hopes with which a year ago he had begun his ministry. He realized that he was but a poor ecclesiastic, for he could not feel that loyalty which others felt to a Kirk which was mainly the work of men's hands. " They have lamentably perverted reason and justice " —he remembered Montrose's words, and yet most of them were honest men and pious men, and maybe their

good on a wide computation was greater than their ill.
It was his unhappy portion to have encountered the ill.
But if the Kirk cast him off he had Christ—" Other
sheep I have which are not of this fold," was Christ's
word—and he must follow with all humility the light
that was given to him. When the main trial came on
he would not relent in his denunciation of the Wood,
and his loss would be well repaid if, like Samson, he
could bring down with him the pillars of Gaza. . . . He
consoled himself thus, but he knew in his heart that he
had no need of consolation, for the thought of Katrine
was there like a live coal.

He came to the manse in the gloaming to find Isobel
waiting for him in the road.

" Heaven save us a' ! " she said, " but there's an
awfu' thing come to Woodilee. They've prickit a
witch, and it's nane ither than puir Bessie Todd o' the
Mains. Guid kens what they did till her, but a' night
the clachan rang wi' her skirlin'. The pricker fand the
Deil's mark on her back, and stappit a preen * intil it
up to the head and nae bluid came, and they burnt her
feet wi' lichtit candles, and hung her by the thumbs
frae the cupples till they garred her own to awesome
deeds. I canna believe it, the puir doited body, but
if the ae half is true she's far ben wi' the Adversary,
and oh, sir, it's fearsome to think what wickedness can
be hidden in the hert o' man. She said the Deil gie'd
her a new name, whilk she wadna tell, and she owned
that ilka Lord's Day when she sat under ye on the
pu'pit stair she prayed to him—' Our Father, which
wert in Heaven.' But whatever her faut it canna be
richt the way they guidit her, lickin' her wi' a bull's
pizzle and burnin' the gums o' her till she yammers like

* Pin.

a bitted powny. If she maun dee, let death come quick.
For the Lord's sake, Mr. David, get her down to the
Kirk Aller tolbooth, for the Shirra is kinder than yon
red brock * o' a pricker. The verra sicht o' his wild een
sends a grue to my banes—and Chasehope standin' by
him and speakin' saft and wicked and smilin' like a cat
wi' a mouse.''

David's heart sickened with disgust. Chasehope
had turned the tables on him; he had diverted suspicion from himself by sacrificing a half-witted woman.
And yet this Bessie Todd had been a member of the
coven—he had seen her grey locks flying in the Wood.
Chasehope was presiding at the examination and torture; he would no doubt take good care that no word
of the truth came out in her delirium. And Isobel, who
had denied with violence his own charges against this
very woman, seemed to believe her confession. She was
revolted by the cruelty, but convinced of the sin. That
would no doubt be the feeling of the parish, for who
could disbelieve avowals which must send the avower
to a shameful death?

" Where is the wretched woman? " he asked.

" They have her lockit up in Peter Pennecuik's
girnel. . . . They've gotten a' they want, and they
say that the Shirra has been sent for to carry her to
the Kirk Aller steeple, whaur they confine the warlocks. . . . They're in the girnel now, and the feck o'
Woodilee is waitin' at the door. Will you stop for a
bite? . . ."

David waited only to stable his horse, and to buckle
on the sword with which he had girt himself on the
night of the second Beltane. He ran so fast towards the
clachan that he was at Peter Pennecuik's house before

* Badger.

Isobel, labouring in his wake, had turned the corner of the manse loan.

The night had fallen dark, but from inside the girnel came a flicker of light. David had once before seen a witch hunt—in Liberton as a boy—and then there had been a furious and noisy crowd surging round the change-house where the accused was imprisoned. But the Woodilee mob was not like that. It was silent, almost furtive. The granary was a large building, for it had once been the barn of the Mains farm; it was built of unmasoned stone cemented with mud, and had a deep roof of thatch; through the chinks of both walls and roof came thin streams of light. The spectators did not press on the door, but stood in groups some paces back, as hushed as in the kirk of a Sabbath. The light was too dim for David to recognize faces, but he saw that one man stood at the door as keeper, and knew him for Reiverslaw.

He had been drinking, and greeted the minister hilariously.

" We've gotten ane o' the coven," he whispered thickly, " ane you saw yoursel' in the Wud."

" But Chasehope is among her accusers."

" I ken, but we'll get that kail-worm too, in the Lord's guid time. At ony rate we're sure o' ane o' the deevils."

" You fool, this is a trick of Chasehope's to divert attention from the Wood. This miserable woman has only confessed bairnly faults, and on that he'll ride off scot free."

The truth penetrated slowly to Reiverslaw's foggy brain, but in the end he saw it.

" God's curse on him, but ye're maybe right. What are ye ettlin', sir ? Gie me the word and I'll come in by and wring the truth out o' him wi' my hands at his gutsy thrapple."

" Bide where you are, and let none leave this place unless I bid you. I will see if I can get justice done."

But when Reiverslaw opened the heavy door to let him enter, the first glance told David that he had come too late. The great empty place had straw piled at one end, and on a barrel in the centre a flickering lantern. By it, on an upturned barrow, sat the pricker, a paper in his hand and an inkhorn slung round his neck, his face wearing a smirking satisfaction. He had once been a schoolmaster, and at this moment he looked the part again. Behind him, sitting on kegs or squatted on the floor, were a dozen men—Chasehope at his elbow, Mirehope, the miller, Peter Pennecuik, Nether Fennan— David saw only a few faces in the dim light. Daft Gibbie by some means or other had gained entrance, and had perched himself in a crevice of the wall, whence his long shoeless legs dangled over Chasehope's head.

On the straw behind the lantern lay the witch. Her grey hair had fallen round her naked shoulders, and that and a ragged petticoat seemed her only covering. Even in the mirk David could see the cruel consequences of torture. Her feet were black and swollen, and her hands with dislocated thumbs were splayed out on the straw as if they were no longer parts of her body. Her white face was hideously discoloured in patches, and her mouth was wide open, as if there were a tormenting fire within. She seemed delirious, for she gabbled and slavered uncouthly to herself, scarcely moving her lips. Every now and then her thin breast was shaken with a frenzied shivering.

At the sight something gave in David's head. He

felt the blood rush above his eyebrows, and a choking at the back of his throat. Always a hater of cruelty, he had rarely seen its more monstrous forms, and the spectacle of this broken woman awoke in him a fury of remonstrance. He strode to the lantern and looked down on her, and then turned away, for he sickened. He saw the gimlet eyes of the pricker—red like a broody hen's—and behind him the sullen secret face of Chasehope.

"What devil's prank have you been at?" he cried. "Answer me, Ephraim Caird. Who is this mountebank, and what have you done to this unhappy woman?"

"All has been done decently and in order," said Chasehope. "The Presbytery is resolved to free this parochine of the sin of witchcraft, and this worthy man, who has skill in siccan matters, has been sent to guide us. There is a commission issued frae the Privy Council, as ye may have heard, to try those that are accused, but the first needcessity is to find the witches and exhort them to confession. This woman, Elspeth Todd, is convict out o' her ain mouth, and we've gotten a memorial o' the ill deeds she owns to. Word has been dispatched to the Shirra, and the morn nae doot he'll send and shift her to Kirk Aller."

The man spoke smoothly and not discourteously, but David would have preferred oaths and shouting. He put a great restraint on his temper.

"How did you extort the confession? Answer me that. You have tortured her body and driven her demented, and suffering flesh and crazed wits will avow any foolishness."

"We followed the means sanctioned by ilka presbytery in this land. It's weel kenned that flesh sell't to the

Devil is no like common flesh, and the evil spirit will no speak without some sort o' compulsion."

David snatched the paper from the pricker and held it to the lantern. It was written clearly in a schoolmaster's hand, and though oddly and elliptically worded he made out the sum of it. As he read, there was silence in the place, except for the babbling of the woman and the mowing of Daft Gibbie from his perch.

It seemed to him a bedlamite chronicle. The accused confessed that she had been guilty of charming, and had cured a cow on the Mains by taking live trouts from its belly. She had "overlooked" a boy, Hobbie Simson, at Nether Fennan, and he had sickened and lain for three months on his back. She had made a clay figure of one of the ewe-milkers at Mirehope and stuck pins into it, and the girl had suffered from pains and dizziness all summer. She had shot cattle with elf-bolts and had cursed a field on Windyways by driving round it a team of puddocks. The Devil had trysted with her on a rig of Mirehope's, and had given her a name which she would not reveal, and on the rig there had been ever since an intractable crop of thistles. Her master visited her in the likeness of a black cat, and she herself had often taken the same likeness, and had travelled the country at night sitting on the crupper of one of the Devil's mares. By means of the charm of the seven south-flowing streams and the nine rowan berries she had kept her meal-ark full in the winter famine. She confessed to having ridden John Humbie, a ploughman of Chasehope's, night after night to a witch-gathering at Charlie's Moss, so that John was done with weariness the next day and unfit for work. The said John declared that he woke with the cry of "Up horsie" in his ear. At these gatherings she admitted to having baked

and eaten the witch-cake—a food made of grey bear
and black toad's blood and baked in the light of the
moon, and at the eating had sung this spell :

" Some lass maun gang wi' a kilted sark ;
　　Some priest maun preach in a thackless kirk ;
　　Thread maun be spun for a dead man's sark ;
　　A' maun be done ere the sang o' the lark."

She admitted that she had taken the pains of childbirth
from women—but what women she would not say—and
that then the child had been born dead, and had so
become a " kain bairn " for the Devil.　Last, and most
damning, she had between her shoulders the Devil's
secret mark.

Some sentences from the document David read aloud,
and in his voice there was bitter scorn.　He believed
most devoutly in the menace of witchcraft and in a
Devil who could take bodily form and divert the course
of nature to seduce human souls, but this catalogue of
sins seemed to him too childish for credence.　It was
what any woman crazed with pain might confess in
the hope of winning respite.　Most of the details he
remembered from his boyhood as common talk ; the
witch-cake rhyme he had sung himself ; the charm to
fill Bessie's meal-ark during the winter he knew to be
false, for she had nearly died of want, and he had fed
her from the manse kitchen. . . . He had seen her in
the Wood, and yet there was no mention of the Wood.
Chasehope had been present at the torture, and doubtless his fell influence had kept her rhapsody away from
the point of danger.　The poor soul was guilty, but not
of this childishness.

He looked at her as she lay, mindless, racked, dying
perhaps, and an awful conviction entered his mind.

She was a human sacrifice made by the coven to their master. . . . He had read of such things, he half-remembered tales of them. . . . Perhaps she was a willing victim—he had heard of such—coming forward with a perverted joy to confess her shame. The torture—that would be to stimulate her imagination. Isobel had always said she was weak in her mind. . . . She might have been chosen by lot in the kirk on Hallowmasse'en. . . . Chasehope was not her inquisitor, but the dark priest who conducted the ritual.

His anger and disgust rose to a fury. He tore the paper into little pieces and flung them in the pricker's face.

"What doubly damned crime have you committed?" he cried. "You have tortured a wretched weak woman and taken down her ravings for truth. You have maybe killed her, murderer that you be! Your sins cry out to God, and yours above all, Ephraim Caird, whose hands I have myself seen dipped in the blackest witchcraft."

Chasehope's face was smiling blandly.

"I kenna what right ye have to meddle, sir," he said. "The paper ye've torn is but a copy. The memorial itsel' will be in safe hands this nicht. Wad ye set yoursel' up against the Presbytery and the law o' the land, you that have been suspended this day, as is weel kenned, frae your rights as minister o' this parish? Ye'd best gang hame to your bed, sir, and pray that ye may be delivered frae the sin o' presumption. This woman will bide the nicht in this place under lock and key, till the Shirra sends for her."

"She will go with me to the manse this night—and, please God, I will nurse her back into life."

There could be no question of the consternation of the audience—it almost equalled his own. Chasehope alone kept his composure; the others stared in horror and growing anger.

"That will no be permitted," came from the lowering Mirehope, and "A bonny minister," cried another, "to file his house wi' a dirty witch. He maun himsel' be ower great wi' the Deil." The pricker twisted and grinned, and his eyes watched approvingly the spasms of the woman on the straw.

David was carried out of himself, and before he was aware of it he had drawn his sword.

"She goes to the manse. I will suffer no let or hindrance in this plain duty. Whoever opposes me will rue it."

"Wad ye deforce the session?" Mirehope shouted in a voice like a bull and got to his feet. From the idiot on his perch came an unexpected encouragement. "Fine, sir. Fine, my bonny Mr. David," cried Gibbie. "Stap your sword in his wame. I'll uphaud ye wi' my staff, for the puir kimmer was ill-guidit. I couldna sleep a wink a' nicht for her skellochs."

A voice broke in on the storm, and David saw that it was the new tenant of Crossbasket.

"Put up your blade, sir," he said. "There's no need for fighting among Christian folk. These honest men have been following the light vouchsafed to them, and if there's blame to be cast it's on this pricker chiel that comes from I know not where."

There was something in the quiet tones which fell like oil on yeasty water. David settled back his sword into its sheath, Mirehope sat down again on his keg, Chasehope turned his head to the speaker with the first sign of discomposure he had yet shown.

"Ye'll forgive me, neighbours," Mark continued, "since I'm but new come to the parish, but I've seen

a hantle o' the world and I would be wae to see honest
men run their heids against a stone wall. The woman
may be a' you say and waur, but it looks as if her hand-
lin' had been ower sair, and I'm muckle mista'en if she'll
no be a corp ere morning. Consider, friends.—This is
no a court constituted by a Privy Council commission ;
it's nae mair than a private gathering o' well-wishers to
the Kirk and the Law. In my time I've meddled ower
much wi' the Law for my comfort, and I ken something
about the jaud. The Law has no cognizance of a pricker
or onything like him, and if well-meaning folk under his
guiding compass the death of a man or woman that has
not been duly tried and sentenced, the Law will uphaud
it to be murder, just as muckle as if a caird had cut a
throat at a dyke-side. I greatly fear ye've brought
yourselves into its danger by this day's work."

Mark spoke with an air of anxious and friendly
candour that called for no opposition. Indeed it was
plain that more than one of his hearers had similar
doubts of their own.

" The wife's weel eneuch," said Mirehope. " Ye'll no
kill a tough auld greyhen like that wi' a raxed thumb or
brunt taes."

" I hope you're richt, neighbour," said Mark. " But
if she suld dee, what will ye say to the Shirra—and what
to the Court o' Justiciar ? Ye've taken doun frae her
mouth a long screed o' crimes, but I'm of the minister's
opinion, ·that they're what ony distrackit body wad
admit that wasna verra strong in the intellectuals and
fand her paiks * ower sair for her. Lord bless me, but
they're maist o' them owercomes I heard at my grannie's
knee. I counsel ye in all friendliness to let the minister
do his best to keep her in life, or it sticks in my mind that

* Punishment.

Woodilee will mak' an ill showing when the King's judges redd up the business."

Chasehope angrily dissented, but he had few supporters. Most of the others wore an anxious air.

"I come to the matter of the pricker." Mark's homely wheedling tones were like those of a packman in an ale-house kitchen. "I ken nocht about him, but I canna say I like the looks o' him. I doubt if I was strapped up by the thumbs and had yon luntin' een glowering at me I wad speak wi' strange tongues mysel'. It's no that difficult for a pawky body to gar a weaker vessel obey his will. . . . Get up off that barry," he said sharply. "Stand ayont the licht till I have a look at ye."

The words came out like a crack of a whip-lash. The atmosphere of the place had suddenly changed, the woman's mutterings had ceased, and, as David stood back from the lantern, he saw that Mark had moved forward and was beside the pricker, a yard from him, with the light between them, and the faces of both in full view of the rest. The one shambled to his feet and set his hand to his head as if to avert a blow, while the other, his dark face like a thundercloud, stood menacingly over against him.

"Look at me," Mark cried. "Look me in the een if there's that muckle smeddum in your breast."

The eyes of the pricker were like small dark points in his dead-white eyeballs.

"Ye're one Kincaid, but ye've gone by mony names. Ye've been a dominie and a stickit minister, a thief and a thief-taker, a spy and a witch-finder, and ye'd fain be a warlock if the Deil thocht your soul worth half a bodle. . . . Turn your een to the licht, and keep them there. . . . Answer me ere the Pit opens for ye. Was there ever a word in your mouth that wasna as false as hell? Say 'I am a liar, like my father the Devil afore me.'"

"I am a liar," the man croaked.

Mark stretched out one hand and passed it over the pricker's brow.

"What's aneath here?" he asked. "Honest banes? Na, na, rottenness like peat." To the horrified spectators he seemed to pass his hand backwards and forwards through the man's head as if a knife had gone through a pat of butter.

"What's in your een?" he cried, leaning forward. "I see the fires of hell and the worm that dieth not. God! the bleeze o' them is keekin' through!"

For a moment it seemed to all that a ruddy glow of flame leaped to the roof, and Daft Gibbie in his agitation fell from his seat and rushed to the door. The idiot flung it open and screamed beyond Reiverslaw to the waiting crowd. "Come inbye, every soul o' ye. The pricker that tormented puir Bessie is getting his paiks, and Glee'd Mark is drawin' hell fire out o' him. Come inbye and see the bonny sicht."

Reiverslaw and a dozen others entered the granary; the door remained half open and the night wind swept up the dust and chaff of the floor and made the red light seem a monstrous wavering cloud that hung like an infernal aureole over the wretched man.

Mark had him by the shoulder. "And what's this?" he cried, tearing his shirt aside and showing his bare throat. "As I live by bread, it's a Deil's pap!" Certainly to the audience it seemed that above the breast grew a small black teat.

The creature was in an extremity of terror. Fear had so drained the blood from his eyeballs that the pupils seemed to burn with an uncanny brightness, even after the red had gone out of the light.

"There's nae bull's pizzle needit to make this wauf * body confess." Mark's iron grip was still on his shoulder. "If ony neighbour has ony misdeed in his mind, I'll warrant to wring it oot o' the pricker as glib as a bairn's schule-lesson. I'll mak' him own to the Black Mass in the kirk on Hallowe'en. . . . There's nane speaks? Weel, we'll leave the dott'rel to his ain conscience."

He relaxed his grip and the man dropped gibbering and half-senseless on the floor.

"There's your bonny pricker," said Mark to Chasehope. "There's your chosen instrument for getting truth out o' auld wives. Do as you like wi' him, but I counsel ye to get him furth o' the parish if he be a friend o' yours, or the folk will hae him in the deepest hole in Woodilee burn."

Chasehope, white and stammering, found himself deserted by his allies, but he still showed fight.

"I protest," he cried. "I kenna what hellish tricks ye've played on a worthy man——"

"Just the same tricks as he played on the auld wife —a wee bit o' speirin'."

"It's no my blame," said Chasehope, changing his ground, "if I have leaned on a broken reed. The man was sent here by folk that vouched for his worth. And nevertheless, whatever the weakness o' the instrument, the Lord has wrocht through him to produce a confession——"

"Ay. Just so," said Mark dryly. "But what kind o' instrument is yon to procure the truth? Will ye get caller water out o' a foul pipe?"

* Feeble.

" The Lord works——" Chasehope began, but Mark broke in on him. His dark mocking face, in which the squint of the left eye was now most noticeable and formidable, was thrust close to the other's.

" See here, my bonny man.—Ye can get ony mortal daftness out o' man or woman if ye first put fear on them. Ye've seen the auld wife and ye've seen the pricker. Do *you* come forrit forenent the licht. Ye're a buirdly chiel, and weel spoken o' for canniness. Ye can keep your thumbs unraxed and your hide unscorched for me, but by the God abune us I'll warrant that in ten minutes by the knock I'll hae ye confessin' fauts that will keep the haill parish waukrife till Yule. . . . Will ye thole the trial ? "

The big man shrank back. " Na, na. I kenna what spell the Deil has gien ye, but ye'll no lay it on me."

" So muckle the better for yoursel'." Mark turned to the others. " Ye've a' seen, neighbours, that my spell, as he ca's it, was nae mair than just an honest speirin'. I'm loth to think that this clachan should suffer for what has been done this day, so the sooner we get the wife to bed and weel-tended the better for us a'."

" She shall go to the manse at once," said David. He had been examining the tortured woman, who had passed into unconsciousness, and it seemed to him that her heart beat very faintly.

" That will be wisest, no doubt," said Mark, but at this point Chasehope found support in his protest. Mirehope, Nether Fennan, and the miller exchanged anxious looks.

" Take her to Alison Geddie," they cried. " She has a toom * bed, and it's near by."

* Empty.

"She will go to my own house," said David, "and be nursed by my own hand. I trust no man or woman of you after to-day's devilry."

The place had filled up and it seemed to him that the better part of the parish were now onlookers. It was clear that a considerable number were on Chasehope's side, for the mention of the manse had wakened a curious disquiet in many faces. David solved the problem by dragging out from the back of the granary a wooden sledge used for drawing peats. He covered it with straw and laid the woman on it.

"Reiverslaw!" he cried. "You take the one end and I'll take the other."

The farmer advanced, and for a second it looked as if he might be prevented by force. He turned fierce eyes on the crowd. "Ay, sir. I'll dae your bidding. . . . And if ony man lifts his hand to prevent me, he'll get a sarkfu' o' broken banes."

The strange cortège moved out into the darkness, without opposition. It may have been the honest feeling of the majority that let it go ; it may have been the truculent Reiverslaw, or David with his white face and the sword bobbing at his belt : but most likely it was the fact that Mark Riddel walked by the minister's side.

Bessie Todd died just before morning. Isobel received her old gossip with tears and lamentations, laid her in the best bed, washed and salved her wounds, and strove to revive her with cordials. But the trial had been too hard for a frail woman far down in the vale of years. David watched all night by her bedside, and though at the end she became conscious, her mind was hopelessly unhinged, and she babbled nonsense and scraps of childish rhymes. If he could not pray with her, he prayed beside her, pleading passionately for the departing soul.

As Isobel straightened the body and closed the eyes, she asked anxiously if there had been any space given for repentance.

David shook his head.

" Puir thing, she got the Devil's fee and bountith, and muckle guid it did her. Let's hope, sir, that afore her mind left her she had grace given her to renounce him and creep to the Mercy Seat. . . . We'll gar some folks in Woodilee look gash * for this. There was a time, Mr. David, when I wad have held ye back, but my word now is Gang forrit, till ye rive this parish wi' the fear o' God, and sinners we ken o' will howl on their knees for as quiet a death-bed as Bessie's."

* Ghastly.

CHAPTER XVII

WOODILEE AND CALIDON

THE pricker disappeared from the parish in the night.
The dead woman was buried decently in the kirkyard,
and her male kin attended the funeral as if there had
never been a word against her fair fame. There was
indeed a certain revulsion of feeling among plain people
in Woodilee. Bessie had been liked ; she was regretted
and pitied ; the downfall of the pricker seemed to
invalidate her confession. But there was a party—
Chasehope was the leader—who held that solemn things
had been trifled with and that the minister had gone
far to bring God's curse on the parish. He had laid his
hand to his sword like a malignant, and had made light
of an awful confession before the pricker had been dis-
credited. Bessie might have been innocent of witchcraft, but in his plea for her he had shown a discreditable
leniency towards the sin. Women might be old and
frail, but if they were leagued with Satan it was enough
to put them beyond the pale of Christian sympathy.
The minister was patently rebellious and self-willed, a
scorner of the yoke of Kirk and Word.

But the night's events caused a notable increase in
one reputation. The new tenant of Crossbasket had
shown himself an ill man to counter. He had the
interests of the parish at heart and had given wise

advice, and he had confounded the pricker with a
terrible ease. Clearly a man with power ; nor was there
reason to think that the power was not given him from
on high. A hard man to gainsay, as even Chasehope
had found. His friendliness had made him popular,
and folk were slipping into neighbourly ways with him.
Soon he would have been " Mark " to most, and " Glee'd
Mark " behind his back. But from that night formality
and decorum invested him ; he was " Crossbasket "
even to the children, and the humbler doffed their
bonnets when he drew near.

He came to David one evening when the candle was
lit in the study.

" What arts were yon," the minister asked, " that
turned the pricker from a man into a jelly ? "

Mark had sat himself in a deep armchair covered
with black leather, which had been David's father's
and had come to the manse from the Pleasance after
the roup. He had crossed his legs and let his head lie
back while he puffed his tobacco-pipe. He laughed as
he answered :

" A simple divertisement, but good enough for such a
caddis-worm. A pinch of Greek powder in the lantern,
and for the rest a device I learned among the tinklers
in Hungary when some of us gentleman-cavaliers had
to take to the hills and forests for a season. But the
body was easy game. The sight of my een was enough
to melt his wits. . . . Chasehope's another kind of lad
—there's metal there, though it's maybe of the Devil's
forging. . . . But for the moment we've fairly houghed
his shelty."

" You saw how distraught he was," Mark continued,
" ay, and others beside him, when you offered to carry
the wife to the manse. The reason wasna ill to seek.

When she was being tortured to confession, Chasehope
was beside her and mastered her with his een. . . .
She was one of the coven, you tell me. But once in
your hands he was feared she would tell things of more
moment than the blethers they wrung out of her. . . .
She didna speak? Ay, I thought she was ower far
gone. It was maybe as well that the puir thing died,
for after the handling she got there was small bodily
comfort left for her."

"By her death her tormentors are guilty in God's
sight of murder," said David.

"No doubt. And maybe also in the sight of the Law.
That's why I say we have houghed Chasehope's mare
for him. He canna ride off on a pretended zeal for
witch-hunts, for this one has notably miscarried. This
pricker business is looked askance at by those that ken
best, and it's certain it has no countenance frae the
Justiciar. They've killed the wife with it, and their
pricker will not show face again in this countryside.
What becomes, think you, of the braw commission of
the Privy Council that Chasehope had the procuring
of? The thing is begowked before it is begun. The
ministers of Kirk Aller and Bold and yon knock-kneed
haverel, the laird of Killiequhair, will e'en hae to content themselves at home, and Chasehope, in place of
hiding his sins behind his zeal for burning witches, is
left with his repute a wee thing touched, like a bad egg.
There's folk in the parish beginning to speir questions
that never speired them before."

"I am convinced that the woman Bessie Todd was a
human sacrifice, decided on by the coven, and maybe
accepted of her free-will. I have heard that every now
and then they must pay such a teind to Hell. . . . She
was weak in the mind, remember."

"I had the same notion myself. No, I wasna there when the pricker was busy, but them that were tell me that he put the feck of the words intil her mouth. That would consort with what I've heard of the black business elsewhere. She was doomed to die, as surely as if she had stood in the doomster's cart. . . . But I have found out another thing. Our neighbour Chasehope is a King-Deil."

"What in Heaven's name is that?"

"You may well speir. He is the priest of the coven, but he is more, for he is a kind of Deil on his own account. That is why you saw them in the Wood bowing before him and nozzling him like dogs. There's been King-Deils before this in Scotland. Francie Stuart was one—him that was Earl of Bothwell in the days of James the Saxt, and he had a braw coven down by Dunbar and the Bass."

"And the man an elder of the kirk!" David exclaimed. "The words of Scripture are never off his lips, and more than once he has reproved me for sin."

"That's the lad. There's a holy pleasure to be gotten out of hypocrisy. And yet—and yet! I'll wager that Chasehope has no doubt but that he is a redeemed soul and will get an abundant entrance at the hinder end. That Kirk of yours has so cunningly twisted religion that a man can grow fat in his own sins and yet spend his time denouncing the faults of others, for he is elected into grace, as they call it, and has got some kind of a title to Heaven. I'm a plain body that canna see how God and the Devil can be served at the one time, but there's many a chiel makes a trade of it. They've gotten one creel that holds their treasure in Heaven and one full of the lusts of the flesh, and though they ettle to coup the latter before the day of death, they are confident that it winna canker what's in the other creel. It's queer doctrine, and maybe I havena riddled it out right, for I'm loth to believe that an honest man could uphold it, though I've heard it often propounded with an unction that made my flesh creep."

"You speak not of the Christian doctrine of election, but of its perversion," said David solemnly.

"Weel, it's the perversion that has gotten the upper hand these days. The Kirk has made the yett of grace ower wide for sinful men, and all ither yetts ower narrow. It has banned innocence and so made a calling of hypocrisy, for human nature is human nature, and if you tell a man that ilka honest pleasure is a sin in God's sight he finds a way to get the pleasure and yet keep the name for godliness. And mind you, the pleasures he enjoys with a doubtful conscience will no long be honest. There will be a drop of black ink in the spring water that makes it drumly, and ere he kens he'll be seeking a stronger brew. The upshot will be that folk who sit under you in the kirk will dance in the Wood on the auld heathen holy-days, and the man whose word gangs furthest with the Presbytery will be hugging lusts to his bosom that would make a common foot-sentinel spew. For they've all their sure title, as they call it—they're all elected into grace, so what for should they fash themselves ? "

Mark's face was smiling, but his voice had a note in it which was not humour.

"You laugh," David cried, "but I'm nearer weeping."

"I laugh, but it's to prevent me cursing." The other's jaw had set and there was a smouldering fire in his eyes. "I tell you the Cities of the Plain were less an offence to Almighty God than this demented twist

of John Calvin that blasts and rots a man's heart. For
if it makes here and there a saint, it is like a dung-
heap to hatch out sinners."

David was suspended from officiating in the kirk, but
he was still a placed minister and there was no embargo
upon his utterances elsewhere. So while every alternate
Sabbath Mr. Fordyce came over from Cauldshaw to
occupy the pulpit, and in defiance of the Presbytery ate
his dinner at the manse, on the others David preached
in the kirkyard. Twenty years later these sermons in
the open air were remembered, when Mr. Fordyce, then
far advanced in age, was driven from Cauldshaw to
hold preachings in the Deer Syke. . . .

There was a novelty in the practice which brought
many the first day ; and on later Sabbaths the audience
increased, for David had never delivered such discourses
in the Woodilee pulpit. One famous sermon was on the
peril of trifling with salvation. A soul was not saved
by an easy miracle, but must mount hardly and painfully to eternal life ; to accept grace lightly was to cast
scorn upon the atonement of the Cross. But doctrine
figured little, nor were there any of the forecasts of hell
and judgment which were the common proof of an
earnest minister. "He is a guid dowg," Richie Smail
was reported to have said : "he wad wyse folk gently
to Christ." Something of the joy in his own heart
revealed itself in a peculiar tenderness ; often there
were wet eyes among his hearers, and the children,
squatted on the grass or on the flat gravestones, forbore to whisper and fidget and listened with a grave
attention. His elders did not attend ; indeed, with
the exception of Peter Pennecuik, they forbore even
to grace the orthodox ministrations of Mr. Fordyce.

Chasehope and his friends walked the five moorland miles to Bold to sup on the strong fare of Mr. Ebenezer till such time—early in the New Year, it was believed —as the Presbytery pronounced final judgment on their minister.

Woodilee had split into two factions. There was the party of the Session, who held David to be a malignant, or at best a Laodicean, one who gave a doubtful sound of doctrine, a rebel, a despiser of authority, a preacher of a cold morality. To this side belonged many of undoubted piety who had been shocked by his defiance and gave ready ear to whispered scandal. Of David's party were respected professors like Richie Smail and Rab Prentice, several godly women, a decent hind or two, and a tail which was neither godly nor respected. Among his supporters were some whom he suspected of dealings with the Wood, and in general he had with him all that was least esteemed in the parish. To have Reiverslaw—who was again drinking hard—as his prophet, and Daft Gibbie as his fugleman, did not enhance the credit of his cause. Between the Jews and the Samaritans there were no dealings. Isobel, now a hot partisan, had quarrelled on this score with her nearest and dearest, and, encountering Jean of Chase- hope-foot in the clachan and being goaded by her tongue, fell on her tooth and nail and chased her into Peter Pennecuik's kailyard. Amos Ritchie, too, had declared his colours, and woe be to the man who in his presence spoke ill of the minister. He was no longer employed by the farmers around the kirkton, so the smithy fire was mostly unlit, while the smith did odd jobs at Reiverslaw and Calidon. Only the new tenant of Crossbasket mixed amicably with all. On the road he had the same greeting for Chasehope as for the minister, and he would drink a stoup at Lucky Weir's with Amos or Mirehope, Reiverslaw or the miller, in all good-fellowship. But this popularity rested more perhaps on fear than on affection. Dark whisperings began to spread. " What ken we o' Crossbasket ? " said one. " Nae doot he's frae Teviotside, but whaur was he afore that ? He never learned that glower on Jed Water." " He's a pawky carle," said another, " and ye canna get far ben wi' him. There's mair in his heid than the Word ever learned him. I wadna wonder some fine day to see him gang off in a fuff and a lowe. Ye say he has the speech o' a guid Christian ? Weel-a-weel, a soo may whistle, though it has an ill mouth for it."

By late November winter should have closed in upon the glen with an iron hand. The first frosts should have stripped the trees, and the first snows lain at the dyke-back. But that year it seemed as if the seasons had gone widdershins. November was bright and calm, and the harvest, delayed by October rains, was soon gathered. Oats and bear, flax and rye—the little crops were housed within a week, and, since the snows tarried, it was the middle of December before the cattle were in the byres and yards and the sheep brought down to the infields. The countryside presented a strange spectacle. Heather lingered in bloom, and the leaves were on the ashes and hazels till long after Hallowmass. When they did fall there were no frosts to crumble them, and they lay in great drifts in the woods and by the roadside, and children dived and scrambled among them. There were swallows still in the thatch in November, and Amos Ritchie, when he went out to the moss to intercept the travelling skeins of wild geese, found that the curlews and plovers had not yet flitted to the seashore and that there were no wildfowl to be seen in all the blue heavens. Morning after morning the sun rose clear as in June, the nights were mild and starlit, herbs which should have been snug below the earth sprouted prematurely, the hedgehog and the badger had forgotten to go to sleep, and only the short hours of light showed that it was midwinter. Reiverslaw, always a scorner of precedents, kept his sheep on the hills, where the pasture was as rich as in summer-time.

But the old and the wise frowned and shook their heads. One said it was such a year as '71, of which his grandsire had told, when winter did not begin till February and did not end till June. Another recalled " saxteen fifteen, named the Lown Year, when there was nae frost, and a blight o' worms and cawterpillars and hairy objects fell on the land." And every wife in the parish, when at Christmas the grass was still rank and high and hips and haws still hung on the bushes, quoted dolefully the saw that " a green Yule makes a fat kirkyard."

But if there was a presage of calamity in it for the thoughtful, it was weather of a rare beauty for those who had the heart to enjoy it. There was no sickness in the parish and as yet no hunger, so David's pastoral duties were light. He was on the uplands most of the day, and now his feet took him away from the Hill of Deer and the north ridge of Rood and across the glen to the hills between Calidon and Aller, for there he could meet Katrine with no fear of interfering parishioners. The garrison had been withdrawn from Calidon, since Nicholas was known to be out of the country and Mistress Saintserf was regarded as well affected, but David did not go there. So long as the short afternoons were crystal under a canopy of blue and the sun set behind

Herstane Craig in gold and crimson, the place for lovers was the hill, for there the world was narrowed to themselves.

But the minister's conscience smote him at last, and on New Year's morning he presented himself at Calidon door. By arrangement Katrine was not there, and from her aunt he got the tempestuous welcome which custom ordained as appropriate to the season.

"Sit ye down, sir, and prie our shortcake and October. Yours is the first stranger foot that has crossed this threshold, and it's surely propitious that it should be a minister's. Our ain Mr. James is lyin' again, for this lown weather doesna 'gree wi' him, though it's hard to say what 'grees wi' him, for the creature's body is sair failed. . . . It's mony a day since we cast een on ye here, Mr. David, and siccan days as they've been for me and mine."

She descanted on the troubles of the autumn, her success in saving Calidon from being sequestrated—"Peter Dobbie, him that's our doer, is far ben wi' Wariston, ye maun ken, and worthy Mr. Rintoul in the West Kirk said a word in the right lug "—on the difficulty in getting funds to Nicholas Hawkshaw at Utrecht, on the garrisoning of Calidon. "They punished our yill, but they fashed us little, for they were sair hadden down by Katrine." But she said nothing of Mark, though in the end she had been made privy to that business, and she did not hint at the trouble in Woodilee which was the talk of the country. Behind all her garrulity lurked a certain embarrassment, and it did not make David's task the easier.

At last he took his courage in both hands.

"I came here this morn for a purpose," he said, and with halting voice and a fiery face he made his confession.

The old woman regarded him with eyes that strove to express amazement and failed ; it was clear that she had had her suspicions.

But her words when she spoke were those of one who had been startled out of all propriety.

"Heard ye ever the like ? " she cried. "Man, d'ye ken of whom ye speak ? Katrine is a leddy born— there's nae aulder or prouder stock in the land—and ye're the oy * o' the miller o' the Roodfoot, and ye seek to make her your marrow.† We ken that the warld is coupit upside-down these days, but this fair cowes a'. Guid faith, ye're no blate."

David held his peace, for he had no answer. He felt in the pith of his bones his immense audacity.

"How would the lassie set wi' a manse, think ye ? " she continued. "She's been brocht up amang papists and prelatists, and though she's had mony a swatch o' the Gospel frae honest Mr. James, she's no muckle wiser than a babe. Forbye, she's a daft quean that wad never mak' a 'sponsible minister's wife. Think ye that the King's court and dancin' and glee-singin' and ridin' on a horse is a guid preparation for a moorland parish and a fower-room house ? How will ane that's been used to velvet and pearlins tak' wi' linsey-wolsey and drugget ? "

"That is for Katrine to decide," he said humbly. "I have heard that true love can glorify a cot-house."

"Havers ! " she cried. "There's a decency in a' things and ye canna mate a blood-horse wi' a cadger's powny. Wedlock, as I weel ken, is nae business o' kissin' and rhymin', but a sober contrack, and if twa folks are gaun to live cantily thegither, they maun see that mair than their hearts are weel agreed. There maun be a chance—there's nae certainty in this perishin' world—

* Grandson.   † Mate.

o' a bien doun-settin', and a sufficiency o' gear, and a life that will be guid for baith. What say ye to that? A minister's wife! Guidsakes, the Session wad think her a randy, for she'd lauch at their solemnities, and your brither ministers, wha are maistly cotters' sons, wad be fleyed by her gentrice, and the folk wad be as feared o' her as a chuckie o' a pyet. Ye're a man o' sense, Mr. David. Ye canna deny that the thing is past a' reason."

"Oh, Mistress," said the unhappy David. "There's truth in what you say—I cannot gainsay it. But I plead that true hearts may break down every obstacle, and Katrine's and mine are as true to each other as the dial to the sun. There was a time when you were young yourself, Mistress—you mind that then there was no rule for lovers but their love."

"I mind weel," she said more gently, "but it's for auld folk to be eident and save the young frae folly. . . . I'll no deny that I would be blithe to see Katrine provided for. She's a fine lassie, but forbye mysel' she has nae near kin to mind her, now that Nicholas is put to the horn and hidin' amang the Hollanders. Fine I wad like to see her in safe hands. . . . But what can ye offer, Mr. David? It's no as if ye were on firm ground yoursel'. They tell me ye've cast out wi' your Session and are bickerin' wi' the Presbytery, and ony day may be turned out o' Woodilee and maybe excommunicat by the Kirk. That's a braw prospect for a wife. Wad ye have Katrine tak' a creel on her back, like a tinkler quean, her that has in her the bluid o' the Black Douglas and the auld kings o' Scots? Ye've made a bonny hash o' things, for ane that's ettlin' to be a bridegroom."

"I am set about with perplexities, and the hands of many are against me. But I have Katrine on my side— and I was in hopes that I might have you, Mistress."

" I'm no against ye," she said, and there was kindness
in her eye. " Never think that. I've heard the clash
o' the country and I've riddled it out, and by my way o't
ye've taken the richt road. I ken nocht about the Wud,
but I ken something o' the tods and foumarts o' Woodilee,
and for the business o' glee'd Mark Kerr it's no a Hawkshaw or a Yester or a Saintserf would cast a stone at ye.
But it's solemn truth that ye've gotten on the wrang side
o' the Kirk, and the Kirk is your calling, Mr. David. . . .
Ye maun ken that I've had mony a crack wi' our Mr.
James anent ye, and if it's the pure Gospel word I'm
seekin' it's to him I'll gang and no to Kirk Aller. I'll tell
ye what he said. ' Mr. David,' says he, ' has his plew
on the wrang rig. He wad hae made a grand sodger, and
if he had been a papist he wad hae made a guid monk.
He has the makings o' a saint and he has the makings o' a
warrior, but a manse is no the place for him. For,' says
Mr. James, ' he canna like me withdraw himsel' into his
closet—he is ower hale o' body and het in spirit for that
—and he canna walk doucely as the Kirk ordains. For,
if he sees wrang he maun set it richt, though the Kirk
tells him to bide still, and he'll no put his conscience in
the keeping o' ony Presbytery. He's ower staunch a
Presbyterian,' says he, ' for the Kirk of Scotland as at
present guidit, whilk is a kind o' Papery wi' fifty Papes
instead o' ane.' "

" Maybe that's the truth," said David.

" Ay, it's the truth, and I'm blithe to hear ye acknowledge it. . . . But we'll hae the lassie in, for this crack
concerns her maist. The cunnin' limmer to keep sae
mum and begowk her auld auntie ! "

When Katrine appeared, her cheeks a little flushed
and her eye bright, she was greeted by Mistress Grizel
with surprising gentleness.

" What's this I hear o' ye, lassie ? Ye've gotten a joe and never telled me ! . . . Na, na, my lamb, dinna be feared that I'll flyte on ye. It's a road we maun a' travel, and nae doubt wedlock is a holy and blessed state and a hantle better than spinsterhood, for a woman maun either be guidit by a husband or be subject to a' and sindry. But it's a serious step, and wants carefu' and prayerfu' thocht. I've had a word wi' Davie—for I tak' the liberty to ca' him Davie as if he were my ain son—and as in duty bound I've set forth the difficulties. I say naething against ye as a man, Davie. Ye're wise-like and weel-spoken, and ye've gentle ways, if ye hae na gentle bluid. But I say muckle against ye as a minister, and I canna picture Katrine as the leddy o' a manse. Forbye there's the solemn fact that ye've made Woodilee ower het a bit to bide in, and what ye've done there ye'll dae in ony ither parochine in the land. . . . Sae hearken to me, sir. Ye've mista'en your trade, like mony another honest lad, but the faut can be mended. Ye're young eneuch to start in a better."

Katrine had moved to David's side and laid her hand on his shoulder. " Aunt Grizel would have you forsake the Kirk for the world," she laughed.

" But I am solemnly vowed to God's service," he said.

" Nae doot," said Mistress Grizel. " But a man serves his Maker as weel in buckskin as in a Geneva gown—better, if a' tales be true. This is the counsel of ane that wishes ye weel, you and that denty lass at your elbuck. Mak' your peace wi' the Kirk—submit yoursel' to the Presbytery—ye need gie up nane o' your views, but submit yoursel' to the lawfu' authority. Tell them that ye'll be guidit in your public doings by them that has been set ower ye. . . . Troth, they'll no be sweir to mak' a brig for ye, for they dinna want a scandal in the Kirk.

They'll censure ye lichtly for a thochtless callant and
the thing will drap.　By that course ye'll dae nae violence
to your conscience—ye'll just be humblin' yoursel' before
your elders in the Lord, as we're commanded."

"But what of the witchcraft in Woodilee?" he asked.

"Let it gang by the board.　It's no you or ten like
you will clean out that dirty nest.　Leave it to the
Almighty, whose judgments are slow and siccar." *

"You would have me sit silent in Woodilee in the
midst of that iniquity?"

"Na, na.　I would have ye get out o' Woodilee as
fast as a bird when the thack's burnin'.　We've Mr.
James's opinion, whilk ye canna controvert, that ye were
never meant for a minister.　I'se warrant it will be made
easy for ye—the Presbytery will no object, and Calidon's
the chief heritor, and I'll get a word spoken to Mr.
Rintoul.　Ye'll leave wi' a guid name, at peace wi' God
and man, and there's a' braid Scotland for ye to find a
habitation. . . . Peter Dobbie tells me that your father,
honest man, made a hantle o' siller and that ye've heired
the haill o't.　Gang down the water to the auld Yester
lands, and buy a bit estate and set up Katrine in her forebears' countryside.　Ye're young and yauld and there's
muckle guid work to be done in Scotland by ane that
lives in the fear o' God, be he laird or minister."

David turned to Katrine, but her face was impassive.
From her he would get no guidance.　Like her aunt, she
awaited his answer.

For a moment he wavered.　On one side he saw peace,
comfort, a new life with his beloved in a new place, the
cutting of a tangle which constricted his youth; on the
other—a thankless fight, where victory was wellnigh
impossible, a sordid struggle which would darken the

* Sure.

sunlight for both and taint all the springs of joy. He dropped his head on his breast and suffered for an instant the anguish of indecision. Then he spoke and his eyes were on Katrine.

"I cannot. I would be going back upon my vows— I would be false to my faith—I would deserve to be cried out upon as a coward—I would be making terms with the Devil."

"Thank God," said the girl, and her arms were round his neck.

The old woman stared at him, coughed dryly, and then very deliberately took her seat in the big armchair which had been Nicholas Hawkshaw's. The two stood before her like prisoners brought to judgment.

"Ye'll tak' that puir lassie and expose her to the ill-will o' the Kirk and the countryside.—Ye'll set her up as a mark for clash and scandal.—Ye'll condemn her to a wearifu' battalation that can have but the one end, for those that are against ye are mair than those that are for ye. A man may fecht stoutly his lee lane, but he is sair trauchled by a wife."

"I will reply," Katrine cried. "I am a Yester. What cognizance does Yester bear, Aunt Grizel?"

"Azure a chevron or between three garbs of the same, and for badge a lion guardant, wi' the ditton 'Thole feud.'"

"My motto is my answer. Would you have me shame my kin and run from a challenge?"

"But what kind o' challenge, my lamb? Ye'll be nae Black Agnes o' Dunbar—but a minister's wife, fechtin' against lees and clypes and fause tongues and ignorance—the cauld law o' the land and the caulder laws o' the Kirk. Ye'll hae to thole and thole wi' never a back-straik o' your ain, and keep a smilin' face and a

high heid when your heart is sick. Ye maun bow to
them ye scorn and bend the knee to them that your
guidsire would have refused for horse-boys, and be
servant to the silliest body that summons ye in the name
o' Christ. Have ye made your market for that, my doo?
There never was Yester—or Hawkshaw neither—that
feared feud, but can ye thole sic dreidfu' servitude, day
in day out, in a wee house in a dreich parochine wi' nae
company but hinds and wabsters? "

The girl looked at David and there was that in her
eyes which made him both exultant and very humble,
so that he longed at once to sing and to weep. She
turned to the Bible which lay on the great table, ran a
finger over its pages and read, and the words were those
which Ruth spoke to Naomi :

" Intreat me not to leave thee, or to return from following after thee : for whither thou goest, I will go ; and
where thou lodgest, I will lodge : thy people shall be my
people, and thy God my God : where thou diest, will I
die, and there will I be buried : the Lord do so to me,
and more also, if ought but death part thee and me."

" So that's the way o't," said the old woman. " Weel,
I've said my say. Ye're a pair o' fules, but there's maybe
waur things than fules in God's sicht. . . . Davie, lad,
get down on your hunkers and I'll gie ye my blessing—
the blessing o' a warldly auld wife that yet has orra glints
o' better things. . . . Man, I kenna where ye got it, but
there's gentle bluid in ye. Your common body would
have chosen the saft seat."

CHAPTER XVIII

THE PLAGUE

In the first week of the New Year the miraculous weather showed no sign of breaking. The sun from rising to setting shone temperately in a clear sky, the nights were little less warm than May, and even the old folk cast the blankets from them and opened the doors of their press-beds; the peat-stacks and the fuel-stacks were scarcely touched, and the fires smouldered only for cooking; the burns were shrunken to summer size, and the spawning fish could not pass the shallows of Rood. But a change had come over the mind of the parish. Men no longer called down blessings on the fine open winter, for such weather seemed in defiance of nature, and an uneasy anticipation of portents weighed on their spirits. The sun did not warm, the unclouded skies did not cheer, the hard roads did not invite to movement. A curious languor fell upon Woodilee.

It seemed as if the same apprehension were felt by the natural world. The cattle and sheep, in spite of the good pasture, grew thinner than in the rigours of winter. The packman's pony turned away from the rich bite by the roadside. Though the air was cool and tonic, beast and man sweated with the smallest exertion. David, tramping the high moors, found that he was more weary after five miles than after twenty in the summer heats. The deer from Melanudrigill had none of their winter boldness, and indeed all wild animals had become shyer of the presence of man than the oldest inhabitant remembered. But all were aware and restless ; there were more worm-casts on the turf than in spring, and migrant birds, which usually tarried long in the sheltered glen, now passed high in air for the south. David saw many a drove as he opened his window in the morning. Even the fieldfares, which Amos Ritchie used to snare in the Mirehope fields, did not come within sight of his bird-lime. . . . A brooding strangeness had come into the air, and apathy silenced the very tykes in the village street. Neighbours rarely gathered at Lucky Weir's for a mutchkin, though it was thirsty weather ; men seemed to be afraid lest what they saw in another's eye might give substance to their own fears.

Peter Pennecuik, sitting on the stone by the smithy door and mopping a wet forehead, watched Amos drop his tools heavily as he returned from a job at Reiverslaw.

" What mak' ye o' the weather ? " he asked.

Amos straightened his back.

" I dinna like it. The gillyflowers in my yaird are ettlin' to bloom. My grannie had a verse o' auld Thomas the Rhymer—what was it ?—

> A Yule wi'out snaws,
> A Januar' wi' haws,
> Bring the deid thraws."

" There's a judgment preparin'," said Peter, " but whatna kind o' judgment I daurna guess. Certes, it's no canny."

" I've heard o' nane ailin', but there's seeckness comin'. I can smell it in the air, and the brute beasts can smell it, for they're sweir to come near Woodilee.

There's no a tod or a maukin on a' the Hill o' Deer. D'ye no find a queer savour in the countryside, Peter? There's wind enough to shake the saughs, but the warld smells like the inside o' a press-bed when the door's steekit. Oh for a snell, dirlin' blast! There's something rotten and stawsome and unearthly about the blue lift and the saft air. It's like withered floo'ers on a midden. . . . If there's nae seeckness yet, there's seeckness on the road. I maun awa' in and see to Ailie, for this morn she was complaining o' a sair heid."

Two days later the child of a cotter at Mirehope returned from school in the manse kitchen and to his mother's amazement beat his head against the door. He fell asleep on the wedder's skin beside the fire, and when he was wakened for his supper his cheeks were flaming and he seemed to have difficulty with his speech. He was put with the rest into the box which was the children's bed, and all night filled it with his cries, so that the others sought peace on the floor. In the morning his face and throat were swollen, his eyes were sightless, and he struggled terribly for breath. Before noon he was dead.

In this way came the plague to Woodilee.

Its coming was realized in an instant, for the sinister weather had prepared the people for calamity. Before the dark the rumour of the breaking out of the pest was in the uttermost sheilings. With it went the word that Peter Pennecuik had sickened, and that another child at Mirehope and one of the Chasehope ewe-milkers were down with it. . . . Next day the place was a beleaguered city. Johnnie Dow, the packman, hearing the news at Cauldshaw, diverted his round to Kirk Aller, though thirty pounds Scots were owing to him in Woodilee. The roads were blocked as if Montrose's kerns commanded them. As it was winter-time there was little work on hand, and even that little was not done. A Sabbath hush fell on the glen, people shut their doors and sat within at their prayers, and that best seeding-ground for plague, a lively terror, was amply prepared.

Peter Pennecuik died in eight hours. There was no heart in the man, and in sickness his command of pious phrases fell away from him, and he passed out of life in a whimpering misery. It was not an edifying death-bed for one who had been a notable professor. But very soon Peter was forgotten—for he was an old man and ripe for his end—as the young and strong were, one by one, struck down. Amos Ritchie's wife, Ailie, followed —the less to be wondered at, for she had always been frail. But when Jess Morison at Chasehope-foot, dark-browed, high-coloured, and not yet twenty, swooned as she drew water at the well, and died in delirium before evening, fear in the parish became panic. The young herd at Windyways, the trimmest lad in the glen, and the miller's man, who looked as gnarled as an oak and as strong as a mill-wheel, followed. But the tragedy was the children. Two of them were struck down for each grown-up person, and perished with the speed of plucked flowers. . . . It was another kind of peril from that which old folk remembered in the year '10, for no pox attended it nor any of the usual sores. The ordinary first symptom was a blinding headache and a high fever ; then came a swelling of the throat and glands and a quick delirium. But in many cases there was no outward swelling ; the mischief seemed to descend straightway to the lungs and produce a severe hæmorrhage. In such cases there was no final delirium ; the patient died with clear mind and little bodily pain in an extreme languor. The first type commonly seized the young and full-bodied ; children and old folk followed, as a rule, the second course. But both were fatal: in a week out of fifty-nine smitten, fifty-nine were dead.

There was no doctor to be had in all the countryside. The leech at Kirk Aller, sent for by David, refused to come within a mile of Woodilee, and the old women, the usual medical authorities of the village, had nothing but senseless concoctions and—in secret—more senseless charms. Presently even these were forgotten and the place lay in a stupor of fear under a visitation from Heaven. Cottages which the pest had entered were by popular consent shut to the world, so that they became a hot-bed of infection for the other inmates. A man who had sickness in his dwelling dare not show his face in the street except under cover of night. There was no neighbourly assistance asked or given. The members of a stricken family had to conduct their life in a dreadful isolation, till they too sickened; there were shuttered dwellings where life was slowly blotted out, and the village only learned that the end had come for all by the fact that the chimney ceased to smoke. . . . At first an attempt was made to bury the dead decently, the remaining members of a household undertaking the task, but the spread of the pestilence soon made this impossible. The dead were laid in byre and stable beside the startled beasts, sometimes by the poorer households in the kailyard, and David more than once found a staring unshrouded corpse in the nettles of the manse loan. There were cottages where all the inmates were dead and unburied, with a lean cat mewing round the barred doors. . . . And all the while the soft blue weather continued, and the wind came balmy from the hills over those silent fields of death.

At first the stupor of Woodilee was shot with an awful apprehension of divine wrath, and the people sought to propitiate their Maker by humbling themselves before Him, and—even the least devout—by constant prayer and the reading of Scripture. But this mood did not long survive. The fury of the blast which smote them drove all religion out of their minds, and left them stark and numb with mortal fear. To begin with, David was welcomed in the house of death, he was summoned in haste, his coming was watched for; even if his ministrations did no good to the unconscious sufferers they seemed to comfort the others. But presently he found himself an unregarded intruder. Whenever he knew of a case he hastened to it, but the panic-stricken eyes of the living looked at him as blindly as the glazing eyes of the dying. His prayers even to himself seemed idle; at any rate they fell upon dulled ears. What contact could he establish with the sick in the delirium or languor of death, and with those who waited on the same fate with the wild despair of beasts in a trap? What use to point to God when God overshadowed them as a merciless tormentor? And all the while he was in a fever of anxiety. More than one of the dead were among those whom he had remarked in the Wood. Men and women were hastening to judgment with their sins heavy on them—sins unrepented and for ever unrepentable. He, their minister, had to stand feebly by and see souls descending into damnation.

The thought drove him frantic, but it alone gave him power to continue in his fruitless duties, for in this trial he found the flesh very weak. It was not that he feared death, even death by plague, but that a horror of Woodilee had fallen on his spirit. His shrinking from the Wood, his hatred of the sins of the Wood, his quarrel with the Session, the distrust in which he was held by many of his congregation, the episode of the pricker and Bessie Todd's death—all combined to make the place reek for him of ugliness and decay. The pest seemed merely to add rotting carcasses to rotting souls. . . . Then the pity of it would overcome him, when he thought of children whom he had taught and honest folk who had been kind to him, now cold in death. He was helpless to cure either body or spirit. He had no leechcraft—what would it have availed if he had, for he remembered the Edinburgh doctor by his father's bed?—and his spiritual ministrations were as idle as wind. . . . Above all he felt himself a prisoner shut into a noisome cage from which there was no escape. None dare leave or enter Woodilee. One afternoon in a mood of despair he climbed the Hill of Deer for a glimpse of the outer world. There lay Calidon on its windy braes, but Calidon was now as distant for him as the moon. There lay the hills in whose spacious wildernesses no pest lurked, for there were no unclean mortals to harbour it, and beyond them was the world where men might live in daylight and honour. As he looked down on Woodilee a haze seemed to lie over it. Was it the effluvia of the plague, a miasma which walled it round more impenetrably than stone walls and iron shutters? . . . He struggled to conquer his shrinking. "Faithless servant," he told himself, "faithless even over a few things! David Sempill, you rebel against the Lord's will not because of the sufferings of your poor folk, but because of your own pitiable discomfort. Think shame, man, to be such a whingeing bairn." For he had realized that the root of his trouble was that he was severed from Katrine.

But that evening Katrine came to him.

While he sat for a little in his study before starting on his melancholy visits, he heard Isobel's voice below high-pitched in excitement. Then he heard another voice which took him down the stairs three steps at a time. The girl, booted as he had seen her in the mist on the eve of Hallowmass, stood in the light of Isobel's candle, one gloved hand raised in protest and with an embarrassed smile at her lips and eyes. To David it seemed the first smile that he had seen for an eternity.

"Awa' hame wi' ye, my leddy," Isobel cried. "Ye canna come here, for the pest's in ilka bite we eat and sowp we drink and breath we draw. Awa' wi' ye, an' keep your mouth tight steekit till ye're ower the Hill o' Deer. Oh, haste ye, or ye'll be smitten like the lave, and ye're ower young and bonny to dee."

"Katrine, Katrine," David exclaimed in agony. "What madness brought you here? Have you not heard that half the parish is sick or dead? There is poison in the very air. Oh, my dear, come not near me. Wrap a fold of your cloak over your mouth and never slacken rein till you are back in Calidon."

The girl drew off her gloves. Her eyes were on Isobel.

"I am his promised wife," she said. "Where should I be if not by his side?"

The news left Isobel staring. "His promised wife!" she stammered. "Heard ye ever the like—the manse o' Woodilee to seek a mistress from Calidon! . . . But the mair reason why ye suld tak' tent. There's nae place for a bonny doo like yersel' in this stricken parish —ye canna help ithers and ye may get your ain death. Awa' hame, my braw leddy, for the minister has eneuch to trouble him without concern for his joe."

The girl walked to David's side and put her hand in his arm.

"You will not forbid me," she said, and her face was still smiling. "I do not fear the plague, and I do not

think it will harm me, for it smites those who live in
foul hovels and I am always about the hills. But I do
fear this loneliness. I have not seen you for two weeks,
David, and I have been imagining terrible things. I
have come to help you, for I have known the pest
before—many times in France, and in Oxford too. I
know what precautions to take, for I have heard wise
men discuss them, but you in Woodilee from all I hear
are no better than frightened bairns."

"But your aunt—Mistress Saintserf——"

"Aunt Grizel knows of my coming. She has given
me this pomander of spices." She touched a trinket
which hung from her neck by a gold chain.

David struggled to salve his conscience by energy in
dissuasion, and though his heart cried for her presence
it was torn too by fear for her safety. He commanded,
pled, expostulated, but she only turned a smiling face.
She sat down before the peat-fire and stretched out her
feet to the hot ashes.

"You will not drive me away, David," she said.
"Would you forbid me from a work of necessity and
mercy—and you a minister?"

In the end he gave up the task, for here was a resolution stiffer than his own, and his strongest arguments
faltered when he saw her smile, which was like sunlight
in a world of darkness and grim faces. He found himself telling her how the plague had begun and of the
nature of its course—the lack of leeches and medicines,
the dearth of helpers, the households perishing silently
indoors. She listened calmly, and did not blanch even
at the tale of the shuttered cottages and the unburied
dead.

"A pretty mess your folk have made of it," she said.
"You have turned Woodilee into a lazar-house and

given the pest a rare breeding-ground. Never mind
your spiritual consolations, David. Let the miserable
bodies come before the souls. You say you have no
leech to cure the sick, and that maybe is as well, for I
never yet heard of leech that could master the plague.
But if you cannot cure, you may prevent its spread.
Our first task is to safeguard those who are not yet
smitten. If you shut up a cottage where there is one
sick man, you condemn every member to death. That
must be stopped without delay—and for God's sake let
us bury the dead—bury or burn."

"Burn ? " he cried out aghast.

"Burn," she nodded. "Fire is the best purifier."

"But we shall rouse the place to madness."

"Better that than death. But we want helpers—
bold men who fear neither the pest nor an angry people."

He shook his head. "There are none such in Woodilee. The bones of all are turned to water."

"Then we must stiffen them. . . . There is the one
whom we now call Mark Riddel. It was he who told
me of your trouble, for he was at Calidon yesterday on
his way back from Annandale. There is the black-
avised man, too, at Reiverslaw. . . . Are there none
more ? "

The girl's briskness was rousing David's mind from
its torpor.

"Amos Ritchie, maybe."

"That gives us three—four with yourself—and four
resolved men can do wonders. Others will fall in once
the drum is beaten. Rouse yourself, David, and be as
eager to save bodies as you ever were to save souls.
And do not forget to pray for a change in this lamentable
weather. A ringing frost would do more to stay the
pest than all the leeches in Scotland. . . ."

She departed as suddenly as she had come. "I dare not come by day," she told him, "for if Woodilee heard of a stranger its panic would be worse. We have to do with terrified bairns. But I will be here at the same hour to-morrow night, and by that time you must have gathered your helpers."

David did not return from his visitations till the small hours, but he brought back the first piece of good news. One of the hinds at the Mains, after lying for two days in delirium, was now quit of the fever and in a wholesome sweat—sleeping, too, a natural sleep. It was the first case of a possible recovery, and he was aware how much a single life saved would do to quiet the broken nerves of the parish. Also Katrine's advent had lifted him out of the slough of despond in which he had been sunk for weeks. She had spurred him to action, and shown him a duty which he had been too blind to see. He fiercely repressed the anxiety with which the mere thought of her presence in that tainted place filled him. He dare not forbid the exercise of courage in another—even in one who was dearer to him than life.

Next morning he went to Reiverslaw, but got no comfort. Andrew Shillinglaw met him out of doors, and made it very clear that he had no desire to come too near him. The conversation was conducted at a distance of a dozen yards.

"Na, na," he cried. "I'm off this verra day to Moffat, and I'll no set foot in Woodilee till the pest has gane. Ye ask ower muckle, Mr. Sempill. It's maybe *your* duty to gang among them—though ye ken as weel as me that the haill parochine is no worth the life o' a tinkler's messan—but it's no duty o' Andra Shillinglaw's. I never could abide the reek o' the folk, and they have doubtless gotten what they deserved."

"Ay, I'm feared," he admitted in answer to David's appeals. "Ilka body has something that puts the grue on him, and with me it's aye been the pest. I'll face steel and pouther, angry men and angry beasts, but I'll no face what gars a man dee like a ratton in a hole. And what for should I face it for folk that are no a drap bluid's kin to me?"

The man spoke loudly and violently, as if a little ashamed of himself, and went into the house, where David could hear the bar falling.

From Amos Ritchie he had a different answer. Amos since his wife's death had gone about with bent shoulders and a grey face and had sat for long hours in his smithy beside a dead fire. There David found him and propounded his request.

"I'll do your will, sir," was the answer. "I've sae little left to live for that I've the less to fear. But there'll be need o' mair than you and me, for the parish is dementit, and daft folk are ill to guide. The first thing is to get the deid buried. For God's sake dinna speak of burnin', for though the body is but our earthly tenement, burnin' is ower like the Deil's wark."

That night Katrine came again, and with her Mark Riddel. The soldier had lost something of his bluff composure, and a troubled eye met David's.

"I have been listening to a sermon on courage," he said ruefully.

Katrine pointed a mocking finger at him.

"He would run away," she said, "he the old soldier of a hundred battles."

"'Deed and I would. A hundred battles, nor a thousand battles, wouldna reconcile me to the pest. I could name you many a bold captain who at the rumour of pestilence shifted his leaguer, though he would have held his ground before all the Emperor's armies. But it seems I must take my orders from this child, when I hoped to slip off cannily to a cleaner countryside. . . . Ugh, Katrine, my dear, I wish you had set me an easier task than to sweep the midden of Woodilee and turn sexton."

"It's an armed and mailed sexton you must be," she said. "You may have to put reason into the folk with the flat of your sword. Comfort yourself, Mr. Mark, this task is not so much unlike that you were bred to."

The soldier grew visibly more cheerful when he heard that there were only three volunteers for the business. "There's trouble brewing, then," he said, "and it's God's mercy that I've won a certain respect in the parish, for it looks as if more persuasion would be needed than a good word and a clap on the back. When do we start our dowie job, for I confess I would sooner be at it than thinking of it ? "

"A lean man like you, all bone and whipcord, need not fear," said David.

"Tut, man," said Mark impatiently, "fear is not in the question. My trouble is that I've a nice stomach and a fastidious nose. Death, whether it comes by pest or steel, is the same to me, and that's a thing worth less than a strae. . . . God's curse on this weather ! . . . To work, Mr. David, or I'll be rueing my bargain."

For three days and nights the three men wrought at their repulsive task with niggardly intervals for food and sleep. They made a list of the stricken houses and forced their way into them, even when the doors were bolted. The dead were buried—some in the kirkyard, some in near-by fields, and this duty fell especially on Amos Ritchie, who performed it with dogged fidelity. Now and then there was trouble—a crazed wife or

mother would refuse to part with the body of a husband
or child, and in some cases the minister had to intervene
with stern appeals. More difficult was the business of
keeping houses, where the sick lay, open to the air and
light. David and Mark had to drive cowering sons out
of doors with threats of violence, and in some cases with
violence itself. One obstinate household had their door
smashed by Amos's axe ; another was turned neck and
crop into the byre that a sick woman might have peace
and air. The three men constituted themselves a relieving force, and had often to do the fetching of food
and water. Terrible were the sights revealed behind
many of those bolted doors and windows, and, though
Amos seemed unaffected, the other two had often to
rush to the air to check their nausea. Thanks they got
none, rarely even curses ; the miserable folk were too
sunk in despair for either. Yet it is likely they would
have failed, had not the news of recoveries got about.
Besides the hind at the Mains, two children had now
weathered the storm and were reported to be mending
fast. The communal mind of Woodilee, which up to
then had been blank fatalism and lethargy, was now
shot with gleams of hope. The pest might have worked
itself out and be on the decline : the corridor was still
long and black but there was a pinprick of light at the
end of it. . . . Also Mark Riddel in himself was a cogent
persuasion. The dark keen face and the reputation of
mystery and command which he had won at the witch-
pricking were arguments sufficiently potent, apart from
the long sword which he wore at his side. For in this
work the douce tacksman of Crossbasket had disappeared ; it was the captain of Mackay's who gave orders
and saw that they were obeyed.

By Candlemas it was clear that the tide had turned,

for there were more on the way to recovery than dying. Well it was that the change had come, for the weather now broke—not, as David had prayed, in wholesome frost, but in perpetual drenching rains. The downpour had come in an instant ; within half an hour during the night the wind had shifted, the sky had clouded, and the fall had begun. It was the night, the even of Candlemas, which the three men had chosen for their work of burning. Now that people were beginning to move about the streets again, it was essential to get rid of centres of infection, and two of the worst were cottages in the clachan where all the inmates had died. Such houses could only be purified by burning, and about ten that night fire was put to them. Dry as tinder, they blazed furiously to heaven, and there were those in the parish, dabblers in witchcraft, who must have turned scared eyes to the glow which was fiercer than any that the altar in the Wood had known. . . . But in an hour came the rain, and the murky smoke-wreaths were turned to steaming embers.

It was a proof of the returning strength of the parish that the burning of the cots startled it out of apathy. Woodilee feebly and confusedly began to take stock of things, and tongues started to wag again. The numbness of loss, the languor of fear, gave place to recrimination. Who was responsible for the calamity of the pest ? It must be a mark of the Lord's displeasure, but against whom ? They remembered that their minister lay under the ban of the Kirk—had been forbidden to conduct ordinances—was convicted of malignancy and suspected of worse. In their search for a scapegoat many fastened upon David. Practical folk said that he had been in Edinburgh in the time of plague, and had maybe brought back the seeds of it. The devout averred that the uncanny weather had followed upon his public sins, and that the pest had come close on the heels of the Presbytery's condemnation. Was there not the hand of God in this, a manifest judgment? The ways of the Almighty were mysterious and He might ordain that the people should die for the sins of one man. Even those who had been on David's side were shaken in their confidence.

To crown all, came the events of the past week. To his critics there was no reason in his doings: they believed the pestilence to be a visitation of Heaven, to be stayed not by the arm of flesh, but by fasting and prayer. He had been assiduous in his futile visiting, it was true, and he had buried the dead; but he had broken in on their suffering with violent hands, and had herded men and women like brute beasts. Doors and windows, open to the February rains, attested his methods; by his act two cottages, once snug and canty, were now grey ashes. . . . Amos Ritchie in such matters was but a tool; Mark Riddel was too much feared to be the mark of censorious tongues; but David, still their titular minister, was a predestined target.

And as the village crept back to life, and those who had escaped took heart to do a little work again, and the convalescent staggered to their doors and looked on the world, there arose stranger rumours. The minister was all day out and about—praying on occasion, but more often engaged in homely tasks like cleaning up a kitchen and boiling water for those who were too frail to help themselves. Dark looks and ugly mutterings often followed him, but he was too intent upon his work to take heed of them. The general sullenness he set down to the dregs of grief and terror. That was for the daylight hours, but—it was whispered—after nightfall he had a companion. There were stories of a woman, a creature beautiful and young, who sang in a honeyed voice, and appeared especially at the bedsides of the children. At first few credited the tale, but presently came ample confirmation. She had been seen at three houses in the clachan, at the Mirehope herd's, at the Mains ; with her had been the minister ; and the bairns to whom she had spoken cried for her return. . . . The old and wise shook their heads. There was no such woman in the parish or in all the countryside. And some remembered that the minister in the back-end had been observed to meet with a woman in the Wood, and that she had seemed to those who saw her to be no mortal, but the Queen of Elfhame.

The truth was that no commands of Mark, no protest-ations of David, could keep Katrine out of the village. She saw the reason for not appearing in the daylight, for a stranger in Woodilee—above all such a stranger as she—would have been too much for the brittle nerves of the parish. But after nightfall the case was differ-ent, and when with David she had once stood by the bed of a sick child, nothing could prevent her making a nightly duty of it. Into those sodden woeful house-holds she entered like a spring wind ; the people may have marvelled, but they were still too apathetic to ask questions, and they felt dumbly her curative power. Among unkempt pallid men and frowsy wild-eyed women the face bright with the weather, the curls dabbled with rain, the cool firm arm, the alert figure, worked a miracle, as if an angel had troubled the stag-nant waters of their life. Her hand on a child's hot brow sent it into a peaceful sleep ; her presence gave to the sick the will to live and to the fearful a gleam of courage. What they thought and said when she had gone will never be known, but for certain they longed for her coming again.

On the 18th day of February the pestilence took its last victim—an old woman, the mother of the Windyways herd, and the earth was still fresh on her grave when the rain ceased. The wind swung to the north, and the black frost for which David had longed settled on the land. It put an end to the pest, but it bore hard on the convalescent, and the older and feebler died under its rigour. In the pure cold air the taint seemed to pass from the land, and the problem of David and his helpers was now a straightforward fight with normal ailments and the normal winter poverty. Stock during the visitation had been scarcely tended, and the byres and infields were full of dead beasts; while in the general terror the customary frugality of the parish had been forgotten and many a meal-ark was empty. There was need of clothing and food, of fuel and cordials, and it did not appear where they were to come from.

There was no help to be looked for from outside, for to the neighbourhood Woodilee was like a leper settlement; none would have dared to enter the place, and had a Woodilee man shown his face in another parish he would have been driven back with stones. Mr. Fordyce managed to send to David more than one distressful letter, lamenting that for the sake of his own people he could not lend his brother a helping hand; but save for that, from the 8th day of January to the 15th day of March, there was no communication with the outer world. In this crisis Mark Riddel wrought mightily. He had ways and means of getting supplies from distant places, and his pack-horses, guided by himself or Amos Ritchie, brought meal and homespun blankets from quarters which no man knew of. David exhausted the manse stores, and Isobel kilted her coats and, with a charity seasoned by maledictions, kept her pot or girdle continually on the fire. But it was the house of Calidon that provided the main necessaries. Its brew-house and its girnel, its stillroom and its cellars, not to speak of Mistress Grizel's private cordials, were plundered for the sake of a parish which Mistress Grizel could not refer to without a sour grimace. When Katrine rode to the manse of a night she would bring with her usually a laden shelty.

The end of the plague was for David a harder season even than its height. For with convalescence Woodilee seemed to lose its wits. Before it had sat dazed and broken under the rod ; now it woke to an ardour of self-preservation. At the beginning the people seemed to be careless of infection ; now the survivors were possessed with a craze to live, and fought like terrified animals to get out of danger. They could not leave the parish bounds, but those that were able fled from the village. The leaky sheilings on the hills, occupied by the ewe-milkers during the height of summer, gave lodging to many, and several died there of the violence of the frost. The outlying farms were believed to be the safer, so Mirehope and Nether Fennan had many undesired tenants in their outhouses. The result was that, in a season of convalescence, when nursing was especially needed, the bedridden were often left deserted. David tried to enlist men and women who had either escaped the plague or had been for some weeks recovered, but he got only fierce denials or an obstinate silence. The place had become brutish, and the selfishness of beasts seemed to have become the rule of life.

21

The one exception was Chasehope. During the worst weeks the clachan had had no news of him, but it was rumoured that he had made a fortress of his farm-town, and had assiduously tended his own people. At any rate at Chasehope there had been only one death. Now he appeared in the street, and to David's amazement it was clear that he came on an errand of mercy. His house seemed still to be well provided, and he brought with him a certain amount of provender. This he did not bestow indiscriminately but only on certain families, which David guessed to contain members of the coven. To these he spoke with authority, and he used his power to put reason into the distracted.

He alone in the place seemed to have no fear of infection—to be careless of the risk which had sent panic abroad among the others. He passed the minister with a grave salutation, and showed no wish to give or ask for help ; he had some business afoot which was his private concern. But the fact stood out that this man, alone in Woodilee, had mastered fear.

Once in a cottage where a child was recovering he came upon David and Katrine. The girl was sitting on a stool by the bed making a toy out of reeds for the child's amusement, and singing a French nursery song about Cadet Roussel and his three houses. David lifted his eyes from admiring the grace and swiftness of her hands to see Chasehope's heavy white face in the glow of the firelight. The latter doffed his bonnet at the sight of Katrine, and murmured some civility. Clearly he knew her, for he picked up a reed from the floor. " Frae the Calidon mill-dam, belike," he said.

" You are the one man in Woodilee who has courage," David said. " You are no friend of mine, Ephraim Caird, but I give you the praise of a stout heart."

" Why should I be feared ? " the other asked. " Why should I dread to walk even in the valley of death if His rod and staff are there to comfort me ? "

" Why should you? But many professors are of a different mind."

" They are but poor professors, then. I fear no ill, for I am in the Lord's hand till His appointed time."

" But many who do not fear death fear to die by the pest."

" Ay, but I have my assurance. I have the Lord's own promise, Mr. Sempill. I ken as weel that no pest can touch me as that my name is Ephraim Caird and my habitation is Chasehope. It's the lack o' sound doctrine that gars folk turn cowards—they dinna lippen enough to the Lord—they havena a firm enough grip o' their calling and election. I have my compact sure, and I ken that the Lord will no gie me a back-cast. I can rejoice even in this sore affliction, for He hath demanded a sacrifice, and what is man to question His will ? Dear in His sight is the death of His saints—ay, and of sinners, too, for His judgments are not exhausted. There's mair to come, Mr. Sempill—take tent o' that, sir—the conviction is heavy on me that the wind o' His displeasure has still a blast to blaw."

The pale eyes had almost the green of a cat's in the dim light, and the bald brows above gave the whole face the air of a mask, which at any moment might slip and reveal nightmare lineaments. The child in the bed looked up as he spoke, saw his face and screamed in terror, and Katrine, after one glance behind her, was busied in crooning consolations. . . . In that moment David had a revelation. This man, secure in his election to grace, secure against common fear, was likewise secure against common reason. He was no hypocrite. To him the foulest sin would be no sin—its indulgence would be part of his prerogative, its blotting out an incident in his compact with the Almighty. He could lead the coven in the Wood and wallow in the lusts of the flesh, and his crimes would be but the greater vindication of God's omnipotence. . . . In that illuminating instant madness had looked out of his eyes.

CHAPTER XIX

THE SACRIFICE

As March drew to its close the wheels of life began once again to run creakingly in Woodilee. The frost disappeared under a week of south-westerly gales, and then the wind moved to the east and blew dry and blighting, so that the lean beasts shivered in the infields. The gross unseasonable herbage of the winter had gone, and it promised to be a backward spring. The men went out feebly to the farm-work, and the ploughing began, though the draught-oxen were so poor in condition that the work moved slowly. The siege, too, was raised. Johnnie Dow once again showed his cautious face in the clachan and brought news of the outer world; the pack-horses again struggled through Carnwath Moss; and there came word from Kirk Aller that the meeting of the Presbytery to adjudicate on David's case was fixed for a day in April. Mr. James rode over from Cauldshaw and the kirk was opened, but David did not renew his preachings at the kirkyard gate.

The truth is that he was weary to the bone. Mark Riddel met him one morning on the road and drew rein sharply at the sight of his face.

" Man, David, you're like a ghost. You've worked your body ower sore these last months, and if you dinna take care you'll be on your back. You and Katrine are two inconsiderate bairns. You've both of you done the work of ten men, and you'll no listen to wiser folk. Take my advice and get furth of this woeful parish till your body is rested and your mind quieter."

" I am summoned to my trial at Kirk Aller in a week's time."

" And that's the crown of it ! That's what you get for wearing yourself to skin and bone for a thankless folk. There are times when I scunner at my native land. There's a rumour that Montrose has escaped abroad and is now at the Emperor's court, and if it werena for you and Katrine I could find it in me to join him. There's a blight on the country which affects even a brisk heart like mine, and I'm getting mortal sick of the eternal crack of nowt and wedders."

But though Mark came to the manse every evening and would have nursed him like a mother, David could not relax the tension of body and spirit. He slept badly, and in spite of Isobel's coaxing ate little ; his nights were filled with wild dreams, and, worse, these dreams seemed to pursue him in his waking hours. He felt no special ailment of body to which he could attribute his distress, beyond an extreme fatigue. He would take long walks by day and night, but though he returned from them very stiff and weary, they did not bring him healthful sleep. He tried to master himself, to laugh at himself, but the malaise would not be expelled. . . . He was the prey of childish fears, looking nervously for something malign to come out of the dark or round the corner. And presently the barriers of the real seemed to crumble. He saw faces where there were none, he listened to voices in the deepest silence. Once, coming at night up the manse loan, he heard footsteps on the dry earth approaching him. They grew louder, passed and died away behind him, and he realized that the footsteps were his own.

A word of Chasehope's stuck evilly in his memory. The Lord had demanded a sacrifice, but the sacrifice was not yet complete, the man had said. The word tortured him and he could get no relief from thinking, for the thing was beyond thought. An oppression of coming disaster weighed on him. He told himself that his enemy had meant no more than the Presbytery trial, but he could not lay the ghost. Something darker, more terrible, hung on the skirts of his imagination. Chasehope was no doubt mad, but truth might lurk in madness ; a maniac saw that which was hidden from others. It was for Katrine that he feared, and what he feared he could not give a shape to—there lay the agony of it.

Presently his old dread of the Wood returned—that dread which he thought he had exorcised for ever. He had defied it, but what if it should prove too strong for him ? In his distraught thoughts the pestilence seemed to have come out of it—Chasehope had moved unscathed through the weeks of plague—Chasehope and the devils he served were the plague's masters. Was there some other terror still in its depths waiting to be loosed on him ? He had moments of clear-sightedness, when he despised himself for his folly, and realized that to be thus faint of heart was to acknowledge defeat and to abase himself before his enemy. But the conviction returned, stronger than will or reason, and David would walk the hill with clenched hands and muttering lips, or in his closet struggle in blind prayer for a comfort that would not come.

After Katrine's nightly visits to Woodilee had ceased the minister had meant to go daily to Calidon. But with this new mood of terror upon him he was ashamed to face the girl; and he had sufficient manhood to put restraint upon his longings. The time came, however, when anxiety conquered scruples. He rode to Calidon with a fluttering heart, an excitement rather of fear than of joy.

Mistress Saintserf faced him grimly.

"What have ye done wi' my bairn?" she demanded. "She is fair broke wi' ridin' the roads and tendin' the riff-raff o' Woodilee—and the haill parochine no worth a hair o' her heid. Christian charity, says you—but there's bounds to Christian charity! Ye're a bonny lad to tak' so little care o' your joe."

Presently she condescended to details. "She has nae strength, the puir thing—clean worn out like an auld bauchle.* Yestreen I garred her tak' to her bed, and she's lyin' as biddable as a wean, and her for ordinar' sae sweir to bide still. . . . Na, ye canna see her. But dinna fash yoursel', my man. She's no sick—just weary wi' ower heavy a task. A long lie in her bed will put her richt, and a change in this dowie weather. Pray for a bit blink o' sun. . . . Ye're lookin' gey gash yoursel'. Ye'd be nane the waur o' a week on your back."

As David rode homeward he remembered the last words and laughed at their irony. A week in bed, when he could scarcely endure three hours in a night! Mistress Saintserf's news had put him into an agony of apprehension. He stabled his horse and set out to work off his anxiety by bodily fatigue, but it grew with every mile he walked. Weariness, he told himself, was only natural after such a winter's toil; was not he himself worn out, and did not even Mark Riddel con-

* Shoe.

fess to a great fatigue? But he could not console himself with such thoughts. At any moment she might fall into a fever, and then—he remembered with dreadful distinctness the stages of the malady. Was this the last lingering effort of the pest?—he had heard of such cases coming weeks after the thing seemed to have been stayed. And always there rose in his mind Chasehope's prophecy of a sacrifice still to come.

He would fain have gone back to Calidon and waited for news. Instead he sent Isobel with a message to Mistress Grizel. His housekeeper was noted as a skilful nurse and an amateur leech, and he begged that she should be allowed to help in waiting upon Katrine. The sending of her did something to ease his mind, for it was a direct piece of service to his beloved; moreover, if Isobel was in Calidon he could go there as often as he wished and have speech with her, for he was a little ashamed to reveal to Mistress Grizel his lack of fortitude. Meantime he could fend for himself, and cook what food he needed.

The time passed on leaden feet and the hours of darkness were one long sleepless nightmare. Next day he was early at Calidon and found Isobel with a composed face. "Ye needna tak' it sae sair, Mr. David," she assured him. "The leddy's no that bad. Nae doot she's sair weary, but the feck o' the time she sleeps like a bairn, and there's nae fever. There's strong bluid in her that will no be lang ere it conquers the weakness. But losh, sir, ye've the face o' a bogle. Awa' hame wi' ye and lie doun, or I'll no bide anither hour in Calidon. Are ye takin' your meat? Dinna look at me like a glum wean, but dae as I tell ye."

David returned to the manse, and under the influence of Isobel's cheerfulness fell asleep in his chair and slept till the late afternoon. He awoke freshened in body, but with a new alarm at his heart. Isobel had said there was no fever, but that meant that she dreaded fever. . . . By this time it might have come. Even now Katrine might be delirious. . . . He realized how swiftly during the pest fever had succeeded listlessness.

Nevertheless the hours of sleep had given him a greater power of self-control, and he curbed his instinct to ride forthwith to Calidon. He wandered through the house and out into the glebe, striving to fix his mind on small and homely things. It was the third day of April, but there was no sign of spring. The dislocation of the seasons had given the earth an autumnal air, for the shoals of fallen leaves lay as if it were November, and the frosts had not bleached the herbage. He remembered how a year ago at this time he had wandered on the hills and felt with joy the stirrings of new life. To-day the world was still clamped in bonds, and death was in the bare trees and the leaden sky. What had become of his high hopes ? All gone save one— and that the dearest. A year ago he had had no thought of Katrine and had been happy in other things. Now these had been turned into ashes, but he had got Katrine in their stead. If she were to go—— ? The thought so chilled his heart that he fled indoors, as if in the house he could barricade himself against it.

In his study he turned over his books. He tried to pray, but set prayer was idle, for every breath he drew had become an impassioned supplication. He had out his notes on Isaiah and the prolegomena which he had completed, but his eyes could scarcely read them. How small and remote these labours seemed ! Every now and then a quotation from the prophet stood out in his manuscript, and these were as ominous as a raven's croaking. *Burning instead of beauty . . . Their faces shall be as flames . . . Through the wrath of the Lord of hosts is the land darkened, and the people shall be as the fuel of the fire . . . This is the rest wherewith ye may cause the weary to rest.*

He turned from his notes in awe and took up his secular books. One he opened at random and saw that it was the *Aeneid*, and the words which caught his eyes were " manibus date lilia plenis." Small wonder that the book had opened there, for it was a well-thumbed passage ; but he shuddered as if he had cast the *sortes Virgilianæ* and had got a doleful answer.

In the evening he found himself some food, and since the dark was full of ghosts for him he lit many candles and banked up the peats on the fire. He was in a strange mood, rapt out of himself, suffering not so much pain in his thoughts as a fever of expectation. His fingers drummed ceaselessly on his knees ; as he looked into the glowing peats he saw forms and figures that seemed to mock him ; to his unquiet ears a wind was blowing round the house—a wind that talked— though the night was very still. And always there was in his head, like the refrain of a ballad, the words " Burning instead of beauty."

He did not see Mark Riddel till the man was beside him and had touched his shoulder. Then he started up with a cry and encountered a grave, perturbed face.

" You had better come to Calidon," Mark said. " Katrine . . . she has taken a turn for the worse. She has been in a fever since midday."

It was the news he had been expecting, and David rose obediently.

" I'll go on foot," he said. " I can run faster than any horse. "

Mark looked at him anxiously. "You'll do no such thing. You'd faint or you were across the Hill o' Deer. Bide where you are and I'll saddle your beast."

The two set off at a gallop, but in the rough parts of the road Mark slackened and took David's bridle. "Hold up," he cried. "It'll no mend matters if you break your neck."

David asked only one question. "Have you got a leech?" he said.

"I'll have no leeches. Your country botcher would only bleed her, and she hasna the strength for that. Grizel and yon wife Isobel are all the leeches that are needed, and I'm not without skill myself. Keep up your heart, David. All is no tint yet, and it's a young life."

At Calidon gate David spoke again. "Is it the pest?"

"I canna tell, for the pest has many shapes to it. Weakness and fever—there's no other signs, though God kens that's bad enough."

He was taken straight to her chamber by Isobel, and found there Mistress Grizel, a silent, stern-faced guardian. Katrine lay tossing in high delirium, moaning a little, and moving her arms feebly on the coverlet. A bandage of wet cloths was on her brow, and as David laid his hand on it he felt the pulse of the fever beneath. Her long dark lashes lay on her flushed cheeks, but every now and then her eyes would open in a glassy stare. He took her hand and it was dry and burning.

"We maun let the fever rin its course," said Mistress Grizel. "She maun fecht her ain battle without the help o' man. God be kind to my bairn," and she kissed the hot lips.

"Ye'll be puttin' up a prayer?" she turned to David.

"I cannot pray . . . I can only watch. . . . I beg you to let me watch here beside her."

"Have your way. There's little need o' speech if there be prayer in the heart. Isobel will get ready your chamber, for ye canna leave this house."

Presently David was in the sickroom alone, and if he could not pray he spent the hours on his knees. Isobel and Mistress Grizel returned from time to time; once Mark came and put his hand on the girl's brow. The night passed and the dawn came, but still David knelt at a chair by the bedside, his head sometimes in his hands and sometimes lifted to gaze at the face on the pillow. He was tortured with the sense of his frailty. A sacrifice, another sacrifice, was required, and for what sins but his own? He had been lacking—oh, he had been lacking in every Christian grace. In those black moments he saw himself as the chief of sinners, his struggles to rise foiled by a dragging weight of self, his ardours half-hearted, the fruits he brought forth but poor pithless stalks, his errors dark and monstrous like birds of night. He was not conscious of any special sin—only of a deep unworthiness which made him unfit to touch the hem of her garment. . . . Had ever any one so made music in the world by merely passing through it? And now—burning instead of beauty. . . .

Mr. Fordyce came over from Cauldshaw in the evening. He spoke to David but got no answer—it may be doubted if his words were understood. But an invitation to follow him in prayer was rejected, so Mr. James prayed alone—"for Thy handmaiden who is in the pangs of a great sickness—and for him Thy servant to whom her welfare is especially dear." The prayer seemed to David to make an enclosure for Katrine and himself apart from the world. . . .

Mark took him to his room and made him lie down on his bed. He gave him a bowl of spiced ale which David drank greedily, for he was very thirsty. Maybe the posset contained some innocent drug, for he slipped into dreams. They were pleasant dreams, shapeless and aimless, but with a sense of well-being in them which soothed him, so that he woke to Mark's pressure on his arm with a vacant smile. But one glimpse of the real world—the corner of a four-post bed, torn arras, and the skirts of Mark's frieze coat—brought down on him the dark battalion of his cares. He had no need to wait for the spoken word ; Mark's eyes were message enough.

" Come ! The fever has abated," were the words.

David's brain was sluggish : the words seemed to be at variance with the speaker's face ; for a moment he had a bewildered spasm of comfort.

" She is recovered ? "

" She is dying," said Mark. " It is now the afternoon. She is going out with the daylight."

The small lozenged windows, though there were two of them, lit the room faintly, for the sky was lowering and grey. Mr. Fordyce had returned, and poured out his soul at the bed-foot, but presently he grew silent like the others, for there was a hush in the room which made even the words of prayer a sacrilege. . . . The flush had gone from the girl's face, and the waxen cheeks and the blanched lips told of a mortal weakness. Her hand was in David's, as passive as a plucked flower. The lashes were quiet on her cheeks, and her faint, difficult breathing scarcely stirred the coverlet.

In that final hour peace of a kind entered into David's soul. He was truly humble at last, for all the flickerings and unrest of human desires were stilled. The joy which he had scarcely dared to hope for, the possession of that

bright and rare thing, was now confirmed to him. Katrine
was securely his for ever. . . . At the very end her
eyes opened, and if they looked a little blindly at the
others they seemed to enfold him in a passion of love.
There was even the glimmer of a smile. And then the
gloaming crept round them, and, as Mark had foretold,
she went out with the daylight.

The quiet was broken by the loud wailing of the
two women, for the composure of even the iron-lipped
Mistress Grizel now failed her. Mr. Fordyce stilled it
with an uplifted hand. "The lamb is safe folded," he
said.

Mistress Grizel, after the fashion of her kind, must
speak. "She was a kind lassie and had nae thochts
but guid thochts, and if she was maybe no that weel
instructed in sound doctrine, it was nae faut in her . . .
she was aye blithe to hearken to Mr. James——" She
stopped short at the sight of David's face.

"She is now at the right hand of the Throne," he said,
"and I say that in the face of every minister that ever
perverted the Word. She was made in the image of
her Lord, and she has gone to meet Him."

Later in the evening the mind of the practical Mistress
Grizel turned to the dismal apparatus of death. "She'll
better lie in Cauldshaw in the Hawkshaw buryin' ground.
There's room in the auld vault, the mair as it's no likely
Nicholas will lay his banes there."

"Nay, but she will not lie in Cauldshaw." David's
face had a strange calm in it and his voice was toneless
and steady. "She will lie in the part of the greenwood
which was her own, in the place she called Paradise.
I know her wishes as if she had told them to me. I will

not have her laid in any kirkyard vault. . . . She is too young. . . . She is not dead but sleeping."

Mistress Grizel protested, but half-heartedly. Mr. Fordyce had little objection to raise. " It is not the way of our Kirk," he said, " to consecrate ground for the dead. All earth is hallowed which receives Christian dust. But lest the graves of the departed be forgotten, it has been the custom to gather them together in some spot under the kirk's shadow. In a wild wood among bracken and stones it will be ill to keep mind of a place of sepulchre."

" I will not forget it."

" But when you yourself are dead and gone . . . ? "

" What matters it then ? " He could have laughed at the meaninglessness of human fashions. He felt that Katrine and he were in a sphere of their own, safe for ever from intrusion, a sphere independent of time and space, even of life and death. But Paradise had been the spot where their love had first been born ; it had become in the mind a symbol and a mystery ; let Paradise therefore receive the earthly covering of the blessed spirit, for even the blessed have their terrestrial shrines.

So it came about that by night—for Mistress Grizel would not permit a ceremony so unconventional in daylight—and by the light of the torches of Jock Dodds and Edie the falconer, the girl was buried near the spring in Paradise, with David and Mr. Fordyce at the grave's head and foot.

To the former it was all a waking dream. The solid earth had become for him bodiless ; the sun's progress, human speech, rain, wind, the ritual of daily life, no more than a phantasmagoria : reality lay only in that inner world where Katrine still lived for him. He abode solitary in the manse, and refused to let Isobel return.

Indeed he begged Mistress Saintserf to keep her and be kind to her.

" 'Deed I will do that, and be glad to do it, for she's a skilly auld body and a great stand-by in the house. But, Davie, my man, what is to come o' you ? I was lookin' to get ye as a guid-son, and the Lord kens Calidon needs a man about the place—what wi' the forty thousand merks to be paid for Nicholas's fine . . ."

But she saw that her words fell on unheeding ears. David's eyes seemed to be looking beyond her to an infinite distance.

CHAPTER XX

THE JUDGMENT

DAVID rode to Kirk Aller to face the Presbytery in a blustering day of April rains. The wind blew high from the south-west in the leafless branches, and tossed the rotting leaves which should long ago have been powdered by frosts and snows. Aller was red with spate, and in the haughs the flood-water lay in leaden shallows. The birds, who should have been riotous in the bent, were few and silent; scarcely a plover or a curlew piped; only from the gnarled firs of the Wood came the croak of a nesting raven. It was a day to deaden a man's spirits, but David regarded it not. He was still in his secluded world, a chamber barred to all memories but one. He had no clear vision of the home of the blessed dead, and what he had would have been held unorthodox by the Kirk. Now he thought of her in a Platonic mood as inhabiting all things lovely and pure, a spirit as rare as the lingering light of sunset. But more often he pictured her as an embodied saint admitted into the fellowship of Christ, wrapped round with a richer love than mortals knew but reaching out warm hands to his loneliness. And the words that came to his tongue were the lines of Peter Abelard:

"O quanta qualia sunt illa sabbata
   Quæ semper celebrat superna Curia";

but the sabbaths he dreamed of were not the sabbaths of the Kirk.

The world, the tangible world, was broken for him in fragments. His chamber was not only shut to its winds, but it seemed set in a high tower from which common realities showed infinitely small and distant. The Presbytery—the General Assembly—the Kirk—seemed tiny things vanishing down the perspective of an inverted spy-glass. He was armoured against censure, for it was idle to censure one who was overwhelmed by his own unworthiness and who at the same time saw all human authorities diminished to cockle-shells. He had no fears and no hates : God had smitten him, and, humble under that awful rod, he could view with indifference the little whips of his fellows. He did not blame them— why should dust accuse dust ?

In his detachment only one thought affected him with any passion. He retained his horror of the Wood. If he were to fall he would fain have brought down with him that unholy temple. For Chasehope he felt no hatred except as its high-priest ; the man himself, with his crazy twisted soul, was rather a mark for pity. But he would fain have rid Woodilee of that incubus. . . . He had failed, and Chasehope was the victor—Chasehope and the Wood. For a moment his mind returned to realities, and he questioned himself if he had left anything undone. This day his original libel would come before the Presbytery, and he had the right to call his witnesses. But where were they ? Reiverslaw had been absent two months from the parish and had not yet returned, and without his testimony Richie Smail and Rab Prentice were meaningless voices. He could give his own witness, but that the Presbytery had already officially rejected. Let it go—the Almighty in His own

time would be his vindication—he who was filthy let
him be filthy still. . . .

> " Ubi molestiis finitis omnibus
>   Securi cantica Sion cantabimus."

But even in his secret world regret penetrated and irked
him, for Melanudrigill was nigh to the greenwood and to
Paradise.

The old kirk on the brae above the Aller bridge was
crowded to its full. Never had been so large a meeting
of Presbytery, both lay and clerical, for the case of the
minister of Woodilee had made a great talk all winter
in the glens. Woodilee itself, now purged of its taint,
was strongly represented by four members of Session,
and in a prominent place at the Moderator's elbow sat
Ephraim Caird. As David entered heads were averted,
but as he advanced to the seat prescribed for him he
found that Mr. Fordyce was his neighbour—Mr. Fordyce
heavily muffled in his ancient plaid, and with a face
whose ordinary sick pallor seemed to be flushed with a
timid excitement. He seized David's hand, and his own
was hot and nervous, and his lips moved as if he were
praying under his breath.

The forty-third Psalm was sung, there were two
lengthy readings of Scripture, and then Mr. Muirhead,
the Moderator, constituted the Court and prayed for
guidance. David's attention wandered, though he tried
to supplement the public supplication with his own. . . .
His eyes seemed to have become distorted and the whole
assembly had gone crooked. The fathers and brethren
were no more than a gathering of death's heads, their
voices were like the creaking of wheels and the scraping
of boughs and the grinding of stones. The Moderator's
massive visage was the mask behind which his brain

ticked small and foolish like a clock. The minister of Bold was only a child, a petted, noisy child. The grave countenances around him seemed shot with fear and confusion ; almost it seemed he could look into their hearts and see terrors and jealousies writhing like coils of worms. . . . He rubbed his eyes and forced himself to attention. The Moderator was speaking of the charge against Chasehope and others anent the Wood.

" We have your written libel, Mr. Sempill," he said. " It is your right to implement it by the calling of witnesses. Have you them here ? "

" My principal witness, Andrew Shillinglaw in Reiverslaw, has left the parish because of the pest and is not yet returned. Without him I can do nothing." David's voice, to his own surprise, came out full and clear.

" Do you seek a postponement ? "

David shook his head. " What boots it ? The Lord will judge the wickedness in His own time and in His own way. But I would ask that the matter be put to him whom I have accused as principal, and that he deny or affirm it on his solemn oath."

" You hear that, Ephraim," said Mr. Muirhead. " I'm loth to put such a task on one of your noted godly walk, but it would maybe conduce to the satisfaction of the Court if you would formally and finally give these monstrous charges a solemn denial."

Chasehope rose and called his Maker to witness that there was no word of truth in the accusation. His voice was steady, his expression of a decent gravity. He looked towards David, and there was not a quiver in the large placidity of his face.

" The Court is content," said Mr. Muirhead. " Have you anything to add, Mr. Sempill ? "

" The Lord will yet judge between us," said David.

"That matter can therefore be dismissed," said the Moderator in a voice in which solemnity wrestled with satisfaction. "We proceed to the charges against our unhappy brother."

He set forth—not unfairly—the counts against David. The principal was that abetting of malignancy with which the Court was already familiar, and which David had admitted and justified. But he added new matter.

"It has come to my knowledge," he said, "through the praiseworthy vigilance of our friend Chasehope, that there is further incriminating evidence on this score. In the recent melancholy visitation at Woodilee, our brother was guilty of strange deeds and in strange company. It seems that he harled the poor folk out of their bits of dwellings, on the plea that when they crept together they fomented the pest. Thereby it is alleged he spread the taint of the malady, and sorely troubled many a death-bed. Further, he violently and wrongfully broke open doors that were barred to him and set fire to cothouses where the sick had lain, thereby destroying gear which was not his and depriving the folk of their lawful habitations. I have here an attested statement setting forth the wrongs complained of. What answer do you make to that, Mr. Sempill?"

"I admit the acts, and reply that by their means and by God's mercy the pest was stayed."

There was a murmur of disapproval throughout the gathering, and Mr. Muirhead cast up his eyes to Heaven.

"More of this sinful pride! As if the hand of the Lord was stayed by breaking in the doors and burning the thack of honest folks' houses! But these are matters which are properly for the civil courts, and do not come within the cognizance of this Presbytery. What deeply concerns us is the company in which it is alleged that these acts were done. Mr. Sempill had as his helper one Amos Ritchie, a dweller in Woodilee, of whom I had hoped better things, and one Mark Riddel, a new-come tenant of the mailing of Crossbasket. We have had news of this Riddel before. He took a leading part in defending a woman accused of witchcraft in the back-end, and—though it seems that the witch-pricker was a poor creature with some irregularities in his conduct—yet it cannot be denied that the words and doings of the man Mark Riddel on that occasion gave great offence to godly folk in Woodilee and led to the just suspicion that he himself had meddled with unlawful matters. . . . Who think you that this Riddel turns out to be ? Who but that Mark Kerr that was a colonel with Montrose and a notorious malignant and has been sought all winter by the arm of the law. Chasehope has riddled out the whole black business, and has those that will swear to the man. Information has been dispatched to the Procurator-Fiscal, and it's like that by this time hands will have been laid on him."

" I fear that he has gotten clean away," said Chasehope. " The word this morn was that there was no reek in the Crossbasket lum."

" He'll no gang far," said the Moderator, " for the countryside will be up against him. Now, Mr. Sempill, what say you on this count ? Did you ken the true nature of this man Mark Riddel ? "

" I knew that he had been a soldier of Montrose. What mattered his past if he were willing to help in a work of Christian duty ? "

" Christian duty ! " The Moderator's face crimsoned with wrath. " The words should choke in your throat, sir. You dare to call it Christian duty to harry the living and perplex the dying for some whim of your own ignorant heart? You found a yoke-fellow worthy of you. It is borne in on me that you and your presumption and your slackness of walk and doctrine have been the cause of this sore dispensation in Woodilee. Upon your head, sir, lie the deaths and sufferings of your afflicted people."

He checked himself with an effort and proceeded in a calmer tone.

"No evidence need be called on the main counts, for they have been admitted by the panel. By his own confession David Sempill, lately ordained minister of the Gospel in Woodilee, is guilty of the grievous sin of consorting with and abetting the declared enemies of Christ's Kirk in Scotland. Under the specious plea of charity—whilk is a favourite device of the Enemy to delude mankind—he has given shelter to one whose hands were red with the blood of the saints, and has endeavoured to cumber the work of purging the accursed thing from our midst. Moreover, he has lately shown what was in his heart by further and intimate converse with the ungodly. I do not speak of other errors, of harsh and un-Christian conduct towards his congregation, of lack of judgment, and of a weakness in doctrine, whilk, if not actual heresy, is its near neighbour. I deal with the gravamen of the matter, a sin openly committed and indeed acknowledged and gloried in."

Mr. Muirhead pursed his lips, and a sigh of approval rose from his hearers.

"But it is needful at all times," he went on, "to temper mercy with justice. Our brother is young and has no doubt been led astray by evil conversation and by over-much carnal learning. There is yet room for repentance, and the Kirk is merciful to the penitent. If he will make full confession of his sins and renounce and abhor them and humbly seek forgiveness from an

offended Jehovah, this Court will doubtless be prepared
to deal tenderly with him. It would not consist with
decency that he continue in the charge of Woodilee, but
the matter of excommunication might be dispensed
with. For let him understand clearly that if he persists
in his contumacy he will be outcast not only from the
ministry of Woodilee but from membership of the Kirk
of Christ."

His voice had become sensibly gentler. If his main
object was to avoid too great a scandal in the Church,
there may have been a spice of pity for the youth and the
haggard face of the accused.

" I acknowledge myself most heartily to be the chief
of sinners," said David.

" There must be more than a general confession," said
the Moderator. " You must condescend upon the trans-
gression. You must in this place confess the heinous-
ness of your guilt on the precise counts I have expounded,
admit your grievous errors and your abhorrence of them,
and humbly submit yourself to judgment."

" Nay," said David. " I cannot admit that to be sin
which I hold to have been my duty."

Again from the assembly came a sound like sighing,
but now it seemed to have a note of wrath in it, as if
the breath came through clenched teeth. The Moderator
shut his eyes as if to ward off an unbearable spectacle.
Then he looked down on David with his brows drawn
so that they made a line bisecting his great face.

" Man, man," he said, " you are far from Christ.
You confess your sin, but you hug to your bosom one
darling iniquity which you proclaim a grace. You are
blinded and self-deluded, and I see no hope for you in
this world or the next. You are an outcast from the
commonwealth of Israel."

He inclined his head to Chasehope, who had plucked at his arm and now said something in his ear.

"I am reminded," he went on. "Malignancy is not all the sum of the sins of this unhappy man. There was a charge which I had hoped there would be no need to press, but which in his condition of resolute impenitence I am bound to bring forward. He was seen in the back-end to frequent the Black Wood in the company of a woman, and it is alleged—nay, it can be proved by many witnesses—that in his doubtful work during the time of pestilence a woman was in his company. To public sins he would seem to have added private lusts. Answer me, sir, as you will answer some day to your Maker, who and what was the woman, and where is she to be found?"

The words scarcely penetrated to David's brain, for he had already slipped away from the crowd of moody faces to his secret world. But in the hush that followed ths question another voice spoke, a voice high-pitched and tremulous but as startling as a trumpet.

"She is with the angels in Heaven." Mr. Fordyce had dropped his plaid from his shoulders, and stood up with raised arm, his eyes burning in his pale face. His repute as a saint was so well established that at any time he would have commanded silence, but now he spoke in a quiet so deep that his hearers seemed to be frozen in their seats. Even the Moderator stopped in the act of settling his bands, and his hand remained at his throat.

"I will speak and not be silent," said the voice. "The woman whom you would accuse with your foul tongues is this day with her Lord in Paradise. Well I kenned her—she was Katrine Yester and she abode at Calidon—there was none like her for gentleness and

grace. She was the promised wife of David Sempill—
and in the time of calamity she left her bien dwelling
and her secure life and wrought among the poor folk
of Woodilee—ay, as Christ left His Father's house to
succour sinful men. . . . She is far ayont us for ever-
more, and in the New Jerusalem she will be so near the
Throne that blessed will I be if I get a glimpse of her."

The words—which when remembered later were accounted a horrid blasphemy—cast at the moment a
strange spell over his hearers. The hush was broken by
many turning their heads, as if they could not endure
the sight of that prophetic face. Even the Moderator
dropped his eyes ; Chasehope stared at the speaker with
half a smile on his lips.

" Fools, fools ! " the voice went on. " I have been
ower long silent because of the infirmities of my flesh.
One came among you preaching Christ and you have
stoned him, as the Jews stoned Stephen outside the walls
of Jerusalem. I pray that it may be given him, like
Stephen, to see the heavens open and the Son of Man
standing on the right hand of God. . . . I tell you that
there's those among us now that will burn in Hell for
this day's work. Blind, blind . . ."

He choked, his face coloured with a rush of blood,
he swayed and would have fallen had not David caught
him. The cessation of the haunting voice restored the
assembly to its senses. Murmurings began, and the
Moderator dropped his hand from his throat and found
speech.

" This is most unseemly. Our brother is sick and has
forgotten himself. Let the work of the Court proceed."

David lifted the half-fainting Mr. Fordyce in his arms.
He bowed to the Moderator. " My presence is no
longer needed," he said. " I have no more to say and

am in the hands of the Court.   Meantime I must look
to my friend."

He left the kirk with his burden.

He took him to the little inn in the Northgate and
put him to bed.   The landlady was a kindly soul and
promised to tend him well ; there was no serious illness
—excitement and emotion and an unaccustomed effort
had drawn heavily upon Mr. Fordyce's small reserve
of strength—he needed only rest to be himself again.
David found a Cauldshaw man just setting off up the
water and sent by him a message to ease the mind of
Mrs. Fordyce, and tell her that her husband would return
on the morrow.   When he left him he was sleeping.

This business occupied his time till late afternoon,
and gloaming had already set in before he rode out of
Kirk Aller.   The Presbytery business was long since
concluded and the kirk on the brae was vacant and
locked.   The members had departed, for the yard of the
Cross Keys, which in the morning had been like a horse-
fair, was now empty.   The wind, which had been growing
in violence all day, had now reached the force of a gale,
and as David turned the corner above the gorge where
the Aller breaks from the hills into the haugh, it met him
full in the face.   He pulled his hat low on his head and
looked back.   The little town, very bleak and grey in
the chill April evening, lay smoking with its hundred
chimneys.   The sight affected him with a painful regret.
It seemed a last look upon the life from which he was
now an outcast, a life which eighteen months ago he had
so warmly embraced.

He was coming out of his abstraction now and looking
at cold realities.   Mr. Fordyce's outburst in the Presbytery had shattered his secret world.   Katrine was in

bliss and he was left alone on the bare roads of earth.
Very solitary he felt ; his father was dead, Mark Riddel
was a fugitive, Reiverslaw had failed him, his Church
had cast him out ; there was no place for him, it seemed,
in all the habitable globe, no work to his hand, no
friend to lean on.   He was looking at life now in a light
as bleak as that April day which was now vanishing
from the hills. . . . He seemed to have lost the power
of feeling.   He had no grudge against his enemies, no
hatred even for Chasehope ; his humility had become
so deep that it was almost the abnegation of manhood.
He was very tired and had lost the will to contend.
" Katrine, Katrine ! " his heart cried.   " I'm not wanted
on earth, and there's no comfort here for the comfortless.
O my love, that I were with you ! "

The night grew colder as it advanced, and the wind,
which commonly he welcomed, now cut him to the bone.
He drew his cloak round him, and tried to urge his horse
to a better pace.   But apathy seemed to have fallen
on beast as well as on master, and it jogged funereally,
as if in no hurry to leave the chilly out-of-doors for the
manse stable.   There was a moon behind the flying
rack of the sky, and there was light enough to see the
dark huddle of the hills.   Only where the track dipped
to the trees by the riverside was there any depth of
shadow.

It was in one such patch of blackness that David
heard the sound of a horse behind him.   Presently
the rider was abreast of him, and even in the dark it
seemed that he recognized him.   " Guid e'en to ye,
Mr. Sempill," said a voice, but a gust of wind made
it hard to recognize it.   The new-comer fell into step
beside him, and when in a minute they came out of the
trees David saw that it was Chasehope.

" You are late on the road, friend," he said.

" I had weighty business on hand," was the answer. The man was in a good humour, for he was humming a tune.

" This has been a waesome day for you, Mr. Sempill," he went on. " Ye have set yoursel' up against God's law and man's law, and ye have taken a mighty fall. I bear no malice—though weel I might if the Lord hadna gi'en me grace to forgive. What I have done in your case I have done painfully as my solemn duty. But there's pardon even for the chief of sinners, and it's not to be believed that one like yoursel' that had once a title in Christ can be cast away. Seek mercy where it is to be found, Mr. Sempill."

Chasehope spoke fast like one under the influence of drink, but the man was temperate, so it must have been some excitement of the spirit. In the dim light David could not see his face, but he knew the kind of light that was in his eye, for he had witnessed it before.

" I speak in all loving-kindness," he went on. " If ye're of the Elect, you and me will meet before the Throne. I would hold out a hand to a stumbling brother."

David made no answer, but his silence did not check Chasehope's flow, for he seemed to be burdened with that which must have vent.

" What have ye made of it wi' your railing accusations ? Bethink ye of that, Mr. Sempill. What has become o' your uncovenanted Reiverslaw, and your Glee'd Mark wi' his warlockry, and the bonny may ye trysted wi' ? Ane is vanished like a landlouper, and ane will soon ken the wuddy,* and ane is under the mools."

David spoke at last, and had the other had ears to

* Hangman's rope.

hear he might have detected a strange note in the minister's voice.

"You speak the truth. I am indeed friendless and forlorn."

"Friendless and forlorn! 'Deed that's the word. And wherefore, Mr. Sempill? Because ye have flung yoursel' against the rock o' the Elect who are secure in the Lord's hands. What said the worthy Moderator after ye had gone? He likened the Kirk to the stone spoken of in Matthew twenty-one and forty-four: 'Whosoever shall fall on this stone shall be broken: but on whomsoever it shall fall, it will grind him to powder.'"

"There was another word spoken—that some for this day's work would burn in Hell."

Chasehope laughed his rare and ugly laugh. "Hoots, man, that was just puir Mr. Fordyce, and a'body kens him. No but what he has the root o' the matter in him—but he's a dwaibly body wi' nae mair fushion than a thresh." *

"Nevertheless he spoke truly. Hell is waiting for some, and maybe this very night."

Again Chasehope laughed. "Is Saul also among the prophets?" he asked. "Who are you, a minister outed and excommunicat, that you suld take to the prophesyin'?"

"God makes use of the feeblest pipes to proclaim His will. I tell you, Ephraim Caird, that this very night judgment may overtake you."

This time Chasehope did not laugh, but moved his horse a little apart.

"Do you daur to threaten me—— ?"

"I threaten no man, but God threatens you."

* Rush.

"Awa' wi' you! I have a firm assurance. And if ye daur lift hand on me——"

"Be comforted. My hand will not be lifted."

The man seemed to recover his composure, for he edged his horse nearer and thrust forward his face.

"Ye've aye hated me. I could see it in your een the first day at the manse."

"I have never hated you. There is no man living in whose company I would rather ride this night. I love you so dearly that I would save your soul."

"You to speak of savin' souls!" Chasehope began, and then stopped. For there was something in David which struck a chill even to his excited mind. The quiet masterful voice cut into his wild gabble like iron into peat. If there was madness in the man, there was a fiercer madness in the minister, for in the last minutes David's weakness had fallen from him like rags and he had quickened to a flaming zeal. It was a flame of such heat that it burned calmly, but the glow of it, radiating from him, made the other's mere wildfire.

David spoke no further word, but a nervous restlessness came upon Chasehope. He blustered and bragged. See to what a pitch of esteem he had come from following the narrow way! And he whined. He had the frailty of all mortals, but it was atoned for by the imputed righteousness of his Redeemer. He seemed to long for a word of confirmation, and he pawed at the minister's sleeve. But no answer came, and the silence of the other began to unnerve him. His voice had a startled note, he quoted texts as if they were supplications to the stony impassiveness of his companion. When his horse stumbled and he almost collided with the minister, he cried out suddenly, as if in fear.

They had crossed Aller half a mile below Roodfoot,

and had come to the turning of the ways. The clouds had thinned and the struggling moon showed Melanudrigill before them, rising and falling like an ocean of darkness. David kept his horse's head straight for it, and Chasehope, who had been riding on his left, edged his beast across the path.

"Ye'll be for the short road. I'll gang quicker by the back o' Windyways. . . . Losh, that's an awesome wind."

"It is the wind of the Lord's anger."

"Guid e'en to ye, and God send ye a contrite heart!" Chasehope seemed to have recovered courage at the prospect of parting company.

David laid a hand on his bridle.

"Nay, you and I do not twine here. Our road lies yonder."

"Are ye daft, man?" Chasehope cried, his voice strong again. "Who are you to order a man like me?" The voice was strong, but in its shrillness was disquiet.

"I do not order you. Look in your heart and you will find the compulsion. It was not for nothing, Ephraim Caird, that we forgathered this night. The Lord ordained it, and in your marrow you know that you cannot leave me. This night we are in a closer bond than man and wife."

"Havers!" It was the last spasm of bluster, and the voice was weaker than the word. "I'll do no man's bidding. Tak' your hand from my bridle."

The hand was raised, and the other cowered to his saddle-bow, as if to avert a stroke. But the hand did not fall. Instead it gripped his arm, and the grip seemed to crush his bones.

"You fool," said the grave voice. "This night I

have the strength of ten men, for the Lord is in me. I could strike you dead if I were minded, but the command is on me that we ride together."

Chasehope's arrogance had drained out of him, but it had left some dregs of courage. He struggled to compose his voice and recover his everyday demeanour.

"Weel, since ye're so pressin' I'll do your will. There's no half a mile differ in the roads." But the words did nothing to break the spell which choked him. They were like the wry-mouthed bravado of a criminal at the gallows' foot.

No word was spoken as they crossed the haugh and skirted the Fennan Moss, but had there been any one to see he would have noted that David rode erect like a trooper, while Chasehope hung like a sack in his saddle, and that David's knee was hard pressed against the other's, as if the two were shackled.

They came to the edge of the Wood, where the road bent to the right among the pine roots towards the glen of Woodilee burn.

"We dismount here," said David, "for we cannot ride among the trees. The beasts will find their way home."

Chasehope cried out, and his voice now was strangled with terror.

"The Wud! No the Wud! Ye daurna gang there . . ." He raised his arm and would have struck, but David caught his wrist. He overbalanced himself and rolled to the ground and in a second David was beside him. The horses, alarmed by the scuffle, dashed up the track.

Fear made the man violent. He flung himself on David, but for all his weight found himself tossed down like a feather. Was this stern figure with the sinews of iron the minister whom he had despised?

The quiet voice spoke.

" You are gross and elderly and I have the exercised strength of youth. At no time could you hope to strive with me. But this night the might of the Lord is in me and I could break you like a straw. . . . You will come with me, though I have to ding you senseless and carry you."

The man scrambled to his feet and made the place echo with his cries for help. No answer came, except the flap of disturbed night birds.

" Where would ye have me gang ? " he whimpered.

" Into the Wood—to the place you know of. Ephraim Caird, this night I give you the chance of salvation. I may have erred—my eyes may have deceived me—it may not have been you that capered and piped in a dog's mask to yon lost crew. If I have been wrong, it will be proven yonder. If I have been right, you will be given a chance of repentance. We go up to the Mount together that you may choose between Abiron and Jehovah."

Chasehope crouched like a dog. " I daurna—I daurna," he wailed. " I'm a believin' man, but I daurna enter the Wud. . . . It's no the season—there's fearsome things ryngin' in't. Oh, ye dinna ken. . . . Let me gang hame and the morn I'll gang on my hunkers to Kirk Aller and sweir that a' I hae said against ye was a lee. I'll confess . . ."

David's grip was on his arm, but he did not struggle. His legs were loosened, and his whole body drooped like a creature stricken with the palsy.

" I'll make confession—I'll tell ye things that are no to be named—I took the Wud wi' ithers, but I kenned I was a redeemed soul and that the Lord wouldna cast me away. . . . I aye ettled to repent, for I was sure o' the Mercy Seat. . . . It is written that Solomon went after the abominations of Moab, and was yet numbered among the Elect. . . . But I'll hae nae mair o't frae this day. . . . I'll tak' my aith on the Word . . . I'll cast my idols ahint my back . . . I'll burn the books . . . I'll forswear the Deil . . ."

"You will do it yonder," said David.

He had never entered the Wood from this side, and in the darkness the road would have been at all times hard to find, but now he seemed to have a map in his brain and to steer by an instinct. In this backward Spring there was no sprouting undergrowth, but the dead bracken stalks had not yet shrunk to earth, and he waded waist-deep among them. The man beside him had lost the power of resistance. He followed like an obedient hound, without the need of David's grasp on his arm. Often he stumbled, and once he fell into the dell of a burn and had to be lifted out, but he made no attempt at resistance or escape. He walked and sometimes ran, crouching almost double, and as he went he made little moaning noises which might have been prayers.

The wind was wild in the tree-tops, and rushing down the aisles and corries of the hillside made a sound which was now like a great organ and now like muffled drums. Higher they mounted till they reached a broad shelf of more level ground, where the covert was thick and the speed slow. . . . And then, almost before he was aware of it, David found himself looking at an open space with a dark stone in the midst of it.

The moonlight was faint but the glade was clear in its outlines, a patch of grey turf in a ring of inky shadow. The altar was no longer white as in the summer midnight, but dark with the drenching winter rains. A bleak sodden place, it now appeared to David, a trivial place, no more than a common howe in a wood.

But the other seemed to look on it with different eyes. When he saw the stone he gave one shrill cry of terror and collapsed on the ground, burying his face in the moss as if to shut out the sight. David seized him and dragged him forward till he lay by the altar, and all the while his screams rose piercingly above the wind.

" There is no need for confession," the minister said. " You have betrayed yourself. . . . Now I know with the uttermost certainty that it was you I saw here at Beltane and at Lammas."

The man did not raise his head, but clasped David's legs and nozzled him like a fawning dog, while, like a dog, he gave short, terrified yelps.

" Your sin is proven and acknowledged," said David. " Here on the scene of your guilt you will choose your road. I say to you as Elijah said to the people of Israel, ' If the Lord be God, follow Him ; but if Baal, then follow him.' This night you renounce Abiron or renounce Christ."

The man was silent, as if the extremity of fear had frozen his speech. But as David raised him, a shuddering like an epilepsy shook his body. His legs were limp, and David placed him on his knees so that his brow rested on the stone.

" Renounce your master here in his temple . . . I will give you words if you have none of your own. . . . Say after me, ' I abhor and reject the Devil and all his works, and I fling myself upon the mercy of God.' Man, man, it is your immortal soul that trembles above the Pit."

The huddled figure was still silent. Then, after a violent shiver, his voice came back to him. He began to stutter words, words meaningless to David's ear. It may be that it was the renunciation of his gods; but, whatever it was, it was not completed.

For suddenly energy returned to his limbs and he sprang violently to his feet. Madness glowed in his eyes; his head was held for a second in a listening posture.

"They come!" he screamed. "The dogs!—the red dogs!"

David seized him, but at that moment the maniac's strength far exceeded his own. He tore himself free with a rending of his clothes. His face was a limp vacancy of terror in which the eyes glared unseeingly. He leaped into the air, spun round, fell, laid his ear to the earth, and then with incredible swiftness ran uphill from the glade. Once he halted to listen, and then, so bent that he appeared to run on all-fours, and yelping like a stricken beast, he vanished into the shades. . . . In a pause of the wind David heard his movements grow fainter, and he thought he heard too a murmur of voices as at Beltane and Lammas. It seemed to him that these voices were now like the distant baying of hounds.

Lethargy returned upon David's soul. He had done his duty, and at the last moment, like Samson, had brought down the false temple; but what signified it to one who had no further hope or purpose? He walked out of the Wood as steeled to its awesomeness as to the other common emotions of man. His heart had dried up within him, and his vitality had run down like an unwound clock. He had but the one thought— to visit Paradise again and Katrine's grave, and this not for comfort but as a step enjoined by duty to complete the heavy weight of his loneliness. After that nothing mattered. His youth was gone and he was become very old.

He crossed the barrier glen, brushed through the catkin-laden hazels, and came to his sacred glade. There was the well bubbling darkly, and there beyond it was the fresh-made mound of turf. . . . The sight melted something within him. He flung himself on the grass and his dry heart was loosened in tears. As he wept he prayed, and as he prayed he seemed to live once again the bright days when Katrine had sung to him among the flowers. Fragments of her songs came back to him:

> " There's comfort for the comfortless
> And hinny for the bee——"

Was there any comfort for a stricken man on this side of eternity? He had a vision of her face with its proud laughing courage, he heard again her voice coming faint and sweet from behind the hills of death. She was smiling, she was saying something too rare for mortal ears to catch, but it seemed to thaw within him the springs of life.

He lay long on the turf, and when at last he raised his head the dawn was breaking. The wind had fallen, and into the air had come the softness of Spring. A thrush sang in the covert—he thought he caught the scent of flowers. . . . Of a sudden the world righted itself and youth came back to him. He saw brightness again on the roads of life and a great brightness at the end of them, where Katrine was his for ever among the eternal fields.

Rab Prentice, limping out in the early morning to

see to the lambing ewes in his hirsel, had occasion to take a short cut through the hazel shaws. He was surprised to see a man walking with great strides from the coppice, and more surprised to recognize him as the minister. What did Mr. Sempill there at that hour? He watched the figure till it disappeared over the ridge, and then went home much puzzled to his cog of brose.

In after-days Rab Prentice searched his memory for every detail of that sight, and often he recounted it to breathless listeners. For his were the last eyes in Woodilee to see the minister on earth.

CHAPTER XXI

THE GOING OF THE MINISTER

WOODILEE was early astir, for it was to be a day of
portents in the parish. Word had come the night
before of the judgment of the Presbytery—that their
minister was deposed and excommunicated and that
Mr. Muirhead of Kirk Aller and Mr. Proudfoot of Bold
had been deputed to preach the kirk vacant that very
day. There was little work on the farms, for the
lambing had scarcely begun, the ploughing was finished,
and the ground was not yet dry enough for the seed-
bed ; so the whole parish waited at the kirkyard gate.

Resentment was still deep against the minister as the
cause—under Heaven—of the pestilence, and for his
high-handed dealings during that time of trial. There
were also the old grievances against him, so that those
faithful to him were very few. Isobel was at Calidon,
Reiverslaw had gone no man knew where, and only
Amos Ritchie and one or two women were left to
defend him. Strange news had come about the tenant
of Crossbasket. There had been soldiers seeking him
with a warrant for his apprehension ; it seemed that
the decent, quiet-spoken farmer-body was Mark Kerr,
a kinsman of the Lord Roxburghe, whose name had
appeared in many proclamations of the Kirk and the

Estates, and who since Philiphaugh had been zealously sought for through the length of Scotland. Men remembered his masterful ways and declared that they had always known that he was gentrice ; they remembered his handling of the pricker and were confident that they had detected his ungodliness. But that he should have lived among them gave them a feeling of distinction and adventure, and the younger people cast curious eyes towards the empty house of Crossbasket.

It was the first day that Spring seemed to have come into the air, and the congregation, waiting in the kirkyard for the arrival of the ministers, were warmed by a mild and pleasant sun. The elders stood by the gate, each in his best attire, wearing—even the miller—an air of ceremonial gravity.

"This is a great day for Woodilee," said Nether Fennan, "and a great day for Christ's Kirk in Scotland. We cleanse the tabernacle of an unworthy vessel, and woe is me that some o' the bauldest and stenchest Christians have no lived to see it. Peter Pennecuik—honest Peter had nae broo o' Sempill—clouts o' cauld morality, was his word—Peter has gane ower soon to his reward."

"What's come o' Chasehope?" Mirehope asked. "He suld have been here langsyne. He'll surely no be late on this heart-searching day."

"I heard from the Chasehope herd," said the miller, "that Ephraim never cam' hame last night. The wife was sair concerned, but she jaloused it would be Presbytery business."

"But that was a' by and done wi' by three in the afternoon. He would be seein' Edom Trumbull about the new aits. Still and on, it's no like Chasehope to let warldly matters interfere wi' his Christian duty. . . .

Eh, sirs, what a testimony Woodilee will bear the day ! Mr. Mungo is to proclaim the outing, and Mr. Ebenezer is to preach the sermon, and on sic an occasion Bold is like a hungry gled and the voice o' him like a Januar' blast.''

Among the women sitting on the flat gravestones there was less talk of the Kirk and more of the minister. Most were bitter against him.

" They may out him and excommunicate him," cried Jean of the Chasehope-foot, " but wha will restore me the braw bairn that dee'd in the pest whilk was sent to punish him ? Answer me that, kimmers? I wad be the better pleased if I got my ten fingers at his thrapple."

" Weel for you, wumman," said another, " that Isobel Veitch is no here, or it's your ain thrapple would suffer."

" There's a queer tale come up the water wi' Johnnie Dow," said a third. " There was talk, ye mind, o' a lassie that he met wi' in the Wud, and we a' ken that there was a lassie wi' him in the hinder days o' the pest—the fairest face, some folk say, that they ever looked on."

" Tuts, gossip, yon was nae lassie. Yon face was never flesh and bluid. It was a bogle oot o' the Wud, and some says——" The speaker lowered her voice and spoke into her neighbour's ear.

" Bogle or no, Aggie Vicar, it cured my wee Benjie, and nae word will be spoke oot o' my mouth against it. The callant is still greeting for anither sicht o' the bonny leddy."

" Haud your tongues and let me speak. Johnnie Dow says the Presbytery had it a' riddled oot, and it seems it was nae fairy but a leevin' lassie. And wha

think ye she was ? Nae less than the young mistress
o' Calidon."

The women exclaimed, most of them incredulous.

" But that's no a'. It seems that she and the minister had made it up thegither, and she was promised
till him. Mr. Fordyce o' Cauldshaw telled that to the
Presbytery."

" Heard ye ever the like ? Will Sempill be hingin'
up his bonnet at Calidon and turnin' frae minister to
laird ? The lassie will no doubt heir the place, and it's
weel kenned that Sempill has walth o' gear o' his ain."

" He canna weel do that if he's excommunicat.
He'll aiblins * be for fleein' the country like the auld
laird, and takin' the quean wi' him."

" Ye havena heard the end o' the tale," said the
first speaker. " Dinna yatter like pyets, or I winna get
it telled. . . . The lassie is deid—deid three days syne
o' a backcast o' the pest, and the minister is no to
haud nor bind wi' grief. Johnnie said he sat yestreen
at Kirk Aller wi' a face like a corp and took his paiks
as mild as a wean, and him for ordinar' sic an ettercap.
Johnnie thriepit that he had maybe lost his reason."

There was silence among her hearers, and only Jean
of the Chasehope-foot laughed. " She's weel oot o' it,"
she said, " and he's weel served."

" Wheesht, wumman," said one. " The lad has
sinned, but he's but young, and his punishment is
maybe ower sair."

. There was a movement among the crowd, for the
ministers were seen approaching. They were received
by the elders and conducted to the minute session-
house, which was a pendicle on the east wall of the kirk.
The congregation, according to custom, now entered the

* Perhaps.

building, whence could presently be heard the sound of slow psalmody. Robb the beadle waited at the single door till the ministers reappeared, Mr. Muirhead in Geneva gown and bands, Mr. Proudfoot in his country homespun, for he was a despiser even of sanctioned forms. They too entered, and Robb followed, closing the door behind him, but leaving the great key in the lock.

Amos Ritchie arrived, moodily sauntering through the gate. He had been unable to face the kirkyard crowd, knowing that he would hear words spoken which might crack his brittle temper. He reached the door and was about to enter, when the sound of furious hoofs on the road made him pause. The rider hitched his bridle to the gate-post and strode up the path, and Amos saw that it was Reiverslaw.

" Am I ower late ? " the new-comer panted. " What's asteer in the kirk ? "

" Ye're ower late," said Amos bitterly. " Yestreen the minister was condemned and excommunicat by the Presbytery at Kirk Aller, and Chasehope was affirmed a saunt for want o' you to testify against him. This day Muirhead and Proudfoot are preachin' the kirk empty."

" God be merciful to me," Reiverslaw groaned. " I only got the word last nicht, and I've left weary beasts on the road atween here and Langholm. . . . Where is the minister ? Where is Mr. Sempill ? "

" The Lord kens. He's no in the manse, for I was there at skreigh o' day, and he hasna been seen since he left Kirk Aller. . . . What does it matter ? The puir lad has his name blastit, and Woodilee loses the best man that ever walked its roads. . . . Are ye for in ? "

" I'm for in," said Reiverslaw grimly. " If I canna help the minister I can mishandle some that hae brocht him doun. I'm thinkin' Chasehope will hae sair bones or nicht."

The two slipped through the door and stood in the dusk at the extreme back of the crowded kirk. The first exercises having been concluded, Mr. Muirhead was reading from the pulpit the finding of the Presbytery. The misdeeds of the minister were set forth *seriatim* with the crooked verbosity of a legal document. Then came the pith :

" Wherefore the Presbytery of Aller, in the name of the Lord Jesus Christ, the sole King and Head of the Church, and by the power committed by Him to them, did, and hereby do, summarily excommunicate David Sempill, at present residing in the parish of Woodilee, delivering him over to Satan for the destruction of the flesh that the spirit may be saved in the day of the Lord, and the Presbytery did, and hereby do, enjoin all the faithful to shun all dealings with him as they would not be found to harden him in his sins, and so to partake with him in his judgments."

The Moderator read the words with a full voice and with relish. He outlined briefly the civil consequences attaching to excommunication, and dwelt terrifyingly on the religious state of one cut off from communion with Christ and his Kirk. Then he proceeded to depose the minister *in absentia* from the charge and to declare it vacant till such time as a successor was appointed. The appointment would be in the free gift of the people, subject to confirmation by the Presbytery, since Nicholas Hawkshaw, the chief, indeed the sole, heritor, was an outlaw and a fugitive. He concluded with prayer, a copious outpouring in which the godly in Woodilee were lauded for their zeal, condoled with in their sufferings, and recommended for a special mark of the Lord's favour. Then he drew the skirts of his gown delicately around him, and gave place to the minister of Bold.

Mr. Proudfoot chose for his text Second Kings, the tenth chapter, the twenty-fourth verse, the second clause of the verse : " If any of the men whom I have brought into your hands escape, he that letteth him go, his life shall be for the life of him." It was a theme that suited his genius, and never had he spoken with more freedom and power. Scripture was heaped upon Scripture to show the guilt of half-heartedness in God's cause (" Curse ye Meroz, said the angel of the Lord ") ; the other charges against David he neglected, and concentrated on the awful guilt of unfaithfulness to the Kirk in her hour of trial. The bulk of the world lay prone under the foot of Satan, but in Scotland the Lord had set His poor people erect and committed His cause to their charge, and woe be to them if they faltered in that trust. At this point Mr. Proudfoot almost attained sublimity. There was a crusading zeal in his voice ; his picture of the stand of the faithful remnant against the world was the vision of a stout heart.

He passed to David and his backslidings. He drew the minister as a weakling, beginning no doubt with an honest purpose, but soon seduced from the narrow path by the lusts of the eye and the pride of life. " Oh, is it not pitiful," he cried, " in this short and perishing world, with the Pit yawning by the roadside and the fires of Hell banked beneath us—is it not pitiful and lamentable that the soul of man should have other thoughts than its hard-won salvation ? What signify profane learning and the delights of the eye and the comforts of the body and even good intents toward your fellows, if at the hinder end the Judge of all will ask but the one question: Have you your title in Christ?"

In especial, he dealt scornfully with the plea of charity. There could be no charity towards sin. The accursed thing must be destroyed wherever found, and were it the wife of a man's bosom or the son of the same mother the sinner must be struck down.

The congregation listened as if under a spell. So intent were they that neither the people on their stools nor the Moderator in his chair nor the preacher in the pulpit noticed that in the dim back-end of the kirk the door had opened and some one had entered.

But it was in the close of his discourse that the gale came upon Mr. Proudfoot's spirit. Now he was at his application. The history of Israel was searched to show how Jehovah the merciful was yet merciless towards error. Agag was hewn in pieces—the priests and worshippers of Baal were slain to a man—the groves were cut down and ploughed up and sown with salt. . . . So rapt were preacher and people that they did not observe that a new-comer was among them moving quietly up the kirk. . . . The minister of Bold concluded in a whirl of eloquence with his favourite instance of Barak the son of Abinoam—how with ten thousand men of Naphtali and Zebulun he went down from the mount Tabor and fell upon Sisera, the captain of the hosts of Canaan, so that not a man was left. He likened himself in all humility to Deborah the prophetess; he called upon the people of the Lord, even as she had called upon Barak, to rise and destroy the Canaanites without questioning and without respite. " Let us smite the chariots and the host with the edge of the sword, for in this day hath the Lord delivered Sisera

into our hand, and let us pursue after the remnant
even to Harosheth of the Gentiles ! "

" Harosheth of your grannie ! "

The minister's voice had stopped, and in the profound hush that followed, the four words fell with a
startling clearness. The blasphemy of them was not
decreased by the tone, which was of measureless contempt. The scared eyes of the people saw Mark Riddel,
for whom soldiers were now beating the countryside,
standing easy and arrogant before the pulpit, and those
near him drew away their stools in panic. He had not
the look of a hunted man, and though his presence had
always won him respect in Woodilee he seemed now
to have expanded into some one most formidable and
unfamiliar. He wore the same clothes as he had worn
in field and market, but he held himself very differently
from the friendly crony who had sat in Lucky Weir's.
At his side, too, swung a long sword.

Mr. Proudfoot looked boldly down on him.

" Who are you that dares to cast scorn upon the
Word ? " he asked in a firm voice.

" Not on the Word," was the answer, " but on the
auld wives that pervert it." He nodded over his
shoulder. " They ken me fine in the parish. I was
baptized after the Apostle, and for my surname ye can
choose Kerr or Riddel as it pleases you."

The Moderator sat with a flaming face. " It is
Mark Kerr the malignant. I summon all law-abiding
and Christian men to lay hands on him and convey
him to a place of bondage."

But no one stirred. The dark face with the laugh at
the lips, the fierce contemptuous eyes, the figure compact
and light with a strength which the toil-bent shoulders

of Woodilee could never equal, the repute for magical skill—these were things terrible enough without the long sword.

Mr. Muirhead rose. "Then I and my brother will get us forth of this place. Come, Mr. Ebenezer," and he gathered the skirts of his gown.

"Nay, friends," said Mark, " ye'll bide where ye are. And the folk will keep their seats, till I give them leave to skail." * He swung the key of the kirk door in his hand as he spoke. "Sit ye doun, Mr. Muirhead. Sit ye doun, worthy Mr. Proudfoot. You billies have the chance ilka Sabbath o' sayin' your say and no man can controvert you. This day for a change ye will have to hearken."

In justice to the two ministers, let it be said that it was not the sword that kept them in their places. Neither lacked courage. But this man who stood confronting them, the very sight of whom seemed to paralyse the folk of Woodilee, this shameless malignant had a compelling something in his air. He spoke as one having authority ; though he used the broad country speech he had that in his voice which, whether it spring from camp or court or college, means command. Very sensitive to this note in their disciplined Kirk, the two ministers listened.

What fell from Mark's lips was discussed secretly for many a day in the countryside. Publicly it was rarely mentioned, for a more awful blasphemy, it seemed, was never spoken in the house of God. He told two pillars of the Kirk and a congregation of the devout that they had all failed utterly to interpret God's Word ; that they were Pharisees faithful to an ill-understood letter and heedless of the spirit ; that they were fools bemused

* Disperse.

with Jewish rites which they did not comprehend and Jewish names which they could not properly pronounce. " It's nothing but a bairn's ploy," he cried, " but it's a cruel ploy, for it has spilt muckle good blood in Scotland. If ye take the bloodthirstiness and the hewing in pieces and the thrawnness of the auld Jews and ettle to shape yourselves on their pattern, what for do ye no gang further ? Wherefore d'ye no set up an altar and burn a wedder on't ? What kind o' kirk is this, when ye suld have a temple with gopher and shittim wood and shew-bread and an ark o' the covenant and branched candlesticks, and busk your minister in an ephod instead of a black gown ? Ye canna pick and choose in the Word. If one thing is to be zealously copied, wherefore not all ? . . . Ye fatted calves ! . . . Ye muckle weans, that play at being ancient Israelites ! "

This was too much for Mr. Proudfoot.

" Silence, blasphemer," he cried. " In the name of Him that snappeth the spear asunder I will outface you." He stumbled down the pulpit stairs, and would no doubt have flung himself on Mark had not old Nance Kello who sat at the foot impeded him and given Mirehope time to catch his coat-skirts. He stopped, breathing heavily, about three yards from Mark, and as he stood, it was not the sword that a second time deterred him. He felt dimly that this outlaw had come to wear a fearful authority. It was not the tacksman of Crossbasket that spoke but the captain of Mackay's—not the farmer of Jed Water but the kinsman of Roxburghe and the brigadier of Montrose.

Mr. Proudfoot turned to his colleague and saw that the Moderator's eye was puzzled and uncertain. He bethought him of his chief ally in the parish. " Where is Chasehope ? " he cried. " Where is Ephraim Caird ? "

The answer came from an unlooked-for quarter. Daft Gibbie sat crouched in a corner of the kirk, and those near him had marked his unwonted silence. He did not gabble as usual, but sat with his great head in his hands, murmuring softly and rolling his wild eyes. But at the mention of Chasehope he suddenly found voice.

"He's up in the hills," he cried. "I seen him at skreigh o' day at the buchts o' the Drygrain and he was rivin' a yowe and cryin' that it was a hound o' hell and that it suldna devour him. He was a' lappered wi' bluid, and when he seen me he ran on me, and his een were red and he slavered like a mad tyke and his face was thrawed oot o' the shape o' man. Eh, sirs, puir Gibbie was near his end, for I couldna stir a foot, but afore he wan to me there cam' anither sound, and as sure as death it was like a hound's yawp. At that he gangs off like the wund, and the next I seen o' him he was skelpin' through the flowe moss, cryin' like ane in torment, and I stottered hame to get Amos Ritchie to tak' his flintlock and stop yon awfu' skellochs. I'll never sleep till I ken that the lost soul o' him is free o' the body."

"Another has told my tale." Mark spoke in a voice out of which all scorn had gone, a voice penetratingly quiet and solemn. "I too have seen him that once was Ephraim Caird and I shudder at the swiftness of the judgment. There is no man or woman in Woodilee that does not ken that he was the leader of the coven that practised the Devil's arts in the Wood, but he had a name for godliness and he had the measure of the blind fools that call themselves ministers of God.—Sit still, sir! I would be loth to draw on an unarmed man, but my sword ere this has punished vermin. . . . He has sworn falsely against the innocent, and yestreen at Kirk Aller he prevailed. But in the night the Lord sent forth His vengeance—ask me not how, for I do not know—and this day he is running demented on the hills, pursued by the dogs of his own terrors. Go and look for him. You will find him in a bog-hole or a pool in the burn. Bury his body decently, but bury it face downward, so that you speed him on his road."

There was such a silence that the rasp of a stool on the earthen floor struck the hearers like a thunderclap. One voice—it was Amos Ritchie's—came out of the back of the kirk.

" Where is the minister ? " it asked.

" He is gone where ye will never see him more," said Mark. " A prophet came among you and you knew him not. For the sake of that witless thing that is now going four-foot among the braes you have condemned the innocent blood. He spent his strength for you and you rejected him, he yearned for you and you repelled him, he would have laid down his life for you and you scorned him. He is now beyond the reach of your ingratitude."

" Unless he be dead," said Mr. Proudfoot, " he is not beyond the reach of the law, and if he be dead he has fallen into the hands of a living and offended God."

" Man, man," said Mark gently, " you and your like have most lamentably confounded God and Devil."

" And you yourself," cried the Moderator, struggling valiantly to assert himself against an atmosphere which he felt inimical, " are within a span of the gallows."

" We are all and at all times within a span of death. . . . To you, reverend sirs, I have no more to say. You will gang your own ways, and some day others will play the tyrant over you and give you your ain kail through the reek. In that day of humiliation you will repent of

what you did in your pride. . . . To those who have
been partakers of the iniquity of the Wood I wish no
less than the fate that has overtaken their master. . . .
To the poor folk of Woodilee I leave their minister's
blessing, and may they have whiles a kindly thought of
one that loved them."

He turned at the door. " You will bide here till you
are released. The ministers can while away the time
excommunicatin' me. Guid day to you a'."

Amos Ritchie and Reiverslaw slipped out after him,
and the key was turned in the lock. Amos wept bitterly,
and Reiverslaw's dark face was working with suppressed
tears.

" You have to live on in this parish," Mark said.
" I need not involve you in my own peril. Let the
bodies out in half an hour. No one saw you enter,
so you will get no discredit by this day's work. Say
you found the key by the roadside."

Amos turned on him with a distraught eye.

" Where is Mr. David ? What have ye done with him ?
. . . We ken nocht o' you—ye come and gang like bog-
fire—there's some says ye're the Deil himsel'. If ye've
wiled a saunt doun the road to Hell——"

" Be comforted," said Mark, laying a hand on Amos's
arm. " I think I have helped to open for him the gates
of Paradise."

EPILOGUE

THE Reverend John Dennistoun in his once-famous work *Satan's Artifices against the Elect* (written in the year 1719, but not published till 1821, when the manuscript came into the hands of Sir Walter Scott) has a chapter on the disturbances in Woodilee. In his pages can be found the tradition which established itself during the next fifty years. He has heard of the doings in Melanudrigill, but he lays no blame for them on the parish. The power of the Kirk has been sufficient to sanctify Chasehope ; in Mr. Dennistoun's pages he appears as an elder of noted piety, who was the chief mark for the enmity of the Adversary and who was, as that Adversary's last resort, driven crazy by hellish assaults on his person till his life ended in a fall from the rocks in the Garple Linn. There is no mention of Reiverslaw, and Amos Ritchie is treated with respect, for Amos carried his grandfather's matchlock to Rullion Green, played a notable part in the Killing Time, was an ally of the Black Macmichael, and has a paragraph to himself in *Naphtali*. Mr. Dennistoun represents the trouble as a deliberate campaign of the Devil against a parish famed for its godliness, and David as an unwitting instrument. The minister of Woodilee he portrays as a young man of good heart but of small experience, unstable, puffed up in his own conceit. He records that there was a faction in the place that took his side, and that his misfortunes, justly deserved as they were, were not unlamented. He mentions as a foolish fable the belief of some that he had been carried off by the Fairies ; he notes too, without approval, the counter-legend that he had been removed bodily by the Devil.

On one matter Mr. Dennistoun has no doubts. Mark Kerr is the villain of his pages : the lieutenant of Satan, or, as many believed, Satan himself ; one at any rate who was sold irrevocably to evil. Of the real Mark Kerr's antecedents he is aware, but he is inclined to the belief that the figure that appeared in Woodilee was not Montrose's captain but another in his semblance. He makes a sinister tale of Mark's doings—his uncanny power over the minds of the people, his necromancy in the case of the witch-pricker, his devilries during the pest (these are explained as mere purposeless cruelties), his crowning blasphemy in the kirk, when he outfaced two godly ministers and spoke words of which the very memory made honest folk tremble. He is inclined to attribute to him also the warlockries of the Wood. When he disappeared on that April day he returned to the place whence he had come.

On this point Mr. Dennistoun reflected faithfully the tradition in Woodilee. Old folk for generations, with sighs and a shaking of the head, would tell of the departure of him who had so sorely troubled the Elect. The tale no doubt grew in the telling, and the children would creep close to their mother's knee, and the goodman would stir the peats into a glow, when grandfather with awe in his voice recounted the stages in that journey of the lost. . . . Sandy Nicoll saw him in the gloaming moving with leaps which were beyond a mortal's power across Charlie's Moss. Later, at the little lonely ale-house of Kilwauk, he was observed by a drover to cross the

peat-road, and the drover—his name was Grieve—swore
to his dying day that beside the traveller moved a coal-
black shadow. There was a moon that night, and
Robbie Hogg, herd in Glenwhappen, saw the fearful
twosome—man and shadow, man and devil—flitting
across the braes of Caerdrochit. At one in the morning
a packman, late on the road, saw the figure on the Edinburgh highway, and, though he had been drinking and
was therefore a doubtful witness, remembered that he
could not be clear whether it was one man or two, and
had been sobered by the portent. . . .

At this point, when all that remained was an awful
imagining, it was the custom of a household where the
tale was told to sing with dry throats the twenty-third
Psalm.

Three hours after the fuddled packman was left
rubbing his eyes, two men entered the back room of a
little hostelry in Leith within a stone's throw of the
harbour. The dust of moorburn and the April roads
was on them, and one of the two was limping and
very weary.

The only occupant of the room was a man in a great
seaman's coat who was eating a hasty meal. He rose
to his feet with an exclamation.

" Mark ! " he cried. " In the name of God, man . . ."

" When does the sloop sail ? "

" In the next hour with the tide."

" The Lord be thanked ! . . . You'll have this gentleman and me as fellow-passengers, Patie . . ."

" Wheesht, man. They ken me in this place as Jens
Gunnersen, a skipper out of Denmark. . . . I'm for
Bergen."

" Bergen be it. All roads are the same for us that lead

forth of this waesome land. A bite and sup would be welcome, Patie, and two ship's cloaks to cover our landward clothes. . . . I'm for the wars again, old friend, and I've gotten a braw recruit, but the tale can bide till we're on shipboard."

But three hours later the telling had not begun. Two men with wistful eyes leaned over the stern bulwarks, and watched the hills of Lothian dwindle in the bleak April dawn.

THE END

PRINTED IN GREAT BRITAIN AT
THE PRESS OF THE PUBLISHERS

NELSON'S NOVELS

Select List of some of the most famous modern novels. These volumes contain as much reading matter as the full-sized novel now issued at 7s. 6d. net. Set in clear type, and strongly bound.

At 1s. 6d. net

ARNOLD, MRS. J. O.	**Garth**
ARNOLD, MRS. J. O.	The Woman in Blue
BAILEY, H. C.	Springtime
BAILEY, PAUL	The Man Who Turned Mex
BALFOUR, ANDREW	By Stroke of Sword
BALFOUR, ANDREW	The Golden Kingdom
BELL, J. J.	Wee Macgreegor
BENNETT, ARNOLD	The Loot of Cities
BENNETT, ARNOLD	Helen with the High Hand
BENSON, E. F.	Thorley Weir
BENSON, E. F.	The House of Defence
BENSON, E. F.	The Image in the Sand
BENSON, E. F.	The Relentless City
BENTLEY, E. C.	Trent's Last Case
BIRMINGHAM, GEORGE A.	The Inviolable Sanctuary
BIRMINGHAM, GEORGE A.	The Simpkins Plot
BOWEN, MARJORIE	A Knight of Spain
BOWEN, MARJORIE	The Leopard and the Lily
BOWEN, MARJORIE	A Soldier from Virginia
BOWEN, MARJORIE	The Sword Decides
BOWEN, MARJORIE	The Carnival of Florence
BOWEN, MARJORIE	The Haunted Vintage

[Continued

NELSON'S NOVELS AT 1s. 6d. net
(Continued)

BOWER, B. M.	The Range Dwellers
BOWER, B. M.	Chip of the Flying U
BOWER, B. M.	The Happy Family
BOWER, B. M.	The Lonesome Trail
BOWER, B. M.	The Lure of the Dim Trails
BOWER, B. M.	Her Prairie Knight
BOWER, B. M.	The Long Shadow
BOWER, B. M.	The Flying U Ranch
BRAINERD, ELEANOR	"How Could You, Jean?"
BRAMAH, ERNEST	The Secret of the League
BRANDANE, JOHN	My Lady of Aros
BUCHAN, JOHN	John MacNab
BUCHAN, JOHN	Huntingtower
BUCHAN, JOHN	The Path of the King
BUCHAN, JOHN	Midwinter
BUCHAN, JOHN	Prester John
BUCHAN, JOHN	The Three Hostages
BUCHAN, JOHN	Salute to Adventurers
CAPES, BERNARD	Jemmy Abercraw
COBBAN, MACLAREN	The Red Sultan
COMSTOCK, HARRIET J.	Janet of the Dunes
CONRAD, JOSEPH	Romance
CRAWFORD, F. MARION	A Roman Singer
CROKER, B. M.	Mr. Jervis
CROKER, B. M.	A Rolling Stone
CROKER, B. M.	Married or Single
CULLUM, RIDGWELL	The Saint of the Speedway

[Continued

NELSON'S NOVELS AT 1s. 6d. net

CULLUM, RIDGWELL	The Man in the Twilight
CULLUM, RIDGWELL	The Luck of the Kid
CULLUM, RIDGWELL	The Riddle of Three-Way Creek
CULLUM, RIDGWELL	The Candy Man
DAVIS, J. FRANK	Almanzar
DE LA PASTURE, MRS.	Erica
DORRANCE, JAMES FRENCH	
	The Long Arm of the Mounted
DOUGLAS, O.	Penny Plain
DOUGLAS, O.	The Setons
DOUGLAS, O.	Pink Sugar
DOUGLAS, O.	Ann and Her Mother
DOYLE, A. CONAN	The Refugees
FINDLATER, M. and J.	Crossriggs
HARLAND, HENRY	My Friend Prospero
HARRADEN, BEATRICE	Catherine Frensham
HARRADEN, BEATRICE	Interplay
HARRIS, CORRA	Making Her His Wife
HARRIS, CORRA	A Daughter of Adam
HEWLETT, MAURICE	The Forest Lovers
HEWLETT, MAURICE	The Queen's Quair
HILL, HEADON	Her Grace at Bay
HILL, HEADON	The Hate of Man
HILL, HEADON	The One Who Saw
HILLGARTH, ALAN	The Princess and the Perjurer
HOPE, ANTHONY	Second String
HOPE, ANTHONY	Father Stafford

NELSON'S NOVELS AT 1s. 6d. net
(Continued)

HOPE, ANTHONY	Simon Dale
JACOB, VIOLET	The Interloper
JACOBS, W. W.	Ship's Company
JACOBS, W. W.	The Lady of the Barge
JACOBS, W. W.	Many Cargoes
JACOBS, W. W.	Sailors' Knots
JACOBS, W. W.	Deep Waters
JACOBS, W. W.	A Master of Craft
JACOBS, W. W.	At Sunwich Port
LEWIS, ALFRED H.	Wolfville
LEWIS, ALFRED H.	Wolfville Days
LEWIS, ALFRED H.	Wolfville Nights
LYNDE, FRANCIS	The Fight on the Standing Stone
MALET, LUCAS	The Gateless Barrier
MARSHALL, ARCHIBALD	Exton Manor
MASEFIELD, J.	Lost Endeavour
MERRICK, LEONARD	A Call from the Past
MERRICK, LEONARD	The House of Lynch
MONROE, ANNE SHANNON	Behind the Ranges
NICHOLSON, MEREDITH	The House of a Thousand Candles
NICHOLSON, MEREDITH	The War of the Carolinas
NORRIS, FRANK	The Octopus
NORRIS, FRANK	The Pit
NORRIS, FRANK	Shanghaied
NORRIS, W. E.	His Grace
OLLIVANT, ALFRED	Old For-Ever
OLLIVANT, ALFRED	Devil Dare

[*Continued*

NELSON'S NOVELS AT 1s. 6d. net
(*Continued*)

PARKER, SIR GILBERT	The Battle of the Strong
PARKER, SIR GILBERT	The Right of Way
PARKER, SIR GILBERT	The Seats of the Mighty
PARKER, SIR GILBERT	The World for Sale
PEMBERTON, MAX	The Great White Army
PHILLPOTTS, EDEN	The Children of the Mist
POOLE, ERNEST	The Harbour
"Q"	The Ship of Stars
"Q"	The Splendid Spur
"Q"	Lady Good-for-Nothing
ROBERTS, MORLEY	The Grinder's Wheel
SABATINI, RAFAEL	The Sea Hawk
SAVILE, FRANK	The Road
SCOTT, MRS. DAWSON	Madcap
SEDGWICK, ANNE DOUGLAS	Valerie Upton
SELTZER, CHARLES A.	The Coming of the Law
SELTZER, CHARLES A.	The Trail to Yesterday
SELTZER, CHARLES A.	The Two-Gun Man
SILBERRAD, UNA L.	Sampson Rideout, Quaker
SILBERRAD, UNA L.	The Good Comrade
SILBERRAD, UNA L.	Ordinary People
SNAITH, J. C.	The Crime of Constable Kelly
SNAITH, J. C.	The Van Roon
SOMERVILLE AND ROSS	All on the Irish Shore
SOMERVILLE AND ROSS	Some Experiences of an Irish R.M.
SOMERVILLE AND ROSS	In Mr. Knox's Country
SOMERVILLE AND ROSS	Mount Music

[*Continued*

NELSON'S NOVELS AT 1s. 6d. net
(*Continued*)

SOMERVILLE AND ROSS	Further Experiences of an Irish R.M.
SOMERVILLE AND ROSS	The Silver Fox
SOMERVILLE AND ROSS	An Irish Cousin
SOMERVILLE AND ROSS	Some Irish Yesterdays
SOMERVILLE AND ROSS	The Real Charlotte
STEVENSON, BURTON E.	The Holladay Case
TARKINGTON, BOOTH	The Gentleman from Indiana
TURLEY, CHARLES	A Band of Brothers
TWAIN, MARK	Huckleberry Finn
TWAIN, MARK	Tom Sawyer
VACHELL, H. A.	The Other Side
VACHELL, H. A.	The Paladin
WALPOLE, HUGH	The Dark Forest
WALPOLE, HUGH	The Duchess of Wrexe
WALPOLE, HUGH	Fortitude
WEYMAN, STANLEY J.	Count Hannibal
WEYMAN, STANLEY J.	A Gentleman of France
WEYMAN, STANLEY J.	The House of the Wolf
WEYMAN, STANLEY J.	The Red Cockade
WEYMAN, STANLEY J.	Sophia
WEYMAN, STANLEY J.	The Wild Geese
WHITE, STEWART EDWARD	The Rules of the Game
WHITELAW, DAVID	The Little Lady of Arrock
WILLIAMSON, C. N. and A. M.	Scarlet Runner
WILLIAMSON, C. N. and A. M.	The Lightning Conductor
WILLIAMSON, C. N. and A. M.	Love and the Spy
WILLIAMSON, C. N. and A. M.	Lord Loveland Discovers America

THOMAS NELSON AND SONS, Ltd.

London, Edinburgh, New York, Toronto, and Paris